DILLY

THE RELUCTANT HEIRESS

Complete and Unabridged

MAGNA
Leicester

First published in Great Britain in 2021 by
HarperCollins*Publishers*
London

First Ulverscroft Edition
published 2021
by arrangement with
HarperCollins*Publishers*
London

Copyright © 2021 by Dilly Court
All rights reserved

This novel is entirely a work of fiction. The names,
characters and incidents portrayed in it are the work
of the author's imagination. Any resemblance to actual
persons, living or dead, events or localities is entirely
coincidental.

A catalogue record for this book is available
from the British Library.

ISBN 978–0–7505–4867–0

Published by
Ulverscroft Limited
Anstey, Leicestershire

Printed and bound in Great Britain by
TJ Books Ltd., Padstow, Cornwall

This book is printed on acid-free paper

*For Barbara Blisset whose wonderful book on
Walthamstow and her memories of living there
were inspirational.*

1

East India Docks, London 1858

Katherine Martin stood on the upper deck of the steamship *Aldebaran*. She took a deep breath of the none-too-clean London air, tainted by the stench of the river mud and the manufactories on the banks of the Thames. It was a cold and rainy February day and the monochrome tones of her surroundings were a complete contrast to the heat, dust and vibrant colours of India, but it was home, and freedom from the terrors she and her parents had encountered at the start of the uprising. They were some of the fortunate ones whose loyal servants had helped them to escape from Delhi moments before the rebel army attacked. Kate recalled with a shudder the night when they had left the luxurious home of her uncle Edgar, who held a senior position in the East India Company. It had been a long and terrifying journey, but somehow, and with the help and goodwill of many villagers along the way, they had arrived in Bombay. They had stayed at the home of Sir Robert Audley, Uncle Edgar's solicitor, and a letter of introduction to the manager of Uncle Edgar's bank had been enough to secure funds for their return to London, travelling first class, and the basic necessities of clothing.

'Don't just stand there, Kate. I've sent Fellowes to find a cab.' Sir Bartholomew Martin tapped the deck with his silver-headed malacca cane. He was not a patient man. How he had managed to hold on to the wretched stick throughout their hair-raising experiences was still a mystery to Kate. However, she was used to her father's bursts of ill temper and she brushed past him, heading to where her mother was waiting at the top of the companionway.

'Are you all right, Mama?' Kate asked anxiously. 'You look very pale.'

'It's the half-light, my dear. I'll be fine when we get home. I long for a comfortable bed and a hot bath, and especially a change of clothes. I will put everything we've been forced to wear for all these weeks in the missionary barrel at the church.'

'I don't know,' Kate said, smiling. 'Having only two or three choices does make dressing much less of a chore.'

'You see the bright side of every situation, Kate.' Arabella Martin sighed and glanced anxiously at her husband. 'Your papa looks angry. What has upset him now?'

'He's just miffed because Fellowes is taking his time.' Kate kept a straight face with difficulty. Her father, who had been a magistrate in Delhi for three years, was used to having his orders obeyed instantly and without question.

'Perhaps our luggage has been lost,' Arabella said anxiously. 'Maybe that's why Fellowes is taking so long.'

'We only have three cases and a carpet bag. I'm sure I could carry most of them on my own.' Kate leaned over the side and waved. 'There he is now, and I think he's found a carriage. We'd best hurry

2

or someone else might snatch it, and I want to get you home as soon as possible, Mama.'

'Come along, ladies. What are you waiting for?' Sir Bartholomew shooed them down the steps to the next deck as if he were herding sheep.

★ ★ ★

Fellowes, Sir Bartholomew's valet, was guarding the hackney carriage as if it were made of solid gold, but there was considerable competition for its services. The former passengers of the *Aldebaran* staggered around with a rolling gait, as if the ship's deck were still beneath their feet, as they sought desperately for transport to take them to their final destination.

'Get in, Arabella,' Sir Bartholomew said testily. 'You, too, Katherine. Don't dawdle.'

Kate faced him angrily. 'Can't you see that Mama is exhausted?'

'Don't use that tone with me, miss. You may be twenty-one, but you're under my jurisdiction until you marry. Then some other man will have the task of keeping you in order.'

Fellowes raised an expressive eyebrow as he helped Kate into the cab, barely allowing Arabella time to settle her voluminous skirts around her.

'Thank you, Fellowes,' Kate said loudly. 'You may sit next to me.'

'Fellowes will sit up with the driver.' Sir Bartholomew fixed his servant with a stern gaze.

'Of course, sir.' Fellowes closed the door.

Kate cast a worried glance at her mother, who had suffered from chronic malaise during their

3

time in Delhi. The climate in India had not suited her, but perhaps now they were back in London her mother's health would improve. Kate sat back, gazing out of the window at the mean streets that surrounded the docks as the cabby urged his horse to a brisk trot. When they had left England three years previously, they had sailed from Southampton. Although they had lived in the centre of London at the time, Kate had never been this far into the East End. It was quite shocking to see such poverty, with barefoot children running wild. Feral dogs and cats were slinking around in the shadows, snarling and fighting over the tiniest scrap of food. Kate had seen poverty in India, although she had never been allowed to go out and explore on her own. She suspected that care had been taken to avoid the poorest quarters of the cities she had visited, but she was appalled now to see small, ragged children and the elderly begging on street corners in such terrible weather.

She closed her eyes to shut out the unpleasant sights, casting her mind back to happier times when life seemed to be a round of parties and balls at the barracks. Kate turned her head away from her parents as tears seeped through her closed eyelids. She was transported back to the candlelit ballroom where she had first met Subedar-Major Ashok Patel, who had been assigned to ensure that she and her family had everything they needed during their time in Delhi. He had bowed over her hand, and when their eyes met she knew that she had found her destiny. Ash had held her hand as if he would never let her go, and at that moment she would have been prepared to

4

follow him to the end of time. His dark eyes, lit by glints of pure gold, had kept her captive and his handsome face still haunted her dreams. They had danced every dance that magical evening, although it was against all the rules, and had caused heads to turn. A young lady of her class was not supposed to mix with the natives, which was something that her mother had drummed into her even before they had arrived in India. The divisions were there for a reason and must be obeyed. Despite the fact that Subedar-Major Patel had earned his promotion by his gallant actions in skirmishes on the North-West Frontier, he was, Sir Bartholomew had said at length, not a suitable companion for any daughter of his. Kate had been forbidden to see Ash again. However, the old saying 'love laughs at locksmiths' had proved true and they had managed to meet in secret. Ash told her later that his commanding officer had also warned him of the consequences of such a liaison, but the objections of their elders hardly seemed to matter.

Over a period of several months Kate had spent as much time with Ash as possible. She discovered that he was an Anglo-Indian. His mother, the daughter of an English employee of the East India Company, had died in childbirth. Ashok's father, a captain in the cavalry, had been killed in action some years previously. His family were as much against mixed blood marriages as Ash's maternal grandparents, and Ash had been sent to boarding school. Kate remembered comparing him to a cuckoo in the nest, and when she had explained the metaphor they had both laughed at the ridiculousness of the

5

social mores that were affecting them even then.

Kate leaned her head against the cold window glass; recalling the good times only intensified the agony of their parting. It was Ash who had risked everything to help them get away that terrible night, but he had insisted that it was his duty as a soldier to return to his unit. The tenderness of their last embrace still burned upon Kate's lips, and the salt tears that trickled down her cheeks now had the bitterness of gall. The long sea voyage had kept her in total ignorance of the progress of the rebellion and there was no way of knowing whether Ash was alive or dead. Kate was alone in her misery, for there was no one in whom she could confide. She knew she would get no sympathy from either of her parents.

The hackney carriage trundled onwards, rumbling over cobblestones, each turn of the wheel and every hoof beat taking Kate further away from the ship, which was her last connection with India and the man she loved. She shot a surreptitious glance at her parents, but her father was glaring into space and tapping his malacca cane impatiently on the floor of the cab, and her mother was lying back with her eyes closed. Kate dashed her tears away on the back of her hand and struggled to compose herself. Her heartbreak was hers to bear on her own, and she would have to find an alternative way of living her life. Marriage for her was out of the question. She could not imagine any man taking Ashok's place in her heart, but there must be something she could do that would give her a new purpose.

The carriage was slowing down and as she

6

wiped the steamed-up glass she realised that they were pulling up outside her old home in Finsbury Square. Lights blazed from the windows on all floors and the front door opened to reveal a uniformed footman.

'Papa, we're home at last,' Kate said with a heartfelt sigh. 'Mama, wake up. We've arrived.'

Fellowes opened the cab door and Sir Bartholomew alighted first. He marched up the front steps, leaving Kate to help her mother from the carriage, while Fellowes paid the cabby. Henry, the footman who had served the family for many years, moved swiftly to assist them.

'You'll have to excuse the state of the house, my lady,' he said earnestly. 'We only got the letter informing us of your imminent arrival this morning. Mrs Marsh and the servants are in a real state.'

'Oh dear.' Arabella's eyes filled with tears. 'Well, never mind, Henry. All I want is my nice comfortable bed, a warm fire and a hot drink.'

'I'm sure we can arrange that, Mama,' Kate said softly. She tucked her mother's limp hand through the crook of her arm. 'We can manage, if you would help Fellowes with the luggage, please, Henry?'

'Of course, Miss Katherine.'

'You must be exhausted, Mama.'

'I am perfectly capable of walking up the steps into my own home.' Arabella teetered off, swaying slightly as she crossed the pavement and ascended the steps to the front door.

Kate followed her parents into the elegant five-storey house that had been her childhood home. She could hear her mother's querulous voice and the deeper responses from their housekeeper, Mrs

Marsh. Housemaids were scurrying from room to room, their arms filled with holland covers. There was no sign of her father, and Kate felt safe in assuming that he had gone straight to his study.

'I have had a fire lit in your bedchamber, my lady.' Mrs Marsh turned to Kate with a pained expression.

'We only heard of your arrival this morning, Miss Katherine. I've had to hire maids and scrub women because we weren't prepared.'

'My mother is worn out,' Kate said firmly. 'We'll have to employ a new lady's maid as soon as possible, but in the meantime have you someone who could fill that position on a temporary basis?'

'There's my daughter, Jenny. She's only sixteen but she worked for Lady Dalrymple for a few months, so she knows how things should be done.' Mrs Marsh lowered her voice. 'She only left because Sir Horace was rather free with his attentions, if you know what I mean?'

'That must have been very disturbing for her. I do remember Jenny. She was a skinny little thing who was always singing.'

A reluctant smile deepened the creases on Mrs Marsh's lined face. 'That's my Jenny. A ray of sunshine, if you'll pardon the expression. Shall I send her up to my lady's room?'

'By all means, and she should take a pot of tea and some bread and butter. Cake would be nice, if you have any.'

'Leave it with me, Miss Katherine. What about yourself and Sir Bartholomew?'

'I expect my father will dine at his club, and I'll be happy with a light supper.'

'There's a fire in the morning parlour. I didn't know whether you'd get here today or tomorrow. We're all at sixes and sevens.'

Kate could see that Mrs Marsh was genuinely upset at the lack of preparations. 'That suits me very well. I'll be retiring to my room early — it's been a long journey and an equally tiring day.' She did not add that the emotional strain of leaving the man she loved and not knowing if he were alive or dead had affected her more than she would have thought possible.

'I'm sure we all understand, Miss Katherine. We've been reading about the terrible goings-on in that country in the newspapers. Thank the Lord you were all spared and have come home safe and sound.'

'Yes, indeed.' Kate realised that Mrs Marsh was eager to learn more of their escape, but she could not bring herself to talk about it now, or perhaps ever. Some things were best forgotten, if that were possible. 'I'd better let you get on, Mrs Marsh. It's good to be home.'

Mrs Marsh inclined her head and turned away slowly, but if she hoped that Kate would change her mind and pass on more information she was doomed to disappointment.

Kate set off towards the morning parlour. The house seemed too large, too echoing and too cold. She missed India and the privileged life she had led there: it was another world and a land of extremes. Until the uprising each day had been an adventure — now she had come back to reality. The smell of carbolic soap mingled with that of beeswax polish, and there was a hint of burning soot in the stuffy morning parlour.

An hour later, after a supper of soup followed by bread and cheese, eaten on her own, huddled by a desultory fire, Kate went upstairs to her bedroom. The curtains had not been drawn and she went over to the window, gazing down into the square. It was quite dark now and the trees in the residents' private garden had a fairy-like quality, shimmering in the gaslight. A few tender young leaves fluttered bravely against the chilly wind, and the first early tulips stood to attention like soldiers on parade in the well-kept flowerbeds. She drew the curtains and was relieved to find a nightgown laid out for her on the bed. She was about to undress when there was a timid knock on the door.

'Come in.'

A young woman, barely more than a girl, rushed into the room and came to a halt by the bed. 'Ma thought you might need a hand to get undressed, miss.'

'You've changed quite a bit since I last saw you, Jenny,' Kate said, smiling.

'So have you — that's if you don't mind me saying so, miss?'

'Not at all. We've both grown up a lot in three years. I believe you are going to be my mother's maid, until she can find a replacement for Bennett.'

'Yes, miss. That's right. But I could be your maid, too, if you so wish.'

Kate thought of the beautiful Mira, who had been assigned to her in Delhi. Mira had anticipated Kate's needs, fulfilling her duties with

10

serene dignity and grace. There could be no comparison, of course, but there was something about Jenny's eagerness and simple honesty that was both warming and refreshing.

'I think that would be a very good idea, Jenny. You may start by bringing me a jug of warm water so that I can wash off some of the city dirt before I go to bed. In India my maid used to float rose petals in the washbowl.'

Jenny wrinkled her nose. 'Funny habits them foreigners have. I wouldn't fancy washing my face with all them greenfly swishing around in the water, not to mention the odd bug.' She left the room, allowing the door to swing shut behind her.

Kate laughed for the first time since she had left Delhi, and then she began to cry. The tears that she had shed since parting with Ash were nothing compared to the heart-broken sobs that now shook her whole body. She collapsed on the bed, unable to control her pent-up emotions for a moment longer, but the storm of crying had passed by the time Jenny reappeared with the water. She set the jug down on the washstand and moved to the side of the bed.

'You're tired out, miss. Upsadaisy, now. Let's get you washed and into your nightie. I was just the same as you after I come back from Lady Dalrymple's place. Run all the way, I did, and when I come home I didn't know if I was to get a clip round the ear or a cuddle. Got both, as it happened, but Ma never made me go back there.' Jenny helped Kate to her feet and undressed her, talking all the time so that there was no need for

11

Kate to respond other than a nod every now and then.

When Kate was settled in bed, propped up by a soft bank of pillows, Jenny stood back with a nod of approval. 'That's better. I'll fetch you a nice hot cup of chocolate, shall I? I knows that Ma has some in because I was sent out special to fetch some when she got the letter to say you was arriving today. Your ma just drank a cup and she lay back in bed and was asleep afore I got to the door.' She left the room without waiting to see if her suggestion had been accepted.

Kate sighed and closed her eyes. Sometimes it was nice to be treated like a child again. Tomorrow she would organise herself and start a new life back in London. She would put all thoughts of Ash, India and the events she had witnessed from her mind. It would all be forgotten — it must be forgotten, or she would go mad with grief. She drifted off into an uneasy sleep.

★ ★ ★

There was a strained atmosphere next morning at breakfast. Sir Bartholomew was hidden behind the pages of The Times, lowering it only to ask someone to pass the butter or marmalade. Arabella looked pale with dark shadows under her eyes, and Kate was concerned.

'Did you sleep well, Mama?'

'Yes, although I think I was overtired.'

Sir Bartholomew rattled the crisp pages of the newspaper. 'Might we take breakfast in silence? I have only a few minutes to study current affairs before I have to leave for my chambers.'

'You are not returning to work today, are you, my dear?' Arabella asked wearily. 'Surely you will allow yourself one day of rest after the long journey.'

'Nonsense. Of course I must. I'm not a gentleman of leisure, Arabella. Thanks to the rebellion my position with the East India Company is no longer tenable, and I need to re-establish myself in my old practice. Heaven knows what state it's in financially after leaving Harte in charge for three years.'

Kate toyed with the buttered eggs on her plate. She was not hungry, but she knew it would cause a fuss if she did not eat.

'I thought you trusted Peregrine Harte, Papa.'

Sir Bartholomew shot her a warning glance. 'This has nothing to do with you, Katherine.'

'But he's such a nice young man,' Arabella said timidly. 'You always spoke highly of him, my dear.'

'Niceness doesn't necessary equate with efficiency, Arabella. But I wouldn't expect either of you to understand anything about business. That's my prerogative, and I intend to go to Lincoln's Inn this morning and surprise Harte and the rest of those who work for me. They will have to account for themselves if I'm not satisfied with their performance.' Sir Bartholomew folded his newspaper and laid it on the table as he rose from his seat. 'Don't allow the servants to dispose of this — I'll study it later, after dinner. By the way, I have a fancy for lamb collops — tell Cook — and apple pie with custard. I want proper English food again.'

'Yes, dear. I'll speak to Cook this morning.'

Kate waited until her father had left the dining room. 'Why do you let him speak to you like that, Mama?'

'It's just his way.' Arabella turned away to dab her lips on her white damask table napkin, but not before Kate had seen her mother's eyes redden with unshed tears.

'You have allowed him to bully you, and now he does it all the time.'

'He is the head of the household, Kate, dear. You will have to give in to your husband when you marry. It's how things are done.'

Kate pushed her plate away. 'Not by me, Mama. If a man tried to dominate me like that I would not put up with it.'

A wan smile curved Arabella's lips. 'So you say now, but it's different once you have a wedding ring on your finger. Your husband will own you and all that you possess, and any children you may be lucky enough to have will belong to him. That's the law, and I don't think it will ever change, because men make up the rules and we women have to abide by them.'

Kate had a sudden vision of the fighting she had witnessed outside her uncle's palatial residence in Delhi, and she shuddered. 'Then it's time women stood up for themselves.'

'Don't let your father hear you saying things like that, Kate. He would be most displeased.'

'Yes, Mama, I know.' Kate bit back the harsh words that sprang to her lips. She was tired of seeing her mother browbeaten and bullied without uttering a word of reproach, but she also knew

14

that nothing she could do or say would change either of her parents. 'Is there anything I can do to help today? You really should rest.'

'If you would speak to Cook and tell her what your papa has requested for dinner tonight that would be an enormous weight off my mind. I think I might go to my room and rest for a while longer. I'm sure Mrs Marsh can handle things perfectly well without me.'

'Yes, of course.' Kate stood up, leaving her food barely touched. 'I'll go now.'

'You need not worry unduly about money, my dear,' Arabella said hastily. 'Despite what your papa said about his chambers' finances, we still have an income from your late grandfather's estate, although, of course, your uncle Edgar inherited the bulk of the fortune.'

'That's a comfort, Mama. At least I know that you will be looked after, no matter what.' Kate left the room and headed along the corridor to the green baize door that separated the family above stairs from the servants' quarters and kitchens.

A burst of steam enveloped her as she entered the large room in the basement. Cook was sprawled in a chair by the range while a young kitchen maid struggled to knead a large mound of bread dough.

'Don't tickle it, you stupid girl. Pummel the dough, pretend it is your worst enemy—' Cook broke off as she spotted Kate standing in the doorway. She heaved herself to her feet. 'Excuse me, Miss Kate. I didn't see you there.'

There was a sudden awkward silence, and a young slavey emerged from the steamy scullery, wiping her hands on her already wet apron.

Kate held up her hand. 'Please don't stop on my account. I've come to give you the order for dinner tonight, Mrs Pugh.'

Cook swallowed convulsively and the colour deepened on her red cheeks. 'I've already started boiling the ox head, Miss Kate. I haven't had time to order meat from the butcher.'

'My father has requested lamb collops followed by apple pie and custard. I'm sure that isn't beyond the bounds of possibility.'

'But the stew is already simmering on the hob, miss. We wasn't expecting you until tomorrow and I got no one to send to market to get what I need to make such a meal.'

'If you give me a list I'll go,' Kate said firmly. 'I have nothing else to do.'

'But you can't go to market on your own, miss. It just ain't done.'

'I can do anything I want, Mrs Pugh.'

'I'll go with Miss Kate.' Jenny bustled into the kitchen. 'I've just helped Lady Martin upstairs to her room, so I'm not needed for a while.'

'You're getting above yourself, Jenny Marsh. You ain't officially a lady's maid, you know.'

'Yes, she is, Mrs Pugh,' Kate said firmly. 'Jenny is my mother's personal maid and mine as well. I will go to market, and Jenny will show me the way. She can help me to carry the items you require. Jenny, please make a list while I get ready to go out.'

★ ★ ★

16

It was a bright morning, still very chilly by Kate's standards, but the sun was shining and it was good to be out of the house. Jenny knew all the back-streets and she suggested that they should walk rather than take a cab to the market. The route took Kate through areas she had not known until now, and when they finally cut through Lincoln's Inn on their way to Clare Market, Kate was shocked to see the poverty of the surrounding narrow streets and alleyways. The stark contrast between the sedate environs of Lincoln's Inn and the narrow, poverty-stricken streets took her breath away. Jenny, however, seemed quite at home and unafraid of the men who gathered together, huddled over burning braziers, calling out in a way that would have caused Kate's mother to faint with horror. Jenny merely laughed as she steered Kate to the butcher's shop that she said Cook preferred, and having purchased the meat they bought vegetables and apples from one of the many costermongers' stalls.

Jenny knew the pieman who walked amongst the crowd selling his wares, and she persuaded Kate to buy one and see if she agreed that it was the best she had ever eaten. In the end they shared a pie with a glistening golden crust, stuffed with tasty beef and onions. Kate tried to ignore the hollow-eyed stare of the ragged, barefoot children who followed them like hungry birds ready to swoop on fallen crumbs. She bought a bag of buns from a passing vendor and tossed it to the nearest child, who was lost beneath a sea of flailing arms and legs as the others fell on him in an attempt to steal the food.

'Best walk on, miss,' Jenny said in a low voice.

17

'Don't stop for nothing.'

They had reached the comparative safety of Lincoln's Inn when a stern voice called Kate's name.

'Oh, my goodness,' she said with her mouth full of pie. 'That's my papa. What shall I do now, Jenny?

He'll have a fit if he knows I've been to the market.'

'Run,' Jenny said, laughing. 'Run as fast as you can.'

2

Kate needed no further encouragement, but she was hindered by her voluminous skirts, and her tight stays made it almost impossible to catch her breath. The heavy basket of groceries also impeded her movements, and she was in danger of losing the contents. It seemed for a moment as if they had escaped, but as they emerged into the Strand, Kate found her father's junior partner barring her way.

'Good morning, Kate.' Peregrine Harte stood before them, looking impressive with his black gown blowing in the wind like a raven's wings and his white wig covering his hair. 'Your father would like to speak to you.'

'Good morning, Perry.' Kate eyed him curiously. She had known Perry when he started pupillage in her father's practice, and she was not going to be intimidated by the barrister's wig and gown. 'You may tell my father that his request for a certain dinner menu necessitated a trip to the market, and I'm on my way home.'

'I'm merely the messenger,' Peregrine said with a wry smile.

'Then you've said your piece. Please let me pass.'

He backed away. 'I'll tell Sir Bartholomew that his dinner tonight depends upon your getting the ingredients back to the kitchen.'

Kate met his amused gaze with a reluctant

smile. 'It would be simpler if you said you couldn't catch up with me. My father will cross-examine you until you enter a plea of guilty.'

'Ah, but I have had three years at the bar since you and I last met. I will stand my ground.'

'I'm sure you will,' Kate said automatically. 'Come, Jenny. I think we'd better hail a cab or Cook will be sending out a search party.'

Perry stepped into the road and raised his hand to attract a cabby's attention. 'I hope we meet again soon, Kate, but in more relaxed circumstances.' He strode off in the direction of the court building.

The cab drew to a halt at the kerb and Kate climbed in first, giving the cabby instructions to take them to Finsbury Square, and with a flick of his whip the vehicle moved off, barely allowing Jenny time to settle herself on the seat. Kate sat in silence as they travelled through the streets that had once been so familiar to her.

'Is that man in a wig your friend, Miss Kate?'

Jenny broke the silence, causing Kate to turn to her with a start.

'Perry?' She shook her head. 'I wouldn't call him a friend, exactly. I knew him before we went to India. He did his pupillage at my father's chambers and became a fully fledged barrister before we left the country. He's done well for himself.'

'He seems to like you, miss,' Jenny said shyly. 'I think he's ever so good-looking.'

'I suppose he is.' Kate found herself comparing Perry's English good looks with Ashok's dark handsomeness, and she sighed.

'I suppose he's very rich, like your family, miss.'

Kate was about to deny their affluence, and then she recalled the narrow lanes and alleys surrounding Clare Market, and the poverty she had seen on the way home from the docks. For once, she had nothing to say. Even so, the ragged adults and undernourished children scrabbling about beneath the costermongers' barrows for scraps of food was something she would find hard to forget. The horrors of the uprising seemed like another world, but London was her home, and she found herself unprepared for the reality she now faced. It seemed impossible that she had grown up in the city without ever noticing the huge differences between those who had money and those who had next to nothing. She returned home knowing that her life had changed inexorably.

★　★　★

When Kate awakened each morning in her comfortable bed, she knew that today would be exactly the same as the one that had just passed. She was restless and desperate for news from Delhi. She accosted the postman every day, but the letter she longed for did not arrive, and she had no idea whether Ash was alive or dead. For all she knew, if he had survived the battles, he might now be languishing in some military hospital, badly wounded and fighting for his life.

The newspapers were filled with lurid accounts of the atrocities on both sides, but Kate dared not allow herself to imagine how she would feel if she learned that Ash had been killed in action. They might never meet again, but she would like to think of him living a long and happy life.

As for herself, Kate knew that she must do something to fill the void created by their separation. She toyed with the idea of seeking employment, but the professions were male dominated, and young women from well-to-do families were expected to remain dutifully at home until they married. Kate was aware that most parents went out of their way to introduce their unmarried daughters to suitable young men, but her father had his sights set firmly on becoming a High Court judge and was rarely at home. Her mother had met up with old friends who were avid fund raisers for a new lead roof on their local church and other worthy charities, and she spent most afternoons at meetings or taking tea with like-minded ladies.

Kate was left very much to her own devices, with little chance of establishing a social life of her own. Her father saw no point in spending money on entertaining, and despite Arabella's pleas, he turned down invitations to dine with acquaintances. He refused to take his wife and daughter on frivolous outings to the theatre, although occasionally he might suggest they accompany him to a lecture at the Royal Society, which Arabella found the courage to decline. The fact that her parents had embraced life in London to the exclusion of herself made Kate even more determined to make her own way. She was desperate to return to Delhi even though the situation was still perilous, but the pin money given to her by her father was her only source of income. She scoured the 'Situations Vacant' columns in The Times, hoping to find a family who needed a governess or even a lady's maid to accompany them to India, but after two months she was beginning to lose hope.

Perry was a regular visitor to the house in Finsbury Square, but he came only when he needed to discuss cases in private with Sir Bartholomew. Even so, he always found time to chat with Kate and she looked forward to seeing him, although not for any romantic reason. Perry brought a breath of fresh air into the stuffy household, where the only lively person was Jenny Marsh. Without Jenny's cheerful chatter and plain common sense, Kate doubted if she would have survived the first weeks at home. Despite the many letters she had sent to her uncle in Delhi, she had not had a single reply, and she had begun to fear the worst.

One morning, unable to bear the stress any longer, Kate went to her father's study where she found him studying a document with Perry.

'What is it, Kate?' Sir Bartholomew said crossly. 'You know better than to interrupt me when I'm discussing a client.'

'Yes, I'm sorry, Papa. I just wondered if you'd heard from Uncle Edgar. I'm very anxious about him.'

'My brother can take care of himself. Given the circumstances, I wouldn't expect to receive any communication from him until the present situation is resolved.'

Perry cleared his throat. 'I have all the information I need, sir. If you'll excuse me, I'll return to chambers.'

'Yes, of course.' Sir Bartholomew waved him away. 'And you should be helping your mother, Kate. I'm sure she has a committee or something for you to join.' He turned away and picked up a sheaf of papers, and Kate knew that she had been dismissed. She left the study, followed by Perry. He caught up with her as she was about to cross the entrance hall.

'It must be a worry for you, Kate. I mean, you're obviously very fond of your uncle, and judging by what the newspapers say, things are bad out there at the moment.'

'Yes, I love my uncle. He was always very kind to me. He never married and I suppose I'm the nearest thing he has to a daughter.'

'I'm sure the army will protect him. The uprising will be put down soon.'

'That's not what the papers say. I knew so many people in Delhi. I can't bear to think what might have happened to them.'

Perry put his head on one side, studying her with a thoughtful frown. 'Do you want my honest opinion, Kate?'

'I don't know,' she said warily. 'It sounds as if it will be something I might dislike.'

'You ought to know me better than that. What I think is that you are stuck in this mausoleum of a house, day in and day out, and it's no life for a lively minded female like yourself.'

She nodded. 'Well, I won't disagree with that. What do you suggest I do about it?'

'For a start you could come with me now. I'm taking on a case of a man who is accused of stealing items from the docks where he works as a carter. He lives in East Smithfield, and that's where I'm going. I think the case might interest you.'

'I'll get my bonnet and shawl,' Kate said eagerly.

The opportunity to get out of the house and do something different from the boring daily routine was too good to miss.

* * *

'Why are you going to so much trouble for this person?' Kate asked as the hansom cab threaded its way through the heavy traffic. 'Surely a man of your standing doesn't normally call at clients' houses?

Unless, of course, they are very wealthy.'

'You are very cynical for one so young.'

'You're forgetting that I grew up in a household where my father was quite ruthless when it came to making money. Even as a child I could see that he was in competition with his elder brother. Uncle Edgar inherited the family fortune and Papa had to make his own way in the world.'

'Which he has done very successfully.'

'Yes, I suppose so, but you haven't answered my question. What is so special about this new client of yours?'

'Ted Harris is my cousin.'

Kate stared at him in disbelief. 'Your cousin? But you said he lives in East Smithfield and he's just a carter.'

'My mother's family were all carters or porters working on the docks. My father was a barrister from a good family. It was a love match between my parents and they married despite opposition on both sides.'

'And it worked out well?'

'They were the most devoted couple I've ever

25

met, and when my father died my mother simply pined away. It was sad for me, being an only child, but at least they were reunited, or so I always hoped.'

'But your cousin's family are very poor.'

'I know what you're thinking, Kate. They are also very proud and have never accepted any money from my father. Maybe now I can redress the balance a little. If my cousin Ted goes to prison his family will starve.'

'He has children?'

'Eight of them at the last count. I don't uphold criminal activities of any kind, but there are some circumstances when I believe even the most law-abiding citizen can be tempted. With a wife and all those children to support, I can understand how the temptation to cheat the system might get the better of any man.'

Kate stared straight ahead as the cab negotiated the overcrowded city streets, heading towards the river. 'I never realised how much difference there was in the way people live in London,' she said slowly. 'I saw poverty in India, but we led such a privileged life that it didn't affect me as perhaps it should have done. Then, when we arrived back home, it was as if I opened my eyes for the first time, and in the past couple of months I've realised what an enormous gulf lies between the rich and the poor.'

'I dare say your parents kept such sights from you while you were growing up,' Perry said reasonably. 'I wouldn't want a child of mine to see some of the things I've witnessed.'

Kate turned to him in surprise. 'But you must

have had a privileged upbringing like myself.'

'When I was studying law at university I used to walk the streets at night. I ventured into some of the most squalid, poverty-stricken areas of the city, and I saw how the poor exist. That is why I take on as many cases similar to that of my cousin's as I can, without damaging your father's interests, of course.'

'Does he know what you're doing?'

Perry shook his head. 'No, but while he was in India I had free rein. Now he's returned to London your father is more interested in becoming a High Court judge than worrying about cases not his own.'

Kate nodded. 'Well, I won't say anything. I agree entirely with what you're doing, although I very much doubt if Papa would be happy if he found out.'

'I will tell him when the time is right.' Perry tapped on the roof of the cab. 'The first house on the left, cabby. Just past the streetlamp.' He leaped to the ground as the cab came to a halt, and then assisted Kate to alight.

She stood on the narrow pavement, taking in her surroundings while Perry paid the cabby. They were very close to St Katharine's Dock, and from the end of Nightingale Lane she could see a forest of ships' masts and tall cranes. The noise of barrels rolling over cobblestones, the rattle of chains and the hoots of steam whistles accompanied the shouts of men working on land and on the water. She wrinkled her nose as the noxious smell of raw sewage rose from the river mud, competing with the pleasant aroma of roasting coffee beans and molasses. Nightingale Lane itself was lined with a jumbled assortment of warehouses, cottages, pubs and ships' chandlers. Ragged children, some little more than babies, played in the gutter, despite the through traffic of horse-drawn vehicles and hand-carts. The street was crisscrossed with washing lines hung with dripping undergarments, aprons and sheets, all flapping idly in the light breeze. A window above them opened and a woman emptied a bowl of dirty water into the street, narrowly missing Kate.

'Come on.' Perry took her by the hand and led her to a house that was squashed between a pub and a small iron foundry. The noise of hammering was deafening and sparks flew out of the open door like a firework display. Kate kept close to Perry, wondering what would be thrown at them next.

He rapped on a door, the panels of which were splintered at the base as if attacked by someone wearing hobnail boots, and it was opened just far enough for a young child to peer at them suspiciously.

'It's me, Nellie. Uncle Perry.'

'Ma, it's Uncle Perry.'

'Good morning, Aunt Ivy.' Perry stepped inside and Kate followed him. She had to blink to adjust her eyes to the dim interior, and the rank smell of a tallow candle made her hand rise instinctively to cover her nose. The small room was sparsely furnished with a moth-eaten curtain draped over the cracked windowpanes, and damp patches formed interesting patterns on the walls, as if nature had decided to decorate the dreary surroundings. The bare floorboards were scrubbed clean, but lacked any kind of rug to add colour or comfort.

'Have you got any news? Is Ted coming home?' Seated by the empty grate, a woman with a baby suckling at her breast attempted to rise, but sank back on the seat. 'I'm sorry, I didn't know you'd brought a guest.'

'Please, don't mind me,' Kate said hastily.

Perry bent down to pick up a golden-haired toddler. 'You've grown since I last saw you, Charlie.'

'Who are you, miss?' Nellie asked, fingering the fine woollen cloth of Kate's skirt.

'Nellie, that's rude.' Ivy shot a wary glance at Kate. 'I'm sorry, miss. We don't get many visitors.'

'That's all right,' Kate said gently. 'I'm sorry to intrude, ma'am.'

'This is my friend Kate Martin, Nellie.' Peregrine kissed Charlie and placed him back on the floor. 'Kate's father is my head of chambers, Ivy.'

'Pleased to meet you, Miss Martin.' Ivy glanced anxiously round the shabby room. 'You must excuse us. I haven't had time to tidy up.'

'You have lovely children, Mrs Harris.' Kate smiled down at the small girls who were seated cross-legged on the floor.

'They're twins, miss.' Nellie ruffled the hair of the nearest child. 'This here is Polly and the naughty one is Emma.'

'Leave the lady alone, Nellie,' Ivy said wearily. 'She don't want to hear all that.'

'It's all right, Mrs Harris. I like children.' Kate picked Charlie up and gave him a hug, but she set him down again when the smell from his soiled

29

nappy assaulted her nostrils.

'Where are the others, Ivy?' Perry sat down in the chair opposite Ivy, leaning towards her with a sympathetic smile. 'Are they out working?'

Ivy nodded. 'Frankie cleans gents' shoes. May and Jimmy sell matches and bootlaces outside the station. They bring in just about enough to keep us fed each day, but it's hard to manage without Ted. You don't think they'll put him in prison, do you, Perry?'

'I have to be honest with you. What he did isn't in doubt, but I'll put his case to the magistrate tomorrow, and I'll do my very best to see that he gets off as lightly as possible. He broke the law, Ivy, and there's no getting away from it.'

'Even though all the others help themselves to things all the time?'

'Ted got caught and it's only a matter of time before others suffer the same fate.' Perry put his hand in his pocket and took out a leather pouch, which he placed in Ivy's lap. 'This will help tide you over for the time being.'

Ivy shook her head. 'I can't take your money. It ain't right.'

'We're family, my dear. You would do the same for me if the circumstances were reversed.'

'That's never going to happen, but ta ever so. I don't know what we would have done without you.'

Perry rose to his feet. 'You won't have to worry about that. I can help and I will to the best of my ability. I just hope that Frankie isn't dipping pockets or anything stupid, otherwise he'll end up in prison, too.'

Ivy shook her head. 'He's a good boy. My nippers know the difference between right and wrong. It's just that Ted had been laid off for two weeks and we was desperate, that's why he did what he did.' She shot a glance in Kate's direction. 'You ain't said nothing. I bet you're standing there all prim and proper, judging us and thinking we brought it on ourselves.'

'No, indeed I am not,' Kate said earnestly. 'I was wondering if I could do anything to help.'

'We don't need your charity, miss.'

'Ivy, that's unnecessary. Kate is sincere in what she says.'

'If Ted receives a harsh sentence there'll be no alternative for us other than the workhouse.'

'There must be someone who could help,' Kate said anxiously. 'My mother is on all sorts of committees at the local church. Maybe there is something like that around here?'

'No, miss. You just don't understand.' Ivy shifted the baby to her other breast. 'There's nothing to be done for the likes of us. Nothing at all.'

'I'm so sorry,' Kate said with a break in her voice.

'Don't waste your sympathy on me, miss. People will say we got what we deserved.'

'That's defeatist talk, Ivy,' Perry said firmly. 'I understand how you feel, but you mustn't give in. You have the children to consider.'

Ivy leaned back in the chair and closed her eyes. 'Do you think I don't know that? I wake up every morning wondering how I'm going to put food in their mouths.'

'You have enough money in that pouch to stop

you worrying for the time being at least. I'll be there to do what I can for Ted, and whatever the magistrate decides, I'll come straight to you afterwards and we'll talk more then.'

'Ta, Perry. You're a good man.'

'Goodbye, Mrs Harris,' Kate said softly. 'I hope all goes well tomorrow.' She relented and picked up Charlie. Despite the unpleasant odour, she kissed him on the cheek before setting him back on the floor.

It was a relief to be outside in the street. The air was cooler although the stench was equally bad, but at least she was away from the sheer misery and despair that seemed to engulf the Harris family.

'Are you all right, Kate?' Perry tucked her hand in the crook of his arm as they walked briskly towards the main road. 'You look a bit pale.'

'I'm all right, but there must be something to be done to help the poor woman.'

'I'm doing everything I can.'

'I could see that, but she has all those children to care for on her own. Has she any sisters or a mother who could help her?'

'Ivy came from the Foundling Home, so she has no one except Ted. His parents died years ago and I'm his only relative in London. Ivy is very much on her own, which is why I took you there. You were looking for something to occupy you, so maybe you can think of something that would help her but without appearing to be charity. Poor Ivy only has her pride left to cling to, and that must be in shreds now.' 'I'll think hard, Perry. I really will.'

Next morning, accompanied by Jenny, Kate took a cab to the magistrates' court. It was still early and there were plenty of spare seats in the public gallery. Jenny admitted to being nervous, but Kate was eager for Ted Harris's case to begin. She sat on the edge of her seat during the proceedings, which were pitifully short, and despite Perry's eloquent words the magistrate sentenced Ted to nine months' hard labour. The mitigating circumstances had been ignored and Ted's punishment was obviously intended to be a warning to others. He left the court room with his head bowed. Perry looked up as he was about to leave the court room and he acknowledged Kate with a weary smile before making his way towards the exit.

They met outside on a pavement bathed in late spring sunshine, but Kate felt a cold shiver run down her spine as she thought of Ivy and her children.

'It doesn't seem fair,' Kate said angrily. 'Poor Ivy. How will she manage?'

Perry shrugged. 'It's the law, Kate. I did what I could, but Ted knew the risk he was taking, and he was guilty of theft. You know that I'll do everything I can for Ivy.'

'There must be some sort of Parish Relief she could apply for.'

'I'm afraid not. The Poor Law Act put a stop to that, and Ivy's only alternative would be the workhouse, which is why I'll do my utmost to support the family. The older children do their best. I just hope they don't fall into the hands of ruthless men who will exploit their innocence and their need to help their mother.'

'Can they read and write? Surely they should attend school?'

'Crikey, miss. You don't know much about being poor, do you?' Jenny had been silent until this moment, but she spoke suddenly, causing both Kate and Perry to turn their heads. 'I don't wish to speak out of turn, but only the better off can afford to let their young 'uns go to school, even if it's for free.'

'You're right,' Kate said ruefully. 'I'm shocked by what I've seen and heard, but there must be a way to help people like Ivy and her children. If they could get an education they might find better jobs, with higher wages. Don't you agree, Perry?'

'Of course, I do. But one has to be realistic, Kate. Families such as my cousin's live hand to mouth. What little the older children earn means the difference between paying the rent or being evicted; between eating enough to keep body and soul together or starvation.'

Kate shook her head. 'I understand what you're saying, but there must be a way to help them.'

Perry patted her on the shoulder. 'If you can think of something I, for one, will be eternally grateful, but Ted's family's situation isn't unusual. I dare say it's replicated all over the country.'

'I can't do anything for the whole of England, but if I can find a way to help Ivy and her children I will,' Kate said firmly. 'The poor woman will be devastated when she learns that her husband is being sent down for nine months.'

'I'm going to visit her this morning, but first I must see you safely home, Kate.'

'Thank you, but Jenny and I will be fine on our own, and you have something more important to do.'

'If you're certain ... ' Perry said doubtfully. 'But I'll see you again soon.'

'Yes, indeed, and please remember that I'll do anything I can to help Ivy. Come, Jenny, I feel like walking home. Why waste money on a cab fare when it can be put to better use purchasing food for the Harris children?'

'Kate, stop.' Perry hurried after them. 'Ivy won't accept charity, you know that.'

'We'll see,' Kate said cheerfully. 'Goodbye, Perry. I'll see you soon.'

3

Kate had no experience of charity work and she decided to put Ivy's case to her mother. They had just finished luncheon and were seated at the table, waiting for the maid to bring them coffee.

'I don't know why a young woman like you would want to bother with the lower classes, Kate,' Arabella said impatiently. 'You ought to be thinking about getting married. In a couple of years you'll be on the shelf, and who will look after you when your father and I are no longer around?'

'This isn't about me, Mama,' Kate protested.

'You could join me and the other ladies in the committee to raise money for the church roof.'

'I'm hardly likely to meet my future husband at a committee meeting, Mama.'

'Don't try to be clever, Kate.' Arabella gazed at her daughter with a frown puckering her brow. 'It's a shame that your father doesn't like entertaining, which I must admit makes it difficult for you to meet eligible bachelors, but some of my ladies have sons who must be looking for wives.'

'Thank you, Mama, but I really don't want to sit around waiting for the right man to come along. I'd like to do something useful. I need to keep busy.'

'I know you were fond of that native chap in Delhi, my dear.' Arabella's frown melted into a sympathetic smile, and she reached out to lay her hand on Kate's. 'But it could never have amounted to anything. You do realise that, don't you? Your father would never have agreed to such a match.'

'Yes, Mama.' Kate withdrew her hand, hoping that her mother had not noticed how the mere mention of Ash made her tremble. Any vague hopes that Kate had cherished regarding support from her mother had been dashed long ago.

Visibly relieved, Arabella smiled. 'I'm glad we had this talk, Kate. I was worried about you having your head turned by an ambitious young man, but fate stepped in and resolved the matter before it became a real problem.'

'I don't think fate had anything to do with the uprising, and we wouldn't be here now if Subedar Major Patel had not risked his own life to help us escape.' Kate rose from the table. 'I just hope that Uncle Edgar and our friends in Delhi are all safe and well.'

'As do I, Katherine. There's no need to take that tone with me. I'm very glad we're back in London, and you'll thank us one day for saving you from a terrible error of judgement. Going native might be all right for men who are far from home, but totally out of the question for a young woman like yourself.'

'For your information, Mama, Ashok Patel is an Anglo-Indian. His mother was English, the daughter of a respected writer working for the East India Company.'

Kate left the room, biting back tears of anger and despair. Even allowing for the long sea voyage, she would have expected to receive word from Ash by now. Every day she waited eagerly for the arrival of the post, but with no word from

Delhi she was beginning to fear the worst. She could hear her mother's plaintive voice calling her name, and for a moment she was ashamed of her outburst, but she had only spoken the truth and for that she was not going to apologise.

Kate needed to escape, even if only for an hour or two, and she was about to go upstairs to collect her bonnet and shawl when Jenny came hurrying from the direction of the back stairs.

'Is everything all right?'

'We're going out. Will you fetch my bonnet and shawl, please?'

'Wait there. I'll be two shakes of a lamb's tail.'

Kate had to smile. There was something about Jenny's seemingly inexhaustible good humour, and her total disregard for the strict rules of behaviour that servants were supposed to obey, that was both refreshing and amusing.

Minutes later, dressed for a walk on a sunny afternoon, Kate set off, accompanied by her maid. It was all very proper, but Kate's reason for stepping out was something of a rebellion.

'Where are we going, miss?' Jenny asked eagerly. 'Are you going to visit that family you told me about?'

Kate shook her head. 'No, but I've just had a brilliant idea.' She came to a halt and hailed a hansom cab. 'Get in, Jenny.'

'Where to, miss?' The cabby leaned towards her. 'Where d'you want to go?'

'Do you know of any empty premises to rent near the docks?'

'A young lady like you don't want to go there, miss.'

'Yes, I do,' Kate said firmly. 'Do you know of any such places?'

'It ain't the sort of area what I'd like any daughter of mine to explore, miss.'

'Then it's fortunate that we aren't related, cabby.' Kate jingled the coins in her reticule. 'I can pay, and if it makes you feel better you may wait for us and bring us back to Finsbury Square.'

'Don't say I didn't warn you, miss. Better hop in quick. Me horse is restless and I got a living to earn.' Kate climbed in to sit beside Jenny.

'What are you up to, miss?'

'Wait and see.' Kate could hardly contain her excitement. Her idea was not a new one; in fact she had visited the lending library the previous week, even before she had met Ivy Harris. Her research had confirmed what Perry had told her previously: parish soup kitchens had been banned by the Poor Law Act of 1834, but one run by charity had been opened a few years earlier in Leicester Square, and some other charities were doing a similar thing in different parts of the East End. As far as she knew, there were none so far in the area she had in mind, and that was why she wanted to go there now.

The cab drew to a halt in Cable Street and the cabby opened the trap door in the roof. 'Are you sure you want to get out here, miss?'

Kate leaned forward in order to get a better view of the premises with the large 'To Let' sign in the window. 'Yes, that's exactly what I'm looking for.'

'It's a rough area, miss,' Jenny said nervously. 'I wouldn't want to walk these streets on me own, particularly after dark.'

Kate climbed down to the pavement. 'I intend to open a soup kitchen, Jenny. We'll open at midday and close immediately after serving food to those who are in desperate need.' She glanced up and down the street, and she had to agree with Jenny, although she was not going to say so. 'You can stay in the cab, if you wish. I'm going to knock on the door and see if anyone is there. I want to look inside and see if it's suitable.'

With obvious reluctance, Jenny stepped down onto the pavement. 'Your papa would have a fit if he knew what you're doing. I doubt if your friend Mr Harte would think it proper, either.'

Ignoring Jenny's protest, Kate hammered on the door with her fist, and she stood back at the sound of footsteps and the turning of a key in the lock.

'Who's there?' A querulous male voice demanded.

'I'm interested in renting the premises,' Kate said boldly. 'I'd like to see inside.'

The door opened to reveal a tall man with a mane of black hair tied back with a piece of string. His jacket was patched at the elbows and his trousers had the shiny texture incurred from years of wear. He glanced up and down the street.

'Are you sure you wasn't followed?'

Kate stared at him in surprise. 'Who would follow us?'

'You ain't here on behalf of Mad Monks, are you?'

'There are mad monks in this neighbourhood?' Kate wondered if the man was slightly deranged.

'Monks is a person of ill repute.' He eyed her curiously. 'If it weren't him was it Harry Trader?

40

Monks is bad enough but you don't want to get on the wrong side of Harry Trader and his gang. This is his place, so take my advice and push off.'

'No, sir,' Kate said patiently. 'I don't know either of those people and I have nothing to do with any sort of gang or gangster. Now may we come in, please?'

'Never let it be said that Augustus Spears kept a young lady standing on the pavement. I was once a soldier in Her Majesty's army. I know me manners.'

He opened the door wide enough to allow them to enter, but he slammed it shut as quickly as he could without knocking Jenny over. 'Help yourselves,' he said, sighing. 'I'm just the caretaker now. I look after the place.'

The first thing that Kate noted was that the premises had gaslight, which was a definite advantage. It was a large empty room with lime-washed walls and a high ceiling. Behind it was an equally large kitchen with a range and a stone sink with a pump.

'This is ideal,' Kate said enthusiastically. 'What was it used for previously, Mr Spears?'

He stood in the doorway, watching anxiously as she opened the back door. It led into a small yard with a ramshackle shed at the far end, which was presumably a privy.

'Many things,' he said vaguely. 'People come and go.'

'It must have been something.' Jenny turned on him impatiently. 'Was it a shop selling boots and shoes, or food of some sort?'

He shrugged. 'It's been all of those. It never

stays open for long.'

'What is the rent?' Kate asked, coming straight to the point.

'Ten shillings a month.'

'It takes me a year to earn that much,' Jenny whispered. 'It's too dear, miss.'

'That is rather a lot,' Kate said thoughtfully.

'Perhaps that's why the occupants don't stay for long.'

'It's the gangs, miss.' Spears tapped the side of his large red-tipped nose. 'Mad Monks and Trader's lot are always trying to outdo each other. Very bloody it gets sometimes, if you'll pardon the expression.'

'That must be hard on the people living round here.' Kate shuddered at the sight of two rats fighting over a scrap of food in the back yard, and she slammed the door, turning the key in the lock. 'This place needs a good clean up.'

'I don't think we'll be staying long enough to raise a duster,' Jenny said in a low voice. 'This ain't the sort of area for you, miss. My ma would have a fit if she knew we was here now, let alone starting up a soup kitchen.'

'Soup kitchen?' Spears moved a step closer. 'Is that what you had in mind, miss?'

Kate winkled her nose. It was obvious from the odour that hung about him like a greenish cloud that Augustus Spears was a stranger to soap and water. 'Yes, it is. That's if I decide to take on this premises at such an exorbitant rent.'

'It ain't up to me. I just do what the owner tells me.'

'Then I suggest you tell that person that I'll pay

six shillings a month and his premises will be put to good use feeding the destitute.'

Spears shook his head. 'I dunno if that will make any difference, miss. Ten shillings is the going rate.'

'You won't know until you try, Mr Spears.'

'Who shall I say is asking?'

Jenny nudged Kate in the ribs. 'I wouldn't tell him if I was you, miss.'

'You're right, of course.' Kate moved towards the door that led out into the street. 'A lady, is all he needs to know. I'll call by tomorrow afternoon for his response.' She opened the door and was relieved to find the cab still waiting, although the horse was pawing the ground as if eager to be on the move.

'Finsbury Square, please, cabby.' Kate climbed inside followed closely by Jenny.

'Are you sure about this?' Jenny asked urgently. 'Look around you. Half these buildings are near derelict, and the gangs that old man spoke of might object to our presence.'

'We'll be helping people,' Kate said firmly. 'That's the only thing that matters to me. Having seen that poor family yesterday has made me determined to put my time to good use. If the owner refuses to let the place to me, then I'll look elsewhere, but I won't be put off, not for a minute. I've no money to give those less fortunate than myself, but a full belly will help to keep body and soul together.'

★ ★ ★

43

Kate had expected an icy reception when she reached home, but her father greeted her with a genuine smile and her mother seemed to have forgotten their difference of opinion earlier that day.

'Guess what, Kate?' Arabella said, clasping her hands together. 'Your papa has been appointed as judge in the Central Criminal Court. Isn't that wonderful?'

'Congratulations, Papa. I'm sure you deserve the honour.'

Sir Bartholomew smiled modestly. 'Well, I have to admit that I've worked hard to earn the position. I put myself forward before we left England, and now my chance has come.'

'It has indeed, my dear.' Arabella clasped her husband's arm, smiling up at him. 'We must celebrate.'

'I've invited Perry to dine with us tonight, Arabella. That will be enough. One doesn't want to appear ostentatious.' Sir Bartholomew strolled off towards his study with a definite swagger in his step.

Kate took off her bonnet and handed it to Jenny. 'Have you engaged a new lady's maid, Mama?'

'Yes, as a matter of fact I have. Miss Barnet will be starting tomorrow. I won't need Jenny's services then. She can go back to being a housemaid.'

'But she's to be my maid, Mama. You promised.'

Arabella's smiled faded. 'I don't remember promising anything, Kate. You assume too much. Of course she will help you when needed, but you are hardly a debutante. You are "a spinster of this parish", I think is the correct way to describe your

44

position in the family. You are dependent upon your papa for everything, and I think you would be well to remember that.'

Kate knew this to be true, but her mother's harsh words acted as a reminder that she had not forgotten their previous exchange of words.

'I'm hardly likely to forget the fact, Mama.'

Arabella recoiled as if Kate had hit her a physical blow. 'That's no way to speak to your mama.'

'But you may say spiteful things to me and I'm supposed to bear your comments in silence. I'm sorry, Mama, but as you pointed out, I'm a grown woman now, and I expect to be treated like an adult and not a wayward child.'

'Oh! I won't listen to this. I'll tell your father what you just said to me.'

'Please do, and if he's as good a judge as he's supposed to be, I'm sure he will see my side of things. I don't wish to argue with you, Mama, but I have feelings, too.'

Arabella threw up her hands and hurried off in the direction of her husband's study.

'I'm sorry, miss.' Jenny emerged from the vestibule. 'I brought that on you. I didn't mean to eavesdrop but I couldn't get to the back stairs without being seen.'

Kate turned to her with a wry smile. 'It wasn't your fault, Jenny. But you heard what my mother said. I am a person of no account in this family.'

'It's not for me to say, miss. But I'd be very upset if Ma spoke to me like that.'

'Mrs Marsh probably thinks for herself, Jenny. My mother simply voices my father's opinions.

45

I'll be in my room if anyone wants me.'

'Yes, miss. Of course.'

* * *

Kate was tempted to have her evening meal sent to her room, but she decided that would be childish and only cause more of a rift between herself and her mother. Before Kate met Ashok she had never challenged her parents' authority, but now, for the first time, she questioned the right of a husband to dominate his wife and children to the extent that they obeyed him slavishly. Perhaps it had something to do with the fate of Ivy Harris, burdened by a feckless husband and the demands of bearing a child each year, and Ivy's humble acceptance of her lot. Despite her desire to rebel, Kate knew that she would have to apologise to her mother if there was to be any peace in the household. What she would keep secret, for the time being at least, was her ambition to start a soup kitchen in one of the roughest areas in East London.

She dressed with care and without Jenny's assistance, although she could not manage the coiffure created by Jenny's nimble fingers, and she allowed her long, blond hair to fall naturally to her shoulders, held back from her face by a pearl-encrusted comb, her only jewellery. With a last critical glance in the tall cheval mirror, Kate picked up her skirts and made her way downstairs to the drawing room.

Perry rose to his feet and his appreciative smile went a long way to soothing Kate's turbulent emotions.

'Good evening, Kate. May I say how charming you look?'

'Thank you, Perry.'

Kate could feel her mother's eyes upon her and a quick glance confirmed her suspicions — Perry was being assessed as a prospective son-in-law. A few months ago he would have been at the very bottom of a list of eligible young men, but Kate sensed a feeling of desperation in her mother and it made her feel extremely uncomfortable. However, if Perry noticed an atmosphere in the room he was far too tactful to bring it to her attention.

'Sit down, please,' Arabella said impatiently. 'We'll have a glass of sherry wine while we're waiting for Sir Bartholomew. He had some papers to attend to, Peregrine.' She signalled to Jenny, who had been standing stiffly to attention, waiting for instructions.

'Thank you, Lady Martin, that would be much appreciated.' Perry pulled up a chair for Kate and another for himself, and he accepted a glass of sherry from Jenny, acknowledging her with a nod and a smile.

Kate admired the easy way he had with everyone, and she warmed towards him.

'Have you had a trying day, Perry?'

He laughed. 'In all senses of the word, Kate.' He turned to Arabella, raising his glass. 'It's been a good day for Sir Bartholomew. He's certainly earned his new appointment.'

'Here he is now.' Arabella half rose from her seat by the fireplace, her face wreathed in smiles as her husband entered the room.

Sir Bartholomew waved away Jenny's offer of a glass of sherry. 'Fetch the brandy decanter and a couple of glasses.' He turned to Perry. 'I'm sure you'd prefer a glass of cognac, Peregrine.'

'Thank you, Sir Bartholomew, but I'm quite happy with sherry. Although perhaps we ought to be celebrating your undoubted achievement with champagne. Had I given it a thought I might have brought a magnum with me.'

Sir Bartholomew accepted a glass of brandy from Jenny and he slumped down on the sofa. 'No need. A fine cognac beats all other tipples.' He sipped his drink with an appreciative sigh. 'But you're right in one way, I do have cause to celebrate, and so do you.'

'Me, sir? I'm not sure I understand.'

'I can't believe you haven't considered the implications of my new appointment. I will be presiding at the Old Bailey, and you will be head of chambers, with all that goes with that somewhat dubious honour.'

'I hadn't considered it until this moment, sir.'

'Then you must. Do you think you are ready to take the responsibility?'

'I've been doing it with some success while you were in Delhi, Sir Bartholomew. I am more experienced now and much more confident in my own abilities.'

'Splendid. Then there is just the question of the funds needed to buy me out, but we'll discuss that privately. This evening we are simply celebrating.'

Kate stared at her father in dismay. 'Did you say that Perry owes you money, Papa?'

'Of course he does, my dear. This is business

and it doesn't concern you.'

'But I thought that he would simply take over, Papa.'

'That shows how little you know about anything in the world of commerce, my dear. I built up the practice and anyone taking over from me would have to pay for the goodwill. Isn't that so, Peregrine, my boy?'

'Of course, sir.' Perry cleared his throat nervously. 'But it might take me some time to raise the amount you might require.'

'I'm sure you will find the way.' Sir Bartholomew beckoned to Jenny. 'Refill our glasses, and then you can go to the kitchen and find out how long dinner will be. I'm famished.'

★ ★ ★

Dinner that evening was a strained affair. Kate could see that in spite of what he said, Perry was shocked by her father's assumption that he had been aware of the debt he was about to incur. She waited until Perry had taken his leave of her parents, and she followed him from the room.

'You didn't know about the money, did you?'

'I must be very naïve,' he said ruefully. 'But all this has happened so quickly that I honestly hadn't given it a thought. Although, of course, your father is well within his rights to ask for payment.'

'I could see that you were taken aback. The point is, can you find the money to buy Papa out?'

'I don't have much choice, Kate. I'll do my utmost to raise the necessary sum.' He gave her

49

a searching look. 'But what about you? I thought you seemed out of sorts when I arrived earlier this evening.'

She had decided to confide in him, hoping that he might know of a philanthropic backer to finance her scheme, but this was obviously not the time. She managed a weary smile. 'I expect I was a bit tired, that's all. I've had rather a busy day.'

'Ahem.' Henry hovered at Perry's side.

'Thank you, Henry.' Perry acknowledged the footman with a brief smile. He put on his hat and tipped it at a rakish angle. 'Good night, Kate. I'll see you again very soon, I hope.'

She smiled. 'You can count on it, Perry. I might need some legal advice.'

'Call in at my chambers at any time. It will be more private there and we can talk.'

★ ★ ★

Later that evening, alone in her room, Kate counted the money she had saved from her monthly allowance. Her father was not overgenerous, but neither was he mean, and he was quite open about his purely selfish motives for having a well-turned-out daughter. Kate knew that this was partly due to her beloved uncle Edgar, who had criticised his brother for being parsimonious, and it was he who had insisted upon her being given a generous amount of pin money. Her father had continued this on their return to London, but she suspected that this was part of his plan to see her married off to someone rich and influential. Whatever happened, and no matter how much her parents disapproved, Kate was determined to marry for love, and if she could not be with Ash, she would remain single.

The coins lay on her satin coverlet, glinting in the firelight, and she counted them once again. There was one pound and ninepence halfpenny. If she could reach a reasonable bargain with the owner of the premises in Cable Street she would have enough money left to make a start. Quite how she would finance the charity when her cash ran out was another matter, but she would face that when necessary. She placed the coins in her reticule and tucked it under her pillow — a habit that she had developed during her three years in Delhi where it was not unknown for monkeys to enter buildings and steal anything on which they could lay their tiny fingers.

She rang the bell for Jenny to release her from the confines of her tightly laced stays.

★ ★ ★

Kate was up early next morning, and set off for Cable Street on her own this time. She would have taken Jenny, but it would cause trouble both above and below stairs if she went against her mother's wishes. Kate missed Jenny's company, but she would have to work upon Mama's better nature if she wanted to have her own personal maid. First and foremost she would have to swallow her pride and apologise.

However, once set upon a mission, Kate was determined to see it through, and she hailed a cab. This cabby made no comment on her destination and he dropped her off outside the premises, accepting the fare but refusing to wait for her.

'I'd be losing work if I sat around waiting for passengers. I got a living to make, miss. I got nippers to feed, so I'll be on me way.'

Despite her protests he drove off and she was left alone in the alien surroundings of Cable Street. She was assailed on all sides by unfamiliar noises from the docks, together with the rumble of trains as they headed towards the end of the line at the Minories, and the sound of booted feet pounding the pavements. The people who trudged up and down Cable Street were poorly dressed, especially when compared with those who lived and worked in the more affluent area of Finsbury Square. Kate was getting very odd looks from passers-by as she waited for Augustus Spears to answer her knock on the door, and she shifted nervously from one foot to the other. He came eventually and somewhat reluctantly allowed her to enter the building. It was half-past nine in the morning, but he was still wearing a grubby nightshirt beneath a faded and equally dirty woollen dressing gown. His bare feet pattered on the tiles as he padded into the kitchen where a desultory fire sputtered and spat sparks as flames licked the damp kindling.

'What time of day d'you call this?' he demanded crossly. 'I ain't even had me first cup of tea this morning.'

'I'm sorry to inconvenience you,' Kate said tactfully, 'but I wanted to find out what your employer said to my offer.'

Spears ran his hand through his long, untidy hair. 'I never thought you'd come back. This ain't the place for the likes of you, miss. Go home and do whatever it is that young ladies like you does while the rest of us works ourselves to death.'

Kate looked round at the grubby floor, the dirty fingermarks on the walls and the peeling paintwork. It did not look as though Augustus Spears over- exerted himself in any way. Even his attempts at making a pot of tea were sloppy, and it was obvious that the milk was on the turn. Lumps of curdled cream floated on the top of the murky brown liquid in his cup, but he drank it with relish.

'If you'll tell me if the landlord will accept my offer I'll give you my answer and be on my way,' Kate said reasonably.

Spears opened his mouth to answer, but the sound of someone rattling the back door made him spin round so violently that he spilled his tea down the front of his nightshirt.

'It's Trader,' he said nervously. 'You'd best nip out the front door, miss. You don't want nothing to do with Harry Trader.'

4

Kate was about to tell him that she was going nowhere until she received an answer when the door burst open. A tall, broad-shouldered man, wearing a navyblue reefer jacket and a peaked cap pulled down over his brow filled the doorway with his presence.

'Harry, my dear friend,' Spears said in a shaky voice. 'To what do I owe this honour?'

'Who is this?' Trader demanded, glowering at Kate.

She was not about to be cowed by a bully and she stepped forward, facing him with a defiant stare. 'My name is Kate Martin and I'm the prospective tenant of these premises.'

He stepped inside, pushing his cap to the back of his head to reveal dark hair waved back from a high forehead. His blue-green eyes, the colour of which put Kate forcibly in mind of the Indian Ocean, gleamed with amusement.

'Why would a young lady like you want to rent this run-down place?'

'Exactly what I said.' Spears clutched his dressing gown closer around his body, eyeing Trader nervously. 'Can I do anything for you, Harry?'

'You can get the main room upstairs ready for a meeting tonight, Spears. When I say ready, I mean clean and tidy and a good fire going. Last time I came here it was a disgusting mess.'

'Yes, sir. I does me best.'

'If that's what you call your best you'd better find yourself another job.'

'Do you own these premises?' Kate stared at Harry Trader in dismay.

'Not good enough for you, Miss Martin?' Trader grinned, revealing a row of even white teeth. 'There's the door. I suggest you leave now.'

'I'll go upstairs and start cleaning,' Spears said hastily.

'No, wait.' Kate caught him by the sleeve. 'You said you'd speak to the owner and it's obvious that you did nothing of the sort.'

'You can ask him yourself.' Spears retreated into the front room, then there was the sound of his bare feet thudding on the wooden stair treads.

Kate turned to Trader, arms akimbo. 'Your man asked for an exorbitant rent.'

'You are persistent, I'll give you that. But you still haven't told me why you would want to rent rooms in Cable Street.'

'I intend to open a soup kitchen for the poor and destitute,' Kate said firmly. She waited, watching his reaction carefully. She half expected him to laugh and dismiss her plan as being ridiculous, but he appeared to be considering her proposition.

'A soup kitchen. What could be a better front than that?'

'What do you mean?' Kate asked nervously. Harry Trader had succeeded in dismissing all her preconceived ideas of what a gangster looked like and how one behaved. This man might have been a sea captain on leave from his vessel, or a well-to-do merchant. He was well spoken and clean-cut, not at all the sort of person she might have imagined running a criminal gang.

'What did that scoundrel ask for? I mean how much rent did he quote?'

'Ten shillings a month, Mr Trader. I told him it was too much and I intend to run the place as a charity.'

'Ten shillings — the old crook. I'm supposed to be a villain but he is the bad fellow in this. Spears would cheat us both. I've no doubt he would take ten shillings from you and hand me five, which is what I charged the last tenant.'

'What happened to that person?'

Trader threw back his head and laughed. 'He tried to cheat me, too. He's inspecting the Thames bed as we speak, although I doubt if he'll find much to interest him in the river mud.'

'You mean you drowned him?'

'Heaven forbid! No, I pay others to do my dirty work, as you might call it. Remember that, Miss Martin. I am a very bad man, so beware.' The laughter lines deepened at the corners of his eyes, even though his tone was serious.

Kate put her head on one side, regarding him with a candid gaze. She suspected that he was laughing at her, and it made her wary. 'I'll remember that, Mr Trader.'

'Now you know exactly who I am and what you might expect if you rent the front room and the kitchen, do you still want to pay me five shillings a month rent?'

'Yes, I do,' Kate said simply. 'But only if you promise to keep away from my clients. They will come here because they are facing starvation — I 'don't want them to be recruited to your gang.'

'You drive a hard bargain, Miss Martin.' Trader moved towards her, holding out his hand. 'Do we have a deal?'

Kate opened her reticule and took out five shillings, which she placed on his palm. 'A month in advance, Mr Trader.'

'It's usual to shake on a business agreement,' he said, smiling. 'I can see I'll have to give you lessons in bargaining.'

'I doubt if you could teach me anything of value.' Kate hesitated. 'But I will require a door key.'

Trader shook his head. 'Spears will let you in. That's what he's paid to do, amongst other things. We'll give it a trial for a month. If at the end of that time either of us is dissatisfied, the arrangement will be terminated. Is that what you consider fair, Miss Martin?'

'Perfectly,' she said briskly. 'I'd like to start tomorrow, unless you have any objections.'

'You may begin whenever it suits you. I'll watch your progress with interest.'

He opened the street door, bowing her out with exaggerated gallantry.

★ ★ ★

Kate arrived home to find her mother in the entrance hall with a small, thin woman of indeterminate age and Henry standing stiffly to attention. Judging by her mother's expression, Kate knew she was in even more trouble.

'Where have you been all morning, Kate? And

57

why were you out on your own? You know that's simply not done.'

'I'm sorry, Mama. I had urgent business to attend to and you've demoted Jenny, so I don't have a personal maid.'

'Nonsense. Of course Jenny is your maid,' Arabella tossed her head. 'Miss Barnet will wonder what sort of establishment she has come into if we cannot afford such a small luxury.'

Miss Barnet blushed and bobbed a curtsey. 'No, indeed, my lady. Such a thought never occurred to me.'

Arabella turned to Henry, frowning. 'Why are you standing there like a dummy? I told you to show Miss Barnet to her room, and take her luggage with you.'

'Yes, my lady.' Henry clicked his heels together and picked up two large carpet bags. 'This way, if you please, Miss Barnet.'

'You should have been here to assist me, Kate. You knew that Miss Barnet was starting today. I was relying on you to explain her duties. You simply cannot come and go as you please without telling anyone.'

Kate took off her bonnet and looped her shawl over her arm. 'As a matter of fact I am involved in some charity work, Mama. You told me that I ought to be doing something worthwhile, and that is what I went out for this morning.'

'I feel quite faint after dealing with the servants on my own. I'll sip a glass of sherry wine while you tell me exactly what sort of charity work you're involved in.'

'Yes, Mama. Do you mind if I go to my room

first and deposit my bonnet and shawl?'

'I do mind, because you'll stay there until it's time for luncheon, and I won't be any the wiser. You may ring for Jenny and she'll see to your garments.' Arabella stalked off towards the morning parlour.

Kate realised that she was cornered and explaining her motives for starting the soup kitchen would not go down well with her mother. If she mentioned the exact location she could imagine the shocked looks, the long lectures and the ultimate end of her plan. It was frustrating in the extreme, but as an unmarried daughter she was very conscious of the role she had to play. She followed her mother to the morning parlour.

Arabella seated herself in an armchair by the fire while Kate filled two glasses with sherry and handed one to her mother. In need of Dutch courage, Kate took a rather unladylike swig of her sherry. She knew that she was about to face a cross-examination equal to any meted out in a court of law.

'Well,' Arabella said, sipping her drink, 'I'm waiting for an explanation, Kate.'

'The charity feeds the poor and needy, Mama,' Kate said truthfully. 'It's to be run from a premises not too far from the Royal Mint.'

'Which premises? Who is the owner?'

'I believe he is a well-known businessman.'

'What is his name? Have I heard of him?'

'He prefers to remain anonymous, Mama.'

'But I assume he is the patron of this charity.'

'In a manner of speaking, yes, he is. And he's very wealthy.'

'Is he married?'

'I could hardly ask that, Mama. But he was not wearing a wedding ring.'

'I want to know his name, Kate. He might be anybody.'

Kate hesitated. She dare not mention Harry Trader, although it was unlikely that his notoriety would have spread this far, it was possible that he might be known to her father. She crossed her fingers behind her back. 'Augustus Spears, Mama. Augustus Spears, Esquire.'

'Then you must invite Mr Spears to dine with us one evening. If you make the invitation to him and his wife we will know if he is attached or not.'

'Yes, Mama. Would you like another sherry?'

Arabella held out her glass. 'After the morning I've had, I need a little sustenance. Miss Barnet is very biddable, but a little slow on the uptake. Maybe I ought to keep Jenny and let you have the new person.'

'But Miss Barnet came with an excellent reference from Lady Charlton. Jenny is just our housekeeper's daughter. Surely you must take precedence, Mama?'

'Yes,' Arabella said wearily. 'I suppose you're right.'

Having successfully diverted the conversation away from the soup kitchen, Kate refilled her mother's glass and placed it in her hand. 'Is it all right if I go and change out of my street clothes?'

'Yes, but I'm still not convinced that getting involved in this so-called charity is a suitable occupation for you, Kate. I think your papa will agree with me.'

For once, and to Kate's astonishment, her father did not share his wife's concerns about the proposed soup kitchen. At dinner that evening he listened to Kate and applauded her public-spirited intention to feed the poor.

'Bartholomew, I'm shocked,' Arabella said crossly.

'I thought you would support me in this.'

'If our daughter is going to be a bluestocking, she might as well do something for others, Arabella. Besides which, Kate's active involvement in a charity will reflect well upon me, and when it becomes known might further my chances of being a High Court Judge. I might even be put forward for a baronetcy.'

Arabella's eyes shone with excitement. 'Do you hear that, Kate? Your papa is always right. He understands the wider issues here.'

'You don't object then, Papa?' Kate said incredulously.

'On the contrary, my dear, I might even make a small contribution to the charity. I dare say you need some sort of equipment to start preparing meals for those who need them.'

'Yes, Papa. Pots and pans and such. I was going to ask Cook to make me a list.'

'I'm sure we must have dealings with a local ironmonger. You may choose what you want and have it put on my account, Katherine. Never let it be said that Bartholomew Martin is a penny-pincher.'

'The man who owns the property is very

61

wealthy, so Kate tells me. Although I've never heard of him.' Arabella turned to Kate, eyebrows raised. 'What is his name? I've forgotten already.'

Kate took a deep breath, hoping that Spears had not come to her father's attention in the criminal world.

'Augustus Spears.'

'I've never heard of him,' Sir Bartholomew said slowly. 'Are you sure you have the right name, Katherine?'

'Yes, Papa.' Kate thought quickly. 'I think he might be recently returned from the colonies, having made his fortune in . . . ' Kate thought hard, 'in guano, I believe.'

'It's strange that he chose to buy property in the Minories,' Arabella mused. 'I don't know that area well, but I have heard that it's not the sort of place one would wish to live.'

Kate could see her father mulling this over and she spoke quickly. 'But it is just the right place for a soup kitchen, Mama. After all, there would be no point in opening one in Finsbury Square, would there?'

'Of course not. What an idea.' Arabella picked up the silver bell and rang it. 'I wonder what Cook has prepared for dessert.'

★ ★ ★

Next morning, having visited the local ironmonger and purchased the necessary equipment with the promise that it would be delivered immediately to the premises in Cable Street, Kate and Jenny visited the market to buy the items that Cook deemed necessary for a good nourishing soup. With baskets overflowing with vegetables, some cheap cuts of meat and beef bones, they took a cab to Cable Street, stopping first in Nightingale Lane.

Kate alighted on her own and knocked on the door of the Harrises' cottage. After a minute or two it was opened by Ivy herself with a baby in her arms and the twins, Polly and Emma, clinging to her skirts. Her eyes widened when she saw Kate.

'Miss Martin. What brings you here again?'

'I know you're very busy with your family, Mrs Harris, but I really need your help.'

'Me?' Ivy glanced over Kate's shoulder. 'Is this one of my cousin's jokes? If it is, it ain't funny.'

'No, of course not, Ivy. I may call you Ivy, mayn't I?' Kate did not wait for an answer. She bent down to retrieve Charlie, who had made a break for the freedom of the street, and she hauled him back into the house. 'I'm starting a soup kitchen in Cable Street. It's not too far from here, but I realise now that I don't know how to make soup. I have all the ingredients, but neither Jenny nor I have ever cooked anything in our lives.'

A glimmer of amusement lit Ivy's pale grey eyes, but was replaced instantly by a look of defeat. 'I would help you, miss, but I can't leave my babies on their own.'

'Of course not,' Kate said hastily. 'You must bring them, too. There's plenty of room and they can play while we work. You will all be fed and I will pay you a small amount each day for your labours.'

'Did Perry put you up to this, miss?'

63

'He knows nothing about it, Ivy. I promise you, it was all my idea.'

'It's too far for the little ones to walk. I'm sorry, miss. I'd love to help — and the money would be more than welcome — but you can see my problem.'

'I have a hackney carriage waiting for us. There's room for you and the babies if you can be ready quickly.'

A rare smile lit Ivy's pinched features. 'If you'll hold on to Charlie, I'll bring baby John, Nellie and the twins.'

* * *

Spears opened the door and his jaw dropped when Kate and Jenny entered the premises, followed by Ivy and her children. He muttered something unintelligible and backed away to an open door that concealed a narrow staircase. He closed it after him with a thud that reverberated around the empty room as he retreated to his room upstairs.

Kate took charge immediately, leaving Jenny to take care of the little ones while she and Ivy unpacked the food and sorted out the delivery from the ironmongers, which had arrived earlier. Ivy rolled up her sleeves and began peeling and slicing onions, while Kate dealt with the mountain of root vegetables. It was back-breaking work for Kate, who had never even buttered a slice of bread, let alone prepared soup for a large number of people, but she was determined to make a success of the venture. Ivy stoked the range, which Spears had lit earlier in the morning, and soon they had two huge pans filled with meat and vegetables, topped up with water. Ivy added salt and pepper before placing the lids on the pans.

'I really enjoyed that, miss,' Ivy said, beaming. 'I used to work in a big kitchen before I married Ted. But if we're going to serve soup we should have a slice of bread to go with it, if it's going to be a proper meal.' She hurried into the front room at the sound of the baby crying and Kate followed her.

Jenny rose from the floor where she had been keeping the twins, Nellie and Charlie entertained. She handed the crying baby back to its mother. 'The soup smells good, but shouldn't there be a table or two, and chairs? The diners can't sit on the floor to eat.'

'And bowls and spoons, too,' Ivy added, cradling the baby in her arms.

'Of course,' Kate said, frowning. 'There are bowls and spoons in the box from the ironmongers, but I think you're right. We should offer bread and butter, too.'

'Butter is too expensive but bread on its own is fine.' Ivy hitched the baby over her shoulder, patting his tiny back. 'We could thicken the soup by adding some pearl barley, and we do need some more peppercorns and maybe a spoonful of mace for flavouring.'

'It's more complicated than I thought,' Kate said slowly. 'But I agree we do need tables and chairs. I haven't got the money to buy or even hire them.

I just hope we have enough crockery.'

Ivy shook her head. 'China gets broken. Tin

plates or mugs will do, and as people get used to us they can bring their own.'

'We have to let them know we're here.' Jenny glanced out of the window. 'It's not very obvious and if we don't advertise in some way, no one will come.'

'Oh, bother! I didn't think of all that.' Kate pushed a strand of hair back from her damp forehead with an impatient flick of her fingers. 'I'll get a good scolding at home if I fail at this.'

'You're a grown woman,' Ivy said hotly. 'Don't let them bully you, miss. Your heart is in the right place, and in my book that's all that matters.' The baby began to whimper and Ivy unbuttoned her blouse and put the squalling infant to her breast.

Kate strolled over to the door and gazed up and down the street. Jenny and Ivy had seen the flaws in her plans and they were right, but to fail when she had got so far was unthinkable. She took a step backwards as a familiar figure strode up to the door, and Harry Trader walked in. He came to a sudden halt when he saw Ivy and the children.

'Mrs Harris is a trained cook,' Kate said hastily. 'She's helped me to make the first batch of soup, but we have a problem.'

Harry glanced round the room and nodded. 'I was wondering when you'd notice the lack of furniture.'

'I was so intent on getting the food ready that I forgot,' Kate said reluctantly. 'Perhaps I could hire some tables and chairs.'

'Have you the funds to pay for them?'

She shook her head. 'No, not really.'

'I might be able to help. In fact, I can be of

assistance. The meeting room upstairs is well-equipped. You can borrow what you need.'

'Thank you,' Kate said humbly. 'That's very kind of you.'

He laughed. 'Not really, my dear innocent. As I said before, you and your charity are providing an excellent front for my business, which will keep the police away from here permanently, or so I hope.'

'I thought you were joking. You're actually using us?'

'Of course, and you are taking advantage of my generosity. It works both ways, my dear Miss Martin.'

Kate eyed him warily. 'Just what sort of business are you in, Mr Trader?'

'It's better for both of us that you know as little as possible about my interests. You might let something slip when speaking to your father.'

'Does he know your name?'

Harry's smiled faded. 'Did you mention it?'

She shook her head. 'I had the feeling that he might have heard of you.'

'So what did you tell him?'

There was an edge in Harry's voice that put Kate instantly on the defensive. 'I'm not as naïve as you seem to think, Mr Trader. I told him that Augustus Spears was the owner of the premises, and my father accepted that without comment.'

'You lied to your father to protect a villain like me,' Harry said, laughing. 'Miss Martin, I'm afraid you're on the road to perdition.'

'Well, at least I won't be facing hellfire on my own.'

67

Harry shook his head and, still chuckling, he crossed the room and opened the door to reveal a flight of uncarpeted stairs. 'Spears, bring a couple of tables to the shop, and benches.'

Kate could just make out a mumbling assent from upstairs, followed by the sound of furniture being dragged over bare boards.

'Thank you,' she said grudgingly.

'Make sure he puts them back for this evening's meeting.' Harry opened the street door. 'Good luck with the soup kitchen. I'll send a few people along at midday. There's nothing like a queue to attract others to stand in line.'

'Are you always so cynical?' Kate demanded crossly.

'I'm told it's part of my charm.' Harry stepped outside onto the pavement, tipped his hat and strode off.

'You want to watch him,' Jenny said in a low voice. 'I've met his sort before.'

'Don't worry. I can handle Mr Trader.' Kate was about to close the door, but she was overcome with curiosity and she could not resist watching him as he walked down the street with a swagger in his step. Not that it was any of her business where Harry Trader was headed, but she was suddenly alert and listening to the sweetest music she had ever heard. On the corner of Cable Street and Leman Street, sheltering from a sudden downpour beneath the railway bridge, Kate saw a young girl playing a concertina. Trader stopped to speak to her. She did not look him in the face, but continued to play while nodding in apparent agreement. There was something about his attitude towards

the girl that suggested they were old acquaintances, and he kissed her on the cheek before going
on his way. Kate was tempted to go out and speak
to the talented musician, but someone tapped her
on the shoulder and she spun round to see Jenny
standing at her side.

'What's the matter?'

'Nothing. You was in a dream, miss. But we still
got work to do. Ivy says we need bread to go with
the soup.'

Kate nodded. 'Yes, of course. I have some
money left. If you run to the bakery along the
street I'll help Spears to set up the tables.' She was
about to close the door but the strains of a haunting melody filled the air with sweetness, despite
the din from the docks and the rumble of traffic.
Kate sighed. 'That girl is very talented,' she said
softly. 'I've never heard anything but jigs and sea
shanties played on a concertina.'

'My uncle Joe used to play a squeeze-box at
weddings and funerals, as well as every Saturday
night in the pub, but he didn't make it sound like
that.' Jenny held her hand out for the money. 'Ta.
I'll be as quick as I can.'

'Get some peppercorns and mace, if you can,'
Kate said hastily, but Jenny was already on her way,
and Spears was bumping a table down the stairs,
accompanying each step with a loud expletive.

'Here, you.' Ivy laid the sleeping baby on her
shawl, which she had spread on the floor. 'Mind
your language in front of me nippers.'

'Well, you can come and give us a hand, missis.' Spears paused on the bottom step, apparently
stuck in the doorway. 'I wouldn't have taken you

lot on if I'd known the trouble it was going to give me. I don't hold with charity, anyway. I'm me own charity and I need funds to keep me in me dotage.' 'If you live that long,' Ivy said darkly.

'Let me help.' Kate hurried over to take the other end of the trestle table. 'Perhaps you'd check the soup, Ivy? You're the expert when it comes to cooking.'

'Lift your end, miss,' Spears said irritably. 'Why is women so useless when it comes to anything that needs a bit of brain power?'

Kate used her pent-up energy and frustration to give the table a sharp tug and freed it from its moorings. Spears almost toppled down the remaining steps, uttering a bark of annoyance.

'Lucky for you that you've a pretty face, Miss Martin. Harry Trader's got a soft spot for good-looking women.'

Kate did not know whether to be flattered or infuriated, but she chose to ignore him. 'Let's get the benches down, Mr Spears. It's almost midday.'

He glanced over his shoulder, curling his lip. 'I don't see no crowd outside.'

'The benches, if you please.' Kate left him to get on with the task while she went into the kitchen to unpack the bowls and spoons that the ironmonger had delivered. If they had a sudden rush of customers there would not be enough, but they would manage somehow.

Minutes later Jenny arrived with three large loaves of bread, although she had been unable to find a shop selling the spices. They laid up the two tables that Spears had reluctantly brought down, and there was nothing to do but wait.

Eventually, Kate realised that she would have to do something drastic if she wanted to advertise their presence. In the meantime Jenny and Ivy sampled the soup, sitting at the table with the children, and they seemed to be enjoying their meal. But Kate was too tense to bother with food, and she wrapped her shawl around her head and shoulders.

'I'm going out to bring in some customers,' she said as she opened the door. 'There must be some hungry people round here.'

5

Even as she closed the door behind her, Kate was aware that the music had stopped and she experienced a sharp pang of disappointment. Somehow the girl's playing had touched a chord in Kate's heart and had left her open to a maelstrom of emotion. The pain of separation from Ash, and not knowing whether he was alive or dead, had found expression in the silvery notes that filled the air on a wet day in Whitechapel. The heat and dust of Delhi might be thousands of miles away, but the strains of a sentimental ballad had brought memories tumbling back into Kate's consciousness.

The tap-tapping of a stick on the paving stones brought her abruptly back to reality, and she turned to see the young girl walking slowly towards her. The truth hit Kate with a sudden shock — the talented musician was blind.

'Are you Kate?' The girl's voice was as soft and gentle as her music.

'Yes, I am. How did you know that?'

A smile creased the girl's pretty face. 'Harry told me you were here.'

Kate reached out to lay her hand on the girl's sleeve. 'Why don't you come inside? It's going to rain again at any moment.'

'Yes, I feel it coming, but I'm used to being out in all weathers.'

Kate opened the door and stood aside to allow the girl to pass. 'May I ask your name?'

'I'm Annie Blythe.' She hesitated on the threshold, sniffing the air with an appreciative smile. 'Something smells good.'

'Would you care to be our first customer, Annie?' Kate resisted the temptation to take the girl's fragile hand and lead her to the table. The blind girl's demeanour was one of quiet pride and self-assurance, despite her obvious disability, and Kate knew instinctively that she would not welcome undue attention, however well meant.

Using her stick to guide her, Annie made her way to the table where Jenny, Ivy and the children were seated.

Jenny sprang to her feet. 'You can sit here, love. I've just finished.'

Annie nodded and set her concertina carefully on the table. 'I can pay for my food.'

'Just give us a tune on your squeeze-box,' Jenny said cheerfully. 'My name's Jenny, by the way, and I love a bit of music.' She patted Annie on the shoulder as she walked past her, heading for the kitchen.

'And I'm Ivy. These are my nippers.' Ivy hitched the baby onto her hip as she rose from the table. 'You eat as much as you can, my dear. You look as though you need feeding up.'

Kate held her breath, hoping that this fragile creature with the face of an angel and a halo of fine golden hair, would not take offence at Ivy's remark, but Annie merely smiled.

'It don't seem to matter how much I eat, ma'am, I stay like this anyway. But I am hungry and the soup smells wonderful. You must be a good cook.'

Ivy puffed out her chest. 'Well, I have been told

73

that before. Anyway, I'd best be going now. I don't like leaving the house empty in case me older kids get home before me. I don't want the fire to go out. Coal and kindling costs money.'

'Thank you for everything you've done today, Ivy,' Kate said as she caught two-year old Charlie by the hand and passed him to his mother. 'Will you be here at the same time tomorrow? Bring your other children, if possible.'

'Yes, if you need me. I will.'

Kate put her hand in her pocket and took out a sixpenny piece, which she pressed into Ivy's hand. 'You've earned this today. I wish it could be more.'

'Ta, miss. It's much appreciated.' Ivy herded her children out into the street and they disappeared amongst the crowd of passers-by.

'I hope we will soon become known,' Kate said, glancing out of the window. Rain was falling heavily now, trickling down the window like tears.

'You need to let people know you're here.' Annie lowered herself carefully onto the bench. 'You might have one already, but I think a big sign in the window would help.'

'I hadn't thought of that, but you're right. That's what I should do.' Kate stood aside as Jenny bustled into the room carrying two bowls brimming with hot soup.

'There's yours, Annie. And you should eat too, miss. Sit down and I'll bring some bread.'

Kate took a seat opposite Annie, who was tucking into the soup with evident relish. 'How do you know Harry Trader, Annie?'

'We're cousins,' Annie said, sighing. 'Our side of the family were poor, but my brother, Joe, and

74

Harry were good friends. They joined the army together, but Harry sold his commission and Joe's regiment was sent to India over a year ago.'

'Do you know where he's stationed?' Kate asked eagerly. Of course it was a slim chance. Annie's brother might be stationed anywhere in that large country, but she was desperate for news of Ashok. 'I was in Delhi until a few months ago.'

'I haven't heard from Joe for a long time. I don't know where he is now.'

The small ray of hope that Kate had felt vanished like morning mist. It was highly unlikely that there might be any connection between Annie's brother and Ash. 'I hope you hear from him soon,' Kate said automatically. 'Have you got family living in London?'

'Our parents died some time ago. Aunt Margaret, Lady Lyndon, is very good to me, but I try to be independent.' Annie spooned the soup into her mouth. 'Joe sends money, but sometimes it takes a long time to reach me, so I go out on the streets with my concertina. Anyway, what else would someone like me do to pass the time?'

'You're a talented musician, Annie. Surely you could get well-paid work in the theatre or a music hall?'

'No one wants a blind girl. It's a hard truth, but one I learned a long time ago.'

'But isn't it dangerous for a pretty young girl like you to be out on the streets?'

A smile flitted across Annie's delicate features. 'Not when you're under the protection of Harry Trader. I'd rather have Harry as a friend than an enemy, if you get my meaning.'

75

'I'm beginning to understand,' Kate said slowly.

'He's the best. He's like an older brother, so Joe doesn't have to worry about me. I'm the one who does the worrying.'

'Yes,' Kate said with feeling. 'I understand.'

'You left someone special in Delhi?'

Annie's perceptiveness was startling and it took Kate a moment to gather her thoughts. 'I had many friends in Delhi,' she said cautiously.

'And now you're here in Whitechapel.' Annie mopped up the remainder of the soup with a hunk of bread. 'You might do well to visit the local churches and get the ministers to mention the work you're doing here after their sermons on Sunday.'

'I hadn't thought of that, but it's a good idea.'

'I'll spread the word, but it will take time for people to know you're here.' Annie stood up and reached for her cane. 'There's just one thing you need to be aware of.'

'What's that, Annie?'

'The Trader gang are not the only people who matter round here. You need to keep away from anyone who works for a man named Monks.'

'I've been warned about Mad Monks, but what possible interest could his gang have in my soup kitchen?'

'You've got a lot to learn, Kate. By setting up here, in one of Harry's premises, you've allied yourself to him, whether you like it or not.'

'All I wanted to do was to help people like Ivy. I wanted to make sure that their children didn't go hungry. I don't see why that would upset anyone.'

'I'm sure Harry must have told you this, but by setting up a charity here you've provided cover for

76

his goings-on without attracting the attention of the police.' Annie picked up her concertina. 'But good luck, Kate. I think you're very brave.'

★ ★ ★

Late that evening, taking advantage of the fact that her father had retired to his study to work on some papers, and her mother was dozing quietly by the fire in the drawing room, Kate slipped away and made her way to the old schoolroom on the floor below the servants' sleeping quarters. There was gaslight only on the first three floors of the house, although Sir Bartholomew had announced earlier that he was considering the addition of gas lighting throughout the building, which had become the main topic of conversation during the evening meal.

Neither of Kate's parents had thought to enquire as to the success or failure of the soup kitchen, and that seemed to sum up their interest in their daughter's venture. Kate was not surprised, and in a way she was relieved. The last thing she needed was criticism of her efforts when she had only just begun, and considering her unintentional involvement with the criminal element, it was better if her father remained in total ignorance of her activities. The only difficulty had arisen when her mother brought up the subject of inviting Spears to dine with them, placing Kate in the invidious position of having to promise faithfully that she would bring that gentleman home the following evening. It was the last thing she wanted. Spears was not noted for being co-operative, and he might refuse

— she could only hope that he would.

By the light of a single candle, Kate explored the schoolroom, where memories lurked in deep shadows. A succession of governesses had led to a motley selection of tutors as Kate had grown from childhood to become an accomplished young woman. But she was not here on a sentimental journey, she had come to find paper, pen and ink, and she settled down to make a large poster, as Annie had suggested. Seated at the teacher's desk, Kate gazed into the dim recesses of the schoolroom. In her mind's eye she saw the child who studied on her own, obeying the whims of ageing spinsters, who had little hope of anything better in life. The sharp rap across the knuckles with a ruler, the punishing back brace to make her sit upright, the stinging blows of the cane across open hands — all these memories came flooding back to her.

Kate bent her head over her work, shutting out the past. She was a grown woman now and she would shape her own destiny, but in the meantime she had an aim in life and that was to help Ivy and a wider community. The poster was only the beginning, and it mattered little to her that she would also be helping to shield a criminal gang. Harry Trader might be using her, but, if setting up shop in his premises was the only way to get help to the needy, it was a price she was prepared to pay.

★ ★ ★

Kate and Jenny set off early next morning, heading first for the market and then for the premises in Cable Street.

Spears greeted them with a surly expression that emphasised the deep wrinkles on his face, putting Kate in mind of a pickled walnut. She controlled the urge to laugh with difficulty.

'I suppose you want me to lug the tables back downstairs,' Spears said crossly.

'Yes, if you please, Mr Spears.' Kate managed a smile.

'I don't please. I had to get them back upstairs last evening for the meeting. I've got a bad back, I'll have you know. Every movement is pure agony.'

'I'm sorry to hear that,' Kate said, trying to sound as if she meant it. 'But it is for a good cause.'

'No one considers whether I might need help or not.' Spears stamped over to the door, flung it open and allowed it to slam behind him as he thudded up the stairs.

'I can see that he's not going to be much help today,' Jenny said, grinning. 'I'll go and see to the fire in the range. He's probably let it go out, just to spite us.'

Kate took the rolled-up poster from her basket and shook it out. 'I'll paste this to the window. And I've had another idea, although I don't suppose Spears will find it very appealing.'

'What do you want him to do?' Jenny asked with a twinkle in her eyes.

'I've seen men with billboards strapped to their front and back,' Kate said, chuckling. 'We're going to turn him into a sandwich man.'

Jenny doubled up with laughter, but the sound

of Spears bumping a piece of furniture down the stairs made her beat a hasty retreat to the kitchen. Kate could hear Jenny chuckling even as Spears erupted into the room, cursing beneath his breath as he gave the table a mighty shove.

'It were a bad day when I opened the door to you, miss. I had a nice peaceful life until you walked in and ruined everything.'

'Look at it this way, Mr Spears,' Kate said reasonably. 'While we are here giving free food to those in need, the police are unlikely to raid these premises. Or so I've been told.'

Spears eyed her suspiciously. 'What d'you know about the goings-on upstairs?'

'Nothing, Mr Spears, and it's better that way. Now if we could have the other table and the chairs brought down here that would be very helpful.'

'I ain't your slave,' Spears grumbled as he hesitated at the foot of the staircase. 'You can't tell me what to do.'

Kate knew that he had a point, but she was not about to let him get an advantage over her. 'Mr Spears, I value your co-operation so much so that my parents have invited you to dine with us in Finsbury Square this evening.'

He glared at her suspiciously. 'You don't mean it. You're making fun of me.'

'No, on my honour I meant every word I said. Please come.'

He grunted and shuffled off in the direction of the stairs. Kate was about to follow him when the street door opened and Perry strolled in. Spears shot upstairs as if the devil himself were after him.

'Who was that strange fellow?' Perry took off

80

his top hat and laid it on the table together with his cane. He peeled off his gloves, taking in his surroundings with a critical gaze.

'That was the caretaker,' Kate said hastily. 'But what are you doing here, Perry? Is this a social call? Because if you're hungry we aren't nearly ready to serve up luncheon.'

'I'm sure the soup will be delicious, but this is purely a social call. I wanted to see where you had set up your charity.'

Kate encompassed the premises with a wave of her hands. 'This is where we serve the food. The kitchen is through that door. Take a look, by all means.'

She followed him into the back room where Jenny had begun peeling a mountain of vegetables.

'You seem well organised, but have you had many customers?' Perry retrieved a potato that had rolled onto the floor and handed it back to Jenny.

'Not really,' Kate admitted reluctantly. 'That's why I stuck the notice in the window.' She turned her head at the now familiar sound of Annie's cane tap-tapping on the bare floorboards. 'We're in the kitchen, Annie.'

'I hope she's brought her concertina,' Jenny said in a whisper. 'I love a bit of music.'

'I never go anywhere without it.' Annie stood in the doorway, a smile hovering on her lips. 'I thought if I stood outside and played some lively tunes it might attract attention to your soup kitchen.'

'That would be wonderful,' Kate said enthusiastically. 'This is Annie Blythe, Perry. She's a brilliant musician.'

'Perry?' Annie turned to him as if she sensed his presence.

'I'm an old friend of Kate's,' Perry said hastily. 'Peregrine Harte, but my friends call me Perry.'

Annie moved a step closer to him. 'You work with dusty old books and papers. Are you a lawyer?'

He stared at her in amazement. 'How did you know that?'

'You speak like a lawyer. I can tell by the tone of your voice, and the smell of old books clings to your clothes. I suppose you could be a law writer or a clerk, but your voice gives you away. You are used to making yourself heard across a courtroom.'

'Amazing,' Perry said softly. 'You should work for the police, Annie. You would make a good detective.'

Kate stepped in between them. The mention of the police had unnerved her, and she wondered if Perry was aware that the premises were owned by a notorious criminal. If he knew about Harry Trader he might feel honour-bound to tell her father, and that would be the end of her attempts to feed those most in need. She was about to speak when the outer door burst open and the sound of running feet preceded Ivy and a brood of young children.

'I didn't expect to see you here, Perry.' Ivy reached out to grab the hand of the oldest boy. 'Stay still,

Frankie. We've come at a bad time.'

'Not at all,' Kate said, smiling. The sudden

appearance of the Harris family was a welcome distraction. 'I'm sure we can find something for Frankie and his sister to do.'

'If you'll excuse me speaking out,' Ivy said shyly, 'I thought that my three eldest could go out and let people know we're here.'

'They could hand out leaflets, if you get some printed, Kate.' Perry took a small notepad from his pocket and a stub of a pencil. 'I could get some done quite quickly.'

'If you'll excuse me, Perry,' Ivy said nervously, 'but most folk round here can't read anyway, and they're the ones who most need a free meal. My nippers know who to tell.'

Kate nodded enthusiastically. 'What a good idea. Of course I'll pay your children for their trouble. I know you will be missing the money they usually earn if they help me, so I'll make it up to you.'

'Ta, miss,' Frankie said eagerly. 'Shall us go out now?'

The younger children were eyeing the loaves of bread that Kate and Jenny had purchased on the way to Cable Street, and Kate suspected that they had not yet eaten.

'First of all you must find somewhere to sit and I'll cut some bread for you. I think I might have a pot of jam in my basket, too.'

Frankie and May rounded up the younger children and they sat in a circle on the floor, waiting eagerly while Kate and Jenny prepared the food, passing the jammy bread to Ivy, who distributed it among the children.

'You, too, Ivy.' Kate handed her a crust spread

83

with strawberry jam.

Ivy looked as if she would refuse, but the aroma of the still warm bread was too much for her and she sunk her teeth into it with a sigh of contentment.

'I've eaten, thank you,' Annie said when Kate offered her a slice. 'But I will play a tune for the little ones, if I may?'

'That would be lovely. You play, Annie, and I'll make a pot of tea for us workers.' Kate turned to Perry with a smile. 'What about you? Have you had breakfast?'

He shook his head. 'No, but I have a court session in half an hour, Kate. I just wanted to make sure you were all right. This isn't the best part of town,' he added in a low voice.

'That's why we're here.' Kate followed him to the street entrance. 'You won't say anything of that nature to my father, will you?'

'No, of course not. You're a young woman who knows her own mind. I admire you for that, but be careful, that's all I'm saying.' He picked up his hat, gloves and cane. 'Good luck, Kate. Let me know if there's anything I can do to help.' He was about to leave but he paused, listening to the tune that Annie was playing. 'She is a good musician.'

'Yes, and I've told her she's wasting her talents playing in the streets of Whitechapel, but she seems content to do so.'

'Maybe we can help her. She looks so frail, as if a puff of wind would blow her away.'

'Don't tell me you've fallen in love, Perry?'

'Of course not.' He leaned over to brush her cheek with a whisper of a kiss. 'I'm just speaking

84

the truth. Anyway, I must get back to my dusty books; Annie was quite right. I really should get out of the office more often.' He walked off at a brisk pace, ramming his top hat on his head as he went.

Kate closed the door and went back to the kitchen. She was met by a ring of jammy, grinning faces as the children swayed in time to the sound of Annie's concertina.

Jenny handed Kate a cup of tea. 'What a nice young man. Is he your sweetheart, miss?'

'I knew him before I went to India, but I haven't seen him for three years.'

'He's very handsome,' Jenny said, grinning. 'I wish I had a gentleman friend like him.'

Ivy went round her children with a damp cloth, wiping jam from sticky faces and fingers. 'Right, Frankie, May and Jimmy. You can go out and spread the word that the soup kitchen will be open at midday. May, you can take Nellie with you, but don't let her stray too near the docks or the watermen's stairs.'

'Yes, Ma.' May's small face lit up with pride as she took her younger sister by the hand. 'Come on, Nellie. You and me will bring in more people than Frankie and Jimmy.'

Frankie scrambled to his feet and headed for the street door, followed by Jimmy. 'I'll beat you two, easy. Nellie's just a baby and you're a girl.'

'I'm not a baby and I'll get more people than you do, Frankie.' Nellie pushed past him and raced out into the street.

'Look after each other,' Kate said, smiling as she closed the door after them. She did not hold out much hope that they would bring in the hordes of hungry people, but even a few would be a start.

She moved swiftly to the door that led to the stairs and opened it. 'Mr Spears, we need the other table and benches. Right away, if you please.' She was answered by a muffled grunt and she returned to the kitchen to help Jenny with the soup.

★ ★ ★

When Kate arrived home late that afternoon, after a moderately successful lunchtime service, she was met in the hallway by her mother.

Arabella wrinkled her nose. 'Kate, you smell of onions and you look like a skivvy. For heaven's sake go upstairs, take a bath and change out of those stained clothes.'

'Why? What's the fuss about, Mama?'

'I am not fussing, and don't take that tone with me, my girl. As a matter of fact we have a guest for dinner tonight and I want you to make a good impression.'

'Who's coming?'

'The new curate from All Saints' church. He's the son of a baronet and very well thought of.'

'You're matchmaking, Mama.'

'Don't say it like that, Kate. Your papa and I are trying to make sure that you don't end up an old maid. There, I've said it before, but I fear that's the way you're heading.'

'There's no shame in being an unmarried woman, Mama. Miss Nightingale is unmarried and is very well respected.'

'She has done something in the world, Kate.

You are a judge's daughter with a good education and you are quite presentable. Don't allow a foolish romance to cloud your judgement. We are back in England now and you have a duty to respect the wishes of your parents. Now, please go upstairs and change. I've instructed the maids to fill a bath with hot water.'

Kate could see that it was useless to argue. Life was easier if she humoured her mother and obeyed her father, or at least made it appear that she was compliant with all his dictates. It was one evening out of her life; she would be nice to the curate, and maybe he could send some of his poorer parishioners to her soup kitchen.

Bathed, scented and wearing her smartest dinner dress, Kate made her way to the drawing room.

Sir Bartholomew was standing with his back to the fire, chatting apparently amicably with a tall, thin young man. Arabella was seated primly on the sofa, clutching a glass of sherry.

'Kate come and meet Mr Haroldson, our new curate from All Saints' church.' Sir Bartholomew beamed at her, although Kate knew by his fixed smile that she was expected to behave with the utmost propriety.

'How do you do, Mr Haroldson?' she said dutifully, holding out her hand.

He held it for a few seconds longer than necessary, peering at her through the thick lenses of his steelrimmed spectacles. The firelight reflected off a shiny patch of his balding pate, but his smile seemed genuine. 'How do you do, Miss Martin? It's a pleasure to meet you. I've heard so much about your good works from your dear mama.'

'I'm sure she exaggerates,' Kate said mildly. 'I've only just set up a soup kitchen in Whitechapel. It's quite difficult to reach the people who need help the most.'

'I'm sure I can find many families who will jump at the chance of a free meal. There is so much poverty in that area, although, of course my parishioners are of a much better class.'

Kate was about to ask him what he meant by that remark when there was a knock on the door and Winnie, the latest addition to the staff in Finsbury Square, hovered on the threshold.

'There's a gent here who says he's been invited to dinner, ma'am.'

Kate held her breath. She had completely forgotten Spears. He had not given her an answer to the invitation to dine with them and she had been too busy to repeat the request. He pushed past Nell and barged into the room. He was wearing a slightly green-tinged frockcoat and tight black trousers that made his skinny legs look like sticks. His white shirtfront was creased and his cravat had come untied. Kate stared at him in horror.

'I was invited,' he said, glaring at Arabella and then Sir Bartholomew. 'It ain't polite to keep a guest hanging round outside.'

6

'Who the devil are you?' Sir Bartholomew eyed Spears suspiciously.

'She invited me to dinner,' Spears said sulkily, jerking his head in Kate's direction.

'Good heavens! Surely this can't be the owner of the premises, Kate?' Arabella stared at him with a puzzled frown.

Spears turned on her with a ferocious scowl. 'You toffs think you're better than the rest of us. Anyway, I never said I owned the place — I'm just the caretaker for—'

Kate stepped in between them. 'I'm sorry, Mr Spears.

There appears to have been some misunder-standing.'

'D'you mean I come all the way from Whitechapel only to be thrown out on the street, because your ma and pa are too stuck up to mix with the likes of Augustus Spears?'

'All men are equal in the sight of God, sir.' Harold Haroldson steepled his hands, peering at Spears over the tip of his fingers.

'Who asked you for your opinion?' Spears demanded angrily. 'I come here in good faith and it's obvious I ain't wanted.' He spun round to face Kate. 'I blame you for this — just wait till I tell Harry—'

'I've had enough of this outburst,' Sir Bartholo-mew said firmly. 'If my daughter invited you to dine, then you are a welcome guest, sir. But if you can't behave like a civilised human being I will have to ask you to leave.'

'I apologise if I have done anything to make you feel uncomfortable, Mr Spears,' Kate said hastily. 'If you would rather not stay I'm sure we will all understand.'

Spears shrugged and drew himself up to his full height. 'Apology accepted. I will stay because you owe me a dinner after that long walk from Cable Street.'

'Do take a seat, Mr Spears.' Kate beckoned to Henry, who had been standing stiffly to attention, his face a mask of self-control. 'I'm sure that our guest would like a glass of sherry wine.'

'Brandy,' Spears said firmly. 'I don't drink that fancy stuff — it's only fit for old ladies.'

Arabella had raised her glass to her lips, but she replaced it on the drum table at her side. 'When you've given Mr Spears a drink, go to the kitchen and see if dinner is ready, Henry. We'll eat earlier than usual.'

Harold went to sit beside Spears on the sofa. 'You seem troubled, my friend. Is there anything you would like to share with me?'

Spears edged away from him. 'I come for good grub, not a sermon.' He grabbed the glass of brandy from Henry and knocked it back in one gulp. 'Call that a tot? Give me a proper measure, mate.'

Henry took the crystal goblet and poured a generous measure from one of the decanters on a side table. He handed it back to Spears, but Kate could tell from Henry's tight-lipped expression

90

that he was exercising all his training in self-control.

'Go now, Henry,' Kate said in a low voice. 'Ask Cook to hurry dinner along, if at all possible.'

Henry left the room at a dignified pace, as if determined to emphasise his position in the household being above that of the ill-mannered intruder. Kate avoided meeting her mother's angry gaze; she knew that she was in for a cross-examination when their guests had gone.

She was not looking forward to dinner, but it went better than she expected. Spears sat in silence with his head bent over his food and he demolished everything that was put in front of him with apparent enjoyment. Harold kept up a monologue, talking about his past experiences as a missionary in Africa before he decided to return to London. Kate was beginning to think she would rather be trampled on by a herd of elephants than to sit through another meal listening to the new curate, when Spears pushed his plate away and rose to his feet.

'Ta, your worship and your ladyship. That was a meal to remember. I'll think about that when I'm living on bread and cheese or a meat pie. Anyway, I'd best go now. I don't want to outstay me welcome.'

Kate jumped to her feet. She knew that she would receive a scolding from her mother for doing so, but she was desperate to get Spears out of the house before he mentioned Harry Trader. There had been a couple of uncomfortable moments, and she was afraid that her luck might run out at any minute.

'I'll see you out, Mr Spears. Thank you so much for coming.' Ignoring the warning look from her mother and the startled expression on her father's face, Kate hurried after Spears. Henry jumped to attention to open the front door and Kate followed Spears down the steps to the pavement.

'Why did you invite me here?' Spears demanded angrily. 'Did you do it to make me look a fool?'

'No, I didn't. If you must know I didn't dare tell my parents that Harry Trader is my landlord. Papa must have come across the name during the course of his work, even if we have been out of the country for three years. I would have been forbidden to have anything to do with him, so I said the first thing that came into my head. I told them that you owned the premises.'

A slow grin almost split Spears' face in two. 'And I thought you was so prim and proper. You're just as big a liar as I am.'

Kate decided that this was meant as a compliment, and she managed a weak smile. 'If you say so. Anyway, thank you for not mentioning Harry's name. I know the soup kitchen is a nuisance for you, but it is intended to help people.'

'If you say so, but I never tasted nothing like what we just had. If you ever need someone to make up the numbers at one of your dinners, just let Augustus Spears know. Ta-ta for now, Miss Kate.' Spears shambled off, heading in the general direction of Whitechapel.

Kate returned to the dining room, expecting to be greeted by grim silence and accusing looks from her parents, but she found her father and Harold puffing away on cigars in between sips of brandy.

'Your mother retired early to bed,' Sir Bartholomew said cheerfully. 'She has a headache. We'll be here for a while so don't wait up, Kate.'

Harold rose to his feet, his previously pale cheeks having taken on a ruddy glow, which was probably due to the copious amounts of sherry, wine and brandy that he had consumed during dinner.

'It's been a delightful evening. It was a pleasure to make your acquaintance, Miss Martin. I will certainly draw the attention of my congregation to the soup kitchen in Cable Street.'

'Thank you, sir.' Kate backed towards the doorway. 'Good night, Papa.' She made her escape, hardly able to believe her luck. Her father seemed to have found a new friend, and she herself had been spared the advances of a singularly unattractive clergyman.

★ ★ ★

She made her way upstairs to her bedroom. Perhaps Spears had been right — she had more in common with the criminal element than she had with the clergy. It was a disturbing and yet amusing thought.

★ ★ ★

Gradually, day by day, the word went round about the soup kitchen in Cable Street, and more and more hungry people arrived at noon for a nourishing meal. Kate worked tirelessly, spending all

93

her pin money on ingredients, but she knew that she must find a way of raising funds. She alone could not support the growing numbers of men, women and children who were living on the edge of starvation. She had seen stick-thin children waiting silently in long queues, together with the elderly, and cripples who were barely able to stand. There were charities aimed at helping those who were sick or destitute, but there were a significant number who either did not fall into the right category or who harboured inbred suspicion of anyone attempting to save their souls. The fear of the workhouse seemed to be the main reason for these people clinging desperately to their independence and Kate was determined to do her best to keep them from that fate.

She had plenty of help from Ivy and Jenny when it came to cooking and serving the food, and Annie came every day to entertain the people waiting for their free meal. Spears, who had been a little more co-operative after the meal in Finsbury Square, grudgingly acceded to Kate's request for a door key.

★ ★ ★

She often rose early and walked to Whitechapel to make sure that the fire in the range had not gone out overnight, and she purchased fresh vegetables from costermongers' barrows on the way. But no matter how frugal she was with her money, there was never enough to go round and she often had to ask Cook for scraps or bones to add goodness to the soup. Kate persuaded Cook to teach her how to make bread, and although her first attempts were a disaster, she improved quickly. Every day from then on the delicious aroma of baking bread wafted from the kitchen into the dining area.

★ ★ ★

Kate had risen particularly early one fine June morning. Sunlight streamed through her bedroom window and she could hear birdsong from the Square garden. It was a lovely day, but all was not well. Kate was down to her last few pennies and her allowance was not due until the beginning of July. She rose from her bed, washed and dressed as quickly as possible and let herself out of the house without disturbing anyone. With her wicker basket looped over her arm she set off for Cable Street, stopping along the way to purchase carrots and onions. There was still half a sack of potatoes in the kitchen, but there would be no meat in the soup today.

She let herself into the premises and was about to enter the kitchen when the door that led to the stairs burst open. Harry Trader was in need of a shave and his shirt hung loosely over his trousers as if he had slept in his clothes. He ran his hand through his already tousled hair.

'What are you doing here at the crack of dawn, Miss Martin?'

'It's hardly that, sir. Anyway, I might ask the same of you.' Kate looked him up and down. 'Have you been here all night?'

'That's none of your business, but as it happens I was working late and I must have fallen asleep.'

95

'I'm going to put the kettle on. You look as though you could do with a cup of strong tea. I think I have enough.' Kate carried her basket into the kitchen and placed it on the table before inspecting the fire in the range. The embers were still glowing and with a little gentle persuasion she managed to get the fire going. She filled a kettle at the sink and placed it on the hob.

Harry stood in the doorway, fastening the buttons on his shirt. 'Do you always arrive so early?'

'No, but today I need to make the bread, and then I can make a start on peeling the vegetables.'

He eyed her curiously. 'Where are your helpers?'

'They'll be here soon.' Kate went to the larder and fetched flour, sugar, salt and yeast.

'There's a bakery on the corner. Why don't you buy loaves? Surely it would save time?'

'Yes, but this way is cheaper.' Kate moved swiftly to the range to make the tea. 'There's a jug of milk on the marble slab. Would you fetch it, please?'

Harry raised an eyebrow but he did as she asked. 'Where are the fishes?'

She stared at him blankly. 'What fishes?'

'Well, it seems as if you need a miracle if this amount of food is going to feed the five thousand.'

'It isn't funny,' Kate said stiffly. 'I'm doing my best.' She took the pot to the table and selected two of the least cracked cups from a shelf above the sink.

'I can see that.' Harry pulled up a chair and sat down. 'Where do you get the money to fund all this?'

'I use my allowance.' Kate had a feeling that

96

Harry Trader would spot an untruth, and there did not seem to be any point in lying. She filled a cup and passed it to him. 'That's all the sugar we have, so please don't take too much.'

'Are you telling me that your pin money is the only funding you have for all this?' Harry waved away her offer of sugar.

'If you're afraid I won't pay next month's rent, it will be paid on the dot.'

'But it will be your money? I thought you were running a charity.'

Kate sipped her tea. 'Does it matter, Mr Trader? You'll get the rent, so don't worry.' She put down her cup and went to open the bag of flour, but her bottom lip quivered.

'What's the matter?'

Kate sank down on the nearest chair. 'Weevils. I can't use this flour.' Tears welled in her eyes despite her efforts to suppress them.

Trader took a handful of coins from his pocket. 'My winnings from cards last evening,' he said with a rueful smile. 'I dare say you frown on gambling, but this will buy bread and some meat to add to those vegetable you purchased this morning.'

'Why would you do that? You don't really approve of what I'm doing, I can tell.'

'Now that's where you're wrong. I think it's a very good thing, and it's kept the police away for the last few weeks, so I applaud your efforts. It suits me to be generous.'

Kate was torn between the desperate need to take the money and the desire to throw it back in his face. She had no particular feelings about

97

gambling — it was none of her business what other people did — but taking the funds from him would make her beholden to a known criminal. On the other hand, if she allowed her pride to overrule her heart it would leave desperate people to go hungry. She reached across the table and scooped the money into her hand.

'Thank you, Mr Trader. I'll send Jenny out to buy bread and a couple of large beef bones when she gets here.'

He held up his hand. 'There's one condition.'

'Oh dear. What is it?'

'That you stop calling me Mr Trader, and you allow me to call you Kate.'

She smiled in spite of her attempt to maintain a serious expression. 'I think I can manage that, Harry.'

He drained his cup and stood up. 'Thank you for the tea. Now I need to go and leave you to get on with your good work.' He hesitated in the doorway. 'And I do mean it when I say it's good work. I wish I were as well-intentioned and caring as you are, Kate.'

'I don't know about that.' Kate felt the blood rush to her cheeks and she turned her head away.

'Annie told me how kind you've been to her. Her brother, Joe, asked me to keep an eye on her and you've made my task a lot easier.'

'It's a pleasure to have her here, and people love to listen to her music.'

'Don't worry about next month's rent,' Harry said slowly. 'It's the least I can do, but you need to register as a charity and then you can raise funds legally. Your lawyer friend should be able to help you with that.'

Kate gave him a searching look. 'How do you know about Perry?'

'There's very little that goes on in this area without coming to my attention. Thank you again for the tea.' He turned on his heel and walked away, leaving Kate staring after him in surprise.

Harry Trader was an enigma. Although she sedulously avoided making enquiries into his criminal past, she knew that his gang had a reputation for running illicit gambling clubs and for violence. Her father would be horrified if he knew that she was involved, even if indirectly, with such a person. Although, if she were honest, Harry's reputation made him a dangerous but romantic figure, and his generosity was more than welcome.

Kate was about to count the coins when she heard footsteps and Jenny hurried into the kitchen. She came to a halt, staring at Harry's empty cup and the money on the table in front of Kate.

'What's happened? Did I just see Harry Trader walking down the street?'

'Yes, you did. And thanks to Mr Trader we are back in business. The flour is alive with weevils so I can't make any bread, but he's given us enough money to purchase loaves from the bakery and bones for today's soup. I can also pay Ivy.'

'But if we take money from him, doesn't that leave us obligated to a villain?'

Kate rose to her feet. 'Yes, I suppose it does, but I don't care, Jenny. If I threw this back in his face we would have to close up at the end of the week. As it is I will have to find another way to fund our efforts. My allowance isn't due until the beginning of next month.'

'You've been using your own money?'

'It doesn't matter. We can carry on today and tomorrow. In the meantime I'll have to think of a way to raise funds without asking Harry for more.'

Jenny tossed her head. 'Be careful, miss. That's all I can say.' She held out her hand. 'If you give me some money I'll go out again and get what's necessary.'

* * *

The last drop of soup had been served and there was not a crumb of bread left after the midday session. Jenny was in the kitchen washing up while Ivy helped Kate to tidy the dining area, and the twins and Nellie kept baby John amused, while Charlie gnawed on one of the bones that had flavoured the soup. There was no meat left on it, but that did not seem to bother him.

A sudden commotion outside made Kate run to the window.

'It's a fight,' she said nervously. 'Better take the little ones into the kitchen, Ivy.'

Ivy glanced over Kate's shoulder. 'I know one of those men. He used to work with my Ted on the docks, but he got the sack and joined Trader's gang.' She scooped the baby up in her arms. 'Come with me, girls. And you, too, Charlie.' She grabbed him by the hand and dragged him protesting into the kitchen.

Outside bricks and stones were being hurled and punches thrown. Kate was about to lock the door when two of the men fell against it and the catch gave way. They tumbled into the room pursued by several others, who smashed up tables and chairs, scattering cutlery and tin bowls onto the floor. Jenny emerged from the kitchen brandishing a rolling pin, but Kate snatched it from her.

'Get help before they destroy everything.' She gave Jenny a gentle shove towards the door, but as if on cue, a broad-shouldered man wearing a long black coat and a felt hat pulled down over his brow, strode into the premises, followed by two tough-looking individuals.

'Enough!' the man bellowed, and the fighting stopped abruptly.

'This is an outrage,' Kate said angrily. 'Look at the damage your men have done. This is a soup kitchen, not a boxing ring.'

'You'd better watch your tongue, young woman.'

'I don't know who you are, but this is private property.' Kate faced him, clenching her hands behind her back. She was trembling from head to foot but she was not going to let this man see she was afraid.

'Monks is the name. I dare say you've heard of me.'

'I have heard of you, as it happens, but nothing good.'

He glared at her and then, to Kate's surprise, he threw back his head and laughed. 'They call me Mad Monks.'

'Well, Mr Monks, please take your men and leave. I don't suppose they have any intention of clearing up the mess.'

He moved a step closer to Kate, bending his

101

head to look her in the eye, and a livid scar on his right cheek gleamed palely. 'You're being used, young lady. Trader only keeps you here as a cover for his not-so-respectable activities, but that's all going to end. Cable Street belongs to me and his time here is over. You've been warned.'

Kate was trembling, but she was determined not to allow him to intimidate her. 'I want you to go now.'

'Out of respect to you ladies we will leave, but you can tell Harry Trader that we won't be so polite next time. Make sure you pass on that message.'

'I have nothing to do with Trader and his gang.' Kate tossed her head. 'We are here to help those in need. I'm not interested in your petty squabbles.'

Jenny plucked at her sleeve. 'Don't annoy him,' she whispered.

'Outside,' Monks roared, pointing at his bruised and bloodied men. He glanced over his shoulder. 'You've seen nothing yet, miss. Stay here and you'll find yourself in the middle of a gang war where no one is safe.' He swept out into the street, followed by his men.

Kate gazed in dismay at the four men who lay on the floor. They were bloodied and bruised and in various stage of consciousness.

'Who are they?' Jenny asked anxiously.

'They must be Trader's gang,' Kate said in a low voice. 'I suppose we'd better help them.'

'They're criminals, Kate.'

'Yes, and they're bleeding all over our clean floor. Fetch a bowl of water and some rags.'

'Have they gone?' Spears peered round the inner door.

'Where were you when we needed you?' Kate demanded.

'I'm not stupid enough to take on Mad Moses Monks. I heard you through the crack in the door,' Spears said, shaking his head. 'You've made an enemy there, miss. You'll need to be very careful where you go and what you say in future.' He bent down to help one of the least injured men to his feet. 'Come on, Watkins. Let's get you upstairs. The rest of you, get up and stop acting like little girls. Harry's not going to be very pleased with you, I can tell you that for nothing.' He heaved Watkins towards the stairs, and the other men scrambled to their feet, two of them bleeding profusely.

Jenny handed one a drying cloth she had been clutching. 'You'll need some salve to put on those cuts, mister.'

'Ta.' The man held the cloth to his nose and stumbled off after Spears.

'We should make them clear up the mess,' Kate said crossly as the door closed on them.

'Never mind. We'll get it done quicker without them.' Jenny began retrieving the items strewn all over the floor. 'Send the bill to Harry Trader. That's what I'd do.'

'Yes, you're right. I'll have a few words with him when I see him next.' Kate heaved at one of the overturned tables. 'This mustn't happen again. Go and check on Ivy and the children, Jenny. They must be scared out of their wits, poor little mites.'

It took time to get everything straight again, and some of the mugs were damaged beyond repair. Kate sent Ivy home early, and she was thankful for Jenny's level-headedness and seeming inability to be frightened by anything. When they had finished clearing up Jenny made a pot of tea.

'Come and sit down, miss. I think we've earned a rest and a cup of split pea.'

Kate wiped her hands on a towel. 'Thanks, Jenny. I'll join you in a minute or two, but first I want a word with Spears. I'm not going to wait for Harry Trader to grace us with his presence. I'm going to find out where he lives and I'm going to tell him that if he doesn't give us some protection from other gangs we'll find somewhere else for our soup kitchen.'

'Quite right. I don't see why we have to put up with what just happened.'

'No, definitely not. I'm just thankful that Annie wasn't here today. That's another thing. I want to know where she lives. She might be ill, for all we know.'

'Do you want me to come with you, miss?'

'I'll speak to Spears first and then I'll let you know.'

Kate made her way up the narrow staircase to the first floor. It was the first time she had ventured this far and she did not know what to expect. She found herself on a narrow landing with doors leading off to the right and left, but she could hear raised voices and moans coming from the room straight ahead and she went in without knocking.

It was large and light, with two tall windows, but the smell of blood and unwashed bodies made her wrinkle her nose. The injured men were sprawled in chairs while Spears dabbed ineffectually at the bleeding wounds on Watkins's face.

Kate snatched the bowl of water and the cloth from his hands. 'You're just making it worse,' she said impatiently. 'You're Watkins, aren't you?'

He eyed her warily. 'Yes, miss.'

'Sit down, please. Then I can see what I'm doing.'

'This ain't your problem, miss,' Spears said awkwardly. 'Harry wouldn't like it if he knew you was up here.'

'Harry Trader has a lot to answer for.' Kate dealt with the cuts on Watkins's face, which proved to be superficial. She handed him the cloth. 'Here, hold that to your nose. It'll stop bleeding soon.'

She turned to Spears. 'I want to see Mr Trader urgently. Where will I find him?'

Watkins shook his head. 'Harry don't like people knowing where he lives.'

'I'm not leaving this room until someone gives me his address.' Kate folded her arms, glaring at each man in turn. 'I'm waiting.'

7

Kate did not know what she had been expecting, but Harry Trader's residence came as something of a shock. She had thought vaguely that he might have rooms in one of the less salubrious areas, although perhaps not too close to Cable Street, but the address given to her by Spears took her to Finsbury Circus and a house that was even larger and more imposing than her parents' home. Kate stood on the pavement, staring up at the elegant façade in disbelief. Surely Spears must have been mistaken. Either that or he was making fun of her. However, there was only one way to find out. She raised the lion's-head door knocker and allowed it to fall on the metal plate. The sound resonated throughout what she imagined would be a large entrance hall.

Kate waited but she was suddenly nervous. How would she explain herself if a pompous butler opened the door and demanded to know her business? She could hear footsteps and she braced herself for whatever might happen next.

The door opened and Kate found herself face to face with a small, older woman dressed in black from head to foot.

'Oh! I beg your pardon,' Kate said nervously. 'I think I must have the wrong address.'

'You're looking for my son.' The woman took a step backwards, holding the door open. 'Come in, my dear.'

'No, really,' Kate protested. 'There must be some mistake. I'm looking for Harry Trader.'

The woman laughed. 'Harry is such a tease. Come into the morning parlour and I'll send for some coffee, or would you prefer tea?'

'Coffee would be very nice,' Kate said automatically. She followed the woman who claimed to be Harry's mother across a black and white marble-tiled floor to a room overlooking the street. It was a hot day but, even so, a fire burned in the grate beneath an imposing and beautifully carved mantelpiece. Everything in the room, from the hand-painted wallpaper to the velvet upholstery on the sofa and chairs, and the flower-filled vases on pier tables, spoke of style, elegance and, above all, comfort.

'This is very kind of you, Mrs Trader,' Kate began awkwardly.

Harry's mother chuckled as she sank gracefully onto a chair by the fire. 'It's Lady Lyndon, my dear.

Do take a seat.' Lady Lyndon reached for the embroidered bell pull and gave it a gentle tug.

Kate sat down obediently. 'I don't understand.'

'Harry has his reasons for keeping our name and address a secret. I know nothing of his business activities, and I don't ask.'

'So Harry Trader isn't his real name?'

'No, my dear. Since the death of my husband Harry is now Sir Harry Lyndon, Baronet. Perhaps you can understand now why he likes to use an alias.'

'I think so,' Kate said guardedly. She was beginning to feel as though she had stepped into a

Gothic novel by Mrs Radcliffe. The Mysteries of Udolpho would seem quite tame after discovering that Harry led a double life.

'That's enough about my boy,' Lady Lyndon said cheerfully. 'Tell me about yourself. I don't even know your name.'

'I'm Kate Martin, ma'am. I mean, my lady. I run a soup kitchen giving meals to the poor in Cable Street.'

'Really? How public-spirited of you, Kate.' Lady Lyndon turned her head at the sound of someone knocking on the door. 'Enter.'

A young maidservant stepped into the room. 'You rang, my lady?'

'Coffee and cake, Agnes.'

'Yes, my lady.' Agnes bobbed a curtsey and hurried from the room, closing the door behind her.

'Now then, where were we?' Lady Lyndon gave Kate a searching look. 'You were telling me about your charitable work.'

'Yes, my lady. I'm not sure how much longer it can go on.'

'Why is that, Kate?'

'I've been funding it myself, but we have more and more people coming for a midday meal, and it's taking every penny of my allowance.'

'I see.' Lady Lyndon sat back in her chair, fixing Kate with a calculating look. 'Did you not think of that before you began?'

'No, my lady. I'm afraid I went ahead blindly.'

'And now you're seeking help from my son.'

'Not exactly. Harry, I mean Sir Harry, is our landlord. He owns the building and even though he's allowing us a rent-free month, I'm afraid we can't continue after that.'

'My late husband was, I believe, a shrewd businessman. I know almost nothing about his finances, but I do know that he invested in property. Harry handles the business side of things now.'

'I didn't come to ask for money, Lady Lyndon.'

'What do you want, Kate?'

Kate rose to her feet. She realised that Harry's mother knew nothing of his criminal activities. 'I really shouldn't take up any more of your time, my lady.'

'Nonsense. It's delightful to have young company. I was just about to go for a walk in the gardens when you knocked on the door.' Lady Lyndon dimpled mischievously. 'My servants will be put out when they learn that I let you in. They have very set ideas of what is proper and what is not.'

'But you're a titled lady, ma'am. You must be used to ordering a large household.'

'My father was a humble clerk in the City. We had a maid of all work, which set us a cut above the rest of those living in our street in Clerkenwell, but my mother took in sewing in order to pay for my education. When I was fifteen I went into service with the Lyndon family, which is where I met Lionel, their only son. We fell in love, but the family would never have countenanced such a match so we eloped to Gretna Green. My husband was disowned by his father, but as he only had sisters, Lionel inherited the title and this house when his father died.'

Kate was saved from commenting by the reappearance of Agnes, bearing a tray of coffee and a plate of tiny cakes.

'Will you pour the coffee, please, Kate? My hands are crippled with what my doctor calls rheumatics, although they are a little better with the warmer weather.'

Kate filled two cups and passed one to Lady Lyndon. She picked up the plate of cakes, but Lady Lyndon shook her head. 'No, thank you, my dear. But do have as many as you like. They are Harry's favourites.'

'Thank you, my lady.' Kate sipped the coffee and nibbled a cake, but all the time she was trying to think of an excuse to leave. Lady Lyndon seemed desperate for company and that made it all the more difficult to get away.

'Tell me about your family, Kate.' Lady Lyndon replaced her china cup on its saucer. 'Have you any brothers and sisters?'

'No, my lady. I'm an only child. My father was the chief magistrate in Delhi for three years. We returned from India in the spring.'

'Were you caught up in the troubles there?'

'Yes, my lady. We fled from Delhi at the outbreak of the uprising. We were lucky to escape with our lives.'

'How dreadfully exciting. Although it must have been terrifying. You must tell me all about it.'

'Maybe another time, my lady.' Kate put her plate back on the tray. 'I have things to do that cannot wait.'

'And you haven't seen Harry. May I pass on a message?'

'No, it's all right. Perhaps I'll see him at the soup kitchen in the near future.' Kate rose to her feet, but as she did so the door opened and Harry strolled into the morning room.

'Agnes said you had a visitor, Mama.'

'I believe you know Miss Martin.' Lady Lyndon smiled fondly at her son. 'She came to see you, Harry.'

'Yes, we are acquainted. How may I be of service, Miss Martin?' Harry pulled up a chair and sat down next to Kate.

'You are full of surprises, Sir Harry Lyndon,' Kate said sharply.

Lady Lyndon rose to her feet. 'I was on my way out when Kate arrived, Harry. I wanted some fresh air.'

'You aren't planning to go out on your own again, I hope?'

'I'm not a child, Harry. I don't think any harm will come to me in the gardens.'

'Where is Hattersley? She should accompany you, Mama.'

'The poor woman suffers from terrible headaches. I told her to lie down in a darkened room until she feels better. Now, don't fuss, Harry. I'm going to take a turn around the gardens and you may watch from the window if you're worried about me.' Lady Lyndon bustled out of the room, allowing the door to swing shut behind her.

Harry half rose from his seat, but he sank down again, shaking his head. 'My mother is a most determined woman.'

'But you're worried about her none the less.' Kate watched him closely. She sensed that he was genuinely anxious for his mother's wellbeing. 'Are you afraid that Monks or one of his men might accost your mother, Harry?'

He met her questioning look with a slow smile. 'You are very perceptive.'

'After that fracas in the soup kitchen nothing would surprise me. You should have warned me that we might be a target for your rivals.'

'That wasn't planned,' Harry said hastily. 'As I see it, a fight between Monks' men and mine got out of hand and it spilled into my premises. For that I'm truly sorry. Is that why you came here to find me?'

'No, not really. I came because I might have to give up the soup kitchen. At least until I can find a way of funding it properly.'

'Are you sure it wasn't because of what happened?'

'That didn't help. There were small children in the kitchen, not to mention Jenny and Ivy, who were both terrified, as was I, if it comes to that. But it is mainly because I can't afford to run it on my own.'

'What would you say if I offered to help you?'

'I can't even begin to understand you, Harry. You lead a double life — you're a gang leader in the East End, but you're also wealthy and titled. Why would you risk all this?' Kate encompassed the elegant room with a wave of her hands.

'It's not all it seems,' Harry said slowly. 'My mother doesn't know, but there is no fortune. My late father was an astute businessman, but he was also a gambler.'

'But you have this beautiful house, filled with expensive furniture.'

'All of which I purchased myself through my

112

illegal gambling clubs.'

'Why don't you simply tell her the truth? She seems to be a very resolute, strong-minded woman.'

'She is, but I intend to keep it from her for as long as humanly possible.'

'But what if she discovers the truth about you? Don't you think that would break her heart?'

'I've taken great care to keep my other life a secret. Until now no one has linked Harry Trader with Harry Lyndon. How did you get my address, by the way?'

'It's best you don't know, but I can tell you it wasn't easy. You have no need to worry about the loyalty of your men.'

'I know that, but even so, if you could make one of them talk without putting undue pressure on him, who knows what might happen if Monks got wind of my true identity?'

Kate shrugged. 'I imagine that's a risk you've been taking all along.'

'You're right, of course. I had planned to disband the gang when I had enough money to pay off a loan secured on the house, leaving enough to live on comfortably.'

'It's none of my business,' Kate said hastily. 'You don't have to worry about me, but don't think I approve of your deception or your criminal activities. I'll keep your secret, if only for your mother's sake. She is such a sweet lady.'

'Thank you, Kate. But before you write me off as a complete villain, I want you to know that the end is in sight for my gang. I plan to close the gaming clubs and pay off all those who've been loyal to me, but not just yet. I cannot divulge the reason at the moment, but it will all become clear in time.'

Kate stood up, reaching for her shawl, which she had draped over the back of the chair. 'I believe you have good intentions, but you'll have to forgive me if I doubt your ability to simply walk away. I think you enjoy the excitement and the challenge of pitting your wits against Monks and those like him.'

'Considering how little you know me, that's quite astute.'

Kate wrapped her shawl around her shoulders. 'I really must go.'

'You have an urgent appointment?'

'Not exactly, but I intend to walk to Lincoln's Inn. I need to ask Perry for advice.' She smiled as she noted a flicker of anxiety in Harry's eyes. 'Don't worry, Harry. As I said just now, your secret is safe with me. I merely want some advice concerning setting myself up as an official charity. Then I might be able to raise funds for the soup kitchen.'

'I happen to be going that way, so unless you have anything against travelling in my barouche bearing the family coat of arms, I could take you as far as Lincoln's Inn.'

'I'm not against your title, I just don't approve of the way you're going about restoring the family fortunes, and I'm sure your mother would agree with me.'

'Heaven help me if you two were to get together.' Harry held the door open. 'If I promise to reform will you accept a lift in my carriage?'

'Yes, but I won't hold you to your promise. I have a feeling it would be broken before the end of the day.'

He laughed. 'You have so little faith in me, Kate.'

'As I said, I hardly know you, but it's a hot day and I would be grateful for a ride in your barouche, but you must promise to let me alight in Fleet Street. It's better if we're not seen together. I'll walk the rest of the way.'

★ ★ ★

Lincoln's Inn was an oasis of calm with the noisy, rat-infested slums of Clare Market to the west and the round-the-clock bustle of Fleet Street to the east. Kate walked slowly towards the building that housed Perry's chambers. She was still struggling to equate Harry Trader the gang leader with Sir Harry Lyndon, Baronet, but she knew she must put that aside and concentrate on the more important matter.

She entered the building that had been her father's old chambers and was met by Franklin, the chief clerk. He had known Kate since she was a child and he greeted her warmly.

'As it happens Mr Harte is in chambers, as is your father. Would you like me to announce you, Miss Kate?'

'No, thank you,' Kate said, smiling. 'I think I'll give them a surprise.' She made her way along the narrow, wainscoted passage to the room that her father had occupied before they left for India. It was only three years ago, but it seemed like another lifetime to Kate. She knocked on the door and entered without waiting for an answer. Perry was seated behind the large mahogany desk and her father was standing with his back to the empty grate. Both of them stared at her as if she were a complete stranger.

Perry was the first to recover. He stood up and walked round the desk to greet her. 'Kate, this is a pleasant surprise.'

'What are you doing here?' Sir Bartholomew demanded stiffly. 'You know you aren't supposed to interrupt daily business, Kate.'

'I came to ask Perry for advice, Papa,' Kate said boldly. 'But I can come another time if you are both too busy to hear what I have to say.'

'Nonsense.' Perry pulled up a chair for her. 'Take a seat and tell me how I may be of help.'

Sir Bartholomew cleared his throat noisily. 'As my daughter is here now, I think I ought to give her the news I mentioned earlier.'

'Really, sir? I mean it might be better done in the privacy of your home, don't you think?' Perry faced Sir Bartholomew with a disapproving frown.

'I think I am the best judge of how to treat my own family, thank you.' Sir Bartholomew turned to Kate. 'Take a seat, my dear.'

Kate knew then that her father must have something momentous to tell her. He rarely used any form of endearment when speaking either to her or to her mother, and he had modified his tone from that of a courtroom judge in an obvious attempt to sound fatherly.

'What is it, Papa?' Kate sank down onto the padded leather seat. 'Please tell me.'

'I only hesitate because I know how fond you were of my brother.' Sir Bartholomew tucked his thumbs under the lapels of his jacket and began to pace the floor. 'I received a missive from Delhi this morning.'

'From Uncle Edgar?'

'Not exactly. I'm afraid it's bad news, Kate. Your uncle died in the uprising.'

'Oh, no!' Kate buried her face in her hands as she tried to assimilate the dreadful news.

'Edgar was well aware that there was going to be trouble, and he entrusted his will into my hands, to be opened only in the event of his demise.'

'Please, Papa, don't address me as if I were in court. What has this to do with me? All I can think of is poor Uncle Edgar. He was always so good to me.'

'Evidently,' Sir Bartholomew said drily. 'He thought so little of me, his only brother, and so highly of you, a mere niece, that he has left you his entire fortune. You are a very wealthy young woman now, Kate.'

'Are you certain that Uncle Edgar has died, Papa? Could there be a mistake?'

'I had a letter from Sir Robert Audley, my dear. I'm afraid it is true.'

'How did it happen?' Kate asked faintly. She was devastated by the loss of her much-loved uncle, but Ash had been part of his personal guard, and she was desperate to learn of his fate. Surely if he had died she would have felt something — she would have known, wouldn't she?

Perry filled a glass with water from a carafe on the desk and handed it to her. 'Sip this slowly,

117

Kate.'

Her hand shook as she held the glass to her lips and she drank a little, but set it aside almost immediately. 'Are you absolutely sure, Papa? Might there not have been a mistake, considering the circumstances? I remember what it was like when we fled.'

'I think you should go home and rest, Kate. I had no idea you would take the news so badly, especially as your uncle has seen fit to make you the sole beneficiary of his fortune. I still find it hard to believe that he would bypass me, his only brother, in favour of you.'

Kate was quick to hear the note of bitterness in her father's voice and she gathered her scattered wits with difficulty. 'I think I will go home, Papa. The walk will clear my head.'

'Nonsense, Kate,' Perry said firmly. 'I'll send one of the clerks to hail a cab and I'll see you safely home. You've had a terrible shock.'

Sir Bartholomew slumped down on a chair by the fireplace. 'I wish I'd had such a shock. I mean, of course I'm sorry my brother was killed, but the money would have been very welcome.'

'I don't know how you can stand there and talk about money when your brother has been murdered,' Kate said angrily. 'Shame on you, Papa.'

She walked out of the office without giving him a chance to respond.

Perry caught up with her in the main office. 'Franklin, will you send one of your juniors to hail a cab, please? Miss Martin has just received some bad news. I'm going to see her home.'

'Of course, sir.' Franklin cast a sympathetic

look in Kate's direction. 'I am so sorry, Miss Kate. I'll go myself; the cabbies know me. I send much trade their way.' He hurried from the building, returning moments later to announce that a cab was waiting on the corner of the square.

★ ★ ★

It had been a day that Kate would prefer to forget, with one shock after another. First she had discovered that Harry Trader was a leading a double life and then she had learned that her beloved uncle had been killed in the uprising. Not only that, but suddenly she was an heiress, and Perry had confirmed that it was a substantial sum. Sir Bartholomew had shown him his brother's will. The sad truth was that she did not want the money, even though it would solve all her financial problems. She would rather have had her uncle safe and sound, and of course that wish must include Ashok. She was desperate to learn of his fate, but the only way to find out would be to travel to India, and that was out of the question with the current state of affairs.

Kate sat by the window in her bedroom, gazing down at the shadowy gardens, and the clouds of moths that fluttered around the streetlamps like tiny fairs dancing in the gaslight.

Perry had advised her to take time off from the soup kitchen. He had even offered to lend her money until her funds were available, to enable Jenny and Ivy to continue the good work on their own, if only for a few days. Kate had refused, of course, insisting that hard work would be her salvation, but privately

119

she felt her heart shattering into small shards. She knew she had to go on, even if her life held no meaning for her without Ash. She had hoped that he might come to England looking for her, but now that would never happen. The nagging void inside had turned her into an automaton, similar to the expensive toys that wealthy people brought from France to entertain their guests after dinner. She was a bird in a gilded cage, singing the same song over and over again, or a beautifully dressed doll, who nodded and waved at a given command.

Jenny came to help Kate undress and her silent sympathy was more comforting than any words. She helped Kate into bed and left the room, returning minutes later with a steaming cup of hot chocolate.

'I lost me dad when I was ten years old,' Jenny said softly. 'You never forget them, miss, but it does get easier.' She backed out of the room, closing the door gently.

Kate lay in almost complete darkness, allowing tears to fall unchecked. She was crying for her uncle, but she was also crying for her lost love, and for their children, who would never be born. She could not imagine loving anyone as much as she had loved Ashok Patel. His death was not confirmed, but she knew in her heart that he was gone from her life for ever.

★ ★ ★

Awaking from a fitful sleep, Kate sat up in bed next morning filled with new-found determination. In the dark hours of the night she had come to the conclusion that to give in to despair was not for her. She would face the future with a brave heart, and she knew exactly how to get her own way. She was out of bed before Jenny brought a pitcher of hot water to fill the ewer on the washstand.

'You're not going to Cable Street this morning, are you, miss?'

'Yes, of course. I have to carry on. If I mope about at home things will seem worse. At least I'll have Annie to cheer me with a lovely melody, and Ivy's little ones to make me smile. Help me with my stays, Jenny. I'll go to market on my way to Cable Street.'

'Of course, miss. But first you must have some breakfast. You can't work on an empty stomach.'

'I doubt if many of those who come to us in Cable Street have eaten breakfast. The bread and soup are the only meal that most of them have in a whole day. I've lost someone I loved, and I don't want the money he left me, but I know how I'll put it to good use.'

'You could buy yourself a house of your own, miss. You would be a woman of means, and you wouldn't have to depend on any man to support you.'

'I might do that when I return to England.'

'You're going away, miss?'

'How do you fancy a trip to India, Jenny?'

8

Kate stood on the East India Dock at Blackwall, gazing up at the steamship that would transport her to Bombay. It had been a difficult decision to make in these uncertain times, and her parents were totally against her plan to travel to India. They had refused to see her off and it was Perry who had hired a barouche to bring Kate and Jenny to the docks. He was now busy organising porters to carry their luggage on board. Jenny had been keeping a watchful eye on their possessions, but she came hurrying towards Kate with her bonnet slightly awry and the ribbons flapping in the breeze.

'We should go on board, miss,' she said breathlessly.

'Yes, of course.' Kate knew in her heart that she was doing the right thing, but she was suddenly nervous. Her excuse for travelling thousands of miles was that she wanted to bring her uncle's ashes home.

He had, so they had been informed by Sir Robert, chosen to be cremated in the Indian tradition. Kate's parents had done all they could to dissuade her, but Kate was adamant. She could now afford the passage for herself as well as for her maidservant, and she felt she owed it to her uncle's memory to bring him home. She meant what she said, but she also knew that her real reason for travelling so far was to find

Ashok, or at least to learn of his fate. She could have gone through official channels and written to the authorities, requesting that they check the Indian Army records for the fate of Subedar-Major Ashok Patel, but that would take months, and might possibly be ignored as the unrest and fighting continued. The accounts that Kate read in the newspapers were at least two months old by the time they reached London, and she could not go another day without knowing Ash's fate.

She had set up a bank account for the soup kitchen, leaving Ivy in sole charge. Ivy was to be paid a generous wage to ensure that things ran smoothly. Kate had said fond goodbyes to Ivy and to Annie, promising to return as soon as possible. Annie had begged Kate to contact her brother, Joseph, as she had not heard from him for many months, and Kate had promised with a heavy heart. It was going to be difficult enough to trace Ashok, let alone Private Joseph Blythe, but she would do her very best. Kate had grown fond of Annie, and had she been fortunate enough to have a sister, she would have chosen someone exactly like Annie, whose sweet nature and gentle sense of humour made even the most miserable days seem brighter.

Perry came towards them with a rueful smile. 'Your luggage has gone on board, so I suppose it's time to say goodbye, Kate.'

'Thank you for everything you've done. It was good of you to go to all this trouble, Perry.' Kate leaned over to brush his cheek with a kiss.

He clasped her hands, raising them to his lips. 'You know where to find me when you return. I hope all goes well with you when you reach India, but please don't take any unnecessary risks.'

She smiled. 'I promise.'

'They're calling for all passengers to board, miss,' Jenny said, tugging on Kate's arm.

'I'm coming. I won't say goodbye, Perry. It's too final.'

'Have a safe journey, ladies.' Perry stood aside, allowing them to hurry past him as they made their way to the gangplank.

'If I had a young man who was so eager to please me, I don't think I'd be getting on that boat,' Jenny said darkly.

'Perry is a good friend, nothing more.' Kate negotiated the steep gangplank and was greeted by a steward, who showed them to their respective cabins.

Jenny opened the interconnecting door. 'This is nice, miss. I don't have to walk miles to get to you.'

Kate took off her bonnet and laid it on the narrow bunk bed. 'I hope I'm doing the right thing, Jenny. Maybe my parents were right.'

'There's still time to change your mind, miss. The steward told me there is a bit of a delay before we sail.'

Kate slumped down on the bunk, shaking her head. 'We've come this far so it would be foolish to walk away.'

An urgent knock on the door made them both jump.

'Come in,' Kate said sharply.

A steward poked his head round the door. 'There's a gentleman who wants to see you

124

urgently, miss. He forced his way on board without a ticket, but he says he won't leave until he's spoken to you personally.'

'Maybe it's your father, miss.' Jenny picked up Kate's bonnet and handed it to her.

Kate rose to her feet. 'I'll come right away.' She turned to Jenny. 'You'd best come with me.' Kate followed the steward to the upper deck when she was amazed to see Harry Trader waiting for her with a burly seaman in attendance.

'What is it, Harry?' Kate demanded anxiously. 'Why are you here, and how did you know that we were leaving today?'

'I'd like a few words with the lady in private.' Harry slipped a coin into the seaman's hand.

'Just a couple of minutes, sir. No more.'

Harry nodded. He took Kate by the arm and led her to the top of the gangplank. 'Your father was taken ill in court, Kate.'

'But he was all right this morning at breakfast,' Kate protested. 'Is this a ploy to make me abandon my trip?'

'No, it isn't. I know because I was there. One of my men was in the dock and your father was presiding over the case. He collapsed suddenly and was taken hospital. I don't know any more than that, but I suggest you postpone your voyage.'

'Is it serious?'

'I'm not a medical man, but if I were you I wouldn't want to take the chance.'

'Has my mother been told?'

'I went to Finsbury Square, intending to speak to you and I was told that you were en route to India. It wasn't up to me to inform your mother

125

of your father's illness. You need to come home, Kate.'

She stared at him in dismay. It was obvious that he was telling the truth — Harry Trader had no reason to lie to her. Although, if she left the ship now she might never again have the courage to defy convention and the will of her parents. But her father might be dying and she could not leave her mother to cope on her own.

'Of course, you're right.' Kate turned to Jenny, who was hovering anxiously a few feet away. 'We're leaving the ship.'

'But our luggage, miss ...'

Harry nodded to the seaman. 'We need the ladies' baggage to be put ashore immediately.'

Before the man could speak a uniformed officer strode up to them. 'I heard what you said, sir. This is highly irregular.'

'I'm sure it can't be the first time that something similar has occurred. Please have Miss Martin's luggage and that of her maid put ashore. Unfortunately, due to sudden and unexpected family illness, the ladies will not be sailing with you.'

'If that is the case, please disembark now. We're about to cast off.' The officer jerked his head in the direction of the seaman. 'See to the baggage, Robinson.'

'Aye, aye, sir.' Robinson hurried off, bellowing instructions at the top of his voice.

Harry guided Kate down the gangplank. 'I'm sorry to be the bearer of such bad news. But you can travel another time, perhaps when the political situation has settled down.'

Kate came to a halt. 'Are you sure this isn't a

126

ploy to stop me going to India?'

'No, on my honour. I was there, Kate. I saw the judge collapse and he was carried out of the court-room by two attendants. I believe he was taken to the Charing Cross Hospital in Agar Street.'

'Then that's where we'll go now,' Kate said firmly.

★ ★ ★

Perry was already at the hospital when Kate finally arrived. He came to meet her, his expression serious.

'How is my father?' Kate demanded anxiously. 'I want to see him.'

'The doctors say he needs rest and must not be over-excited,' Perry said gently. 'I saw him for a couple of minutes, Kate. He was barely conscious, but not in pain.'

'What happened? What is the matter with him?'

'I believe they call it an apoplectic fit, but you should speak to Sir Bartholomew's physician. He'll be able to tell you more.'

'Has anyone told my mother?'

'I was about to leave for Finsbury Square when you arrived. Do you want to come with me?'

Harry had been standing at a tactful distance with Jenny but he stepped forward, eyeing Perry suspiciously. 'Are you all right, Kate?'

'I can't see Papa yet, so I'm going home with Perry. I think I ought to be the one to tell my mother.'

'I understand.'

'Thank you for coming to fetch me. It was the

right thing to do.'

'If you need anything, you know where to find me.' Harry shot a calculating look in Perry's direction. 'We haven't met before, although I've seen you in court.'

'I thought I recognised you, Trader. I can't say I approve of the way you're using Kate's soup kitchen as a cover for your criminal activities, but I appreciate the fact that you've gone out of your way to help her.'

Harry faced him with a tight-lipped expression that did not bode well. Kate could see trouble brewing between them — one of them a man who upheld the law, and the other a privileged person who had chosen to become a criminal. It might have been laughable in different circumstances, but everything now took second place to her father's condition.

'If you don't mind, I'd like to go home now, Perry,' she said hastily.

'My coachman will deliver your luggage to Finsbury Square.' Harry stood aside to allow Kate and Perry to pass. 'I have business to conduct near here, or I would take you home myself.'

'You've done enough, Harry.' Kate gave him a wan smile.

Perry waited until they were out of earshot. 'A gang leader must earn more than a mere lawyer, if he can afford a carriage and a coachman, too.'

Kate turned on him angrily. 'Harry Trader is a criminal, of that I have no doubt, but today he did a good thing. If he hadn't been in court and seen Papa collapse, and if he had not come to the docks, Jenny and I would be on our way to India by now. My poor mother will be devastated when she hears the news.'

'You're right, of course,' Perry said mildly. 'We'd better hurry. You need to be the one to tell her — bad news travels fast.'

★ ★ ★

Kate told her mother as gently as possible, but Arabella was distraught and she took to her bed with a cold compress on her forehead and a bottle of sal volatile close at hand. Barnet was kept busy with endless small tasks that were totally unnecessary, and, after her initial attempts to soothe her mother's anxiety, Kate returned to the hospital, accompanied by Perry.

They sat side by side in the gloomy waiting room in total silence. The clock on the wall seemed to have stopped, or else time had stood still, but eventually Sir Jasper Fey, the senior consultant, entered the room. His expression was not encouraging.

Kate jumped to her feet. 'How is he? Will my father be all right, sir?'

'He is comfortable,' Sir Jasper said vaguely. 'I'm afraid I cannot tell you more at this early stage, Miss Martin. I have had patients with a similar condition who have regained most of their faculties, but it is by no means certain.'

'I don't understand.' Kate sank back on her chair, staring at him blankly. 'Are you saying that Papa might not recover completely?'

'It's impossible to say at the moment.'

'May I see him, please, Doctor?'

129

'I wouldn't advise it, not yet anyway, Miss Martin. Come back tomorrow and we will have a better idea of the prognosis.'

Kate was about to argue, but Perry laid his hand on her arm. 'That sounds eminently sensible. Your father is in good hands, and you don't want to upset him, do you?'

'No, of course not. But what shall I tell, Mama?'

'I will be more than happy to speak to Lady Martin.' Sir Jasper opened the door. 'But not today.' 'She's taking it badly,' Kate said in the low voice.

'I don't know what to say to her.'

'Give her a dose of laudanum, that's my professional advice. Lady Martin will benefit from rest and a good night's sleep.' Sir Jasper hurried from the room.

'I'll take you home, Kate.' Perry stood up, holding out his hand. 'There's nothing more to do here.'

She allowed him to help her to her feet. 'I'll get a cab, Perry. You've done enough for my family today.'

'All right,' he said doubtfully. 'But are you sure you can manage?'

'I'll go home and change into something more practical and then I'll go to the soup kitchen. The meal will be over, but I can help them to clear up, and if what Sir Jasper said is true, there's almost nothing I can do for Mama. Keeping busy will take my mind off things.'

'I'm sorry you had to cancel your trip to India, but it's probably for the best.'

'I expect you're right,' Kate said dully.

Fate had once again turned her world upside down, but she refused to think about what might have been. Uncle Edgar had loved India, and he had devoted more than half his life to that country. Perhaps it was better that his ashes were scattered on the land he held so dear. As to finding Ashok, she would never give up hope of their reunion, but now the only option left was to go through official channels. She would return to India at the first opportunity, come what may, but for now there were people who needed her here at home, and her first duty was to her family.

* * *

Sir Bartholomew was discharged from hospital a month later. On a hot afternoon in late July when the pavements sizzled beneath the unrelenting rays of the sun, he was helped from the carriage by Henry and Fellowes, who had been at his side most of the time he had been in hospital. They carried Sir Bartholomew upstairs to a bedroom adjacent to the one he had shared with his wife for the past twenty- two years, and a bed had been placed in the dressing room so that Fellowes could be on hand if Sir Bartholomew needed anything during the night.

Kate had made sure that her father's sick room was aired and made as welcoming and comfortable as possible. Vases filled with summer flowers were placed on side tables, and the drab brocade curtains had been replaced by colourful chintz draperies. Fellowes had shown touching devotion to his master and he rarely left Sir Bartholomew's side. His services were needed even more than before the illness that had struck Sir Bartholomew with such power and speed. His recovery had been very slow and the whole of his left side was paralysed. His speech was slurred and on occasions it was only Fellowes who understood what his master wanted. Kate had found it difficult to be in her father's company for very long, and Arabella's visits to the hospital were even more infrequent, leaving her depressed and tearful for days at a time.

When her father was safely installed in his new surroundings, Kate made sure that he was as comfortable as possible. She left Fellowes fussing over the cushions in the chair by the window, which overlooked the square gardens, and she went in search of her mother.

Arabella was in the drawing room, seated by an open window, fanning herself energetically. 'I hate London in the summer,' she said crossly. 'The heat and the awful smells make life unendurable, and there are flies everywhere.'

'Papa is comfortable in his new room. Will you go up and see him?'

'Yes, but not now. Fellowes is with him and he manages the situation much better than I.'

'Papa has been very ill. He might have died, so I wouldn't call it a "situation".'

'Well, you're so clever, miss. You may call it what you like, but I will choose when I visit my husband. He is well cared for and that is the most important thing.'

Kate sensed that there was more beneath her mother's casual attitude to her husband's condition than she was saying. 'Is there something bothering you, Mama?'

'Sir Jasper came to see me this morning while you were playing the Good Samaritan at the soup kitchen. He told me that he doesn't think your father's condition will improve, and it's quite possible that another such episode might be fatal.'

Kate sank down on a padded footstool. 'Surely he didn't use those words, Mama?'

'It's what he meant, rather than what he said. I'm not a fool, Kate. I understood him perfectly well.'

'Doctors can be wrong. With all the love and care that Papa will receive I'm sure he will make a good recovery.'

'Are you a doctor? No, of course you are not, so don't make predictions that mean absolutely nothing.'

Her mother's hurtful words struck Kate like barbed darts, but she forced herself to remain calm. 'I meant that we will take good care of him, and now he's at home, surely he will recover more quickly.'

'You may think you know it all, miss, but the truth is that your father is unlikely to work again, and now Edgar has bequeathed the family fortune to you, including this house, we will probably have to move to somewhere much smaller and in a less salubrious area. You, of course, can afford to live anywhere you wish.'

'I don't know what you mean,' Kate said slowly. 'Why would you and Papa have to move away? This is your home as well as mine.'

'You say that now, but I wouldn't be surprised if you turned this house into a refuge for the disreputable people you feed at your wretched soup kitchen. You're not a good daughter, Kate. You defy your father's wishes, and mine. I wouldn't be surprised if his illness was brought about by you — you ungrateful child.'

Kate stared at her mother in dismay. She had known all along that Mama disapproved of her work, but she had not been prepared for such a vitriolic outpouring.

'I'm sorry you think that way, Mama. It was never my intention to upset either of you, and Sir Jasper said that Papa's illness could not have been predicted, nor was anyone to blame.'

'You say that because it suits you. I saw the way you acted when you were with your uncle in Delhi. You were all sweetness and obedience then, but look at you now. You're still defying me even at this moment. I'll tell Barnet to start packing up our things now.'

'You'll do no such thing, Mama.' Kate stood up, clasping her hands together in an attempt to stop them shaking. She had never lost her temper with either parent, but now she found herself very close to speaking out. Somehow she managed to remain calm. 'This is our family home and always will be. You have no need to worry about money, or making economies — I will see to everything. All you have to do is to concentrate on helping Papa to get better.

If anyone is going to move out, it will be me.'

Kate left the room without giving her mother a chance to argue, but she was shaking from head to foot as she closed the door behind her. Her mother's words had cut deep and they were totally unfair. She knew her duty to her parents, even though she had seen very little of them while she was growing up. A succession of nannies, governesses and tutors had taken their place, and the only person who had shown her genuine affection and understanding was now dead. Uncle Edgar would have been horrified if he had heard what Mama had just said. Kate brushed tears from her eyes. She was of age now, even though her mother had called her a child. Circumstances had placed her in charge of the household. It was something wished upon her, but she would do her best to look after all those in her care.

* * *

Next day Kate was up early and she ate her breakfast alone in the dining room. Seated at the end of the mahogany table, which would seat twenty or more guests at dinner, Kate looked around at the elegant Sheraton furniture and the gilt-framed oil paintings of pastoral scenes, gushing waterfalls and a stag at bay, in the style of Sir Edwin Landseer. Arabella had been particularly proud of this acquisition, purchased just before the family embarked on the voyage to India. Kate sighed, pushing her plate away. Once again, the contrast of their opulent lifestyle was painful when compared with the way Ivy and her children existed, as well as the hundreds of people who now flocked to the soup kitchen every week.

She rose from the table and snatched her bonnet and reticule from the chair by the door. If she left now she might be able to get away without having to explain why she was leaving so early.

Perhaps it was something that Spears had said the day before, but Kate had been feeling uneasy ever since. He was not the most cheerful person to have around, but yesterday he had been positively gloomy, and he had gone round muttering about the possibility of a police raid on the premises. Kate had never ventured further than the meeting room upstairs, but she thought it was used too infrequently to attract any interest from the constabulary.

She left the house without being seen and hailed a passing cab to take her to Whitechapel. It was still early but the sun beat down mercilessly from a cloudless sky and the odour from the sewers grew worse as the cab headed towards the river. Flies clustered on mounds of horse dung, and the horse pulling the cab flicked its tail and tossed its mane as the tiny tormentors buzzed around its head. Kate held a silver vinaigrette beneath her nose, but the pungent smell of the aromatic vinegar could not quite eliminate the city stench.

She alighted outside the soup kitchen and paid the cabby, but even before she tried the door she sensed that there was something wrong. A mere touch of her fingers on the handle made the door swing open, and she felt a shiver of anxiety run down her spine.

'Spears?' Kate stepped inside. Her voice came back to her in an eerie echo. 'Spears, are you there?' She walked slowly to the foot of the stairs where the interior door hung from a single hinge, and the lock was broken. 'Spears?'

Once again his name came back as if to mock her. She had a vision of him lying on the floor

136

in the meeting place upstairs, battered and bruised after a confrontation with Monks' gang. Her footsteps reverberated on the bare treads as she ascended the stairs, but the room above was empty apart from the folded trestle tables and the neatly stacked chairs. It took all her courage to explore the rest of the first floor, but there was nothing unremarkable. The second- and third-floor rooms were all dusty and sparsely furnished, but when she reached the attic rooms at the top of the premises she was reassured by their emptiness. There had been signs of a scuffle in the room where Spears slept, but it could be that he was extremely untidy, and maybe he always threw his clothes on the floor. Whatever had occurred during the hours of darkness, there was no one here now to bear witness.

Kate retraced her steps and headed for the kitchen. She still felt uneasy, but there was nothing she could do, and there would be hungry people queuing outside at midday. She set about the mundane task of building up the fire in the range and filling pans with water from the pump at the sink. By the time Ivy arrived with the baby in her arms, followed by Charlie and the twins, Kate had peeled a mountain of potatoes and was about to start on the carrots.

'You're here early,' Ivy said cheerfully. 'What happened to the front door? The lock's broken.'

'That's the question I've been asking myself ever since I arrived this morning. Spears isn't here and he never leaves the premises unlocked.'

'That doesn't sound good.' Ivy placed the baby on the floor. 'Take care of your brothers, girls.

Ma has things to do.' Ivy rolled up her sleeves. 'There's nothing we can do about it. I'll start on the onions. It's certainly much easier since we've been buying sacks of vegetables. It saves time and money.'

Kate nodded but she barely heard what Ivy had said. If Spears had been taken by Monks' gang it was quite possible that they would return and claim the property for their own purposes. She took off her apron and laid it over the back of a chair.

'I think I'd better find Harry Trader. We might be in serious trouble.'

'I've heard that there's even worse hostility between the gangs,' Ivy said, frowning. 'Word gets round quicker than you can blink in Nightingale Lane.'

'Nevertheless, this building belongs to Harry, and Spears works for him. I think he needs to know what's happened. I'll be as quick as I can, Ivy. I won't leave you to manage on your own.'

'That's all right, miss. I'll have Annie to help when she gets here. She's getting good at chopping onions and the like, and I think she enjoys helping.' 'Even so, I'll be back before you know it.'

* * *

Kate took a cab to Finsbury Circus. The heat was oppressive as she ran up the steps to hammer on the door knocker. Dark clouds had obscured the sun and there was a sulphurous haze in the air.

Lady Lyndon's butler opened the door, staring blankly at Kate.

'I need to see Sir Harry Lyndon. It's urgent.'

'Then you'd best go to Coldbath Fields Prison, miss.'

9

A distant rumble of thunder sent shivers down Kate's spine. 'Did you say Coldbath Fields Prison?'

'That's what I said, miss.'

'I need to speak to Lady Lyndon,' Kate said firmly. 'Please inform her ladyship that Miss Martin would very much like to see her.'

'Her ladyship is not at home to anyone today.' The butler was about to close the door, but Kate put her foot over the threshold. 'I think she will see me. Please tell her that I am here and it's urgent.'

The butler glanced up and down the street, his brow knotted in a frown. 'You'd best come inside, miss.'

'Thank you.' Kate marched past him. 'I'll wait here.'

He nodded wordlessly and closed the door just as a vivid flash of lightning lit up the entrance hall, followed by a loud crack of thunder. He headed for the wide staircase, mounting it with infuriating slowness, but Kate was prepared to wait. The news that Harry had been arrested had come as a shock, although perhaps it was to be expected. The law was bound to catch up on him sooner or later. As a judge's daughter she should have been pleased, but somehow she had never really thought of Harry Trader as being a criminal.

The butler returned almost immediately. He paused, halfway down the sweeping staircase.

'Her ladyship will see you now, miss. Follow

me, if you please.'

Kate knew where to find the drawing room, but she followed the butler meekly and allowed him to announce her. As she had feared, Lady Lyndon must have received the news of Harry's arrest and she was visibly upset. Her eyes were reddened by tears, and she rose shakily to her feet.

'Miss Martin, it's so good of you to come and see me, but it really is not a good time.'

'I understand, my lady,' Kate crossed the floor, her feet sinking into the thick pile of the Axminster carpet. 'I am so sorry. I've only just heard the news.'

'It will be common knowledge before nightfall.' Lady Lyndon shuddered as a huge crash of thunder made the crystals on the chandeliers tinkle like tiny bells.

'Not necessarily,' Kate said with more confidence than she was feeling. 'There must be something we can do.'

Lady Lyndon mopped her eyes with a tiny handkerchief, trimmed with lace. 'It's a mistake, of course.

The police must have Harry muddled up with someone else.'

Kate moved to the sofa and sat down beside her. 'Undoubtedly, ma'am. You must try not to worry.' 'It's easy to say that, but of course I'm anxious. Harry has always been such a good son, and it's humiliating for him.'

'I have a friend who is a barrister-at-law,' Kate said recklessly. 'I'll ask his advice.' Perry was probably the last person who would have sympathy with Harry Trader, and even less for Sir Harry

Lyndon, but he was the only person she could think of who might be able to help.

'Would you, my dear? Our family lawyer died last year and I've had no need to seek a legal opinion, until now.' Lady Lyndon clasped Kate's hands. 'Will you do something for me, Kate?'

'Yes, of course. I'll do anything I can.'

'Will you go to this dreadful prison and ask to see Harry? I need to know that my boy is being well cared for, but I cannot face seeing him behind bars. I know it's cowardly, but I would simply break down and sob, and that wouldn't help him.'

'What do you want me to say to him, ma'am?'

'I don't have to put words into your mouth, Kate. I just want to know that he's all right. Tell him I'll spare no expense to get him the best lawyer in London.'

'Is there anything you wish to add?'

'No, my dear. I'll leave it to you. Now if you'll get up and ring for a servant I'll have my carriage sent round to take you to that dreadful place. I can't have you going there on your own, especially in such a dreadful thunderstorm.'

'That's very kind of you, Lady Lyndon.' Kate rose to her feet and went over to the mantelshelf to give the embroidered bell pull a gentle tug.

'You'll be safe with Warrender, my coachman, who's been with me for thirty years or more.'

* * *

Coldbath Fields Prison was even worse than Kate could have imagined. Warrender insisted on accompanying her into the compound, having left

142

a very nervous footman in charge of the carriage. Kate might have protested, as she wanted to see Harry on his own, but once inside the prison grounds she was only too glad of Warrender's company. The rain had ceased, leaving the air damp and muggy. Kate had to step over deep puddles to get to the reception area of the grim-looking institution, and the oppressive atmosphere inside was not solely due to the passing storm. It took all the money she had in her purse to pay various bribes, but eventually she was shown to a small anteroom, leaving Warrender standing guard outside.

Minutes later Harry was thrust into the room and the door slammed shut behind him. They stood facing each other uncertainly. Kate was both relieved to see him and angry to find him in such circumstances.

He gave her a wary smile. 'Well, say something, Kate.'

'I came because your mother wished it.'

'You went to see her?'

'I knew that there was something wrong. Spears seems to have disappeared and the premises in Cable Street was broken into some time after we left yesterday.'

'Spears wasn't there this morning?'

'There was no sign of him. There might have been a struggle — it was impossible to tell from the messy state of his rooms.'

Harry motioned her to take a seat at the small table in the centre of the otherwise bare room. He pulled up a chair and sat opposite her. 'I don't expect you to understand, Kate. I imagine you will

143

think I've got my just deserts, but it's my mother I worry for.'

Kate sat down on the hard wooden chair, leaning her elbows on the table as she met his apologetic gaze. 'That's why I'm here. I suppose you deserve to go to prison, although I don't know what you've done to make them pounce on you so unexpectedly.

Are the rest of your men here?'

'Not to my knowledge. I've disbanded the gang anyway.'

'I suppose you've cheated enough people to allow you to live in the grand style.'

'Maybe I simply had a change of heart.'

'I don't believe that for a moment. I think you were scared of getting caught, and now they have you.'

He reached across the table and laid his hand on hers. 'Something has happened to upset you, and it had nothing to do with my incarceration. What is it, Kate?'

The question and the unexpected sympathetic look in his eyes took Kate aback. She snatched her hand free, turning her head away in case he spotted the tears that threatened to spill down her cheeks. He was right: she had left home in an emotional state after her clash with her mother, but she thought she had overcome the feeling of sadness she had experienced so deeply. The news of Harry's arrest had taken her mind off her own problems, but they were still simmering inside her head, and he, of all people, had sensed her distress.

'It was something and nothing,' she said guardedly.

144

'A lot more than nothing, by the looks of you. Now, I deserve to be here — I fully admit that — but someone has upset you and I'd like to know who and why that was. Has your father's condition worsened?'

She shook her head. 'No, he's still the same.'

'Then it must be that mother of yours.'

'You know nothing of my family, Harry.'

'Maybe, but you sometimes let things slip. I suspect that your dear mama does not give you the support that you deserve. Am I right?'

'I didn't come here to discuss my problems. I came on behalf of your mother, who is desperate to have you home. I'm not sure she can cope on her own.'

'I'll be up before the magistrate tomorrow morning, Kate. He'll decide whether to send me to the criminal court for trial, or perhaps he'll issue a fine and tell me to be a good fellow and give up my evil ways.'

'This isn't something to laugh at, Harry. Your mother is distraught, and from what you told me before, you depend upon the money you make from your gaming clubs. Maybe the people who gamble away their fortunes deserve to lose everything, but what will Lady Lyndon do if you go to prison?'

'I'm hoping to grease a few palms, as they say in the trade, and get off with a fine. I've made enough to pay off the debts accrued by my late father.'

'What then? You still have to live. Will you seek honest employment?'

He threw back his head and laughed.

'Who appointed you as my conscience, Kate? I know you're right, but it seems as though you've taken on the task single-handed.'

She rose to her feet. 'If you're going to make fun of everything I say, it's time for me to leave. I'll tell your mother that you are an irredeemable sinner and you will probably spend the rest of your days picking oakum or whatever they do here.'

He caught her by the hand as she was about to walk past him. 'I'm sorry. I'm really grateful for your concern for my mother, but I hope to be able to return home tomorrow.'

She gave him a searching look, and she could see that he was sincere. She relented, just a little. 'You'll need someone to represent you in court.'

'Are you suggesting your lawyer friend?'

'Perry might be persuaded to take your case. He's very good at his job.'

'I'm not sure I want to be beholden to a man who made no secret of the fact that he dislikes me.'

'He doesn't have to like his clients, but he is a very fair-minded man, and well thought of.'

Harry sat back in his chair. 'How praiseworthy. Maybe I'll follow his example and reform.'

'Don't you ever take anything seriously, Harry? Think of your poor mother — she doesn't understand why you're here. Maybe you ought to tell her.'

His smile faded. 'You're right, of course, but the truth is I don't want either of you involved in my affairs.'

'You allowed me to use your premises for the soup kitchen,' Kate said reasonably. 'You said

146

yourself that it suited you to do so.'

'I know, and I'm ashamed to admit it, which is why I want you to get away now. Forget about helping me — I can look after myself.' Harry stood up, taking Kate's hands in his. 'You really shouldn't be dragged into this, and neither should Annie and my mother.'

'What are you saying?' Kate met his earnest look with a frown. 'Surely you must have considered this before you were caught?'

He shrugged and released her hands. 'I was arrogant and thoughtless. I suppose I thought my luck would never change, but it has, and now I must pay the price.'

'You don't believe you'll get off lightly, do you?'

A half-smile curve his generous lips. 'What do you think? You're a judge's daughter, you probably know more about the law than I do.'

'I don't think my papa would be very lenient if you were brought before him in court.'

'Then I want you to do something for me, and for yourself as well.'

'What is it?'

'I own a property on the other side of the River Lea. It's been in my family for centuries but I've spent very little time there since I was a boy. I employ a caretaker and his wife, and they look after the house and grounds, although I haven't visited it for quite a while.'

'Why are you telling me this?' Kate demanded angrily. 'I can't see how it concerns me.'

'It's a rural area, but not too far away. I would like you to persuade my mother to go there until I've got myself out of this tangle.'

'I wouldn't call it a tangle exactly. You could go to prison for years.'

'Thank you, Kate. I do know that, but there is also Monks' gang to reckon with. If they discover my true identity, I need my mother to be somewhere safe, and that goes for Annie, too.'

'What about me, and Jenny and Ivy and her children? We're all involved because of the soup kitchen.'

'I know, and I'm sorry. When I agreed to let the ground floor to you I had no idea that everything would come to a head. Someone has informed against me, and when I find out who it was they'll regret their actions.'

'Do you always resort to violence to solve a problem?'

'I didn't mention physical assault — there are other ways. But I intend to bring the Monks gang to justice. Their actions are despicable and my men are like choirboys in comparison. I want to get Spears out of their clutches. He's loyal and he doesn't deserve the treatment they'll almost certainly hand out.'

'I don't think I want to know about that,' Kate said hastily. 'Anyway, I can't go to your house and tell your mother to pack up and move out of town, and the same goes for Annie. They have minds of their own, and Lady Lyndon seems to have no idea of your criminal activities.'

'It's true that my mother knows nothing and I want to keep it from her as long as possible. Maybe you'd care to wait until after the court session tomorrow. Who knows? I might be home in time for dinner.'

'I think there's more to this than you're telling me,' Kate said slowly. 'But I like your mother and I feel sorry for her. I will wait and see what sentence they hand out to you.'

'If it goes against me, you'll find the keys and the deeds to the house in Walthamstow in a locked box in my room in Finsbury Circus.' Harry took a bunch of keys from his pocket and handed them to Kate. 'It's the small brass key with scrollwork. The others are keys to the premises in Cable Street, and the house in Finsbury Circus.'

Kate took them, eyeing him warily. 'You really don't think it will go well for you?'

'Best be safe, that's my motto.' Harry leaned towards her and brushed Kate's lips with a kiss. 'Thank you, Kate. I know I can trust you.'

She hurried from the room and found Warrender standing outside the door. 'It's all a mistake, isn't it, miss? The master will be released as soon as they discover their error.'

'I hope so,' Kate said evasively. 'But I need to put his case to a lawyer friend. Will you take me to Lincoln's Inn Fields?'

'Of course, miss. You'll find that all of us servants in Finsbury Circus will do anything for Sir Harry.'

Kate held her finger to her lips. 'They don't know his title here, Warrender. Make sure you don't mention it should you come here again.'

'As I said, miss. It's obviously a mistake.'

★ ★ ★

149

Kate was lucky enough to find Perry in chambers, and she wasted no time in repeating the plea for him to represent Harry that she had been silently rehearsing during the carriage ride from Cold-bath Fields Prison to Lincoln's Inn.

'Of course it isn't a mistake,' Perry said angrily when she finished speaking. 'The police haven't arrested the wrong man. I don't believe the cock-and-bull tale that Trader has fed you.'

Kate folded her hands in her lap, meeting Perry's angry gaze with a steady look. 'I think you'd better know the truth, although this mustn't go any further.'

'Just a moment, Kate. You know that I can't withhold vital evidence. I'm not going to court to lie for Harry Trader. He's a common criminal and a gang leader. If he's sent down for a long term it will be what he deserves.'

'You know that I can't ask my father for advice.' Kate watched Perry carefully, looking for the slightest change in his tight-lipped expression. 'Harry Trader allowed me to run the soup kitchen from his premises, but that probably makes me an accessory. If he goes to prison I might be arraigned on charges of aiding and abetting a criminal, or something similar. I only know the terms I've heard Papa use when talking about court cases.'

Perry paced the floor behind his desk. 'What are you saying, Kate? What else aren't you telling me?'

'This must not be used in court. I want you to give me your word.'

'It depends.' Perry came to a halt. 'You'd better tell me everything.'

'Harry inherited a baronetcy from his late father. His real name is Sir Harry Lyndon and his home is in Finsbury Circus where he lives with his mother, Lady Lyndon.'

'You'll be telling me next that he spends most of his time raising funds for charities, instead of preying on gullible fools with more money than sense.'

Kate jumped to her feet. 'If you're going to be facetious I won't bother. Forget that I asked you to represent him. I'll find someone else.'

'Don't be so hasty. I'm growing more interested in this case by the minute. Please sit down, Kate. Finish what you had to say.'

Reluctantly, Kate sank down on the chair. 'He doesn't deny his criminal activities, but I believed him when he said he wanted to bring the Monks gang to justice. What do you say, Perry?'

He was silent for a moment and then he sighed. 'Ordinarily I would refuse such a case, but because you are involved and because your father is in no state to support or advise you, I will represent Harry Trader in court tomorrow. It is, after all, only an appearance before a magistrate, and it should be quite straightforward.'

Kate gave him a beaming smile. 'Thank you, Perry.'

He held up his hand. 'Unless, of course, someone knows the true identity of your villain. That will change everything, and I will stand down from the case. I can't afford to have my reputation damaged in such a way.'

'I understand,' Kate said reluctantly. 'But I am grateful.'

'Does Trader actually own the premises where you've established your soup kitchen?' Perry went to sit at his desk, resting his elbows on the table and steepling his hands.

'I believe he does, but you're making me feel as if I am on trial, Perry. Why does it matter?'

'I suggest you vacate it immediately, Kate. Move elsewhere and walk away from any connection with

Trader and his criminal activities.'

'He told me that he's disbanded his gang.'

'And you believed him, Kate? I think he told you that so that you would feel sympathetic and help him by persuading me to represent him in court.'

'If it's such an onerous task why did you agree to take him on?'

'Because he obviously means something to you, or you wouldn't be here now pleading his case.'

'You're wrong. My involvement with Harry Trader came about by chance, but I do believe that he has a right to the best possible representation in court. Surely innocent until proven guilty is the premise on which our judicial system is based?'

A reluctant smile curved Perry's lips. 'Kate, if women were allowed to study law, you would make a superb barrister.'

'I don't think my father would agree with you, Perry. But I really mustn't take up any more of your time.' Kate stood up. She was satisfied that Perry would do his best and that Harry would have a fair chance of acquittal, or at least a less heavy sentence. She could go to Lady Lyndon with reasonably good news.

'As I said before, you must seriously consider vacating the premises in Cable Street.' Perry rose from his seat. 'The sooner the better, in my opinion.'

'I'll give it some thought,' Kate said tactfully. 'You don't need to show me out. I should know the way after all these years.'

'Your father is much missed. It's not easy to live up to the standard he set.' Perry followed her to the door and held it open. 'How is he doing now? I'd like to visit him if he's well enough.'

'He's about the same,' Kate said, sighing. 'He's no worse, thank goodness, and the doctors think he might improve as time goes by.'

'Then I'll definitely pay a call at your house in the next couple of days.'

'I'm sure Papa will appreciate a visit. Goodbye, Perry, and thank you for agreeing to take Harry's case.'

'I'm only doing it for you,' Perry said drily.

She acknowledged this remark with a brief smile. 'If anyone can get him off, it will be you, and now I must go and tell Lady Lyndon that her son will be well represented in court tomorrow.'

'You've met his mother?' Perry barred her way. 'Are you sure you're doing the right thing, Kate? I would advise against getting too deeply involved with that family.'

'It's common courtesy to put the poor lady's mind at ease. I know what I'm doing, Perry.'

Kate left him standing in the doorway, but she did not look back.

Kate was in the court room next morning, waiting for Harry's case to come before the magistrate. She had not wanted to be there, but Lady Lyndon had been so distraught that in the end Kate had agreed to attend and to report to her the moment she knew Harry's fate. She waited patiently, sitting through several cases, until he was called to the dock, and she held her breath. Despite his confident bearing, he looked pale, tired and unkempt. He glanced up, scanning the public gallery until he saw her, and a genuine smile lit his face. Kate found herself smiling back, but then she caught Perry's eye and she composed herself, staring down at her folded hands. She sat quietly, listening to the charges against Harry Trader being read out and his subsequent plea of "not guilty".

Perry spoke on his behalf, but the magistrate seemed to have made up his mind from the outset and without any further ado, he referred the case to the Crown Court.

'I'm sorry, Kate,' Perry said when they met outside the court room. 'I did my best, but Trader's reputation seems to have gone before him.'

'What do you think it means?' Kate asked anxiously. 'Will he go to prison for a long time, if he's found guilty, that is?'

'It seems likely. I don't want to give you false hope.'

'His mother will be devastated. She really had no idea that he was involved in criminal activities.'

'Keep your voice down, Kate.' Perry glanced around anxiously. 'Anyone might be listening, and I have to prepare the case if I'm to represent him at the Old Bailey.'

'Have you changed your mind about him?'

'No, not entirely, but it will be a challenge.'

'Thank you, Perry. I'm sure that Harry will be very grateful to have you as his counsel.'

'I don't think that grateful is in his vocabulary, Kate, but I will do my best to get him acquitted, if only for your sake.'

Kate eyed him curiously. 'For my sake?'

'If he is acquitted it means that your connection with him through the soup kitchen is quite legitimate, and you are exonerated. I am doing this for you, not for Trader. Now, I have another client to see, so I must go.'

Kate was left speechless as she watched him walk away.

'Ain't that romantic?' Jenny said dreamily. 'He done it for you, miss.'

'I can look after myself, and I'm not closing down the soup kitchen. I won't let all those people down who have come to depend upon us. In fact, we'd better hurry now or poor Ivy will be coping on her own again.'

★ ★ ★

They arrived in Cable Street to find the queue of hungry people stretching almost as far as the railway bridge. Annie was standing outside the closed doors of the soup kitchen, playing a lively tune on her concertina, but it was hard to tell if the music had any effect on those whose bellies growled with hunger. Their grey, pinched faces and stick-like

155

limbs revealed how close some of them were to starvation. Kate was painfully aware that the meal the soup kitchen provided was the only thing keeping the poorest of them from the dreaded workhouse or, even worse, dying on the street.

'Where've you been?' Ivy demanded as Kate and Jenny entered the kitchen.

'I'm sorry,' Kate said humbly. 'Harry Trader was up in court today. I wanted to be there to see the case first-hand.'

'He's a criminal.' Ivy heaved a large pan from the range. 'Help me to get this into the dining room, Jenny. You might slice the bread, Kate. I can't allow the twins to wield a knife.'

'Of course.' Kate laid her shawl on a chair. 'We're here to help, and I apologise again for leaving you to do all the work.'

'Oh, well, I suppose you are paying me, and it's made such a difference. At least I can feed my nippers now, and I don't have to send the older kids out to work if they're poorly.' Ivy hefted the pan into the dining room.

Kate set to work slicing three loaves, and she took the bread into the room where people were queuing up with their cups, bowls or anything that would hold a portion of soup. It was then that she realised there was a disturbance amongst those crowding round the entrance. With the bread basket still clasped in her hands she went to investigate and was almost bowled over when a man hurtled through the doorway, cannoning into her. Jenny caught the basket, but Kate ended up on the floor beneath a body with a nauseatingly familiar smell. She extricated herself and scrambled to her feet.

'Spears! What happened to you?' she cried as he lifted his head. He was barely recognisable beneath a mass of cuts and livid bruises.

'Miss, you got to get away from here,' he said hoarsely. 'They ain't going to leave you alone, no matter what you say. You got to shut up shop and leave. I'm telling you that for nothing. Just look at the state of me if you don't believe what I'm saying.'

10

'Who did this to you, Spears?' Kate asked anxiously.

He raised himself to a sitting position, holding his head in his hands. 'Who d'you think? It was the Monks gang. They were responsible for Harry being arrested, and they want you out of this building.'

'I don't see what they can do,' Kate said slowly. 'Harry owns the premises. They can't argue with that.'

Jenny placed the bread on the table. 'Let's get him into the kitchen, miss. The mob will break down the doors if we don't start serving them.'

'Yes, of course.' Kate helped Spears to his feet, and between them they managed to guide him to a chair in the kitchen.

'I'll clean him up,' Kate said firmly. 'You'd better give Ivy a hand, Jenny. She'll be run off her feet in the dining room.'

'Yes, of course.' Jenny cast an anxious glance at Spears. 'I wouldn't believe everything that one says.'

'I heard that,' Spears muttered crossly. 'I'm in agony here, miss.'

Jenny tossed her head and marched into the dining room, slamming the door behind her.

Kate filled a bowl with warm water from the kettle. 'This will hurt, Spears, but it has to be done.' She proceeded to bathe his bruised and bloodied face, ignoring his complaints.

'I think they broke me arm,' Spears said, groaning. 'Don't you listen to that Jenny woman. I'm telling you to get away from here, all of you. Harry would say the same if he was here. If Harry does time that will leave Monks free to run riot.'

'Are you telling me that Harry has been keeping this other gang under control?'

'I wouldn't say that exactly, miss. Monks has more men than any of the other gangs, and he's vicious, but Harry is a match for him.'

Kate eyed him curiously. 'But why would Harry take on the other criminals in this area? It doesn't make sense.'

'Why do you think Harry has managed to keep his clubs going for such a long time?' Spears tapped the side of his nose. 'There's many a high-up government official and even a few judges who enjoy a night at the gaming tables.'

'Are you saying that the police turn a blind eye to Harry's illegal gaming clubs in return for his help in keeping the other gangs under some sort of control?'

'That's about it, miss.'

'But Harry might go to prison. What will happen then?' Kate rinsed the bloodied rag in cold water before handing it back to Spears. 'Hold this over your swollen cheek. I'll make you a cup of tea and then you'd better go to your room.'

'I wouldn't stay here if I was you. I can't wait to get away to somewhere safe.'

Kate busied herself making a pot of tea. 'If anyone can get Harry acquitted, it's the barrister who's taken on his case, and he happens to be a good friend of mine.' She filled a cup with tea, adding a lump of sugar before handing it to Spears. 'Take my advice and lie down for a while. You're going to be sore for days and you don't want to risk getting into any more fights.'

'It weren't what I'd call a fight,' Spears said gloomily. 'I was set upon and beaten up. That's how they do things.'

'Then let's hope that all goes well when Harry goes to court.'

★ ★ ★

A date was set for Harry's trial in the Crown Court. Kate wanted to attend but Ivy's children had all contracted chicken pox, and she had to remain at home to care for them, leaving Kate and Jenny to run the soup kitchen on their own. Spears had taken to his bed and rarely left the building. Although he would not admit it, Kate realised that he was terrified of going out for fear of encountering the thugs who had thrashed him. In spite of everything she felt responsible for him, and she took him a bowl of soup and a hunk of bread every day at noon. If there was anything left after the midday meal, Kate would leave it in the larder together with a large chunk of cheese and a couple of apples. It had always vanished when she went to look next morning, and she could only assume that Spears had plucked up the courage to come downstairs at some time during the night. His continuing fear of the Monks gang was infectious, and although Kate tried to put on a brave face, she too was nervous. Every time the street door opened and a rough-looking man entered the premises she reached for a rolling pin and was prepared to use it to defend herself or her patrons. They had been left alone so far, and for that she was grateful, although what might happen after the trial was another matter.

A week had gone by and the trial was imminent. Ivy was still at home caring for her children, and her help was greatly missed, but Annie proved to be a willing substitute. She arrived early that morning ready for work and there was no task that she would not attempt. She picked up a large knife and began chopping vegetables for the soup.

'That looks dangerous,' Kate said nervously. 'I don't mean to criticise, Annie, but I'm afraid you might cut yourself.'

Annie smiled and shrugged. 'I can see just a little. It's just a vague outline of objects, but enough to get by.'

'You're very brave.' Kate reached out to lay her hand on Annie's shoulder. 'I don't think I could cope in your situation.'

'Yes, you would. I could stay in my room all day, but that would be awful, and I have my music. I know it makes people smile — I can hear it in their voices.' 'It's a wonderful gift,' Kate said earnestly.

'Harry loved to hear me play.' Annie's blue eyes filled with tears. 'His case comes up in court today, doesn't it?'

'Yes. I'd like to be there, but I can't leave you and Jenny to manage on your own.'

'I wish I could help serve the food, but I would be very slow, and I'd probably spill more soup than I managed to get into their bowls,' Annie

161

said with an infectious chuckle.

'I wouldn't want to leave you two on your own, just in case Spears is right. If any of the Monks gang come here they would be out to cause trouble.'

'It's been over a week since Spears was attacked. Perhaps they'll leave us alone while Harry is away.'

'Maybe,' Kate said doubtfully. 'Anyway, I'll go to the court when we finish here today. At least I can have a word with Perry. He should be able to tell me how he thinks the case is going.'

'I don't want Harry to go to prison,' Annie said, sniffing. 'He's been so good to me.'

'If anyone can get him off it's Perry.' Kate spoke with more confidence than she was feeling. Perry had not been enthusiastic about the case, and he had never attempted to conceal his dislike for Harry, but he was a professional and he would not allow such considerations to affect his work.

Kate could barely wait until the last drop of soup had been served and she went outside to hail a cab, leaving Jenny and Annie to finish clearing up.

The cab ride to the Central Criminal Court seemed to take twice as long as it should, but eventually Kate arrived, paid the cabby, and she entered the building with a sudden feeling of foreboding. Her fears were confirmed when she mounted the stairs and came face to face with Perry.

'Has the trial begun?' Kate asked anxiously.

'It's over.' Perry's handsome features were marred by a scowl. 'Trader changed his plea to guilty, and he didn't advise me of his decision. I was made to look a fool in front of one of the most senior judges in the country.'

Kate clutched his arm. 'Why would he do that? I don't understand.'

'You don't understand?' Perry's voice shook with suppressed anger. 'Neither do I. Anyway, Trader's got what he deserves. I wasn't too happy about taking on the case, and I've been proved right. The man is a charlatan and he deserves the twelve-year sentence he was given.'

'Twelve years?'

'That's right.' Perry's expression softened a little. 'I'm sorry, Kate. I know you consider him to be a much better person than he really is.'

She shook her head. 'I don't think that's so, but I do feel for his poor mother and for Annie, who depends on his help to get by.'

'The fellow obviously thinks a lot of you.' Perry produced a folded sheet of paper from beneath his robe. 'He asked me to give you this.'

'What is it?'

'You won't know until you read it, but if he asks you to look after his mother, you must refuse. She is not your responsibility, nor is Annie. Harry Trader, or however he chooses to style himself, is a man who takes advantage of people. He's fortunate that the case ended swiftly and his true identity was not revealed. Not that it will do him any good in Newgate Prison.'

Kate's hand shook as she took the note from him. She tucked it into her reticule with a casual shrug. 'I'll read it later. Is there anything we can do for him, Perry? Can we appeal the sentence?'

'He's admitted his guilt. You can say goodbye

to Harry for a decade or more. Perhaps he will emerge a better person for his incarceration.'

'You are so smug,' Kate said angrily. 'This is a man's life that has been ruined.'

'I'm sorry, but the only person to blame is Trader himself. He knew what he was doing, and the fact that he's had a good education and comes from a titled family makes him even more culpable.'

'But you said that didn't come out in court.'

'That's right. Maybe Trader chose to plead guilty to keep his identity a secret. Either way, I can't feel any sympathy for the man.'

Kate could see that arguing in Harry's defence would be useless. 'I have to go home, Perry.'

'I'd like to visit your father soon.'

'I'm sure he'll be pleased to see you.' Kate walked away, torn between loyalty to her old friend and annoyance at his attitude. Harry Trader was not a wicked man, of that she was certain. He had fallen into bad ways, but there was a reason for his behaviour. She clutched the letter tightly in her hand, only opening it when she was seated in the hansom cab on the way home.

Newgate Prison
July 1858

My dear Kate,
By the time you read this I will be back in my cell, and likely to remain here for quite some time as I have changed my plea to 'guilty'.
I am sorry for involving you in my affairs, but I know that you have respect for my mother and I would be most grateful if you

164

could bring yourself to break the news of my imprisonment to her personally. I know it is a lot to ask, but I comfort myself with the knowledge that you have a good heart and a generous spirit.

However, London is not going to be safe with the Monks gang at large. I have been doing my best to bring them to justice, but it seems I have failed. I want you to persuade Mama to leave Finsbury Circus and move to the house in Walthamstow together with Annie. For your own safety you must abandon the premises in Cable Street. The Monks gang are vicious and they don't care who they hurt. Now I am out of the way they will attack anyone with close connections to me.

I cannot insist that you should go to Warren House, but I would ask you to consider it seriously if you feel at all threatened. I promise you that this will end, but I cannot be more explicit at this time.

I remain your most loyal friend and admirer,
Harry Lyndon

Kate read the letter again and again, and was still studying it when the cab drew up in Finsbury Square. She paid the cabby and stepped down onto the pavement outside her home. Harry's warning had both alarmed and worried her. Although she had not received any direct threat from the Monks gang, she had seen the state in which they had left Spears, and he was only just getting over the beating. One thing was certain:

she must persuade Lady Lyndon to leave town, at least for the time being. Annie might be more difficult to convince, but perhaps her affection for Harry's mother would be the key. All Kate knew was that she must try. There was, however, one of Harry's instructions that she was prepared to ignore. She would only close the soup kitchen as a last resort.

Henry answered her knock on the door and Kate went straight to her room. She needed time to think, and that meant being on her own for a while. It seemed as though she was always surrounded by people. When she was at home her mother was constantly bemoaning her fate and criticising Kate for working with the poor when her father was an invalid and needed her attention. Jenny was always on hand, too, but Jenny knew when to talk and when to remain silent. Then there was the soup kitchen, which was so hectic that it gave Kate no time to think about anything other than satisfying an increasing number of hungry people.

She had read Harry's letter for the third time and had come to the conclusion that the first step must be to visit Warren House. She could hardly persuade Lady Lyndon to move somewhere that might be totally unsuitable, and the little that Kate knew of Harry's mother was that the lady had a mind of her own. A knock on the door made her jump.

'Who is it?'

'It's me, Jenny.'

'Come in.'

Jenny opened the door, peering into the room

with an anxious frown. 'Did the trial go well, miss?'

Kate shook her head. 'He pleaded guilty. I don't know why.'

'Oh, no.' Jenny's eyes widened. 'Does that mean he'll go to prison?'

'The judge gave him twelve years.'

'I am sorry, miss. I mean, I know he's a villain, but he's a nice man. He always had a cheery word for me and the others. Annie thinks the world of him — she'll be so upset.'

'Don't take off your bonnet, Jenny.' Kate folded the letter and placed it back in her reticule. 'You and I are going to get a cab to Walthamstow.'

'That's across the River Lea and over the marsh. Might I ask why, miss?'

'Harry thinks his mother and Annie will be safer living out of town, but I want to take a look at the house before I try to persuade either of them to make the move.'

'Surely the Monks gang will cease hostilities now that Harry Trader is out of the way.'

'He doesn't seem to think so, and who am I to argue? I know virtually nothing about how the gang laws work, and I don't want to find out. Look what they did to Spears.'

'I don't like him, but I feel quite sorry for him now.'

'Spears is old enough to look after himself. It's Ivy and the children I worry about.' Kate stood up and reached for her bonnet. 'Let's do something positive. I can't bear standing around doing nothing.'

'Shall I ask Henry to have the carriage brought round, miss?'

'No. I think we'll take a cab. I don't want my mother asking questions. She wouldn't understand. I doubt if we'll be there for long and I'll pay the cabby to wait for us.'

★ ★ ★

Warren House was situated at the end of a country lane on the edge of Epping Forest, with open fields leading down to the marsh. The house itself was hidden behind a high red-brick wall with tall wrought-iron gates and a curved carriage sweep.

Kate paid the cabby, securing his promise to wait for them outside with a generous tip.

'I ain't got all day, miss,' he said grumpily.

'We'll be as quick as we can, and there's a bonus for you if it takes longer than an hour.' Kate opened a narrow side gate, lifting her skirts to avoid snagging her lace-trimmed petticoat on a creeping shoot from a bramble. She marched up the overgrown carriage sweep with Jenny close on her heels.

'It looks spooky,' Jenny said in a stage whisper.

They came to a halt in front of the red-brick façade. The whole house seemed to be losing its battle with the ivy that clambered up towards the roof, wrapping its tendrils around the windows as if trying to gain access to the interior.

Kate glanced over her shoulder at what must once have been a lawn, but was now more like a wildflower meadow. 'It certainly needs a little love and attention, but it's off the beaten track and I can see why it could prove to be a good hideaway for Lady Lyndon and Annie.' She rapped on the door knocker several times and there was no answer.

'No one's at home,' Jenny said with a sigh of what sounded like relief.

'Perhaps the caretaker lives at the back of the house. Come along, Jenny. I doubt if any monsters or ghouls abide in Walthamstow.'

Laughing, Kate strolled off along the pathway that led around the house, skirting a shrubbery. The house was considerably larger than she had at first thought, and what might once have been a beautifully kept rose garden stretched out towards a stand of trees and another overgrown grassy area. Rose petals had been scattered by the wind like confetti and their rich scent filled the air, mingling with the brackish odour from the marshes. Kate, however, was not here to enjoy the beauty of nature. She headed for the stable yard at the far side of the house, which had obviously been unused for some time. Moss covered the cobblestones and a stable door hung off rusted hinges, groaning as if in pain.

Kate knocked on the back door and when no one answered she tried the handle. To her surprise the door opened and she stepped into a narrow passageway with a flagstone floor.

'Is anyone about?' she called loudly.

'I say we leave now,' Jenny muttered.

'Ho, there! Is anyone at home?' Kate opened a door, which turned out to be a boot cupboard, although there was only one pair of muddy pattens on the rack. The next door was a preparation room of some sort, again seemingly unused but spotlessly clean, and at the end of the passage she

169

walked through a scullery into a large kitchen.

Seated facing each other on either side of the range, an elderly man and woman were sound asleep and the man was snoring.

Kate cleared her throat. 'Ahem. Good afternoon.'

The woman woke up with a start and she kicked the man, who staggered to his feet, still half asleep.

'I'm so sorry to disturb you,' Kate said hastily. 'I've come here on Mr Trader's behalf.' 'Who?' The woman stared at her suspiciously. 'Don't know anyone of that name.'

Kate realised her mistake. 'I mean Sir Harry Lyndon sent me.'

'Why didn't you say so in the first place?' The old man brushed a stray lock of thinning grey hair off his forehead. 'Martha, put the kettle on. We've got visitors.'

'You do it, Arthur. You're the nearest.' Martha stared suspiciously at Kate. 'Where is Sir Harry? Why has he sent you here today?'

'My name is Kate Martin, and this is my maid, Jenny. I'm here because Sir Harry asked me to come.'

Arthur puffed out his chest. 'Me and the missis have worked for the family for forty years. Arthur Boggis, at your service.'

'I'm very pleased to meet you both, but I'm afraid I am the bearer of bad news. Sir Harry won't be visiting here for quite a while.'

'Why not?' Arthur placed the kettle on the hob. 'He ain't took sick, is he?'

Kate shook her head. 'He has . . . ' She paused; the anxiety on the old couple's faces was too much

170

to bear, and she could not upset them further by telling them the truth. 'Sir Harry has had to go away for a while, but he's quite all right, so no need to worry. He wanted me to tell you that his mother will be staying here for a while with her ward, Miss Blythe.'

'Her ladyship is coming to live here?' Martha exchanged worried glances with her husband. 'What does she want to come to this place for?'

'For her health,' Kate said firmly. 'The air in Walthamstow is much cleaner than that in London. I would like to inspect the rooms to make sure that they are suitable.'

'I keep the house spotless, miss. You won't find a cobweb nor a cockroach. I keep the house ready for the family whenever they choose to arrive.'

'That's exactly what Sir Harry told me,' Kate said hurriedly. 'But I would still like to see the rest of the house.'

'Show the young lady, Arthur.'

Arthur shot a weary glance in his wife's direction. 'You're younger than me, Mattie. You do it.'

'I've got the miseries in me legs, Arthur. You know very well I can't do the stairs like I used to.'

'I'm sure we can find our way round without troubling either of you,' Kate said hastily. 'We'll be very quick and we won't disturb anything.'

'You won't find a speck of dust or a cobweb in this house.' Martha bustled over to the dresser, despite her alleged disability. 'I can't do it like in the old days, but a girl comes in from the village every day, and I make sure she keeps up my high standards.'

'Thank you. I'm sure everything will be perfect.'

Kate headed for the door, followed by Jenny.

'What a pair,' Jenny said when they were out of earshot.

'I'm sure that Lady Lyndon can keep them in order.' Kate led the way through a maze of wainscoted passages that ended in a wide, oak-panelled entrance hall. Sunlight streamed through the lattice windows, creating diamond patterns on the polished floorboards. A heavily carved oak chest stood against one wall and a huge stone fireplace occupied most of the opposite side of the hall. Kate could imagine a blaze roaring up the chimney in winter, but now, in high summer, the grate was filled with greenery placed in a large copper pot.

'It seems that Martha is as good as her word.' Kate ran her finger along the top of the mantelshelf. 'No dust here.'

'Let's see the rest of the house then,' Jenny said, shrugging. 'I doubt if it's like this everywhere.'

They explored several rooms on the ground floor, including a book-lined study, a morning parlour and a dining room large enough to hold a ball. Without exception all were comfortably, if not fashionably furnished, and so clean that Jenny said she could eat off the floor in all of them. The drawing room was scented with roses from a bowl spilling pink petals on the top of a mahogany side table. The furniture was old-fashioned but it was set out as if expecting guests to enjoy its undoubtedly comfortable, if out-dated style. Kate could imagine ladies in sack-back gowns seated at the small ornately carved tables, playing hands of whist or three-card loo.

'She's right,' Jenny said in a low voice. 'The

place is so spotless it looks as if the family still live here.'

'Maybe the ghosts of the Lyndons do haunt this house.'

Jenny shuddered. 'Don't say that. We've got to go upstairs now.'

'Don't be a baby. I was teasing you.' Kate squeezed Jenny's cold hand. 'The house has a very warm and welcoming atmosphere. I'm sure that Lady Lyndon and Annie will be very happy here — if I can persuade them to leave London.'

'I'm not sure I'd want to live this far from the city.' Jenny glanced nervously over her shoulder.

'You can stay here and I'll go upstairs if you're scared.' Kate went to the door and opened it. 'I really like what I've seen so far.'

'Don't leave me. I'm coming.' Jenny hurried after her and they crossed the hall to the wide oak staircase, its treads polished to a satin sheen after more than a century and a half of footfall.

There were six large family bedchambers on the first floor, all with their own dressing rooms, and at least eight good-sized rooms on the second floor, with the servants' sleeping accommodation on the top floor. Kate could not find fault anywhere, and it was clear that Martha Boggis had been telling the truth when she said she kept the house as if the family were still in residence.

They returned to the kitchen where Martha had laid a tea tray with what appeared to be the best china, and a plate of tiny cakes.

'Perhaps you would like to take tea on the terrace as it's such a warm day, miss?'

Kate pulled up a chair and sat down at the

kitchen table. 'Thank you, but we can't stay long, Mrs Boggis. We have a cab waiting to take us back to town, but I have to say that I'm very impressed with the house, and you are to be highly complimented on the way you've kept it. The family could move in today and it would be as if they had never left.'

'I told you not to worry, Mattie,' Arthur said gruffly. 'My wife is very diligent, Miss Martin. She wages war on dust and dirt.'

'I can see that.' Kate reached for the teapot. 'Won't you join us? A cup of tea is most welcome, especially in this heat.'

Jenny sat down next to Kate. 'May I have one of them cakes? They look almost too good to eat.'

Martha's tense expression melted into a smile. 'They are tasty, even if I say so myself. I make them once a month so that when the vicar calls I have something to offer him. The poor man has gone down with some sort of sickness, so he couldn't come today.'

'Do take a seat Mr and Mrs Boggis, or might I call you Martha and Arthur?' Kate filled her own cup and one for Jenny.

'We don't think that's proper, miss, if you'll excuse me being frank.' Arthur moved closer to his wife and slipped his arm around her ample waist. 'We like to do things proper in Warren House. Start as you mean to continue, that's my motto.'

'Do whatever feels best for you,' Kate said easily. 'The house is more than suitable, but can you tell me anything about the village? Would it be a safe place for two ladies to live?'

'Safe, miss?' Martha exchanged puzzled glances

174

with her husband. 'I don't understand.'

'In London there are gangs of men who flaunt the law. I don't suppose any of them come this far to the east, do they?'

'Heavens, no, miss.' Arthur shook his head. 'We get people breaking the law but they are dealt with immediately. This is as safe a place as any you'll find in the whole country. But do you think Lady Lyndon really will want to live here?'

11

'My dear girl, why would I want to leave my home in London?' Lady Lyndon leaned towards Kate with a questioning look in her ocean-blue eyes, so like those of her son.

Kate could see nothing for it but a slightly watered-down version of the truth. 'It's Harry's wish, my lady. He's had dealings in the past with some very bad men who have made threats against him and his family.'

'I don't see why they would do anything to me, my dear. Harry was always very protective, but I think he's worrying unnecessarily.'

'Maybe, but I've seen an example of what these people can do, and I have to agree with your son.'

'I'm sure you mean well, Kate, but this is my home and I have no intention of leaving.'

'Warren House is quite delightful, my lady. It wouldn't be for ever, and by moving to the countryside you would be so much safer from the dangers of cholera.'

'I'm sure that people become ill in Walthamstow, just as much as they do in Finsbury Circus, Kate. I appreciate your concern, but I want to stay in London as I intend to visit Harry in prison.'

Kate stared at her in dismay. 'I don't think that's a good idea. Harry wouldn't want you to expose yourself to the squalid conditions in which he's forced to live.'

'But Harry is a member of the aristocracy.

Surely the authorities wouldn't treat him like an ordinary criminal?'

Kate shook her head. 'I doubt if they care either way, ma'am. But Harry's instructions were clear. He wants you to be safe.'

'And I appreciate his concern and yours, my dear. But I am not going to be driven from my home by some ruffians my son has offended.'

Kate had sudden vision of Spears after his encounter with the Monks gang. To call them ruffians was an understatement, but it was obvious that Lady Lyndon was not going to be easily persuaded.

'I understand,' Kate said patiently. 'However, should you change your mind I know that Mr and Mrs Boggis would be delighted to have the opportunity to make you welcome.'

'What is this? Are you planning a trip somewhere,

Aunt Margaret?'

Kate turned with a start to see Annie making her way carefully across the room.

'Annie, dear. Do come and sit down.' Lady Lyndon rose to her feet and pulled up a chair. 'I didn't expect to see you today.'

'I heard voices. Who is with you, Aunt Margaret?'

'It's Kate, she came to see me because she's worried for my safety. I told her that I'm not afraid. It would take more than a threat from some villains whom Harry has crossed in the past to make me leave my home.'

Kate reached out to touch Annie's hand. 'It's more than that, Annie. You know the situation

177

better than I do.'

Annie's pretty face puckered as if she were about to cry. 'It's true, and that's why I came here today. I wasn't going to say anything because I didn't want to upset you, Aunt Margaret, but I must speak out.'

Lady Lyndon tugged at the bell pull. 'We'll have a nice cup of tea and some cake. You'll feel better then, Annie.'

'No, I'm afraid I won't. These men are very dangerous and because of them I've had to leave my lodgings. You should listen to what Kate has to say.' Annie turned her head so that she was facing Kate. 'Is that what you were planning when I walked into the room?'

'Harry wants his mama to leave Finsbury Circus immediately. He would feel much happier if both of you left London and went to stay in Warren House.'

'Where is that?'

'In a village called Walthamstow. It's in Essex, on the other side of the River Lea. I went there yesterday and I think you would both find it very comfortable.'

'And safe,' Annie added fervently. 'Aunt Margaret, you don't know what the Monks gang are like.'

'No, dear, I don't.' Lady Lyndon returned to her chair and sank down, sighing. 'Surely an apology would suffice? Or perhaps a payment in compensation for whatever wrong they think has been committed against them.'

Kate could see that the time for tact had passed. Lady Lyndon was a stubborn woman and she needed to know the truth. 'I'm sorry to be blunt, your ladyship, but they are vicious criminals. They won't care that you and Annie are women, or that you are a titled lady. They would have no compunction in razing this house to the ground, or they might try to abduct you and hold you to ransom. Harry chose to plead guilty to save your family name being dragged through the courts, but he also knew the risks you were facing, which is why he wants you to leave London.'

'Oh, my goodness!' Lady Lyndon clasped her hands to her bosom. 'Harry was always such a good boy.'

'He's a man now, Aunt Margaret.' Annie said firmly. 'And despite the fact that he's been mixing with the wrong people, Harry is a good man and he loves his ma. I'm willing to go with you, if you'll agree to do as he wishes.'

'But if I leave they might still burn my house down.' Lady Lyndon's eyes filled with tears and her bottom lip trembled.

'I think the building would be safer if you were not in it, ma'am,' Kate said firmly. 'I'm sorry to say these things to you, but Harry was very clear. He wants you to leave London, for the time being at any rate.'

'I see.' Lady Lyndon sat for a moment with her hands neatly folded in her lap. Then she looked up, meeting Kate's earnest gaze with a lift of her chin. 'Heaven knows, the Lyndon family has weathered scandal after scandal over the past two centuries. I'll go to Walthamstow, but only if Harry promises that he will appeal against his sentence. I don't care what people say about us, I want my son back.' She looked up as the door opened and Agnes entered, bobbing a curtsey.

'You rang, my lady?'

'Yes, Agnes. We'll have tea and cake for the three of us.'

Kate shook her head. 'Thank you, but I'd better go now, Lady Lyndon. I need to ensure that the soup kitchen is running smoothly.'

'Of course, my dear. You may see Miss Martin out, Agnes. Then bring the tea, and please tell Cook that Miss Blythe will be staying with us. You'd better advise Mrs Fulton so that she can make the rose guest room ready.'

Kate leaned over to brush Annie's cheek with a kiss. 'I'll be back soon, Annie,' she whispered. 'In the meantime, please do your best to persuade Lady Lyndon to make the move to Walthamstow.'

'I'll try but I can't promise anything. Her ladyship has a mind of her own.'

'I'll go now, but don't let her ladyship go out unattended. If you need someone to help you bring your things here, our footman will be glad to be of service.' Annie nodded and smiled.

'What are you two plotting?' Lady Lyndon demanded. 'I don't like being kept in the dark.'

'It was simply about bringing my belongings here, Aunt Margaret,' Annie said glibly. 'I hope I'm not putting you to any trouble by coming to stay.'

Kate left the room, closing the door behind her. With Annie on her side she might just succeed in persuading Lady Lyndon to move to Warren House, where she would undoubtedly meet her match in Martha Boggis.

Kate left the house, stepping out into the heat of midday. She unfurled her parasol and set off in the direction of Finsbury Square, intending to call in at home before going to Cable Street. The sun blazed down from a cloudless sky and she could feel the heat from the pavement through the soles of her boots. Dust hung in the air, settling on the leaves of the London plane trees, dulling their greenness to pale grey. The smell of effluent made Kate cover her nose and mouth with her handkerchief. At this moment Walthamstow seemed like heaven on earth and Kate had a sudden longing for the peace and freshness of the countryside.

She was almost home when the sound of running footsteps made her clutch her reticule in both hands. Even in the most respectable parts of the city there was the danger of pickpockets and petty thieves, but it was Frankie, Ivy's eldest child, who caught up with her.

'Miss Kate. You got to come with me. Ma's in a terrible state.'

'Whatever is the matter, Frankie? Slow down and catch your breath.'

He grabbed her by the sleeve. 'They set fire to the soup kitchen, miss. It's burning.'

'Is anyone hurt?'

'I dunno, miss. It was that Mr Spears what come to our house. He told Ma and she sent me to fetch you.'

Kate raised her hand to hail a hackney carriage, but it drove past without stopping. They waited a few minutes and eventually a hansom cab pulled up at the kerb.

'Cable Street, please, cabby.' Kate helped

181

Frankie into the cab and she climbed in to sit beside him.

'I ain't never been in one of these,' Frankie said, grinning.

'I heard about the chicken pox. You're obviously much better now.'

'I was the first to get sick, then Jimmy and May. We've all had it, even baby John.'

They lapsed into silence as the cab wended its way through the chaotic tangle of horse-drawn vehicle, handcarts and pedestrians, who seemed to have no fear when it came to barging across the road. Eventually, a pall of smoke made the cabby draw his horse to a halt.

He opened the flap in the cab roof. 'Can't go no further, miss. You'll have to walk the rest of the way.'

Kate paid him and alighted, holding out her hand to Frankie, who ignored it and leaped to the ground.

'The whole street is on fire,' he said gleefully.

Kate ignored his childish enthusiasm for what appeared to be a disaster, and she covered her mouth again, but this time it was to help her breathe in the thick smoke. Her attempt to reach the soup kitchen was foiled by a burly police constable.

'You can't go no further, miss. It ain't safe.'

She came to a halt, staring in dismay at the flames shooting up into the summer sky.

Frankie tapped her on the arm. 'That's the man who come to our house, miss.' He pointed to a bent figure, who emerged from the curtain of smoke, coughing and red-eyed.

'Mr Spears, are you all right?' Kate caught him by the arm as he was about to wander past.

'Miss Martin?' Spears' eyes were bloodshot and runny, and his face was streaked with soot. 'They done it — Monks' gang — but the police don't want to know.'

'Are you hurt?' Kate asked warily. 'Perhaps you should go to the hospital.'

'I ain't hurt, but I've lost everything. I got nothing and no home to go to. I might as well hand meself in and go to prison.'

'Let's get away from here,' Kate said urgently. 'There's nothing we can do.'

'Got nowhere to go.' Spears dashed his hand across his eyes. 'I got no home and only the duds I stands up in.'

'We'll take Frankie home.' Kate grabbed Frankie by the hand. 'I need to speak to your ma, Frankie.'

'She never done it.' Frankie's eyes widened in alarm. 'You can't pin it on any one of us, miss.'

'Silly boy. Why would I think that?'

He shook his head. 'Dunno.'

'We'll go and see your ma.' Kate turned to Spears. 'You'd best come, too. I'll help you get back on your feet, but first you need to get cleaned up.'

'It's the end of me. I should never had fallen in with Harry Trader. It's all his fault.' Spears trudged along behind them, grumbling to himself.

★ ★ ★

Ivy greeted them with a solemn face. 'What a state of affairs, miss. What shall us do now?'

'I don't know, and that's the truth.' Kate studied Ivy's pale face. 'What's wrong? It's not just the loss of the soup kitchen, is it?'

Ivy shook her head. 'Come inside. I don't want the whole street to know me business.' She ushered them into her tiny living room, where baby John slept in a wooden cradle and the twins sat crosslegged on the floor, playing with a roughly carved wooden doll, while Charlie sucked on a lamb bone.

'Where are the others?' Kate asked anxiously.

'Nellie, May and Jimmy are out selling bootlaces. Not that it brings in much these days. I can't manage without the money from the soup kitchen, miss. We'll have to go to the workhouse — there's nothing else for it.'

'You won't do that,' Kate said firmly. She opened her reticule and took out her purse. 'Here, take this, Ivy. It will keep you for a day or two while I try to sort things out.'

Ivy hesitated. 'I didn't ask for charity, miss.'

'I think we can count each other as old friends now, Ivy. Please take it, if only for the children's sakes.'

Reluctantly, Ivy took the coins and pocketed them. 'Are you going to start another soup kitchen?' Spears slumped down on a rickety wooden chair. 'No one asks me how I'll manage. I could do with a cup of tea or a tot of rum.'

'You won't get either here, Augustus Spears.' Ivy glared at him. 'You've only got yourself to care about. I've got eight little ones.'

'That ain't my fault.'

Kate held up her hand. 'There's no point in fighting with each other. How did the fire start, Spears?'

'How d'you think? It were Monks hisself what set the blaze going. I tried to beat it out but the flames took hold and the whole place went up. I only just got out with me life.'

'They know I used to work there.' Ivy clutched Kate's hand, squeezing it until Kate felt as if her bones would break.

'They have nothing on you, Ivy,' Kate said gently. 'You should be safe here.'

The words had hardly left her lips when a missile hurtled through the already cracked windowpane, sending a shower of glass onto the floor, which narrowly missed Charlie.

Ivy scooped him up in her arms, and tears poured down her cheeks. 'We ain't safe anywhere, and all because I worked in a building owned by Trader. You'd better watch out for yourself. Monks is after the lot of us.'

Kate eyed her curiously. 'Why would he want to harm you or me? We've done nothing to him.'

'I don't think that matters,' Ivy said grimly. 'He hates anyone with a connection to Trader. You need to look out for yourself, miss. Monks is a bad man.'

Kate bent down to pick up the brick that had been hurled through the window. 'This was obviously sent as a warning. You must pack up your things, Ivy. Get the children together and be ready for a move. I'll come back later this afternoon with the carriage and I'll take you somewhere safe.'

'Where would that be, miss?'

'I don't know yet, but I promise you that I'll find somewhere for you and the children to live where Monks won't think of looking for you.'

'What about me?' Spears muttered. 'Don't I count?'

'I suggest you stay here and protect Ivy and the children until I return. I'll think of something for you, Spears. Although you must admit you haven't always been of much help to me.'

'I didn't approve of Harry letting you have the ground floor, and I've been proved right.'

Kate moved towards the doorway. 'Just stay here. Keep together and I'll be back in a couple of hours.' She left the small house and walked briskly to the end of Nightingale Lane where she managed to hail a cab.

★ ★ ★

Kate walked into Lady Lyndon's drawing room to find her ladyship relaxing on the sofa, listening to Annie, who was playing a haunting melody on her concertina.

'I'm sorry to interrupt,' Kate said apologetically, 'but this is urgent.'

Lady Lyndon was suddenly alert. 'Kate! What are you doing back here? Have you news from Harry?'

'No, my lady. I've just had some bad news and I need your help.'

'Oh dear! What has happened?'

'Is it to do with Harry?' Annie asked tremulously.

'It's just another example of the Monks gang

186

doing everything they can to make life difficult for anyone connected to Harry. The building he owns in Cable Street, where I've been running a soup kitchen, has been burned down.'

'What are you saying, Kate?' Lady Lyndon sat bolt upright. 'What has this to do with me?'

'Lady Lyndon, the time has passed for being too polite and tactful. The truth is that your son was the leader of a gang who ran illegal gaming clubs. Now, I believe there are mitigating circumstances, but that doesn't matter now. The facts are that Harry's internment has left a number of people exposed to the wrath of a ruthless villain called Monks.'

'How frightening.' Lady Lyndon reached for a bottle of smelling salts and held it under her nose. She sniffed, coughed and dabbed her watering eyes with a hanky. 'Tell me everything.'

'That's the sum of it so far, but the woman who has been helping me to run the charity has been threatened by the gang. Her husband is in prison for theft, but she does not deserve to suffer, nor do her young children.'

'Why are you telling us this, Kate?' Lady Lyndon replaced the small brown bottle on the drum table at the side of the sofa. 'What can I do to help them?'

'I'd like to take Ivy and her children to Warren House. I know it's what Harry would suggest, and it's only temporary until I can find them somewhere else to live.'

'By all means,' Lady Lyndon said, smiling. 'I wouldn't want the poor woman and her little ones on my conscience, but that means there would not

187

be room for myself and Annie. We will be able to stay here with a clear conscience.'

'I'm afraid you might be next, Lady Lyndon.' Kate laid her hand on Annie's shoulder. 'You're both in danger and the obvious solution is for you to go to Warren House, too. It's large enough and you would be safe.'

'Perhaps you should give it some thought, Aunt Margaret,' Annie said softly. 'Kate is telling the truth and I can vouch for the fact that people in Whitechapel are terrified of Monks and his men.'

'I want to see Harry,' Lady Lyndon said, frowning. 'I'll only make the move to Walthamstow if he tells me so himself.'

'Very well.' Kate knew when she was beaten. 'I'll arrange it as soon as possible.'

'Harry won't make me do anything I don't wish to,' Lady Lyndon said smugly. 'In the meantime you are welcome to take your friend and her children to Walthamstow. Perhaps you would like to accompany them, Annie?'

'I would be happy to move to the country, but I would prefer to remain here with you, at least for the time being.' Annie picked up her concertina. 'What would you like me to play for you, Aunt Margaret?'

* * *

Harry entered the small room where a surly warder had told Kate and Lady Lyndon to wait.

'Mama, what are you doing here?' he demanded incredulously. He turned to Kate, frowning. 'Why did you bring her to this dreadful place?'

188

Lady Lyndon rose from the wooden chair, which was the only furniture in the small room and she held her hands out to her son. 'Don't blame Kate. I insisted on seeing you, Harry.'

'Sit down, please, Mama.' Harry pressed her gently back on the seat. 'Why did you want to see me?'

'I'm your mother,' Lady Lyndon said calmly. 'Of course I wanted to know that you were being well cared for.'

Harry laughed, but there was no humour in the sound. 'This isn't a hotel, Mama. This is a place of punishment and I knew what I was coming to when I pleaded guilty.'

Kate cleared her throat. 'I've been trying to persuade your mother to move to Warren House, but she insisted on hearing it from your lips, Harry.'

'Yes, that's the most sensible thing to do.' Harry nodded, raising his mother's hand to his lips. 'It's too dangerous for you to remain in Finsbury Circus, at least for the time being.'

'Monks or one of his men set your premises in Cable Street on fire.' Kate fixed him with a searching look. 'Ivy had a brick thrown through her window, so I'd like to take the family to Warren House, with your mama's permission, of course.'

Harry nodded. 'That's very sensible. You should be there, too, Mama.'

'I don't want to leave my home.' Lady Lyndon's bottom lip trembled. 'I don't want to stay in the country. Warren House was the family home of the Lyndons — I never liked that place.'

'It's a very nice house, Mama,' Harry said gently. 'You'll be very comfortable there and you'll be

189

safe.'

Lady Lyndon slapped his hand away. 'I don't like you being mixed up with evil men.'

Harry kneeled down at her side, ignoring the fact that the dirt from the floor was ruining his expensive trousers. 'I won't be here for much longer, but please do as I ask, Mama.'

'But your sentence was for twelve years,' Kate said anxiously. 'Are you planning to escape?'

He rose to his feet, brushing the dirt from his knees. 'In a way. I'm working with the police to bring Monks to justice. I couldn't tell you before the trial.'

'But what can you do from a prison cell?' Kate met his smiling gaze with a scowl. 'Don't make a joke of this, it isn't funny.'

'No, indeed it isn't.' Harry's smiled faded. 'I'm sorry but I can't tell you more at present.'

Lady Lyndon shook her head. 'I don't understand any of this, Harry.'

He helped her to her feet. 'Go with Kate, Mama. I'm afraid there might be more trouble if Monks gets wind of what is planned for him. I'll feel much happier if I know you are safe, and Annie, too. I hope it won't be for long, but I want you to go to Warren House and stay there until I leave prison.'

'I might be dead in twelve years' time,' Lady Lyndon said plaintively.

'I promise you it won't be anywhere near that long, Mama. It will be a matter of a few weeks or even a couple of months, if I have anything to do with the matter.'

'Are you sure about that?' Kate said warily. 'If what you say is correct, all of us who have had

190

anything to do with you are in danger while this is going on.'

'Yes, I'm afraid that's true. Which is why I need you to be out of London as well, Kate. Warren House is large enough to give shelter to all of you.' He grasped his mother's hands. 'Can I depend upon you to do as I ask, Mama?'

'I suppose so, since you put it so strongly, Harry,' Lady Lyndon said, drawing away from him with a sigh. 'You were always such a good little boy. I don't know what happened to you. I never imagined you would mix with villains.' She walked to the door and banged on it with her fist. 'Let me out. I want to go home.'

12

Next morning Kate was about to leave for Nightingale Lane when Perry arrived, and it was obvious from his grim expression that this was not going to be a social call. He shook his head when Henry offered to take his hat and cane.

'I'm not staying. I want a word with you, Kate.'

'I have an urgent appointment. Can it wait until later?'

'No, it cannot. You know very well why I'm here.'

'Thank you, Henry. That will be all.' Kate waited until the footman was out of earshot. 'Well, what is it, Perry?'

'Why didn't you tell me about the fire? And why did you take Lady Lyndon to Newgate Prison without first asking my permission?'

'I didn't know you needed to be informed if Harry's mother wanted to visit her son. As to the fire, I don't see what it has to do with you.'

'I thought we were friends, Kate.' He moderated his tone, sounding almost apologetic, but not quite. 'Your wellbeing is important to me and it's obvious that the fire was arson. Luckily the building wasn't totally destroyed, but that's not the point. I've seen the police report and I'm only too well aware of the rivalry between the Monks gang and Trader.'

'Then you must know that Harry is working with the police to bring Monks to justice.'

'Of course I do now, but if word of that gets out you will be in even more danger. Just think how it would suit Monks to abduct someone close to Trader, either his mother, Annie or yourself.'

'I've thought of that, and it's not only those closest to Harry. Ivy has had a brick thrown through her window. She and the children are an easy target for the Monks gang, and that's where I'm going now. Don't try to stop me, Perry. I'm going to get them to safety, and then I'll make sure that Lady Lyndon and Annie are taken care of.'

'But who will look after you? Your father is an invalid and he cannot protect you.'

'What are you suggesting? What is your answer to the problem?'

He hesitated for a few seconds, meeting her angry gaze. 'Marry me, Kate. Forget about Trader and his family; forget about soup kitchens. Marry me and let me take care of you.'

'You are asking me to marry you?' Kate stared at him in astonishment.

'Don't look so surprised. You must know that I have feelings for you.'

She shook her head. 'No, it never occurred to me. We've known each other since I was little more than a child, but we were apart for three years.'

'And when I saw you again I knew that you were the woman for me.'

'I suppose a wealthy wife would be a definite advantage in your line of business.'

'Kate! How could you think such a thing of me?'

'I'm sorry if I'm doing you an injustice, but surely love ought to come into it somewhere? You've never demonstrated any particular fondness for me, so why would you want me to be your wife?'

'Just because I haven't showered you with flowers and compliments doesn't mean that I don't have deep feelings for you.'

Kate glanced at the towering grandfather clock that stood in the corner of the entrance hall. As a child it had always scared her, especially at night. The striking of the hour had sounded like the knell of doom, and she had imagined that the door might fly open and a hideous goblin-like figure would leap out to terrify her. But she was a grown woman now and all she saw was the clock face — she was going to be late.

'I'm sorry, but I really have to leave. Ivy and the children are depending on me to take them to a place of safety, so perhaps we could have this conversation at a more appropriate time?'

'I take it that means no to my offer of marriage.'

'Don't put words into my mouth, Perry. I imagine most young women would ask for time to consider such a proposal, especially if it were flung at them so unexpectedly, and so early in the morning.'

'Now you're laughing at me.'

She laid her hand on his arm. 'No, I am not. I'm very flattered and conscious of the honour you do me . . . '

He held up his hand. 'Don't say any more. I've made a fool of myself. I see that now.' Perry strode to the door and opened it. 'I don't know what happened to you in India, but you aren't the same person you were. You've changed, Kate. And not for the better.'

'Then I'm even more surprised that you want to marry me.' Kate marched past him and ran down the steps to the waiting carriage.

* * *

The older children were bubbling with excitement when the barouche drew up outside Warren House, but Ivy was pale and nervous.

'What if the housekeeper don't like nippers, Kate? Did you warn her that we was a large number?'

Kate opened the carriage door without waiting for the coachman to climb down from his box. Frankie and Nellie leaped out first, followed more slowly by May and Jimmy, leaving Kate to help the twins to the ground. Charlie teetered on the top step but Kate caught him before he fell and Ivy clambered out with baby John clutched in her arms.

'Calm down, children.' Ivy sighed. 'Remember your manners or we might get thrown out onto the street, and we'd have to live off grass like cows.'

'We'll go round to the back of the house,' Kate said firmly. 'The children can run round for a while and I'll tell Mr and Mrs Boggis that we're here.' She turned to the coachman. 'I won't be long, Goodfellow.'

'You heard what Kate said.' Ivy rounded up her excited flock, leaving Kate to show them the way.

Let loose in the flower meadow that had once been a lawn, the children gambolled around like lambs, while Ivy perched on a low balustrade. 'I'll wait here, where I can keep an eye on them, miss.'

'I won't be long.' Kate made her way to the kitchen, where, as expected, she found Martha. 'Good morning, Martha. I know it's early but I have a surprise for you.'

'Is Lady Lyndon with you, miss?'

'No, but she will be here later. I have a family who will be staying here for a while. It's not permanent, but the poor lady has eight children and their father is serving time in prison for theft. He's not a bad man but he was desperate for money to feed his family.'

'Stealing is stealing, as far as I'm concerned,' Martha said, pursing her lips. 'I don't hold with robbers, and I don't like nippers.'

Kate's heart sank. She had not expected such a reaction — surely all women loved children? She tried again. 'The Harris youngsters are very well behaved and eager to please. Ivy is a good woman and she's been working hard to keep the family together, but it's vital that she and the children leave London for a while.'

'As I thought,' Martha said, sniffing. 'I can smell trouble, miss. No good will come of it.'

'It's only temporary, and I'm sure the children will benefit from your high moral standards. They will do their bit to help you and you'll hardly notice they're here. After all, there's plenty of room, and you will have Lady Lyndon and Miss Blythe to take care of, so you'll have very little to do with the Harris family.'

'I suppose I haven't got much choice, but I don't know what Arthur will say. If her ladyship don't mind, then who am I to say anything?'

Kate took a heavy purse from her pocket and

196

placed it on the kitchen table. 'There is money to cover their needs and there will be more when it's needed.'

Martha weighed the purse in one hand. 'That feels like a tidy sum, miss.'

'It should suffice. Anyway, the children have not had breakfast, so I hope you might be able to find something for them. They haven't eaten since last evening, and even then it would have been a very frugal meal.'

'Youngsters need good food if they're to grow and thrive. Luckily I've made a big pan of porridge, which would normally last us for days. I might not like children, but I know my duty. Better send them in, miss.'

'You're very kind, Martha.' Kate hurried outside and found Ivy where she had left her.

'Everything will be fine now, Ivy,' Kate said cheerfully. 'Martha Boggis is all right if you know how to treat her. I've told her that this is a temporary arrangement, which it is, of course, although I didn't tell her the real reason for your stay in the country — I think that would have been too much for her to take in. Anyway, I'm sure you can handle Martha and she'll give you a good breakfast.'

'Aren't you staying?' Ivy asked anxiously.

'I have to go to Finsbury Circus and make sure that Lady Lyndon is ready to make the move. Don't worry, Ivy. When her ladyship and Annie arrive, Martha will be too busy taking care of them to bother about anything else.'

'But you will come back later?'

'Yes, I'll travel with Lady Lyndon. I want to make sure she gets here safely.'

When Kate arrived at Lady Lyndon's house in Finsbury Circus it was almost midday. Annie said that the servants had been rushing round for hours, packing things that Lady Lyndon was certain she would need. Kate stood by and watched the last of Lady Lyndon's trunks and bandboxes being loaded onto a cart and she was impressed. Harry's mother might seem to be a quiet, gentle person, but when stirred by the prospect of losing her precious belongings, she was as fierce as any battle-scarred general.

'You must accompany us, Kate,' Lady Lyndon said, wrapping a cape around her shoulders, even though it was a hot afternoon. 'And, of course you will stay.'

'Surely you don't need me to be there,' Kate protested.

'I've avoided visiting that country cottage ever since my husband passed away. I barely know the housekeeper and her husband. I will be living amongst strangers.'

'But, Aunt Margaret,' Annie said hastily, 'you're taking Miss Hattersley with you, and Warrender will be on hand should you require his services. I'll be with you, too.'

Lady Lyndon gave Annie an affectionate hug. 'Yes, my dear. All of that is true, but I'm used to having a whole household at my command. I don't know how we will live with just two servants. It all sounds very compromising to me.'

'Ivy is there already and she will help you, as I said before.' Kate took a deep breath. 'And the older children are quite capable of doing jobs around the house or in the garden. They are used to working.'

'Children?' Lady Lyndon raised an elegant eyebrow. 'How many?'

'There are eight of them, but they are very well behaved.' Kate waited for Lady Lyndon to raise a list of objections. If Martha Boggis disliked children, it seemed likely that her ladyship would feel the same, but Lady Lyndon was all smiles.

'How delightful. I simply adore little ones, although older children can be tiresome at times. However, I might consider hiring a governess for them. If they can all read and write and do simple arithmetic it will help them to get better jobs in the future. I've missed having a baby to hold.'

Annie smiled and tucked her hand in the crook of Lady Lyndon's arm. 'Why are we wasting time here, Aunt Margaret? I think time spent in the country will benefit us all.'

'You'll travel with us, of course, Kate,' Lady Lyndon said firmly. 'Send your carriage home and we will enjoy the journey together.'

Kate was about to refuse on the grounds that she would not have any transport for her return journey to Finsbury Square, when she heard someone calling her name and Jenny rushed past a startled footman, who had been standing by the open front door.

'I thought I might catch you here, miss,' Jenny said breathlessly. 'You're wanted at home urgently.'

'What's happened?' Kate grasped Jenny's hand. 'Calm down and tell me what's wrong.'

'It's your father, miss. He's taken a turn for the

worst.'

'I'll come immediately. Get in the carriage, Jenny.'

Kate turned to Lady Lyndon. 'I'm sorry, ma'am. I can't come with you.'

'That's quite all right, my dear. Your family come first, but I hope you'll join us soon. If it's unsafe for Annie and myself to remain in London, then it must be doubly so as far as you're concerned.'

'I can't think about that now.' Kate laid her hand on Annie's shoulder. 'I'll come to Walthamstow as soon as possible.'

'I hope your pa recovers soon,' Annie said softly.

Kate hurried from the house and climbed into the carriage. 'What happened, Jenny?'

'Fellowes found him unconscious in his bed, miss. The doctor was sent for and he was with Sir Bartholomew when I left the house. Your ma told me to find you, and I just hoped you might still be here with Lady Lyndon.'

'Another few minutes and I might have left with them for Walthamstow.' Kate sank back against the padded leather squabs. 'I've been so busy with the soup kitchen and trying to help Ivy and her family that I fear I've neglected Pa since his illness. I'll never forgive myself if he dies thinking I don't care about him.'

'I'm sure he don't think nothing of the sort, miss.'

Kate had no answer for this and she sat in silence during the short drive to Finsbury Square.

Henry opened the door, his expression grave.

'Is the doctor with my father, Henry?' Kate

asked anxiously.

'I believe the doctor is with Lady Martin in the drawing room, Miss Kate.'

Kate took off her bonnet and handed it to Jenny, together with her shawl. 'I'll be in the drawing room,' she said hastily.

★ ★ ★

The sight of her mother in tears and Sir Jasper Fey standing with his back to the fireplace confirmed Kate's worst fears.

'Mama?'

Arabella looked up, tears coursing down her pale cheeks. 'It's all your fault, Kate. I blame you for your father's condition. Your stubbornness contributed to his illness, of that I'm certain, and now he's dead. Where were you when I needed you?' A fresh bout of sobbing put an end to the tirade and she covered her face with her hands.

'I'm sorry.' Kate could think of nothing else to say. She looked to Sir Jasper for confirmation and he nodded.

'It was a peaceful end, Miss Martin. Your father did not regain consciousness. It made no difference if you were present or not — he would have known nothing about it.'

'Thank you, Sir Jasper.' Kate went to sit beside her mother on the sofa. 'I'm sorry I wasn't here, Mama. I had urgent business, but I wouldn't have gone if I'd known that Papa was so ill.'

Arabella dropped her hands to her lap, her fingers tearing at the fine silk as if trying to punish the material for her distress. 'You always put others before your own family. You are an ungrateful daughter. Go away and allow me to grieve in peace.'

Kate rose slowly to her feet.

'Try not to be upset by your mother's remarks,' Sir Jasper said kindly. 'Grief takes everyone differently. Give her time and I'm sure she'll see things more clearly.'

'I doubt it. I've never been able to please my mother, Sir Jasper, but thank you all the same.'

'There's nothing more I can do. Although I could notify a suitable undertaker, if that would help you?'

'Thank you. Once again I am most grateful.'

'Have you any relatives who could be with you at this time?'

Kate shook her head. 'No, sir. My mother and I are the last in the line on both sides of the family.'

Sir Jasper walked swiftly to the door and opened it. He glanced over his shoulder with an attempt at a smile. 'I'll see myself out, but if there's anything further I can do, just let me know.'

Kate nodded, at a loss for words. His kindness was in stark contrast to her mother's harsh words.

The sound of the door closing made Arabella look up. 'I hope you're happy now. You own everything and I have nothing.'

'I'm sorry, Mama. I don't know what you mean.'

'Don't pretend ignorance, Kate. You know that this house belonged to your uncle. It was part of the estate he inherited, but he allowed us to live here. Now it's yours and I am a penniless pauper.'

'Don't say things like that.' Kate stared at her mother in dismay. 'I'll look after you, of course I will.'

'I'm still a young woman and yet I have to depend upon your charity. I suppose I will end up queuing for food in your soup kitchen.'

'Mama, you're being ridiculous. I can only put it down to shock and grief or you wouldn't say such dreadful things.'

'Go away, Kate. Leave me alone with my grief.'

Kate hesitated but she could see that there was little point in continuing the conversation while her mother was in this mood. She left the room and found Jenny waiting outside.

'I'm sorry, miss. I didn't know that Sir Bartholomew had passed away.'

'It's all right, Jenny. You did right in coming for me.'

Jenny eyed her anxiously. 'Ma would like to know who's in charge now, miss. Lady Martin won't speak to any of the servants and they don't know what to do.'

'I'll go and see your mother, Jenny. I have to be practical and there will be funeral arrangements to make.'

'I suppose we won't be going to Warren House then?'

Kate managed a wry smile. 'I think that Lady Lyndon and Ivy can manage without us. They're both capable women and they will have to contend with Martha Boggis. I'm sorry I won't be there to see it for myself.'

'But is it safe for you to stay in town, miss?'

'I don't know and that's the honest truth, but there's nothing else I can do for the moment, anyway.'

'Ma is in her office below stairs if you wish to speak to her, miss.'

'Yes, you're right, Jenny. I must start as I mean to continue. I'll go and see her now.'

The house in Finsbury Square was in mourning. The clocks had been stopped at the assumed time of death, mirrors were covered in black veils and the curtains were drawn. Kate took her mother to Jay's of Regent Street, a mourning warehouse, where they were both outfitted in black silk trimmed with crepe. Arabella barely spoke to Kate during their shopping expedition, and Kate's efforts to comfort her mother were repulsed with a shrug.

With the help of Mrs Marsh and Jenny, Kate had everything organised down to the smallest detail, but on the day of the funeral Arabella refused to attend the church service. No matter how hard Kate tried to cajole, persuade or shame her mother into accompanying herself and Perry, Arabella would not be shaken.

In the end Kate left the house with Perry and the cortège proceeded to the church, which was packed with mourners. She was surprised by the number of people, mainly from the legal profession, who had taken the time and trouble to attend. Sir Bartholomew in life had not been an easy person to get on with, but it seemed that he was highly respected amongst his peers and Kate wished wholeheartedly that her mother had plucked up the courage to say a last farewell to her husband.

After the interment in the cemetery, Kate turned to Perry in desperation. 'I have intended to invite some of Papa's colleagues and friends back to the house, but with Mama in such a state I don't think it's a good idea.'

'No, indeed. I could suggest we adjourn to an inn to raise a glass to the memory of the departed.' Perry glanced round the mourners, who remained standing in groups, talking in low voices. 'It's all gentlemen, so I think it more appropriate, especially in the circumstances.'

'Yes, you're right. Please do that.' Kate shot a sideways look at Fellowes, her father's valet for more than twenty years. 'Please take Fellowes with you. The poor man looks as though he's been crying. He was devoted to Papa and now he'll have to find work elsewhere.'

'I'll do all I can for him. I do know of someone who is looking for a gentleman's gentleman. Anyway, you should go home, Kate. I'll call to see you later, if I may.'

She eyed him uncertainly. Perry had not mentioned their last fateful meeting, and for that she was grateful. His support before and during the funeral had been invaluable, but she did not want to give him false hopes.

'Might we leave it a day or two, Perry? My mother is obviously taking Papa's death very hard, and I have to respect her wish for privacy, but thank you all the same. You've been such a great help during these past difficult days.'

'Kate, you've done far more for my family. I can never thank you enough for taking care of Ivy and the children.'

'They are safely away from London and won't return until Monks and his gang are arrested and sent to prison. I won't rest easy until that happens.'

'You must allow me to contribute financially to their upkeep.'

'I won't hear of it. What are friends for if they cannot help each other in time of need?' Kate glanced over her shoulder. 'My carriage is waiting, Perry. If you're certain you can deal with the gentleman without me, I'll go home and see if I can comfort Mama.'

He took her hand and raised it to his lips. 'Of course, you must. Just send word to my chambers if you need me, and I'll come immediately.'

She smiled, acknowledging his words with a nod, and walked away, leaving the mourners to follow their own inclinations.

Kate arrived home but the moment she walked through the open front door she sensed that there was something wrong. There was no sign of Henry, and the house was even more silent than when she had left earlier. Her footsteps echoed eerily as she crossed the marble-tiled entrance hall. She went straight to the drawing room, where she expected to find her mother. The sight that met her eyes as she opened the door made her come to a sudden halt, and her hand flew to her mouth to stifle a cry of dismay.

13

Kate immediately recognised the large man with the scarred face, who was obviously terrifying Arabella. Her face was ashen and her eyes wide and staring as she sat upright in her chair, seemingly too scared to move.

'So you've come home at last, miss. Allow me to introduce meself.'

'What are you doing here, Monks?' Kate said angrily.

'You're a bold one and no mistake. I come here to give you a friendly warning.'

'You're frightening my mother. Say what you have to say and go.'

'Not very hospitable, are you, love?' Monks pulled up a chair and sat down, causing the cabriole legs to bow beneath his considerable weight.

'What do you want with us?' Kate demanded.

'This is a house of mourning, as you will have noticed.'

'I can't say I'm sorry for your loss. Your pa was responsible for me going to prison in the first place. He was the prosecuting counsel and I was little more than a boy. It's too late to settle the score with him, but I ain't fussy. You two will do.'

'My husband is dead.' Arabella's voice shook with emotion. 'You must have broken the law to have been in the dock.'

Monks curled his lip. 'That's all you know, lady.

Kindly keep your trap shut. I weren't speaking to you.' He jerked his head in Kate's direction. 'She's the one with the brains, but she's been consorting with my sworn enemy. I know what Trader is up to and you can tell him to leave well alone if he wants to see your pretty face again.'

'You're wrong,' Kate said furiously. 'Harry Trader is in Newgate Prison — what harm can he do you from there? Or is it easier for you to make war on helpless women?'

Monks leaped to his feet. 'One more word from you and you'll feel the back of me hand, miss. You will do as I say if you don't want to end up in the cemetery with your pa. And that goes for her ladyship over there as well.' He pointed to Arabella, who shrank back on her chair, closing her eyes.

'Say what you have to say.' Kate managed to keep her voice calm, but inwardly she was quaking.

'You'll tell Trader to leave off. I know what he's up to. He's a snitch and I reckon he's done a deal with one of the high-ups — the sort what patronises Trader's illegal gaming houses. If he doesn't do what I say it'll be you and your ma who'll suffer.' Monks paused, glaring first at Arabella and then at Kate. 'But I suspect he's too much of a gent to let that happen. D'you understand me, girl?'

'Say yes, Kate,' Arabella cried faintly. 'Say anything to get him out of the house.'

Kate met Monks' gaze squarely. 'I will visit him in prison, and I'll tell him what you just said.'

'Make it sound good, love. I ain't playing

games. I got a reputation to keep up, but if you fail you'd best remember what happened to the soup kitchen.'

'I've said I will speak to him. I can do no more than that.'

Monks picked up his battered top hat and put it on at an angle. 'You'd best try your hardest, girl. You've seen what I can do, so don't think you can get the better of me.' He tipped his hat to Arabella with a mocking smile and sauntered out of the room.

Kate hurried over to her mother, going down on her knees in front of her. 'You mustn't let him scare you, Mama. He's a thug and a bully.'

Arabella gazed into the distance, her breath coming in short gasps. 'He'll kill us and burn the house to the ground.'

'I won't allow that to happen, Mama.'

'You silly girl, how do you think you can stop a man like that? Your father kept the sordid side of his work from me, but I've seen and heard enough of these dreadful people to know that they do awful things. We escaped being murdered in Delhi, but now we're facing danger in our own country and our own home.' Arabella's eyes focused on her daughter's face. 'But it isn't my home, is it? This house and the money that your father should have inherited all belong to you.'

'Mama, stop saying these things. This is still your home. I told you that. I never wanted the money or the house. I'll give it all to you if it would make you happy.'

'Happy?' Arabella's voice rose to a shriek. 'How can I be happy without your father? We loved each other, which is something you can't understand. I know that you refused Peregrine's offer of marriage. He came here to see me, brokenhearted. You are a cruel girl, Kate.'

'He only offered to marry me out of pity and a sense of duty, Mama. Perry doesn't love me any more than I love him.' Kate stood up and backed away. 'This is getting us nowhere. I think the best thing I can do is to get you away from here to somewhere safe.'

'Leave me alone, Kate. I feel one of my headaches coming on.'

'I'll send Miss Barnet to you, Mama.' Kate hurried from the room and made her way to the servants' quarters where she found Miss Barnet in the sewing room.

'Miss Barnet, I've decided that my mother needs a change of scene. I hope a sojourn in the country will help to raise her spirits.'

Miss Barnet looked up from the garment she was mending, her brow creased in a puzzled frown. 'Bereavement can take people in many ways, but I thought that her ladyship was being particularly stalwart, all things considered.'

'An unfortunate incident occurred that has set her back somewhat. I want you to go to her room and pack everything she might need for a reasonably long stay in the country. We'll be leaving this afternoon.'

Miss Barnet's eyebrows curved in astonishment. 'This afternoon?'

'Yes, that's correct. I think you deserve some time for yourself. I will pay you, of course, but perhaps you have some relatives you would like to visit?'

'But Lady Martin needs me. Who will look after her if I'm not there?'

'I'm sure we'll manage, although of course you will be missed. You must leave a forwarding address and I'll notify you when we decide to return to London.' Kate was not in the mood to argue and she left the room, to find Jenny waiting in the passage.

'What's going on, miss?' Jenny demanded anxiously. 'Ma told me that you'd come looking for Miss Barnet. Something's up — I know it.'

Kate took her by the arm and led her along the corridor so that there was no possibility of Miss Barnet overhearing their conversation.

'Monks was here, Jenny. Mama and I have to leave London for a while and I want you to come with us. You know too much and you might also be in danger.'

'Are we going to Warren House?'

'I think that's the safest place. I want you to pack for me and for yourself. Miss Barnet will see to my mother's things, but I have to go out. I need to see Trader before we leave town.'

Jenny nodded. 'I understand. I'll make sure everything is ready for your return, but what shall I tell Ma?'

'You'll think of something,' Kate said, chuckling. 'Make is sound convincing, but don't alarm her, Jenny. It's safer for everyone here if the servants know nothing.'

Jenny grinned. 'I've had plenty of practice. I used to tell Ivy's nippers all sorts of tales to keep them amused when we was at the soup kitchen.'

Her smile faded. 'I just feel sorry for all those folk we had to let down. I hope they found somewhere else to go for a bowl of soup.'

'I've made a donation to a small charity who have started something similar in Spitalfields, so I hope the people we've helped will go there. I'm off to the prison to see Harry Trader, but I'll be back as soon as I can.'

★ ★ ★

The prison seemed even more unwelcoming than it had on Kate's last visit, and she had to force herself to enter the building. The warder on duty appeared to remember her and had obviously jumped to the wrong conclusion. He grinned and winked in a suggestive manner that might have offended her had her nerves not been so fraught. After what seemed like an eternity of waiting in a dismal celllike room that smelled of damp and unwashed bodies, another warder shoved Harry over the threshold.

'Five minutes,' he said tersely, and slammed the door.

'Kate?' Harry stared at her frowning. 'Why have you come here again? This isn't the place for you.'

'I returned from Papa's funeral to find Monks in our drawing room with my terrified mother.'

'The devil!' Harry said angrily. 'If he hurt you I'll—'

'He didn't touch either of us, but he made it clear that he knows you're working with the police. He said if you continued to do so it would be the worst for Mama and myself.'

212

'I'm sorry, Kate. It was wrong of me to involve you in the first place, but at the moment my hands are tied. My sentence was genuine, and probably richly deserved,' he added with a humorous glint in his eyes. 'But my men never hurt or terrorised anyone. They were there to keep Monks and his gang away from my clubs. We kept the peace in a manner of speaking, although admittedly we were on the wrong side of the law.'

'Monks needs to be stopped. I don't expect you to give up your efforts. I'm sure I was followed here, so at least he knows that I kept my word.'

Harry took both her hands in his. 'You must get away from London. This isn't your fight, Kate.'

The warmth of his grasp sent a pleasant shiver down her spine, but this was neither the time nor the place for letting down her guard and she snatched her hands free. 'It became my battle when Monks entered my home and scared my mother. Now it's become very personal, Harry. Your mother and Annie will be at Warren House by now and I'm going to take Mama to join them, whether she likes it or not.'

'You'll stay there, too?'

'I will, although I wish there was something I could do to bring Monks to justice.'

'Leave that to me. Now that I know my mother and Annie are out of danger I can go ahead with my plans.'

'How will I know when it's safe to return to London?'

'I'll get word to you somehow. Who knows? I might be released early due to my co-operation with the authorities.'

She found herself responding to his smile, but Monks' visit to her home had left her on edge, and she must not forget the time. 'I have to go now, Harry. If I'm to get Mama to Warren House before nightfall we must leave soon.'

He nodded. 'Yes, of course. Reassure my mother when you see her, but don't tell her anything. She could never keep a secret.'

Kate was about to reply when the door burst open.

'Time's up, miss.' The warder ushered her from the room before she had a chance to speak.

* * *

It was early evening when Kate, her mother and Jenny set off for Warren House. Arabella had insisted on bringing almost her entire wardrobe and she clutched her jewel case, refusing to let anyone else touch it. Barnet had packed everything but her set expression made it clear that being left behind had offended her deeply. Mrs Marsh sent Jenny off with a basket of provisions that would have kept them well fed for a much longer journey, but eventually the trunks and boxes were strapped to the roof of the carriage and they were ready to leave.

It was getting dark when the carriage trundled along the road that crossed the marshes. Jenny gasped, pointing in wonder at the eerie lights of the will-o'-the-wisp, floating above the boggy ground, but Kate was too deep in her own thoughts to comment. She was as sure as she could be that whoever had followed her to the prison had given up by the time they left Finsbury Square, but she could not help wondering how long they would have to remain in virtual exile. There was no guarantee that Harry would manage to bring Monks to justice from his prison cell, and although Warren House might provide sanctuary for a while, they could not return home. Her mother had spent the first part of the journey complaining bitterly, and then she had fallen asleep. How she would react when she discovered that she was to share the mansion in Walthamstow with Lady Lyndon, Annie, Ivy and eight young children was another matter.

* * *

The first thing that Kate noticed when she alighted from the carriage, was the heady perfume of roses and night-scented stock, adding to the fruity aroma of damp earth and the slightly musty smell of the marshes. The air was cool and fresh and a breeze fanned her hot cheeks, but there was a hint of approaching autumn in the air and a warning that summer was almost over.

'Where are we?'

Arabella's querulous voice from the interior of the carriage brought Kate abruptly back to the present and she held out her hand. 'We're at our destination, Mama.'

'Wherever that might be.' Arabella yawned and stretched. 'I'm so stiff.'

Aided by Jenny, Kate helped her mother from the carriage.

'We must have been travelling half the night,'

215

Arabella said crossly. She gazed at the dark shape of Warren House with the moonlight caressing its roof and reflecting playfully off the top-storey windows. 'This is the back of beyond, Kate. Why have you brought me here?'

'We'll be safe from people who wish us harm, Mama.' Kate rapped on the knocker. She could only hope that Arthur Boggis might venture through the maze of passages to open the front door.

'The house looks deserted,' Arabella muttered. 'It's probably haunted.'

Jenny clutched Kate's arm. 'You don't think there are ghosts and ghouls in there, do you?'

'Of course not.' Kate knocked again, and this time she could hear footsteps on the flagstone floor. 'Someone's coming. Thank goodness for that.'

The door opened and a shaft of lamplight quivered in the darkness. 'Who's there?' Arthur's voice boomed out into the night.

'It's me, Arthur,' Kate said hastily. 'Miss Martin. I've brought my mother with me, and my maid. Sir Harry wishes us to stay here for a while.'

'Sir Harry?' Arabella poked her daughter in the ribs. 'Who is Sir Harry, Kate?'

'I'll explain later.' Kate ushered her mother into the house, stepping in after her, followed by Jenny.

Goodfellow hefted the first of the trunks into the entrance hall. 'Give us a hand, cully?'

'I'm the caretaker here. We haven't got a footman, you'll have to manage on your own — cully!' Arthur turned his back on Goodfellow. 'This is a bit unexpected, Miss Martin. Martha likes to have a bit of warning so she can get a room prepared. We have other guests, as you well know.'

'I'm sure we can manage just for tonight,' Kate said hastily. 'I don't mind sharing with my maid, but my mother is recently widowed and today was my father's funeral. I would like her to have one of the best rooms.'

'Well, if you put it like that, miss, I'll see what I can do.' Arthur lit a candle, which was placed in readiness on a carved wooden chest. He handed a brass candlestick to Kate. 'I'll go and tell Martha that you're here.'

'I can give Ivy a hand to get the beds made up.' Jenny proffered her arm to Arabella. 'If you'd care to lean on me, your ladyship, I remember where the drawing room is situated. I expect you'll find company there.'

'Company?' Arabella turned to Kate, her eyes blazing. 'You didn't mention that we would have to share the accommodation with anyone. Really, Kate, this is too bad. We'll leave first thing in the morning.'

Goodfellow came to a standstill with a heavy box balanced on his shoulders. He looked to Kate for instruction. 'In or out, miss?'

'Bring all the luggage in, please, Goodfellow,' Kate said firmly. 'Mr Boggis will show you to your accommodation.' She turned to Arthur. 'Is Lady Lyndon in the drawing room?'

He nodded. 'Yes, miss, but Ivy and the nippers have gone to bed.'

'Children?' Arabella's voice rose to a pitch that might have shattered glass. 'There are children here? How many?'

'Eight of them, ma'am,' Arthur said silkily. 'Eight nippers running around the house, all of

217

them under the age of nine.' He turned to Good-fellow. 'You'd best come with me. There's room above the stables, but don't get in Warrender's way. He's her ladyship's groom and he's not too happy about being away from London. Just so you know to watch what you say.'

Goodfellow shrugged and muttered something beneath his breath.

'We're definitely leaving first thing tomorrow.' Arabella leaned on Jenny's arm. 'Take me to the drawing room. Do they keep a good cellar here? I need a glass of sherry wine.'

'Come with us, Mama. I'll introduce you to Lady Lyndon. I'm sure you'll both get along really well.'

As they walked slowly towards the drawing room Kate could hear the strains of 'Home Sweet Home' being played on a concertina. She opened the door and they hesitated, listening intently while Annie played the last notes. It seemed to Kate it was an omen, but one look at her mother's face dashed her hopes.

'What have we come to, Kate? Who is that person?'

'Mama!' Kate released her mother's arm. 'That was impolite,' she whispered.

'Don't lecture me on manners. I'm tired and I'm in a haunted house with complete strangers.'

Annie sank down on the sofa, clutching her concertina. 'I'm sorry if my music offends you, ma'am.'

'It was beautiful,' Kate said hastily. 'I'm afraid my mother is overwrought and very tired. It was my papa's funeral earlier today.'

Lady Lyndon rose to her feet. 'My dear Mrs

Martin, how very sad. Please accept my condolences.'

Arabella drew herself up to her full height, ignoring Lady Lyndon's outstretched hand. 'It's Lady Martin, and we haven't been introduced, ma'am.'

'Mama, I think this is not the time to dwell on etiquette. This is Lady Lyndon and the talented musician is Annie Blythe.' She turned to Lady Lyndon with an apologetic smile. 'We will be staying here for a while, ma'am. At your son's invitation, of course.'

If Lady Lyndon was offended by Arabella's attitude she was too polite to make an issue of it. She smiled and sat down. 'I assume we are all being threatened by that dreadful fellow in London.'

'Yes, exactly.' Kate turned to her mother. 'Sit down, please, Mama. Jenny will pour you a glass of sherry wine and then she'll make sure that your bed is aired and ready. You must be exhausted.'

'I am not a child, Katherine. You don't have to speak to me as if I were half-witted. I will take a glass of sherry, for medicinal purposes.' Arabella lowered her voice. 'Did you pack my laudanum? Sir Jasper recommended I take some before retiring.'

Kate exchanged meaningful glances with Jenny.

'I'm sure that Miss Barnet saw to everything, Mama.'

'I'll have a glass of sherry wine, and one for Annie,' Lady Lyndon said eagerly. 'Play us another tune, Annie, dear.'

'I don't want a drink, thank you, Aunt Margaret.' Annie struck up a lively jig.

219

'No, no, no!' Arabella covered her ears with her hands. 'My nerves are already on edge. If you must play that common instrument, please play something soothing.'

Kate took the glass of sherry from Jenny's hand. 'I think the sooner my mother gets some rest the better.'

'Of course, miss. I'll make sure that her room is ready soon.' Jenny hurried from the room.

'Here you are, Mama.' Kate pressed the wineglass into her mother's outstretched hand. 'Try to relax a little. Things will look better in the morning.' She moved swiftly to a side table and poured sherry for Lady Lyndon, which she placed on a small table within easy reach.

'That's a lovely tune, Annie,' Kate said appreciatively. 'It's "Come into the Garden, Maud", isn't it?'

Annie smiled. 'Yes, it's quite new but it's one of my favourites. The words are nice, too, but I can't sing.'

'Nonsense,' Lady Lyndon said, sipping her drink. 'You have a sweet voice, Annie. It's a bit late now, but tomorrow you must entertain us properly. I'll look forward to that.'

Arabella drained her glass and handed it back to Kate. 'You may take me to my room now. I'm in need of peace and quiet.'

Kate knew better than to argue and she helped her mother to her feet. 'I'll say good night, too, Lady Lyndon. I need to sort some things out with Martha before I go to bed. Good night, Annie. Thank you for the lovely music.' She picked up a chamber candlestick and opened the door, standing back to allow her mother to pass.

'Lovely music!' Arabella muttered as she left the room. 'I thought we'd walked into an ale house when I heard that dreadful noise.'

Kate closed the door. 'Mama, I know you're upset and tired, but please try to be civil. Lady Lyndon is Harry's mother and she's a very nice person. You could at least try to get on with her, and Annie is blind.'

'Don't talk to me in that tone of voice, Kate. I don't think I'm going to like it here.'

'We haven't much choice, Mama.'

'I'm going to tell Goodfellow to drive me back to Finsbury Square in the morning. I'd rather face that dreadful creature Monks than be marooned here with that woman and the concertina girl. Heaven knows what it will be like when there are dozens of children running round this dreadful old mausoleum.'

'We'll see how you feel after a good night's sleep.' Kate guided her mother to the staircase. When they reached the first floor she could see an open door.

'That must be your room.'

'Not for long,' Arabella said gloomily. 'I expect the bed is damp.'

Martha emerged from the room carrying an armful of bedding. 'A little notice would have been helpful, Miss Martin. This isn't a hostelry.'

'We came at Sir Harry's invitation,' Kate said firmly. 'Tomorrow morning you and I will settle down and see what arrangement can be made to employ extra help.'

Martha eyed her warily. 'It sounds as if you

might be here for some time, Miss Martin.'

'I'm afraid that is a matter beyond my control.'

'Are we to stand here all night, discussing our business with a servant?' Arabella demanded crossly.

'Your room is ready, your ladyship.' Martha tossed her head and stomped off in the direction of the back stairs.

'Come along, Mama.' Kate ushered her mother into the bedroom. 'Thank you, Martha,' she called over her shoulder.

'Don't pander to her.' Arabella came to a halt, gazing round the shadowy room with obvious distaste. 'I'll sleep here tonight because there's no alternative, but I'm leaving tomorrow, with or without you, Kate.'

14

Kate's room was situated at the front of the house, overlooking the carriage sweep, although by the time she was ready for bed she was too tired to care which direction it faced. Jenny had made up a truckle bed in the adjoining dressing room. She could have chosen a much larger room on the top floor, but Kate realised that Jenny was nervous of sleeping on her own, and she was happy to have her company.

A fire had been lit to dispel any hint of dampness, despite the fact that it was a reasonably warm night. Even in the flickering light from the flames and the glow from two candles on the mantelshelf, the corners of the room were lost in the gloom. The four-poster bed with its damask-covered tester and curtains stood like a welcoming island in a sea of shadows. Even so, the darkness seemed to wrap itself around Kate like a warm blanket and she felt completely at home. When she eventually climbed into bed the feather mattress was soft and she sank into it with a sigh of relief. They were as safe here as they could be anywhere, and Monks was unlikely to find them. She could hear Jenny snoring gently in the next room, and Kate closed her eyes, drifting off into a deep sleep.

She awakened next morning to the chorus of birdsong and the sound of a teacup rattling on its saucer. Kate opened her eyes to see Jenny standing at her bedside.

'What time is it?' Kate sat up to take the tea from Jenny's hand.

Jenny chuckled. 'Well, in London you'd think it early, but here in the country it seems they get up at the crack of dawn and they consider this mid-morning.'

'I slept so well. I haven't had a night's sleep like that for goodness knows how long.' Kate sipped the hot, sweet tea. 'Is my mother up and about?'

'I looked into her room before I went downstairs but she was still asleep. I left her because it will do her good. The poor lady is worn out with grief.'

Kate nodded. 'Yes, I suppose you're right. Anyway, I'll get up as soon as I've drunk this and I'll put on one of my old gowns. I dare say there'll be plenty to do downstairs, and I'm more than happy to help.'

'Your mama won't like it, miss.'

'I can't laze about and I want to make sure that everything is running smoothly. Perhaps my mother will agree to stay if she finds the house comfortable and well run.'

'Surely you won't allow her to return to London? Not with that Mad Monks planning to kill us all.'

'I don't think he'd go that far, although I cannot be certain. The sooner he's behind bars, the better.' Kate handed her empty cup back to Jenny and swung her legs over the side of the bed. 'Thank you for that. Now I'm ready for anything. I'll dress and go downstairs to face Martha.'

'She's banned Ivy's nippers from the kitchen. I think Martha and Lady Martin have got something in common, miss. They don't like children.'

Kate walked over to the washstand and filled the bowl with water from the ewer. 'I can see this isn't going to be easy, Jenny.'

★ ★ ★

Kate entered the kitchen expecting to face an irate Martha, but instead she was greeted by a broad smile.

'I've found something to keep them nippers out of my way, miss.' Martha said, chuckling.

'That was very clever of you. They're good children but they're used to working. I don't think a life of idleness would suit them.'

'As I said to Arthur, the devil finds work for idle hands. I've set them to work in the garden. Morrison is getting too old and rheumaticky to do the job properly. I saw to it the nippers had a good breakfast and the older ones went off as if it was a game to them.'

'What about Ivy and the other children?'

'Ivy's in the stillroom using the rose petals that the nippers have collected. She said she knows how to make rose water and skin cream. She might know how to make perfumed soap, too. Carbolic is good enough for us country folk, but her ladyship has other ideas. I had to tell her that the village shop don't sell them fancy soaps and fragrances. Ever so disappointed she was.'

'I'm sure she can live without such luxuries,' Kate said, smiling.

'Anyway, that's enough of that. Lady Lyndon is in the dining room having breakfast. The bacon and buttered eggs will still be hot, if you care to join her. I'll make some more toast.'

Feeling like a schoolgirl dismissed from class, Kate murmured assent and left the kitchen to make her way to the dining room, where to her astonishment she found Annie sitting at the table with baby John on her lap, while Charlie entertained Lady Lyndon with his attempts to hold a conversation.

'Kate, my dear. Do help yourself to some breakfast. Annie and I have finished but we are being entertained by Charlie and the baby. Annie definitely has a way with little ones.'

Annie dropped a kiss on top of baby John's head. 'He's so sweet and he loves music. He was crying earlier and then I played a tune on my concertina and he was all smiles.'

'Everyone seems to have settled in so well,' Kate said, helping herself to bacon and buttered eggs from a silver breakfast dish on the sideboard. 'It feels as if the old house has woken up after a long sleep.'

Lady Lyndon smiled. 'That's exactly what I said. Of course I hope we can return to London very soon, but this place is really quite pleasant and the air smells delightful. I'm going out into the garden to see what the children are doing.' She rose from her chair. 'How is your mama this morning, Kate? I should have asked you sooner. The poor lady looked very out of sorts last evening.'

'She was still asleep when I came downstairs, ma'am. I'll check on her again as soon as I've had my breakfast.'

Annie stood up, still cuddling baby John. 'I'll come with you, Aunt Margaret.'

'I think Charlie wants to hold your hand,' Kate said, trying not to laugh at the little boy's determination to attract Annie's attention.

Annie reached downwards and Charlie curled his tiny hand around her index finger. He followed Lady Lyndon, leading Annie as carefully as if he understood that she was unable to see. Kate watched them with a smile on her lips. They had barely left the dining room when Martha bustled in carrying a silver rack filled with toast.

'It's a pleasure to have the house filled with people,' she said, beaming. 'I could do without them nippers, but I have to say they've behaved themselves so far.' She placed the toast rack in front of Kate. 'I could make up a tray for your ma, if that would help. I like to clear the dining room as soon as everybody's finished. I have a routine to keep up.'

Kate nodded. 'A boiled egg and some toast would do very nicely, thank you, Martha. I'll take it upstairs myself, and I'm prepared to help around the house.'

'Oh, no, miss. That wouldn't do at all. You're definitely above stairs and we're here to wait on you.' Martha folded her arms across her ample bosom. 'We might be a way out of London, but we do things proper here in Walthamstow.'

'Yes, of course,' Kate said hastily. It was obvious that her suggestion had offended Martha's sense of propriety. 'Perhaps I could help by going to the village. You might need some extra supplies now we're here.'

'I suppose that wouldn't hurt,' Martha said thoughtfully. 'I usually write down an order for

227

Mr Ruggles at the village shop. He makes it up and his boy delivers it, but we are a bit short of flour and lard. A pound or two of cheese would be useful.'

'That's settled then,' Kate said cheerfully. 'I'll go for a walk and get my bearings. It's a lovely day.'

'Very good, miss.' Martha picked up the empty silver serving dish and left the room at her usual brisk pace.

Kate suspected that, despite her grumbles about the children, Martha Boggis was in her element now that her services were needed again. Kate finished her meal and collected her bonnet and shawl from her room. She did not bother Jenny as she intended to go out on her own. Being seen with a servant in attendance would only draw attention to herself, and that was the last thing she wanted. She knew little about village life, but she suspected that the gossips would delight in passing on titbits of information concerning Warren House.

She set out with a wicker basket slung over her arm and a list of groceries in her reticule. Outside the gates was a strange new world of narrow country lanes bordered by deep green forest, farm land and the marshes stretching as far as she could see. As directed by Martha, Kate carried on until the lane widened into a street lined with cottages, a smithy and at the far end she could see the steeple of a church. Cyrus Ruggles' shop was situated opposite the Nag's Head Inn, adjacent to an ancient timberclad house.

Inside the shop the floor was covered in sawdust and Cyrus himself presided over a highly polished counter, behind which shelves were lined with bottles, jars and a side of bacon, waiting to be sliced. A wheel of cheese sat on the end of the counter, and a sack of flour was carefully opened to reveal its contents.

The only other customer was an elderly woman, who turned her head to stare openly at Kate.

'That'll be tuppence halfpenny, Mrs Sloan.' Cyrus rapped on the counter to attract her attention.

Mrs Sloan delved into her pocket and produced two pennies and a halfpenny, which she threw down on the counter. 'That's robbery, if you ask me. How's a poor widow supposed to survive with prices so high?'

'I'm not the one to blame, Mrs Sloan. It's them in the Government who control everything.'

Mrs Sloan grabbed her basket and pushed past Kate. 'I wouldn't shop here, if I was you, dear.' She slammed out of the shop.

'Don't take no notice of her,' Cyrus said, chuckling. 'Dora Sloan likes to grumble, and she likes to gossip. It'll be all round the village now that we have a newcomer in the village, Miss, er . . . '

'Miss Martin,' Kate said, smiling. 'I'm a guest at Warren House.'

He leaned across the counter. 'I heard there was new folk moved in there. That accounts for Martha's large order. Very good for business.'

Kate handed him her list. 'I hope we'll be staying for a while.'

'Have you come from far away, miss?' Cyrus busied himself checking the list and adding the items to her basket.

229

'Not too far, Mr Ruggles.'

He cut a wedge off the cheese and weighed it on his brass scales. 'There, that's two pound of best cheddar exactly. Martha must be doing a lot of cooking. How many did you say there were staying at Warren House?'

'I didn't,' Kate said casually. 'But there's quite a few extra mouths to feed.' She watched him as he weighed tea leaves into a paper poke.

'I'll put all these things on the Warren House account, shall I, miss?'

'Yes, please.' Kate picked up the basket, which was significantly heavier than when she had started out. 'Thank you, Mr Ruggles.'

'It's a pleasure, miss. Anything to oblige.'

Kate left the shop and was walking towards the church, admiring its square Norman tower, when she was accosted by a woman who emerged from the school playground and hurried towards her.

'Just a minute, miss. May I have a word with you?'

Kate came to a halt. 'Can I help you?'

Slightly breathless, the woman clutched the cross hanging on a chain over the high-necked white blouse she was wearing. 'I'm sorry. I should have introduced myself. My name is Elaine Courtney, my husband is the vicar of St Mary's.'

'How do you do?' Kate said politely. 'I'm Kate Martin.'

'You must be one of the guests staying at Warren House. Word gets round very quickly in the village.'

'I was doing some shopping for Martha Boggis, and I thought I'd take a look at the church.'

230

'Everyone is welcome at St Mary's, Miss Martin. I hope we'll see you on Sunday.'

'I expect so, Mrs Courtney.' Kate was about to walk on when the vicar's wife barred her way.

'I believe there are children staying at Warren House. We have an excellent infants' school.'

'I will certainly tell their mother.'

Mrs Courtney eyed her uncertainly. 'I could call on her at Warren House.'

Kate hesitated. The last thing they needed was for the whole of the village to know their business, and she could see that the vicar's wife was filled with curiosity.

'My mother is with me at Warren House. She used to do a great deal of charity work in London with ladies from our local church. I wonder if I might bring her to see you. She is recently widowed and in great need of something to take her mind off her loss.'

'Oh, the poor lady.' Mrs Courtney's sympathetic expression was then replaced by a smile. 'I would be delighted to help her through this difficult time. Why not bring her to see me tomorrow afternoon? I'd love to show her round the church and we can discuss the charitable works that the other good ladies do.'

'Thank you, ma'am. What time do you suggest?'

'Three o'clock would suit me, but if you wish to come earlier I will be at home.'

'We'll see you tomorrow, Mrs Courtney.'

★ ★ ★

231

Kate walked back to Warren House, and although no one else spoke to her, she was aware of curious stares and the fluttering of curtains in the neat row of alms houses. In London it was rare for anyone to show interest in the business of their neighbours. Even so, Kate was amused to be the centre of attention. Martha, on the other hand, pursed her lips and denounced the entire village as a bunch of busybodies. However, she was pleased with the contents of the shopping basket and she studied the bill, frowning when she came to the total.

'Ruggles knows how to charge for things,' she said tersely. 'But he has the only shop for miles, so we have no alternative.'

Kate turned to Jenny, who was peeling potatoes with a pained expression on her face.

'Did my mother eat her breakfast?'

Jenny nodded. 'Yes, I collected her tray about half an hour ago and she'd eaten everything, so she must be feeling better.'

'Did she get up and dress?'

'No. She said she wanted to rest.'

'That's not good. I'll go up and see her.' Kate left the kitchen and made her way upstairs. She found her mother still in bed, propped up on a pile of pillows. 'Do you intend to stay in bed all day, Mama?'

'Don't speak to me like that, Kate. I deserve some respect.'

'Of course you do, but lying around all day won't help.' Kate picked up her mother's wrap and handed it to her. 'Now, why don't you get out of bed and I'll send Jenny up with some warm water so that you can have a wash. Get dressed and come downstairs. It's a lovely day.' Kate walked over to the window and threw it open. She could see the older children racing around in the long grass while Polly and Emma sat on the balustrade making daisy chains. 'The garden could be beautiful if the old man who looks after it has some help. I could hire some strong fellows to cut the grass and attend to the flowerbeds.'

'I don't know why you're bothering, Kate.' Arabella rose reluctantly from her bed. 'Ring for Jenny. I will wash and come downstairs if it means so much to you, but I don't want you wasting your money on paying for gardeners or cleaning women. We're going home.'

Kate turned to face her mother. 'Do you really want to risk that dreadful man breaking into our house again?'

'No, but I don't see why I have to put up with Lady Lyndon and that girl who plays dreadful tunes on her concertina, let alone be pestered by all those children.'

'I'm sure that Lady Lyndon would rather be in her lovely home, too. But we're all in danger if we return to London.'

'And it's come about because of her wretched son. I'm not a fool, Kate. I suspect that the man you call Harry Trader is really Sir Harry Lyndon. I've lived in London long enough to know the names of the wealthy local families. She should be ashamed of him, and you should be ashamed of telling me lies.'

'What untruths have I ever told you, Mama?'

'You told me that Augustus Spears was the

233

owner of the premises where you opened the soup kitchen, but from what has happened it seems obvious that it was your Harry Trader, who is now detained in prison.'

Kate stared at her mother in surprise. 'How did you know?'

'Your papa never discussed his actual clients, but I learned a great deal about the criminal world from him and from reading the newspaper. I suspect that you are more interested in Sir Harry Lyndon than you care to admit, and quite frankly, Kate, that has to end.'

'I don't know where you got that idea, Mama. I am not romantically involved with Harry and never will be.'

'It seems to me that you recovered quickly from your infatuation with that Indian soldier. I suspect it will be the same with Harry Trader, or Lyndon . . . however he likes to style himself.'

'I haven't forgotten Ashok Patel. I'll never forget him, but we are worlds apart. He might have been killed in the conflict, for all I know, and the thought of that breaks my heart. But you can rest assured that I am not about to throw myself at another man, saint or sinner, so let's not talk about it any further.'

'Oh, well, if that's your attitude,' Arabella said huffily. 'Send the girl to help me dress. I will come downstairs, but I am still determined to go home.'

Kate could see that she was getting nowhere and she managed a smile. 'We'll see, but there is someone in the village who is very keen to meet you.'

'Who would that be?' Arabella asked suspiciously.

'Mrs Elaine Courtney, the vicar's wife, expressed a desire to meet you. I told her of your excellent work with the ladies' committee in London, and she invited us to visit her at the vicarage tomorrow afternoon.'

Arabella shook her head. 'I don't know about that. I have no interest in this house or the village. I want to go home.'

'And you shall,' Kate said patiently, as if dealing with a fractious five-year-old. 'As soon as the time is right we will return to Finsbury Square, but in the meantime why not give the ladies of this village the benefit of your considerable experience?'

'Well, if you put it like that, I suppose it won't hurt to meet this person.'

'That's settled then. When you're ready perhaps you'd like to take a walk around the grounds with me. I want to take a look and see what needs doing.'

Arabella eyed her warily. 'It sounds as if you're getting too fond of this old mausoleum, Kate. Remember that we're only visiting.'

'Yes, of course.' Kate moved towards the door. 'I'll send Jenny to you.'

★ ★ ★

Despite all Kate's efforts at persuading her mother to explore the gardens surrounding Warren House, Arabella refused to go outside, using a variety of excuses, and she declined to join Lady Lyndon and Annie in the drawing room, even though the older children were still playing outside. The sight of Charlie being entertained by Annie, and

235

Lady Lyndon cuddling a sleeping baby John, was enough to send Arabella straight to the morning room, where she settled down to read a copy of The Englishwoman's Domestic Magazine that she had brought with her from home. Kate gave up her efforts to make her mother socialise and she went out to explore the grounds on her own.

It was a balmy afternoon in late August when the fierce heat of the summer sun had mellowed to gentle warmth, and the leaves on some of the deciduous trees had already started to change colour. The hum of bees buzzing in great swathes of scented lavender and the twitter of sparrows as the tiny birds went about their daily business was interrupted by occasional shrieks and bursts of laughter from the children. They were obviously enjoying their first experiences of freedom, and Kate listened to them, smiling happily. Bringing them to the country had been the right decision, and Ivy had also settled in with surprising ease. Even at this moment she was busy helping Martha in the kitchen, and it pleased Kate to see how well they were getting on. She had been afraid that they might clash in the workplace, but Ivy seemed happy to take instruction from Martha, and Martha herself appeared to enjoy having a second in command. For the moment all was peace and harmony. Kate could only hope that this was a sign of things to come. Quite how long they would have to remain in Walthamstow was another matter, but for the moment she was content to stay away from the dangers of London.

She continued to walk at a leisurely pace. The gardens, although neglected, had obviously been spectacular at one time. She discovered a walled vegetable garden, which was completely over-grown with weeds and brambles. A greenhouse had been constructed along one side, but that too was sadly neglected. Most of the glass panes were broken, and those that remained were covered in grime, but Kate could imagine it as it must have been years ago, filled with trays of seedlings and ripening tomatoes, cucumbers and even melons. As she let herself out of the walled garden she almost bumped into an old man, who was hefting a wheelbarrow towards a huge compost heap.

'Good afternoon,' Kate said politely. 'You must be Mr Morrison.'

He squinted at her through the thick lenses of steel-rimmed spectacles. 'I don't know you, miss.'

'I'm Kate Martin and I'm Lady Lyndon's guest. I've been admiring the gardens.'

He pushed his cloth cap to the back of his head. 'They was splendid once, miss. But in them days we had at least six men working day in and day out. We produced all the fruit and vegetables for the family, as well as flowers for the house and herbs for the kitchen.'

'That must have been wonderful.'

'Aye, it were, miss. I started here as a lad of eight, working for me dad who was head gardener. Now it's just me to try and keep the weeds at bay, but it's a losing battle.'

'What would you say if I offered to hire some help for you?'

Morrison blinked several times as if struggling to understand. 'Why would you do that, miss? I mean, you're a lady and you're a guest.'

'I am just a visitor, but I can see how much you love this place, and I can feel it all around me. People have enjoyed this garden for a very long time, and it's a shame to let it go back to the wild.'

'A strong boy would be a boon, miss. Maybe a few men at the start to scythe the grass and cut down the brambles.'

'If you can find the people you think would do the job well, I'll be happy to pay them the going rate.'

Morrison seized her hand in his. 'Thank you, miss. There's always men looking for work and I've known them all since they was nippers.'

'That's excellent. I leave the choice to you, Morrison.' Kate squeezed his gnarled fingers and walked on. In her mind's eye she could see the gardens as they must have been years ago, and she sighed happily. At least there was something she could do to repay Lady Lyndon's hospitality. If she could just help her mother to join in with everyone else, life would be so much easier. Kate sighed; she knew she had an uphill task ahead of her.

She continued her walk but the sound of a horse's hoofs on the gravelled carriage sweep made her change direction and she hurried to the front of the house. Perhaps Harry had sent a messenger with good news? Her heart seemed to miss a beat. Maybe it was Monks who had discovered their whereabouts? She broke into a run.

15

Kate came to a sudden halt. 'Perry! What are you doing here?'

He dismounted, looping the reins over the horse's head. 'I came to see how you and Ivy were settling in, and to make sure you wanted for nothing. I feel I haven't done enough for either of you, especially my cousin's children.'

'You needn't worry about them. Ivy seems happy enough and she gets on well with Mrs Boggis, the housekeeper. The children are having a wonderful time and they have roses in their cheeks, even after such a short time.'

'I'm delighted to hear it. Is there anywhere I can leave Tarquin?'

'Yes, the stables are at the far end of the house. I'll show you.' Kate fell into step beside him.

'Goodfellow is still here, but Lady Lyndon sent Warrender back to Finsbury Circus. Goodfellow will look after your horse.' She shot him a curious glance. 'How did you find us? No one was supposed to know where we'd gone.'

'Harry told me where to find you. Only a few people know about this country estate.'

'You knew his true identity all along?'

'I wouldn't take on a client without going into their background, Kate.'

They came to a halt outside the stables, and Goodfellow emerged from the coach house.

'Look after my horse, if you please, Good-fellow,' Perry said, handing him the reins. 'I'll stay long enough to give him a rest before returning to London.'

'Aye, sir. Your horse will be all right with me.' Goodfellow led Tarquin into the stable.

Kate started off in the direction of the house. 'You're welcome to stay for the night, Perry. I'm sure we have room for one more, and you might be able to bridge the gap between Mama and Lady Lyndon.'

He eyed her curiously. 'They don't get on well?'

'You could say that, although I'm afraid it's my mother who's at fault. She simply refuses to have anything to do with Lady Lyndon or Annie, and having Ivy's children in the house isn't helping.'

He chuckled. 'I'm not sure I can do anything, but I'm willing to try.'

'Have you met Harry's mother?'

'No, I haven't.'

'She's a delightful lady.' Kate came to a halt on the terrace at the back of the house. She perched on the balustrade where the twins had abandoned their attempts at making daisy chains. 'Before we go indoors and I make the necessary introductions, please tell me why you came here today. What did Harry say to you?'

Perry stood with his hands clasped behind his back as he gazed into the distance. 'This is a splendid old house. I'd take bets on the fact that you're planning improvements both inside and outside.'

'Don't change the subject, Perry. The house doesn't belong to me, although I do hate to see the garden in such a state, but we'll only be here for a short time. Please answer my question — what did Harry say?'

'He wants you to remain here for an indefinite period. I can't say more than that because I'm not party to his dealings with the Metropolitan Police.'

'So you don't know whether they are closer to catching Monks?'

'I believe they are closing in on him and his gang, but they need to have concrete evidence in order to bring a case against him. Simple affray wouldn't be enough to convict him and his gang. Monks might be called mad, but he's far from that. In fact, he's very clever and extremely cunning, and he knows that Harry's weak point is his mother, and now it's you and your family, too.'

'We are not connected in any way. You know very well that I only used the ground floor of his building to run the soup kitchen.'

'Whether you like it or not, that made you an accomplice. Your charity worked was a perfect cover for him and his men. He might not be a villain like Monks, but Harry Trader was running illegal gaming establishments for at least seven years, and he made a fortune. Monks wants to take over his business and he's prepared to fight for it.'

'So you've just come all the way from London to tell me that we must stay on here. Is that so?'

'Not entirely. That was Harry's message, but I wanted to see you and make sure that you weren't living in dire circumstances.'

'We're quite comfortable and Mrs Boggis keeps the house neat and clean, as if the family were still

241

in residence.'

'You said that your mother is unhappy here. There is a way that you could both return to London and still be safe.'

'I know we will have to wait for the police to arrest Monks and his gang.'

'Better than that, Kate. You could marry me and I would be there to protect you and your mother.'

'You know my answer to that. I haven't changed my mind.'

'Your father asked me to take care of you, Kate. I would try to be a good husband.'

She rose to her feet, eyeing him curiously. 'I don't want you to marry me because of a promise you made Papa.'

'What I don't understand is whether you are hankering after the ghost of a man you met in Delhi, or if you have genuine feelings for Harry Trader.'

She turned on him angrily. 'You'll just have to accept my decision, Perry. You might think you're doing the honourable thing but there never was anything between us, and there never will be. If you can't accept that then I think you'd better return to London as soon as your horse is rested.' She was about to walk away when he caught her by the hand.

'I'm sorry, Kate. I know you don't have any feelings for me, but I would have honoured my promise. If you should change your mind I will be there for you.'

'You simply don't give up, do you?'

He gave her a rueful smile. 'I wouldn't have got so far in my profession if I were someone who gave up at the first hint of trouble.'

'And an independently wealthy wife might prove a definite advantage.'

'I suppose you're right,' Perry said with a wry smile.

'Come in and make yourself pleasant to my mother, but if you even hint at any romantic attachment between us I will never speak to you again. Mama would love to have you as her son-in-law, but don't let that go to your head.'

'I promise not to say anything that might embarrass you.'

'Then follow me. I'll introduce you to Lady Lyndon. You've already met her companion, Annie.' Kate crossed the terrace and opened the door leading into the rear of the house. She led the way to the drawing room where, as she had expected, Lady Lyndon was relaxing on the sofa listening to Annie playing a haunting melody.

Perry came to a standstill in the doorway, gazing in admiration at Annie, or maybe it was her playing that touched him. Kate was amazed to see tears in his eyes. She had never seen this side of Peregrine and it was as if he had lifted a curtain on his feelings and now they were there for all to see. She turned away, embarrassed for his sake, but Annie came to the end of the music and there was a sudden silence, broken by Perry clapping enthusiastically.

'That was really beautiful, Annie.'

'Who are you?' Annie asked nervously. 'Do I know you? Kate, are you there?'

'Yes, of course. I'm sorry, Annie. It's Perry, I'm sure you remember him.'

'I do,' Annie said, smiling. 'You like my playing, Perry.'

'That was wonderful,' Perry said with a break in his voice. 'Really beautiful, Annie.'

'We were carried away by your music.' Kate turned to Lady Lyndon, may I introduce you to my good friend and legal adviser, Peregrine Harte? He is also Harry's lawyer.'

Perry moved forward to take Lady Lyndon's outstretched hand and he raised it to his lips.

'How do you do, my lady? It's a pleasure to meet you.'

'Have you news of my son, Mr Harte?'

'I saw him this morning, ma'am. He is quite well and he sends you his best regards. He asked me to come here and make sure that you were comfortable.'

Lady Lyndon smiled sadly. 'I can't bear to think of him in that dreadful place. Did he say when we might go home?'

Kate met Perry's anxious look with a frown. 'We are all to remain here for a little longer, my lady.'

'I hope he's not suffering too much,' Annie said gently. 'You are sure that they are treating him as well as can be expected?'

Perry turned to her. He held out his hand, then, as if remembering that she could not see the gesture, he dropped it to his side. 'Harry is strong physically and he never allows anything to disturb his equilibrium. I wish I had his ability to adapt to any situation.'

'Are you going to be here for a while, Perry?' Annie said with a sweet smile.

'If it's not inconveniencing anyone, I would

love to stay for the night, but I'm afraid I'll have to leave early in the morning.'

Kate was standing close to the bell pull and she gave it a sharp tug. She knew that she had no reason to be annoyed, having just turned down Perry's offer of marriage, but he was gazing at Annie like a love-struck youth. 'I'll have a room made ready for you, Perry.'

She had spoken more sharply than she had intended but Perry seemed not to have noticed and he went to sit beside Annie on the sofa.

'Would you play another tune, please?'

Annie blushed and picked up her concertina. 'I think Aunt Margaret has had enough of my playing for now. Shall we go for a walk in the garden, Perry?'

'That's a good idea, Annie,' Lady Lyndon said with a nod of approval. 'You go out and get some fresh air. Kate will keep me company.'

'Of course.' Kate took a seat in a chair close to where Lady Lyndon was sitting.

Perry took Annie's hand and tucked it into the crook of his arm in a spontaneous gesture that brought a smile to Annie's pretty face.

'I can find my way about, you know.'

He opened the door for her. 'I'm sure you can. I am the one who needs guidance, Annie. I don't know this big house.'

'Has that young man upset you, dear?' Lady Lyndon asked gently as the door closed on them.

Kate shook her head. 'No. Well, yes, I suppose he has. Perry has twice asked me to marry him, the last time being a matter of minutes ago in the garden, although to be fair he only did it because he promised my father that he would take care of me.'

'I assume you didn't accept?'

'I did not, but that doesn't mean that he ought to fall in love with the first girl he sees.'

'My dear, I do sympathise, but don't take it to heart. Annie is a sweet child and she has that effect on some men. She brings out their protective nature.'

'I suppose so, and I'm being mean,' Kate said with a reluctant chuckle. 'But it doesn't say much for his feelings for me.'

'Maybe you ought to have words with that young man, but don't spoil Annie's moment of happiness. The poor girl has had few enough of those since her parents died and her brother's regiment was sent to India. I know she worries about him constantly.'

'You're right, of course,' Kate said earnestly. 'I think it was just my pride that was hurt. You're very wise, Lady Lyndon.'

'Not really, Kate. One good thing about growing older is that one has seen and experienced many things, although passing on that information is not always welcomed. You are a very sensible young woman. No wonder Harry chose you to support him.'

Kate eyed her warily. 'He chose me? I don't understand.'

'I know very little about Harry's business ventures, but I do know that he would have thought very hard before he allowed you to run the soup kitchen in that rough part of London. He's quite shrewd when it comes to picking the people who

246

work closely with him.'

'But I did nothing, Lady Lyndon.'

'Harry obviously trusts you and that encourages me to do the same. I know that you will do anything you can to see that justice is done, and I support you in every way.' Lady Lyndon sat back in her chair, closing her eyes. 'I think I'll have a short nap before dinner.'

There was nothing left to say and Kate hurried from the room. At a guess, Annie would have led Perry through the house to the terrace overlooking the meadow that had once been a lawn. As she had suspected they were seated together on the balustrade, but the rapt look on Annie's face made it impossible to interrupt their conversation and Kate retreated into the house before either of them noticed her.

It was not until much later that she managed to speak to Perry on his own. Dinner was over and Arabella had pleaded a headache and retired to her room with Jenny in attendance. Lady Lyndon and Annie had gone to the drawing room and Perry was about to follow them when Kate laid a hand on his sleeve.

'Don't go yet, Perry. I want to ask you something.' He came to a halt. 'Have you changed your mind?'

'No, but it appears that you have.'

'I don't know what you mean.'

'Yes, you do. You've had eyes for no one but Annie ever since you met her again.'

'She is a beautiful woman, and so sweet.'

'Just a few hours ago you proposed to me.'

'Kate, I have the highest regard for you and I

247

would have made you a good husband, but you've turned me down twice.'

'It doesn't seem to have upset you.'

'I was trying to do the right thing.'

'So you were never in love with me?'

He smiled and raised her hand to his lips. 'Of course I was — just a little, anyway. You are a beautiful, spirited woman with a mind of your own. I doubt if I could live up to your high ideals but I would have tried. I had no thought of looking for anyone else, and then I saw Annie. I'm sorry if it offends you, but I have to admit that everything changed at that moment.'

'What are you going to do about it? Annie is living here; you are in London.'

'I haven't thought that far, Kate. All I know is that I want to see her as often as possible, but I'm truly sorry if I've hurt your feelings.'

She reached up and kissed his cheek. 'I was a little piqued, I must admit, but I understand how you feel. It was the same for me when I first set eyes on Ashok, although that can never be.' Kate took a deep breath. 'However, that doesn't mean you have to suffer. Annie is a lovely person, and if you win her heart you will be a very lucky man.'

'You are a very special person, Kate. I would have counted myself a very lucky man had you accepted my offer of marriage.'

'Fibber!' Kate said, smiling. 'I don't feel so bad about refusing you now. Anyway, I'm sure you have better things to do this evening than stand here talking to me.'

He kissed her on the cheek. 'I'm going to the kitchen to have a chat with Ivy. I have some news for her, as if happens.'

'About her husband?'

'Yes, I visited the prison and because I was Ted's lawyer I was allowed to see him briefly. He's surviving well and he's determined to go straight. He might even be released a bit earlier for good behaviour.'

'That would be wonderful,' Kate said earnestly. 'Poor Ivy has been so brave and she's worked so hard to keep herself and her children. I really admire her.'

'I'm ashamed that I've done so little to help her, but I will do what I can now.'

'Go and tell her the good news. I'm going to see if I can persuade Mama to join us in the drawing room.'

Kate watched him walk away with mixed feelings. She had never felt anything other than friendship for Perry, but his open admiration had helped during the first bleak days back in England and her enforced separation from the man she loved. So much had happened in such a short time, however, and she was beginning to wonder if she was the same person who had stepped off the ship on that cold and miserable day. She caught sight of her reflection as she walked past a mirror in the passage leading to the morning room, where she expected to find her mother. The image gazed back at her with a rueful smile. Despite heartbreak, life went on and there was nothing she could do other than wait and hope maybe one day she would receive news from Delhi. She had given Ashok the address of her home in Finsbury Square and he had promised to send word, if only that he had survived the bitter conflict. She sighed and walked on. Ash belonged to another world, a completely different way of life. Their stars had crossed but she could not foresee a happy ending.

She opened the morning-room door. 'Mama, why are you sitting in here on your own?'

'I prefer my own company, Kate. You, of course, are welcome to join me, if you can tear yourself away from Peregrine.'

'There is nothing between him and me, Mama.' Kate hesitated in the doorway. 'Please come to the drawing room. What will Lady Lyndon think if you continue to avoid her like this?'

Arabella shrugged and held her book closer to the flickering candle. 'I'm engrossed in this tale by Mr Dickens. I found the book in my room. It's about a man called Mr Pickwick and his friends — it's quite entertaining. Go and join your friends, Kate. I'm quite content to sit here and read.'

'All right, but remember that we've been invited to the vicarage tomorrow afternoon. I hope you'll agree to come. Mrs Courtney is very keen to meet you.'

'I would welcome the chance to get away from this dreadful old house. Now go and entertain Perry. I'm sure he would propose again if you gave him some encouragement.'

Kate knew better than to enter into an argument with her mother and she merely nodded. 'Good night, Mama. I hope I'll see you at breakfast.'

'I've told Ivy to bring me a tray in bed. Your papa knew that I have a delicate constitution, but no one else seems to care.'

Kate sighed and closed the door. Perhaps a visit to the vicarage might give her mother something else to think about.

* ★ *

Elaine Courtney gave them an effusive welcome and Kate could see that her mother was delighted, even though she managed to maintain a casual outward appearance, accepting compliments with a modest smile. They were shown into what was obviously the best parlour with its carefully arranged furniture and heavy red velvet curtains that matched the upholstery on the sofa and chairs. The scent from vases filled with garden flowers was overpowered by the smell of the camphor, commonly used to keep moths at bay. Knowing that her mother prided herself on her sensitivity to strong odours of any kind, Kate could only hope that this one had gone unnoticed. She glanced anxiously at her mother, but Arabella was smiling graciously.

'What a charming room,' Arabella said smoothly. 'How kind of you to invite us to your home, Mrs Courtney.'

'My dear lady, it is so good of you to come. We are a small community, but I have a group of very good ladies who get together weekly to do good works. Your daughter tells me that is what you do so well in London.'

'We have had some success,' Arabella said modestly. 'Maybe I can give you some fresh ideas, if you think they will be well received.'

'Oh, yes. I can guarantee that my ladies will

251

hang on your every word, Mrs Martin.'

'It's Lady Martin,' Arabella said firmly. 'My daughter obviously forgot to mention the fact.'

'I do beg your pardon, your ladyship.' Elaine shot a reproachful look in Kate's direction. 'I would be honoured if you would meet my committee. Would you be free tomorrow afternoon?'

'I'm sure I could manage that.' Arabella turned to Kate, eyebrows raised. 'Have I any other appointments for tomorrow?'

'No, Mama.' Kate maintained a straight face although she was tempted to giggle. She could tell that her mother was enjoying every moment of basking in Elaine Courtney's undisguised admiration.

'Then I would be pleased to attend. I was planning on returning to London, but another day in the country will be quite pleasant.'

'I'll ring for tea. You do take tea, don't you, Lady Martin? I could offer you coffee or chocolate, if you prefer.'

'Tea will be delightful,' Arabella said automatically. She stared past her hostess, frowning. 'Who is that person peering in through your window, Mrs Courtney?'

Elaine and Kate turned their heads to look, and Elaine threw up her hands. 'That is my son, Hedley. He's a captain in the East India Company Bombay Army, but he was on leave at the start of the uprising and has not yet been recalled for service.'

'Why is he staring at us?' Arabella demanded crossly. 'It seems very impolite.'

'You'll have to forgive him,' Elaine said hurriedly. 'Hedley was injured some time ago in a skirmish — a head wound, which has left him with some problems.'

'He seems to be a little nervous.' Kate stared back at the young man, who immediately withdrew and walked away.

Elaine turned away from the window. 'Please don't trouble yourself about my son, Miss Martin. I think Hedley will be returning to his regiment in the not-too-distant future. I'm sure the sea voyage will be beneficial. But where are my manners? Please be seated, ladies.'

Arabella sank gracefully onto the cushions of an ornately carved armchair. 'We were in Delhi at the start of the rebellion, Mrs Courtney. I wouldn't wish to go through that experience again.'

Elaine's hands flew to cover her mouth and her eyes widened. 'Oh, my goodness. How terrible for you. Do tell me about it, if the memories are not too painful, of course.' She glanced at Kate, who was still standing. 'Perhaps you'd like to take a turn around the garden, Miss Martin? It's not very large, but the herbaceous borders are still full of colour.'

Kate glanced at her mother, who seemed quite relaxed and even eager to talk about their time in India. 'Would you mind, Mama?'

'No, my dear. Go outside and enjoy the sunshine while it lasts. It will soon be winter and we will be confined indoors for months on end.'

Kate left the room and let herself out through the front door, but it was not the herbaceous borders that interested her — she was eager to speak to Hedley, who had served in India. It would be

253

a relief to talk to someone who must know the country well. She made her way round the side of the house and came across Hedley standing in the middle of the lawn, staring up into the sky.

'Good afternoon, Captain Courtney.'

He spun round, staring at her with dawning recognition. 'You were in the front parlour just now.'

'That's right, I was.' Kate held out her hand. 'My name is Kate Martin. I'm staying at Warren House.'

He eyed her warily. 'I don't go out in society.'

'I don't know anyone in Walthamstow,' Kate said casually.

'Why are you here?'

'Your mama invited us so that she could meet my mama. They are in the parlour getting to know each other, so I thought I'd leave them in peace, and I love flowers. Your garden is lovely.'

'It is quite pretty, I suppose. I come out here to get away from my parents.' A vague smile replaced the sombre expression in Hedley's dark eyes. 'I served in the East India Company Army for ten years.'

'You must have been very young when you joined up.'

His mouth twisted in a wry grin. 'I was thirteen, and my parents were missionaries. I ran away and joined the army as a drummer boy. My father bought me a commission before they returned to England, and I stayed on — until my accident.'

Kate laid her hand on his arm. 'I'm so sorry. How did it happen?'

'I was thrown from my horse and they say I cracked my skull, but I don't remember any of it.

254

They all think I'm simple-minded because I forget things. Sometimes I don't even remember my name.'

'That's quite shocking. But your mama said you are recovering slowly.'

'Slowly is the right word. I feel, at times, that I'm going to be trapped forever in this peasouper fog that was once my brain.'

'Will you return to India?'

'I don't know. According to my papa, who reads The Times every day, the East India Company Army is going to be disbanded. I'm not sure if there is any prospect of retaining my old rank if the British Army takes over.'

'But you would like to return to India?'

He nodded vigorously. 'I would.'

'As would I, but I doubt if I'll go back. My uncle had a good position with the East India Company in Delhi, but he was killed during the rebellion.'

'I'm sorry,' Hedley said simply.

'Yes, I was very fond of him.' Kate turned away, struggling with her emotions. The loss of her uncle Edgar still brought tears to her eyes.

'I think we should go indoors,' Hedley said, taking her by the hand as if she were a small child. 'There's a slight chill in the air.'

Kate nodded wordlessly. She allowed him to lead her to the parlour door where he bowed and was about to walk away. 'Aren't you coming in with me?'

'No. I think I'll go to my room for a while. Mama won't expect me to join you.' He smiled. 'They are used to my foibles by now. I spend a lot of time on my own. Anyway, it was nice meeting

255

you, Miss Martin.'

'Kate,' she said firmly.

'Kate. I won't forget you.' Hedley walked away, heading for the staircase, and leaving Kate little alternative but to rejoin her mother and Mrs Courtney. She entered the parlour to find her mother and Mrs Courtney chatting amicably over cups of tea.

Elaine looked up and smiled. 'Well, my dear, how did you get on with my son? He must have taken to you because he normally shies away from meeting new people. Perhaps you could come again and spend more time with him? I'm sure that talking to another young person would speed his recovery.'

'I don't think we'll be staying at Warren House long enough to make new friends,' Arabella said firmly. 'It's a pretty village, but my home is in Finsbury Square. We have a very large house, and heaven knows what the servants are doing in my absence.'

16

There seemed little prospect of returning home. Perry advised strongly against it and Monks was still on the run from the police. Until he was caught and imprisoned there was still danger, and they would have to remain at Warren House. Arabella grumbled, but Lady Lyndon was philosophical and Annie positively blossomed, especially when Perry was present.

Autumn had turned the countryside into a kaleidoscope of colour. The marshes were all shades of green and brown, and the leaves on the trees hung like golden coins, ready to be plucked by the next gale. Kate had ridden into Epping Forest on several occasions, sometimes with Perry and Annie, whom he was teaching to ride. Annie was an apt pupil and she revelled openly in the fact that the horse was her eyes, taking her to places where she would never have ventured on foot. Kate was touched by Perry's gentleness and the protective way in which he treated Annie, while allowing her an amount of independence previously denied her. It was a pleasure to ride behind them, listening to Annie's trills of laughter when Perry said something amusing, and his obvious pleasure in her company. Kate's initial reaction had been one of pique, but that had faded almost instantly and she could see now that the couple were well suited. Whenever Perry arrived — which was every ten days or so — Kate always asked for news of Harry, and the answer never varied. Harry was still in prison and Monks was still at large, but the Metropolitan Police were working as hard as they could to bring him to justice.

Kate visited the vicarage at least twice a week to spend time with Hedley. On these occasions she was always accompanied by Jenny, who sat quietly at her side, listening to their reminiscence of India. At first Hedley seemed to enjoy their conversations, but sometimes he preferred to remain in his room, refusing to see anyone. Neither of his parents seemed able to cope with him when he was overtaken by deep depression. Kate could only sympathise and walk away. She had grown fond of Hedley during their short acquaintance, and she suspected that his condition was worsened by the fact that he was desperate to return to his regiment. His mother fussed over him constantly, and when Kate met the Reverend Humphrey Courtney she could understand why Hedley kept himself to himself.

The vicar was a tall, thin man with a loud booming voice and a commanding manner. Kate could imagine that as a missionary he might have frightened naïve peasants into adopting Christianity simply in order to placate him. His sermons on Sundays were impassioned and very long, and although Kate and almost everybody at Warren House attended matins, she had seen Martha and Lady Lyndon nodding off occasionally. Ivy attended with her older children, who had to be bribed with pieces of cake to keep them from disrupting the service, and the little ones were left at home in the care of Tilly, a young girl from the village who had been taken on to help in the kitchen.

The biggest surprise for Kate came when her mother decided that county life was not as terrible as she had first thought. Arabella stopped talking about her old home in Finsbury Square and threw herself into committee work with Elaine Courtney. They were now in the process of organising a sale of work to raise funds for the village children's Christmas party. Arabella had taken it upon herself to visit the large houses and estates dotted around the area, and had managed to persuade several well-to-do ladies to attend meetings and donate items for the sale. Kate could hardly believe the change in her mother from the sad, dispirited widow, to a happy energetic woman with a purpose in life. Despite the differences in their situations, Arabella and Elaine were a partnership to be reckoned with, and Kate wondered if Walthamstow would ever be the same again. There was still a little frostiness in the air when Arabella and Lady Lyndon were in the same room, but Kate continued to be optimistic. The fault was mainly her mother's, but Kate did not expect miracles. Perhaps in time her mother would forgive Harry Lyndon for involving them in the criminal world, and at least they were safe from Monks and his gang.

Kate had fallen in love with Warren House and she continued to put her inheritance to good use. She paid for extra staff to help Morrison in the gardens and now, in their autumnal glory, they were looking quite splendid. She had engaged three daily women from the village to do the heavy work around the house, and a washerwoman came in once a week to see to the laundry. Martha was delighted to be in charge of the servants and Arthur took it upon himself to organise the work outside. Ivy and Martha had formed an alliance and it amused Kate to see them chatting together as if they had known each other all their lives. Elaine Courtney had made sure that Frankie, May, Nellie and Jimmy attended school, leaving the twins, Charlie and baby John in their mother's care. Tilly proved to be a useful nursery maid when Ivy was busy, and for the most part peace reigned in the household, with only the occasional disagreement to ripple the harmony.

With Goodfellow at her side, Kate bought a horse for herself as well as one for Annie, and a pony so that Ivy's children could be taught how to ride. Goodfellow had met Marie Parker, a comely if rather loud-mouthed widow, at church. Since then Kate had not heard him mention his desire to return to London. The cottage formerly used by the head groom was decorated and refurbished to his taste, although Kate suspected that Widow Parker had inspired Goodfellow's sudden interest in domesticity. With the extra horses to care for and a carriage and a dog cart to maintain, Kate hired a stable boy to help Goodfellow.

By now Kate was well known in the village. She enjoyed walking to the local shop to purchase items that might not have been put on the weekly order, and she always stopped to chat to anyone who wanted to pass the time of day. It was pleasant to be greeted by friendly faces. Although she had been born and bred in the city, if she were to be truthful, she enjoyed living in the country and had no real desire to return to the house in Finsbury Square. She still felt that her heart was held captive in Delhi, but she tried not to think of Ashok. Even so, he stole into her dreams and she often awakened to find her pillow wet with tears. However, life had to go on.

As the days grew shorter and colder, Martha and Ivy were busy making preserves from the fruit grown in the walled garden and berries that the children had gathered from the hedgerows. Martha made rosehip syrup, which she swore by as a remedy for coughs and colds, and the kitchen was filled with the tangy aroma. She was an expert when it came to making herbal medicines, and Ivy was an eager learner. In the walled garden Morrison, with the help of his underlings, had built clamps in which root vegetables were stored between layers of soil and straw so that they lasted throughout the winter months. Kate viewed the pyramid-shaped mounds with admiration. She had bought vegetables from costermongers' stalls, but she had never given any thought as to where they came from or how they happened to be available even in the worst of the weather.

The day of the sale in the church hall to raise funds for the village children's Christmas party arrived and everyone, including Arthur Boggis, had been bribed, persuaded or bullied into helping. Even Lady Lyndon was not immune from Arabella's determination to make the event a huge success. Goodfellow decked the Warren House carriage with swags of ivy into which the heads of the last chrysanthemums had been woven, and dressed in his coachman's outfit he drove round the village picking up anyone who was too infirm to walk to the church hall. Martha had found an old tea urn at the back of one of the cupboards and it had been cleaned and polished until the copper shone like molten metal. Martha and Ivy had baked rock cakes and jam tarts, which they laid out on their stall, together with a large jug of milk and a pound of tea, purchased by Kate, plus a whole cone of sugar snipped into small lumps. Refreshments at a halfpenny a time were waiting for the hungry and thirsty people whom they hoped would flock into the sale.

All the ladies from Elaine's committee were on hand to serve the prospective customers, and Annie was seated on the rostrum playing her concertina to welcome everyone with cheerful jigs and popular songs. Lady Lyndon stood next to Annie, preparing to make the opening speech. Kate could see that her mother resented the fact that Elaine had asked Lady Lyndon to officiate, but Arabella was presenting a determinedly pleasant smile despite what she must have been feeling. However, as the landowner, Sir Harry Lyndon, was mysteriously unavailable to attend, his mother was the obvious choice.

Hedley had been persuaded, or more likely bribed by his mother, to attend, dressing imposingly in his captain's uniform, but he looked embarrassed and ill at ease until Jenny asked him to help sell the raffle tickets. They did this together and Kate was amazed to find that they had sold every last one. Even more surprising was the fact that Hedley seemed to be enjoying himself and

Jenny was seized with a fit of the giggles at something her unlikely partner had said. It all boded well for the success of the sale.

It was Kate's job to keep the tea urn topped up with boiling water from the range in the vicarage kitchen. It entailed a swift walk across the lawn and through a gap in the hedge to the back door of the hall, and she had eight-year-old Frankie to help her. They stood together, waiting for instructions from Martha, who was in charge of the urn, with Ivy standing by to pour the milk. It was seven-year-old May's job to pass round the sugar and to keep cheeky boys from stealing the precious and expensive glistening lumps of sweetness.

Arabella and Elaine marshalled the other committee ladies to their stations behind the various stalls, selling all manner of second-hand articles, quite a few of which had come from the large houses in the area. These were the items that many of the village women seemed to prize most, and Kate expected to see Mrs Whitely, the butcher's wife, wearing a bonnet donated by Lady Martin or Lady Lyndon at next Sunday's church service. There were embroidered hankies, fur tippets and lacy woollen shawls, as well as jars of homemade hand cream, lotions and a vast array of cheaper second-hand clothes, caps, gloves and mufflers. The glass jars filled with colourful boiled sweets were temptation enough, but there were also pyramids of sugared almonds, and trays of toffee with vicious-looking pincers to break it into irresistible chunks. Crowds of children jostled for position, although most of them were simply onlookers, having no pennies to spend. Kate could see their small faces alight with pleasure simply imagining the delights of munching on such treats, and she had a bag of farthings saved for this occasion, which she would hand out surreptitiously so that no one went home feeling disappointed.

The doors opened and Kate noticed that everyone who came through the doors was wearing their Sunday best for the occasion, even though it was Saturday. When the hall was crammed with people Elaine Courtney stepped onto the rostrum and patted Annie on the shoulder, which was a signal to stop playing. Elaine clapped her hands to gain the hall's attention, and then she welcomed everyone and thanked them for coming. She handed over to Lady Lyndon, who was dressed like a duchess and looked resplendent in lilac silk trimmed with blonde lace and a purple velvet mantle with a fur collar and cuffs. Her silver hair had been coiffed by Miss Hattersley, who kept herself to herself and took her meals on a tray in her room rather than mix with Martha and the servants. Miss Hattersley was not present, using a headache as an excuse, but she had been well enough to help her mistress dress and to add the finishing touch of a perky little fur hat with a black lace veil.

There was silence in the hall while her ladyship made the opening speech and then the voices rose in a crescendo as everyone pushed and shoved in their attempts to find bargains.

Ivy nudged Kate in the ribs. 'The tea urn is half empty. We're going to need more hot water very soon.'

Kate nodded. 'I'll go and fetch the kettle from

264

the vicarage kitchen. I can't see Frankie; I think he's met up with some friends from his school, but I don't need him yet.' Kate edged her way through the crowd and went outside. It was a relief to be in the fresh air, but it was chilly even though the sun was shining. She hurried across the yard and was about to enter the vicarage garden when a man emerged from behind the box hedge.

'Kate, there you are. I've been searching for you.'

She stifled a cry of surprise, glancing over her shoulder to make sure there was no one about. 'Harry! What are you doing here? Have you escaped from prison?'

He seized her hand and dragged her into the privacy of the vicarage garden. 'No one must know I'm here, not even my mother.'

'You broke out? Are you on the run?' She stared at him in dismay. Harry had always been immaculate and clean shaven, but now he had a straggly beard and moustache, and his face was gaunt, but his eyes still held the same old spark of humour.

'In a manner of speaking,' he said in a low voice. 'But I'll explain everything later. I mustn't be seen.'

'You were taking a chance by coming here in broad daylight. You'd better come into the kitchen,' Kate said hastily. 'They've all gone to the sale so there won't be anyone around.' She led the way across the lawn to the back of the house, checking first that there was no one in the kitchen before she hustled Harry inside. She leaned against the table, looking him up and down. 'You look terrible. I doubt if anyone would recognise you as Sir

265

Harry Lyndon.'

He gave her a wry smile. 'I know, and I probably smell dreadful.'

'Are the police after you, Harry?'

'I'm more worried that Monks will track me down. I have to lie low until he and all his gang are safely behind bars.'

'But if words gets round that you're here it won't be a secret for long.'

'You've learned that already. I'm impressed.' Harry's smiled faded. 'I'll leave now and head back to the house.'

'You've been there already? How did you know where to find me?'

'Morrison was burning dead leaves. I followed my nose and found him in the walled garden. Don't worry, Kate. I've known him since I was a boy. He told me where you were and he also said how much you'd done for him. You've made a friend there.'

'I only did what was necessary . . . But more importantly, what will you do now?'

'I have a plan and it involves you, but we won't go into that at the moment. I'd better make myself scarce before someone comes looking for you.'

'Where will you stay? You wouldn't be able to hide in a house filled with people.'

'Morrison has a small cottage on the edge of the estate. I'll stay there for a while and keep the old fellow company.'

Kate glanced out of the window. 'Frankie is crossing the lawn.' She snatched the kettle from the range and made a move towards the door. 'I'll see you later, unless Constable Middlemiss arrests you on the way home.' She did not wait for his answer and she hurried from the house, meeting Frankie halfway. 'Sorry I took so long. I had to wait for the water to heat up.'

Frankie took the kettle from her. 'I got longer legs than you, miss. They're crying out for more tea in there.' He raced off, spilling water on the ground in his hurry.

Kate followed him, not daring to look behind her. Harry was playing a dangerous game and she was eager to hear the full story, but she must carry on as if nothing had happened. She entered the church hall with a set smile on her face, but they were all so busy that no one appeared to notice her. She might as well have been invisible. It was tempting to leave now and follow Harry home, but Kate went back to her station at the refreshment table, curbing her impatience. She kept glancing at the large, whitefaced clock on the wall, but it seemed as though the hands had ceased to move. However, eventually, when the tables were virtually bare of goods and all the cakes and jam tarts had been consumed, Elaine Courtney climbed onto the rostrum and thanked everyone for coming. She said the money had yet to be counted, but the local children were assured of a Christmas party to remember. She allowed her husband to hand her down amidst clapping and cheers from those who had not chosen to make a hasty retreat. Kate suspected that some items had been quietly pilfered, but as they had been donated free of charge it was not a great loss, and some of those attending looked more in need than the children for whom the money had been collected.

When they were tidying away the garments that had not sold, mainly because the ladies who had given them had put too high a price on the items, Kate suggested that perhaps it would be a good thing to make them into bundles to be distributed to the families whose wants were well known; many of whom were too proud to ask for charity. Elaine agreed, leaving the task to Kate and Martha, who knew everyone in the village and for miles around. Kate had spotted a woollen muffler and a man's cap, which she thought would be suitable for Morrison, and it would give her an excuse to visit his cottage on the way home.

Lady Lyndon and Arabella were the first to leave. Kate was surprised when her mother did not raise any objection to riding in the carriage with Lady Lyndon, but they seemed to be on reasonably good terms, and they departed to a round of applause from those who were left to finish clearing the church hall. Kate, Ivy and the children had to wait for Goodfellow to return with the barouche. Kate climbed in last, having instructed Goodfellow to drop her just inside the gates of Warren House.

'Why do you want to be set down so far from the house?' Ivy asked, frowning.

'I want to give the cap and muffler to Morrison. The mornings are getting colder and he's an old man.'

'I could send Frankie,' Ivy suggested.

'It's a lovely afternoon,' Kate said casually. 'We won't get too many days like this now, and I feel like a walk. Besides which, I had an idea for planting different vegetables in the greenhouse, so I want to talk to Morrison.'

Ivy shrugged and smiled. 'Anyone would think you was the lady of the manor, Kate. You fit into the part very well.'

'I like to keep busy, and it's nice to see everything getting back to how it must have been years ago. Anyway, I think the sale went well,' Kate said, quickly changing the subject. 'You worked very hard, Frankie, and so did you, girls.'

Frankie blushed to the roots of his hair, while Nellie and May giggled and hid their faces as if unused to such praise.

'They're good nippers, most of the time,' Ivy said with a tremulous smile. 'Their dad would be proud of them.'

'How much longer has he got to serve?' Kate asked gently. Although Ivy said little about her husband's prison sentence, it was obvious to anyone who knew her well that she had suffered greatly.

'I'm not sure, but I don't think we'll see him before February. I don't know if they get time off for good behaviour.'

'Let's hope so, Ivy. Anyway, it's only a few months now and you'll be reunited. Just think how happy Ted will be to see the children so healthy.'

'And with book learning,' Frankie added with a cheeky grin. 'I can read if the words aren't too long.'

'I can read better than you,' May added. 'Mrs Courtney said I'm a clever girl.'

'I'm sure you're all doing well,' Kate said hastily. 'You'll give your dad a lovely surprise.'

Ivy took Jimmy onto her lap and gave him a

cuddle. 'What about Harry? Cousin Perry is his solicitor — does he know when Harry will be released?'

Kate had not been expecting this turn in the conversation. 'I don't think Perry knows any more than we do.'

'It's a shame. Harry Trader might be a crook, but he ain't no villain. He used to slip me the odd halfcrown whenever he came to the soup kitchen. I've tried asking Perry about my Ted, but he's always vague. You'd think, being cousins, he'd try a bit harder to get Ted's sentence shortened. He only stole because we was desperate.'

'I know, Ivy.' Kate gave her a hug. 'I'm sure that Perry is doing everything he can for Ted and for Harry.' She sat back against the squabs with Nellie nestled against her, while May and Frankie grew bored and began to squabble, receiving a sharp rebuke from their mother.

It was only a short ride to Warren House, but Kate was eager for it to end, and she alighted the moment the barouche came to a halt. She waited until the carriage passed her before walking off in the direction of the gardener's cottage on the far side of the grounds.

Morrison answered her knock on the door. 'I was expecting you, miss. The master is in the front parlour.'

'Thank you, Morrison.' Kate handed him the bundle. 'I thought these might help to keep you warm when it gets colder — I noticed that your muffler is a little threadbare.'

His eyes filled with tears. 'I ain't had a present since me wife passed away ten year since. Thank

270

you, miss. Much appreciated, I'm sure.'

Kate smiled. 'You're a very important member of staff, Morrison. You've done wonders in the garden, especially now you have more help.'

'I can't thank you enough for hiring the extra men, miss. My old back ain't what it used to be, but I've got a lifetime of gardening knowledge, I just haven't got the strength I used to have.'

'But your experience is invaluable, Morrison. I'm sure Sir Harry has told you that often enough.'

'He was always a good lad, even when he was very young.'

'His presence must be kept secret. No one must know, not even Lady Lyndon.'

'Wild horses wouldn't drag the truth out of me, miss.'

Kate smiled as she entered the small front parlour. Its shabby furnishings and peeling wallpaper matched Harry's scruffy appearance, although she could tell that he had attempted to wash some of the prison grime from his hands and face.

'Well, you look a sorry sight, Sir Harry Lyndon,' Kate said, laughing.

'Thank you, Kate. That makes me feel very much better.'

'I think you need a change of clothes. Do you keep any at the house?'

'Yes, that's one thing I was going to ask you to do for me. You'll find a large clothes press in my dressing room, which is off the master bedroom. Who sleeps there now?'

'I do, but I haven't bothered to look closely at what's in the smaller room. I'm usually so tired that I fall into bed at night and go straight to sleep.'

271

'You're sleeping in my bed, Kate,' Harry said with a wry smile.

She turned away, uncomfortably aware that she was blushing. 'It's very comfortable,' she said in an attempt to sound casual. 'But never mind that. What do you want me to bring you?'

'A couple of changes of clothing will do. I'll come round to the back of the house at midnight. I know the servants go to bed early and I doubt if anyone else will be up and about at that time. If you could fill a valise with my things I'd be your slave for ever.'

She could hear the laughter in his voice and she turned back to face him. 'You might think all this is funny, Harry, but I want to know what your being here might mean to the rest of the family. Do you think that Monks and his men might try to find you?'

'It's possible, but I don't intend to remain here for very long.'

Kate sank down on an armchair, which sagged in the middle. One leg was slightly shorter than the others, so it rocked dangerously, but she was too interested in what Harry had to say to worry about a rickety seat. 'Why? Where are you going? I'm not helping you until you tell me exactly how we stand and what you're planning.'

'If you're afraid that the police will come looking for me — don't worry. My escape from prison was done with their full knowledge, but it must be kept secret. Monks will have a false sense of security if he thinks I am still incarcerated. The net is closing in around him.'

'Does he know that you own this estate?'

'I haven't lived here for years.'

'I don't know why, Harry. I love Warren House and it's a wonderful family home.'

'I was happy here as a child, but when my father gambled everything away, I set my sights on restoring the family fortunes. I do keep an eye on the old place and visit from time to time.'

'Martha was keeping ready for your return with every room clean and aired. She's a jewel of a housekeeper, and Arthur has done his best, too.'

'I know I'm very lucky to have such loyal servants. One day, maybe, I might decide to come and live here and enjoy the quiet life, but not yet.'

'You could hide out here, Harry. Morrison won't say anything, and neither would I.'

'It would be inviting trouble. Someone might see me and then it would be all round the village. Above all, I want to keep my family safe, and that includes you and Lady Martin.'

'I understand. Where will you go?'

Harry hesitated, meeting her anxious gaze in a way that made her fear the worst. 'If I tell you, I want you to keep it a secret.'

'Of course I will. You can trust me, Harry.'

'Some of my clients were men with influence in high places, some of them in the military. I learned that Annie's brother, Joseph Blythe, was badly wounded in the uprising. I intend to bring him home, but I don't want Annie to be told. The poor girl had enough to contend with.'

'You're going to India?'

'I'm travelling on a troop ship, which leaves tomorrow.'

'I wish I could come with you.'

Harry put his head on one side, giving her a searching look. 'Is it that you desire my company, Kate? Or are you still hankering after that Indian soldier?'

'I need to know if Ashok has survived. Is that so terrible? If it's at all possible will you make enquiries for me?'

'I'll do what I can, but I can't promise anything.'

17

At midnight Kate waited on the terrace with a valise packed with Harry's clothes. It was a cold, clear night and the moon hung like a golden guinea in a translucent dark blue sky, pierced with pin-pricks of starlight. After a while she heard a rustle of leaves in the shrubbery and Harry emerged.

'Thank you, Kate. I won't forget this,' he said as he took the case from her hand. 'I've decided to go now and not leave it until daybreak.'

'But how will you travel?'

'I left my horse in the paddock and the tack in Morrison's cottage. I can't promise anything, Kate, but I'll make enquiries about Subedar-Major Patel. I know he means a lot to you.'

'Thank you, Harry.'

He took both her hands in his and for once his expression was serious without a hint of a smile.

'There's always a touch of sadness in your beautiful eyes. If I could banish that for ever I'd be a happy man.'

'I don't know what you mean,' Kate said hastily.

'You left your heart in Delhi — I know that. I can't take you with me, but if I can find Ashok Patel I will.'

'You'd do that for me?'

The smile returned to his ocean-blue eyes. 'I'd do a great deal more, but I know I have to lay his ghost to rest first.' He took her in his arms and kissed her. She found herself kissing him with equal passion.

'I will return, Kate.' He turned on his heel and within seconds was lost in the darkness of the shrubbery.

Kate stood very still, listening to his muffled footsteps on the soft mud and leaves, until she could only hear the sighing of the wind in the trees. Even now she could hardly believe what she had just heard. It was not an outright declaration of love, and yet it had felt as though Harry was laying his heart before her. She retreated to the privacy of her bedroom, but even then she could not escape from Harry Lyndon. The knowledge that she was sleeping in his bed, and that everything in it belonged to him was disturbing, and yet oddly exciting. When she climbed into the four-poster, with its matching tester and brocade curtains, it felt almost sinful. She cuddled down in the blissful softness of the feather mattress and pulled the coverlet up to her chin.

Harry was well able to look after himself. He was heading into danger for the sake of another, and he was prepared to risk even more for her sake. She could still smell the masculine scent of him, despite the lingering prison odour, and the kiss, although brief, still burned on her lips. It felt as though she was being unfaithful to Ashok, although she knew in her heart that their love had been doomed from the start. Even so, she needed to know that he was safe and well, and, even more surprising, Harry knew that without her telling him. She closed her eyes and drifted into a deep sleep.

Despite Kate's worries for Harry's safety during the long sea voyage to India, and what might happen to him when he arrived there, life went on as usual at Warren House. No one, apart from Morrison, knew that Harry had come home, albeit briefly, and Kate doubted if anyone other than his mother and Annie would have been very interested. As far as Kate's mother was concerned, Harry was the cause of all their problems and she would be delighted to see him sail away into danger.

Arabella was basking in the success of the fund raising for the children's party while Martha and Ivy worked tirelessly to keep the house in order. Arthur, in his own phlegmatic way, kept an eye on the work outside and also the stables, as Goodfellow was now openly courting Widow Parker. Kate had never seen Goodfellow so cheerful or so neat and tidy, and he was now clean-shaven, where once he had sported a huge, drooping ginger moustache. Martha was very critical, pursing her lips and tut-tutting over the widow's influence on a middle-aged man. Kate was on Marie Parker's side, but she had the good sense not to argue with Martha. The only person who seemed unhappy with the match was Warrender, Lady Lyndon's coachman, who normally kept himself to himself, but he had obviously a fancy for Mrs Parker too, and he strutted around the stable yard, puffing out his chest and flexing his muscles every time the widow was present. Kate imagined him like a cockerel in the farmyard, exhibiting his charms to a particularly attractive hen.

Lady Lyndon had made friends with some of the well-to-do ladies who had contributed so much hard work to the event in the church hall. She received invitations to their grand houses at least three times a week, and she responded in kind. Kate was always wary of entering the drawing room in the afternoons in case she interrupted a group of Lady Lyndon's friends with their heads together, most likely gossiping about the unfortunate person who was not present that day.

Annie had taken a liking to Hedley Courtney and when she discovered that he knew her brother, Joseph, having met him in Bombay, she was ecstatic. Kate knew how fond Annie was of her brother and the knowledge that Joe was badly wounded weighed heavily on her mind. She was always very careful when talking to Annie, knowing that a slip of the tongue might plunge the poor blind girl into a state of panic. On the occasions when Annie visited the vicarage she was always accompanied by Kate, who sat quietly, paying little attention to Annie and Hedley's conversation. Inevitably her thoughts strayed to her time in Delhi. She read accounts in the newspapers about the dreadful events in the uprising, and she knew she should be grateful for having escaped. She was desperate for news of Ashok and now she also had Harry to worry about. He had left her in a state of confusion as to her true feelings. Before she met Harry she had been clear in her mind that there was only one man in her life. Now she was not so sure.

In order to take her mind off the worries that

haunted her dreams, Kate threw herself into preparations for Christmas. It would be the first time that she had had young children to think about and a large surrogate family to care for. She ordered the carriage and, taking Jenny with her, she set off for a day out in the West End, where there were exciting new shops opening up in Wigmore Street and Oxford Street. But after buying presents for everyone, Kate felt guilty for spending so much money on luxuries, and they visited a soup kitchen in Leicester Square to give a donation. It was an enjoyable day out, but both Kate and Jenny were glad to return to the peace and quiet of Walthamstow.

Goodfellow was unusually cheerful during the drive and Kate was quick to notice the sprig of holly stuck in his hatband. When they arrived back at Warren House, Kate could not resist the temptation to quiz him on his good humour.

Goodfellow handed her down from the carriage. 'To tell the truth, Miss Kate, I'm to be married on Christmas Eve. The vicar has agreed to perform the ceremony in the morning. I'm the happiest man in the world.'

'Congratulations, Goodfellow,' Kate said, smiling. 'Have you made any arrangements for the wedding breakfast?'

'No, miss. Me and Marie were going to the village pub to celebrate with a few friends.'

'Nonsense, Goodfellow. You must bring them here. We'll do it in style. What do you say?'

His cheeks reddened and it was not just from the cold east wind. 'Thank you, miss. Marie will be so happy. Neither of us has got any family — at least none that live nearby, and the rest of them don't speak to us — so we'd be honoured to have our wedding feast here.'

Jenny climbed down to the ground and shook his hand. 'Congratulations, Mr Goodfellow. I can't wait to tell Ma and Mrs Boggis. Ivy will be pleased for you, I'm sure. A party at Warren House on Christmas Eve — who would have thought it?'

★ ★ ★

To Kate's surprise, it seemed that everyone in Warren House was delighted by the idea of a wedding on

Christmas Eve with a party to follow. Everyone, except Arabella, who made it plain that she thought it extravagant and unnecessary. To act in such a manner towards a servant, especially a coachman, would create a precedent and all the staff would expect similar treatment. However, Lady Lyndon was enthusiastic and so was Annie, who offered to provide a musical accompaniment to the wedding breakfast. Martha and Ivy set about making lists of the ingredients they would need to make a feast more suitable for a prince than a coachman, as Kate was adamant that no expense should be spared. It was time that the old house was filled with people who were enjoying themselves.

Christmas was a time for happiness and a wedding was always a joyous occasion, or nearly always. Kate remembered seeing a wedding party in Delhi where the bride and groom had not met until the day of the ceremony. She had noted the

280

bowed head of the young girl, and she had seen tears falling onto the small, tightly clasped hands. Neither Seth Goodfellow nor his intended were in the first flush of youth, but it was obvious that they cared for each other deeply, and Kate was happy for them. She wanted their special day to be remembered for all the right reasons, and she worked hard to make it happen.

The house was decorated with boughs of holly and swags of ivy trimmed with scarlet ribbons. Vases were filled with late chrysanthemums that had survived the first frosts, and a huge Christmas tree occupied the entrance hall, reaching almost to the ceiling. The children had decorated it with brightly coloured glass balls and as much tinsel as they could lay their hands on. Frankie and May had made a silver star and Bob, the stable boy, fetched a ladder from an outside store. Balancing precariously, and cheered on by the children, he fixed the star to the top of the tree.

To add to the excitement, two days before the wedding it had started to snow. A light dusting covered the ground and iced the bare branches of the trees. Perry had joined the family for Christmas, much to Annie's delight, and Kate could not wait to get him on his own. He had barely taken off his greatcoat, hat and gloves when she managed to corner him before he made his way to the drawing room.

'Perry, I want a word with you,' Kate said urgently. He came to a halt. 'What's wrong?'

'Nothing, or at least I hope everything is going well. Have the police caught Monks and his gang?'

'A couple of his men have been apprehended

281

and are awaiting trial, but Monks himself is a slippery character. He's yet to be detained.' 'What do you know of Harry?'

He eyed her warily. 'It all depends on what you mean?'

'Don't play games with me, Perry. You must know that he was released early.'

'Can we talk about this later?' Perry glanced over her shoulder. 'Your mother is on the staircase. I doubt if you want her to know your business.'

'All right. Later then, but I want the full story from you, Perry. I don't like being kept in the dark.'

'Always so impatient.' He patted her on the shoulder as he retraced his steps towards the staircase. 'Lady Martin, how charming you look today. Country air seems to suit you so well.'

Arabella descended the last three steps with the grace of long practice. 'Perry, how lovely to see you. Are you spending the whole of Christmas with us?'

He proffered his arm. 'Yes, I am. London is cold, foggy and dirty. At least it's much cleaner in the country.'

'A few months ago I would have said that's the only advantage of country living, but I find I'm growing quite used to it. I have more friends and acquaintances here than I did in London.'

'I'm very glad to hear it.'

Kate could see that Perry was working his charm on her mother, as usual. She smiled. 'Do come to the drawing room, Mama. It's cold in the hallway.'

'Yes, of course.' Arabella smiled graciously.

282

'I'm even growing used to the Lyndon woman, although I'll never forgive that son of hers for putting us in this situation.'

'You seem to be bearing up heroically, ma'am,' Perry said smoothly. 'When all the villains are behind bars I'm sure you will wish to return to Finsbury Square. I've kept an eye on the house, and the servants who are left are doing a splendid job of keeping the place clean and aired.'

'I should hope so.' Arabella tossed her head. 'It's costing Kate a fortune to keep both households going. She's very generous with the money that should have come to her late father.'

'Mama, please don't bring that subject up again' Kate said, sighing. 'It's the festive season and we have a wedding party on Christmas Eve. At least allow us all to enjoy it without recriminations.'

'You're right, I suppose, but it still rankles, and always will. But you are very generous, I'll allow you that.'

Kate sighed as she followed them into the drawing room. She knew that her mother would never forgive her for inheriting Uncle Edgar's fortune.

★ ★ ★

The day of the wedding dawned bright and cold, with sunlight sparkling on newly fallen snow. Perry had been called back to London the previous evening for some reason that he refused to divulge, but he promised to be back in time for the reception, if not for the wedding ceremony itself. Kate was intrigued, but was too busy with last minute details to demand an explanation.

283

St Mary's church was crammed with wedding guests and well-wishers, and afterwards, in a picture book snow scene, the bride and groom were transported to Warren House in Farmer Watson's cart, which was decorated with evergreen fronds and corn dollies. The rest of the party followed in a succession of carriages, carts and on foot. Braziers placed on either side of the front entrance sent flames dancing in the still, cold air providing a warm welcome for the bridal party.

Tilly and another girl from the village were on duty to take the guests' capes, coats, cloaks and hats as they arrived, and Ivy was ready to hand out mulled wine or hot rum punch to fend off the chill. All the ground-floor rooms were open and log fires blazed up the chimneys creating warmth with the comforting scent of burning apple wood. The newly married couple seemed overwhelmed by the grandeur of the occasion, but Kate ushered them into the drawing room where Annie played them in with a rousing tune that sent feet tapping. After a few glasses of mulled wine or punch the guests, who at first were quiet and respectful, suddenly livened up, and one by one couples took the floor and were soon executing a lively jig.

Arabella sailed past Kate, who was standing in the doorway, enjoying the spectacle of Mr Ruggles, the shopkeeper, capering around like a spring lamb in an attempt to impress Emily, Dora Sloan's spinster daughter. Dora's plans to marry off the plain and awkward Emily had so far failed miserably, but it looked to Kate as if success might be in sight. Perhaps if Emily drank a glass or two of mulled wine she might relax enough to smile and enjoy herself. She might even flirt a little, with encouragement from Cyrus Ruggles. That would give Dora something to talk about when she was in a huddle with her friends.

'They've turned the house into a bear garden,' Arabella said crossly. 'I'm going to the morning parlour.'

'I think you'll find it occupied, Mama,' Kate said in a whisper. 'You'll find almost every room downstairs has been taken over by the wedding party.'

Arabella tossed her head. 'I'm going to my room then. Send Jenny up with a bowl of soup and a slice of bread and butter. I can feel one of my headaches coming on.'

Kate glanced over her shoulder. 'But, Mama, Mrs Courtney is coming this way. Who is that with her?'

Arabella's pale cheeks flamed with colour. 'Oh, my goodness. It's Mr Pomeroy-Smith. Why on earth would Elaine bring him here today of all days? Especially when I'm not feeling my best.'

Kate turned to see the man who had made her mother blush, and was pleasantly surprised. She had never met Giles Pomeroy-Smith, but everyone in the neighbourhood knew of him and his philanthropic works. His family had once owned several mills on the banks of the River Lea and had made a fortune in milling flax seeds for linseed oil. The mills had been sold long ago, but the money had been invested by one of his forebears, who had more than doubled the family fortunes. Kate was not impressed by wealth or position, but Giles Pomeroy-Smith was a good-looking, mature man, with an impressive presence and a charming smile. Kate could see now why he was considered to be the county's most eligible bachelor, and from the look on her mother's face, it was obvious that she was of the same opinion.

'Arabella, there you are,' Elaine cried delightedly. 'I think the whole village has turned out to wish the happy couple well.'

'We certainly have a houseful,' Arabella said drily.

'I don't think you've met my dear friend Giles, have you, Arabella?'

Arabella shook her head mutely.

'How good of you to come, sir.' Kate stepped forward, seeing that her mother was suddenly struck dumb. 'Welcome to Warren House.'

Elaine shot a warning glance in Kate's direction. 'Arabella, may I introduce Giles Pomeroy-Smith? Giles, this is my dear friend Lady Martin.'

Arabella extended her hand and Giles held it briefly, bowing to her with a smile that would have melted the coldest heart.

'How do you do, Lady Martin? It's a pleasure to meet you. Elaine has told me all about your charitable work in the village.'

'How do you do, Mr Pomeroy-Smith?' Arabella fluttered her eyelashes. 'You are something of a legend locally.'

Kate cleared her throat. 'I'm Kate Martin, sir. How do you do?'

She received icy stares from her mother and Elaine, but Giles Pomeroy-Smith turned to Kate with a twinkle in his dark eyes.

'How do you do, Miss Martin? I believe I've

286

seen you riding round the village on a chestnut gelding.'

'Yes, indeed. I find the whole area very interesting, and I've been studying the history of Walthamstow.'

'I have an extensive library at Pomeroy Park. You're welcome to use it at any time, Miss Martin.'

Kate inclined her head. 'Thank you, sir. That's very kind.'

'Haven't you things to do, Kate?' Arabella said pointedly.

'Yes, of course, Mama. You'll excuse me, I need to make sure that the food is being laid out in the dining room. Otherwise we might have a riot on our hands if the guests get too hungry.'

Giles chuckled. 'The cold weather certainly whets the appetite. Perhaps you and your mama would accept an invitation to dine at Pomeroy Park in the near future?' He glanced at Elaine, who was beginning to pout. 'That includes you and Humphrey, of course.'

'Thank you, Giles. We always enjoy dining with you. Pomeroy Park is a beautiful house, Arabella.'

Kate did not wait to hear the rest of the conversation. She was pleased, although slightly surprised, by her mother's obvious attraction to Giles Pomeroy-Smith. Although Mama was officially still in deep mourning, perhaps meeting someone new was exactly what she needed. Burying one's heart in the grave might sound romantic, but Kate wanted her mother to be happy, and if Giles was the man who could make her mother smile again, he was heaven sent. Kate made her way to the kitchen where she found Martha brandishing a carving knife at Frankie, who had jam smeared all round his mouth.

'What's the matter, Martha?'

Martha bristled like an angry hedgehog. 'That young monkey has been stealing the jam tarts. I made them special, like, because I know that Goodfellow has a fancy for them.'

'You do make delicious pastry, Martha,' Kate said diplomatically. 'And your strawberry jam is the best I've ever tasted.'

'Yes,' Frankie murmured, nodding. 'I'm sorry, Mrs Boggis. I gave way to temptation.'

'Just like your pa did, I suppose.' Martha glared at him. 'That's what landed him in the clink, boy. That's where you'll end up if you carry on like that.'

'I burned me mouth on the hot jam.' Frankie's blue eyes filled with tears. 'I'm very sorry.'

'There, you see, Martha. Frankie has had his punishment. A burned tongue is very painful, and he's apologised twice.'

Martha tossed her head. 'Serve him right. That's what I say. He can help by taking the rest of these platters into the dining room, and heaven help him if he pinches any more food.'

'I'll make sure it doesn't happen.' Kate picked up a dish of cold meats and handed it to Frankie, safe in the knowledge that he had a sweet tooth. 'You take that one, Frankie, and I'll take the salver of cold roast beef and lamb.' She ushered him out of the kitchen before Martha could think up a more suitable punishment.

With the food safely delivered to the dining table, Kate sent Frankie to the stables to help Bob with the guests' horses. Frankie had shown promise as a groom and Goodfellow had been more than happy to teach him the rudiments of grooming and tacking up. Such training would serve him well if and when the family returned to London. There was always work to be found in stables, both private and commercial. So far there had been no news of Ted's release from prison, although Perry promised he would keep them informed. He was due to arrive at any moment and Kate could only hope that he might have something positive to tell Ivy.

She was just putting the last touches to the festive dining table when Jenny burst into the room. 'Lady Lyndon sent me to look for you, miss. It's getting a bit rowdy out there and someone just broke one of her ladyship's favourite ornaments.'

'Oh dear!' Kate glanced at the dainty ormolu clock on the mantelshelf. 'I think it's time we announced that luncheon is served. We'll get the bride and groom in first and the others can follow.'

'I've laid up an extra table in the morning parlour,' Jenny said, chuckling. 'There'll be a stampede when I tell them that the grub's up.'

Kate laughed. 'I wouldn't put it quite like that Perhaps we'd better let them come in in groups, so that there isn't a terrible scramble for the food.'

'Leave it to me, miss. My pa was a soldier so mustering is in my blood.'

'Mrs Marsh has never mentioned him,' Kate said thoughtfully. 'At least not in my presence.'

'He was lost to us when I was a nipper.'

'I'm so sorry, Jenny. Was he killed in action?'

'No, miss. He run off with a barmaid from Kent.'

Kate was trying to think of something suitable to say when Ivy rushed into the dining room.

'Things are getting very rowdy, Kate. And I think Mr Harte's just arrived. I spotted what looked like his chaise pulling up to the front entrance.'

Kate threw up her hands. 'All right. First things first. Let's get the bride and groom in here and then the rest of the party. I'll go and meet Perry at the door.'

Ivy and Jenny hurried off and Kate made her way through the groups of very merry wedding guests to fling the door open. On such an occasion it would have been useful to have Henry here, but they had left him in charge at Finsbury Square. She lifted the latch and opened the door to see Perry leap down from the driver's seat, followed more slowly by another man.

Perry came bounding up the steps, grinning widely. 'Look who I've brought with me, Kate. This will be the best Christmas present of all.'

18

Kate eyed the man warily. He was unshaven, his clothes were those of a working man, and judging by the smell emanating from him, neither he nor his garments were too clean.

'I know you, don't I?' Kate said cautiously.

'This is my cousin, Ted Harris. I brought him straight here from prison, Kate. He was released this morning, which is why I went to London last evening. I hope you don't mind.'

Kate glanced at Ted, who was standing behind Perry, looking dishevelled and very wary. She managed a smile. 'You're very welcome, Ted. Come inside out of the cold.'

'Thank you, miss.' Ted followed Perry into the entrance hall and Kate shut the door.

'I'm sure you'd like to greet Ivy in private,' Kate said gently. 'If you'll take him to the winter parlour, Perry, I'll go and fetch Ivy. As you can see, it's all a bit chaotic here today.'

She stood aside as a rather drunken man, whom she recognised as Joss Clarke, the butcher, lurched past her and let himself out through the front door. His wife came to a halt in front of Kate, her round face flushed and beads of perspiration standing out on her forehead.

'I'm sorry, Miss Martin. My Joss can't hold his liquor like he used to. I do apologise.'

'That's quite all right, Mrs Clarke,' Kate said hastily. 'Perhaps you'd better go out and make sure he's all right. If you take him round to the kitchen I'm sure Mrs Boggis will give him some strong coffee.'

'Yes, miss. Thank you.' Mrs Clarke bobbed a curtsey before wrenching the door open. 'Joss Clarke, just you wait until I get you home...' She slammed the door.

'Come with me, Ted.' Perry beckoned to Ted, who hunched his shoulders and hurried after him, leaving Kate to go and break the news to Ivy.

* * *

The news that her husband was waiting for her in the winter parlour caused Ivy to collapse in tears. Kate wrapped her arms around her and gave her a hug.

'You're not teasing me, are you, Kate?'

'No, I promise you it's true. Anyway, I wouldn't be so cruel. He's here and he's been released a bit early, maybe because it's Christmas, or perhaps Perry had a hand in it. Wipe your eyes and go to him.'

Ivy sniffed and blew her nose on a hanky she produced from her apron pocket. 'He won't have any clothes with him. What shall I do?'

'Don't worry about anything. I know where Harry left perfectly good garments and they'll probably fit Ted. Do you want me to send the children to you?'

'Not yet. But what about the party? I should be helping.'

'Nonsense. You've done more than your share of work. Go to your husband and I'll make sure

292

the children get fed. Don't worry about anything, Ivy. It's going to be a perfect Christmas.' Kate shooed Ivy out of the pantry. It would be wonderful for the family to be reunited, but there were others who would spend Christmas apart. However, this was not the time for self-pity; she braced her shoulders and went to marshal the guests who had yet to eat into the dining room.

The platters were piled high with meat pies, sausage rolls, thick juicy slices of roast beef and pork with crisp crackling. Dora Sloan was heard to complain that she might break another tooth but that did not seem to stop her from taking several slices of pork and a great dollop of apple sauce. There were mounds of crusty bread rolls, freshly baked that morning. Kate had smelled the delicious aroma when she awakened. Martha must have been working since the early hours to produce such a feast with only Ivy and Tilly to help her. Despite her dislike for children and her tendency to grumble about everything, Martha was a hard worker and she put her heart and soul into her cooking. The result was obvious as the wedding guests, having demolished most of the savoury offerings, stuffed themselves with cake and plied the young children with shivery red jellies and silky white blancmange.

Giles Pomeroy-Smith and Perry joined in, taking their meal with the villagers, but Arabella, Lady Lyndon and Annie remained in the drawing room, and there was no sign of Ivy or her husband. The children had sensed that something was going on and reluctantly Kate had sent them to the winter parlour. They had emerged joyfully, but also very hungry and were now seated on the stairs, eating off one plate, with May making sure that the younger ones had their fair share. Kate took the opportunity to go upstairs to her bedroom where she rifled through the clothes press in the dressing room, going through Harry's things in search of suitable garments for Ted. She unfolded each item, holding it close to her cheek and inhaling the faint scent that would always remind her of Harry. Their relationship had gone through many changes since they met less than a year ago; her initial distrust of him had given way to grudging liking, and that had deepened into something more. She could not put her finger on her exact feelings for Harry Lyndon, but his parting kiss still burned her lips.

The smoky, peaty scent of his old tweed jacket brought unexpected tears to her eyes. Harry was heading into danger, not only from the hazardous sea voyage, but also from any pockets of insurgents that he might come across in India. The newspapers had published articles declaring that the rebellion had been crushed, but Kate was wary of believing everything she read in print. She folded the items she had chosen into a bundle, and closed the door on the dressing room — that was Harry's domain and one day he would come home to reclaim his position as master of the house. Even so, she wished that he was here now to share Christmas with them.

She made her way downstairs to the winter parlour where she found Ivy and Ted seated side by side on the small sofa, holding hands. 'I think these might fit you, Ted.' Kate set the bundle down on the nearest chair.

'Thank you for looking after Ivy and the nippers, miss.' Ted gave his wife a hug. 'She's a diamond is my Ivy.'

'I wouldn't argue with that,' Kate said, smiling. 'And I'd say that Ivy looked after me, not the reverse. She is a wonderful woman and that's the truth.'

Ivy's sallow complexion bloomed pink and she giggled. 'Stop it, both of you. I just done what I had to do. It was the children what kept me going.'

'Well, from now on I'll take care of you all.' Ted rose from the sofa. 'I don't know how I'll manage it, but I'll find work and we'll get somewhere to live.'

'Like I said before you come in, Kate, I expect our old house has been let to someone else.' Ivy sighed, shaking her head. 'We had to come away in such a hurry, and I couldn't afford the rent now that the soup kitchen is closed.'

Kate stared at her in dismay. 'You should have told me that, Ivy. I'd have paid it for you. But what about your possessions? Will they have gone, too?'

'The furniture, such as it was, come with the house,' Ivy said, with a wry smile. 'We brought with us what we needed most and what was left was only fit for the rubbish heap. I don't mind saying goodbye to Nightingale Lane.'

'I'm sure we can arrange something, but there's plenty of time.' Kate moved to the door and opened it. 'I'm going back to the wedding party, but tomorrow is Christmas Day. It's time to enjoy ourselves and be thankful for what we have, and the people who are dear to us.'

She stepped out into the corridor. She had meant what she said. There was plenty of work still to be done in the grounds of Warren House and she was prepared to pay Ted, should he be willing to join forces with Morrison. Maybe he could take over when the old man decided to retire? Perhaps she could find a cottage nearby for the family to rent. There were always answers to problems; you just had to find them. With that in mind Kate went to the dining room where the bride and groom were preparing to cut the cake that Martha and Ivy had baked and decorated with glacé fruit and nuts.

Outside the light was already fading and the snow was falling again, only this time it was heavier and settling fast. Kate realised that the guests needed to leave right away, but she hesitated, not wanting to spoil the happy couple's moment.

The cake was sliced and handed out, but when everyone shouted, 'Speech!' Goodfellow declined.

'I've just looked out of the window, my friends. I think maybe we should call it a day or some of you won't be able to get home. It looks like we might have a blizzard later and I'm sure that Lady Lyndon don't want to have us all sleeping here on the floor.'

'Anyway, it's Christmas Eve and I expect you all want to get home,' Kate added quickly before anyone had the nerve to argue. There was a sudden hush and even the tipsiest of the guests nodded blearily, agreeing that they had better leave before the snowstorm made the lanes impassable.

Kate went to the drawing room where she discovered that Lady Lyndon had fallen asleep over a glass of port. Arabella was all smiles as she chatted to Giles Pomeroy-Smith and it seemed a pity to disturb them. This left Kate little choice other than to act as hostess and she stationed herself at the front door, shaking hands with everyone as they left and wishing them a very merry Christmas. The last to leave were the vicar and his wife, although Hedley was lingering at the far end of the entrance hall, deep in conversation with Jenny.

'Hedley, we're leaving now,' Elaine called impatiently. 'Come along do, or we'll be snowed in.'

With obvious reluctance, Hedley joined his parents at the front entrance.

'What were you doing, Hedley? We don't consort with servants.' Elaine wrapped her cloak around her, pulling the hood up so that only her nose was visible. 'I'm sorry, Mama, but I like her,' Hedley said sulkily.

'Don't answer back to your mama,' Humphrey countered. 'You know very well how to behave fitting your position, Hedley. An officer and a gentleman would not encourage a servant to think more highly of themselves than they should.'

'I'm surprised to hear you say so, Vicar.' Kate could keep silent no longer. 'Jenny is a very nice, kind and intelligent young woman. Any man would be very fortunate to earn her good opinion.'

'That is very impertinent, Miss Martin,' Elaine said, bristling. 'I'll ask you to mind your own business.'

'No, Mama.' Hedley faced his mother with a stubborn lift of his chin. 'I have been ill and Jenny has made me feel better. She listens to me and she understands how I feel.'

'Has this liaison been going on for long?' Humphrey's voice echoed around the high ceiling of the entrance hall, causing the remaining guests to stop and stare.

'It is not a liaison, Papa,' Hedley said firmly. 'I have been fortunate enough to earn the good opinion of a lovely young woman, and I rejoice in the fact.'

Kate cleared her throat. 'Perhaps this conversation would be better continued at home, Hedley?'

He nodded. 'Yes, you're right, and I'm sorry if it's embarrassed anyone present.' He turned to his father. 'I will be returning to my regiment as soon as possible, Papa, but before that I hope to persuade Miss Marsh to marry me and accompany me on my next tour of duty.'

'The de Courtneys came to England with William the Conqueror, Hedley. You can't sully the family name by marrying a servant.' Elaine held up her hand for silence when Hedley looked as though he were about to argue. 'We'll talk about this at home. Open the door, Humphrey. We're leaving.'

Kate patted Hedley on the shoulder. 'Well said, and congratulations. At least I hope that you and Jenny will be very happy, should she be prepared to take on the role of army wife. She's a wonderful girl and I value her as a friend.'

Hedley smiled, looking almost handsome. 'I know that. She speaks very highly of you.' He squeezed Kate's hand. 'I have to go now, but I'll return as soon as I can. Please tell Jenny that for me.' He glanced over Kate's shoulder to where Jenny was standing at the far end of the hall. He blew her a kiss before following his parents out into the swirling snow.

Kate had to see several other couples out before she managed to speak to Jenny, who was clearing the table in the dining room.

'Is it true about you and Hedley?'

Jenny's cheeks reddened. 'I know I'm not in his class, but we get along so well it doesn't seem wrong.'

'Of course it's not wrong, Jenny. You are as good as he is, if not better.'

'I don't think that Mrs Courtney, or the vicar, would agree with you.'

'Well, they should be grateful that someone cares about their son. He's been through a bad time.'

'He might be a little awkward, miss, but he's got a kind heart and he makes me laugh.'

Kate eyed her thoughtfully. 'He told his parents that he wants to marry you.'

'I didn't know that he felt so deeply. We've only seen each other a few times on our own, and we do get along splendidly. I blame his parents for his condition. His mother bullies him and so does his father.'

'Would you consider being an army wife?'

'Yes, I think I would. Of course I wouldn't want to leave you and Ma, but I think I do love Hedley.'

'You must be absolutely certain, Jenny. As you admitted, you hardly know him.'

'If Mrs Courtney has anything to do with it, that's the last I'll see of Hedley. There are some things you can't fight, and a housekeeper's daughter is not a good match for the son of a vicar who can trace their family back to the Norman Conquest.' Jenny moved aside as a group of happy wedding guests pushed past them, laughing and joking about driving home in snow.

'Merry Christmas, Miss Martin.' Farmer Ball tipped his cap and guided his wife towards the door with their children trailing after them.

'Lovely wedding, dearie,' Mrs Ball said with a drunken grin. 'I haven't enjoyed meself so much since I don't know when.'

Farmer Ball rolled his eyes. 'Come on, love. Let's get you home before we're snowed in.'

Kate stood aside as the rest of the party wandered past her, some of them singing and others more intent on wrapping themselves up warm to face the blizzard.

Giles Pomeroy-Smith shook her by the hand. 'It was a wonderful wedding party, Kate. Your mama must be very proud of you.'

Kate smiled and nodded, but she knew that her mother would find something to criticise. 'It was good of you to come, Mr Pomeroy-Smith.'

'Giles, please. I hope to visit again in the very near future.'

'You would be welcome to join us for Christmas dinner tomorrow, sir. That is unless you have family waiting for you at home.'

'I was too busy adding to the fortune I had inherited to consider marriage. Alas, I am a single man with little to show for my efforts other than a country estate and the trappings of wealth.'

'Then I hope you'll accept my invitation. I know my mother would be delighted to have your company.'

300

'I accept with gratitude.' He raised her hand to his lips. 'Please tell your mother that I look forward to furthering our acquaintance.' He bowed and followed a group of merrymakers out into the cold night. There were a few stragglers, who all thanked Kate for a wonderful party, and last of all came Mr and Mrs Goodfellow.

Seth grasped both Kate's hands in his. 'You'll excuse the familiarity, Miss Martin, but we both wanted to thank you for a splendid wedding party. You've done us proud and we're both very grateful.'

Kate shook his outstretched hand. 'You deserved it, Goodfellow. I hope you're both very happy.'

'They'll be talking about this in the village for months to come,' Marie Goodfellow said happily. 'The only thing is that I've got to leave my cottage, but I'll have to pay the rent until the land agent finds another tenant.'

'That doesn't seem fair,' Kate said, frowning. 'Who owns the property, Mrs Goodfellow?'

'Mrs Goodfellow!' Marie doubled up with laughter. 'I've been Widow Parker for nearly ten years, so Mrs Goodfellow sounds very odd, but good,' she added hastily.

'Who is your landlord?' Kate repeated patiently as a germ of an idea came into her head.

'I believe it belongs to the Church,' Goodfellow said solemnly. 'We was going to ask the vicar if he'd let Marie off paying the rent.'

'How many bedrooms does it have, Mrs Goodfellow?'

Marie puffed out her chest. 'Three all told, and a small attic room. It were a good size when the late Mr Parker rented it for us. We was going to fill the bedrooms with nippers, but it never happened.'

'I think I might have the ideal tenants for your cottage, Mrs Goodfellow. I'll have a word with the vicar after church tomorrow morning, so don't worry.'

'Thank you, miss. I'd be ever so grateful. I had to take in washing to keep up with the rent, and mending, too. I'll be quite a lady of leisure now I'm married to Seth.'

Goodfellow slipped his arm around her ample waist and kissed her on the cheek. 'Come on, love. Let's go home.'

Kate closed the door with some difficulty as a strong wind hurled snow around like a hooligan intent on making mischief. As she made her way back to the drawing room Kate could hear Annie playing carols on her concertina with the children singing the words at the tops of their voices. It was going to be a happy Christmas, but maybe some people would be happier than others.

★ ★ ★

After church on Christmas morning, Kate complimented the vicar on his sermon before broaching the subject of Marie Goodfellow's cottage.

Humphrey's bland smile faded. 'You want me to rent Church property to a former felon?'

'Yes, I do,' Kate said firmly. 'Your brilliant sermon on love and forgiveness really touched my heart, Vicar. Ted Harris is not a bad man. He was desperate for money to feed his family when he

302

committed the crime. He has served his time and surely he deserves a chance to rebuild his life?'

'Yes, of course, but the cottage is my responsibility, and with a family that large there is the possibility of damage to the fabric of the building.'

'The children have been living with us at Warren House for several months now. We've had minor breakages but nothing very serious, and I will undertake to pay for any repairs that are necessary. I can say that with complete confidence, Vicar. Surely, on this holy day, it would be a wonderful thing to give the family a home?'

'Well,' he said doubtfully. 'If you put it like that, I suppose . . .'

'Humphrey.' Elaine abandoned a group of her friends and came hurrying towards them. 'What are you talking about? If it's to do with my son . . .'

'No,' Kate said hastily. 'This has nothing to do with Hedley. I was speaking to Mr Courtney about a Church matter.'

'Yes, my dear, a Church matter,' Humphrey agreed nervously.

'We always discuss such things before making a decision,' Elaine said firmly. 'Anyway, it's Christmas Day and not the time for talking business. Come along, Humphrey, there are people waiting to speak to you. You'll excuse us, Miss Martin.'

Kate managed a smile. 'Of course. Perhaps I could speak to you tomorrow, Vicar?'

'We are very busy for the next few days.' Elaine tucked her hand into the crook of her husband's arm. 'Come, my dear. Another time, Miss Martin.' She led her husband away and they were immediately surrounded by an eager crowd of worshippers.

Kate could see that she would get nowhere with the vicar if his wife had anything to do with it, and she decided it was time to call upon the senior members of the household. Kate was only too well aware that Elaine Courtney fancied herself as the leader of everything in the village, but there was one thing she could not argue with — a title. Lady Martin and Lady Lyndon were a force to be reckoned with.

★ ★ ★

That evening, after a splendid festive meal followed by the opening of gifts that Kate had placed under the Christmas tree, Ted, Ivy and the children retired to the winter parlour where a fire had been lit earlier that day. Kate had suggested they might like to spend some time as a family and both parents had agreed, although Ivy was worried that it might seem rude and ungrateful, but Kate had reassured her. Perry and Annie were seated together by the fire, with Annie doing most of the talking and Perry listening with a rapt expression on his face. Kate smiled, but there was an ache in her heart. She could not help wondering what Christmas would have been like if Harry had not answered the call of duty, but she put all such thoughts behind her as she approached her mother and Lady Lyndon.

For once, upholding the spirit of the day, they were seated side by side on the sofa, talking as if they were old friends.

'Ladies,' Kate said, smiling, 'I need your help.'

'Really? That's the first time in your life you've ever admitted that you were at a loss,' Arabella said, frowning. 'It must be something momentous.'

'Of course I'd be willing to do anything you ask, Kate.' Lady Lyndon beamed at her and took another sip of port. 'What is it you want, my dear?'

Kate pulled up a chair and sat down. 'I have two problems and one of them concerns Mrs Courtney.'

Arabella and Lady Lyndon exchanged meaningful glances.

'That doesn't surprise me,' Arabella said with a wry smile. 'We get along well because she loves to be seen with a titled lady, but if I were just Mrs Martin, I doubt if she would have given me the time of day.'

'My thoughts precisely.' Lady Lyndon nodded in agreement. 'Dreadful woman. I feel sorry for her husband; he seems nice enough, if a little overbearing at times.'

'Yes, exactly.' Kate moved a little closer, lowering her voice. 'Mrs Goodfellow's cottage is vacant, and from what she told me it would be ideal for Ivy and her family, but it belongs to the Church and when I tried to broach the subject to the vicar, Mrs Courtney intervened. She made it clear that I would have to seek her approval as well, which is ridiculous.'

'Ridiculous,' Lady Lyndon echoed.

'You said there were two problems,' Arabella prompted.

'Yes, Mama. The other is perhaps more serious. It concerns Hedley and Jenny. Apparently they've become close but Mrs Courtney will have none of it. She says that the Courtney ancestors came from France at the time of the Norman Conquest and Jenny is not good enough for their son.'

'I suppose most mothers feel that way about their little boys,' Lady Lyndon said thoughtfully.

'But we're talking about Hedley.' Arabella rolled her eyes. 'He's nice enough, but the poor fellow is not right in the head.'

'He suffered a bad injury, Mama,' Kate said defensively. 'He is much better now and he wants to rejoin his regiment, taking Jenny with him as his wife.'

'Well, now.' Lady Lyndon pursed her lips. 'Let's hope the poor girl knows what she's letting herself in for.'

'Jenny is a good servant,' Arabella added. 'I don't know what her mother would say.'

Lady Lyndon placed her empty glass on a side table. 'I am more than happy to help, but what is it you want us to do, Kate?'

'Mrs Courtney respects both of you. I think if you asked her to tea on Monday it would put her in a better frame of mind towards my requests, and it would allow me to speak to the vicar without her at his side.'

'It seems simple enough.' Lady Lyndon glanced at Arabella. 'What do you think?'

'I agree. Anyway, I'm seriously considering taking over running the various committees. Elaine had better grow accustomed to asking my opinion on village matters. I've discovered I have quite a gift for organisation.'

'Then I can rely on both of you?' Kate rose

from her seat.

'Yes, my dear. And you can pour me another glass of port,' Lady Lyndon said, smiling. 'It is Christmas Day, after all.'

Kate picked up the empty glass. 'What about you, Mama?'

'I think I will indulge, Kate. I'm beginning to feel quite like my old self, and Giles has invited me to visit Pomeroy Park next week. Of course, I am still in mourning, but I'm sure that your dear papa would not want me to be miserable for ever.'

Kate filled their glasses and one for herself. She was gambling on her powers of persuasion, but she was almost certain that the vicar would see things from her point of view.

★ ★ ★

Kate's strategy worked. Without undue pressure from his wife, Humphrey Courtney agreed that to give Ted Harris a second chance was the Christian thing to do. The cottage was available and it would be better to have tenants installed right away so that the property did not fall into disrepair during the winter months. Ivy was ecstatic and the children were bubbling over with excitement when Kate accompanied the family to visit their prospective home. Ted was less forthcoming, but he nodded and said that 'it would do nicely', and Kate took this as the best she could expect from a man who kept his inner feelings to himself.

Ivy, Ted and the children moved into Marsh Cottage in the middle of January. Ivy had insisted

307

on giving it a thorough spring clean before they took residence and, with Jenny and Kate's help, they had the place spotless, warm and welcoming. Ivy was to continue working at Warren House, and Morrison was only too happy to have a strong man like Ted to assist him, especially during the long winter months when the old man's rheumatics were most painful. The older children attended the village school, and Ivy continued to bring Charlie and baby John to the house, where Tilly clearly doted on both of them.

Hedley and Jenny saw each other as much as possible, despite opposition from Elaine, but Kate's meeting with the vicar had proved successful, and Humphrey raised no objections to his son's return to duty or his relationship with a servant girl. Hedley had to make several trips to London where he underwent rigorous tests to ensure that he was fit to return to duty, and at the beginning of February he received orders to join his new regiment in Delhi. There was not enough time for the banns to be read and Hedley, with a degree of purpose that Kate could not have imagined he possessed, had attended Doctors' Commons to get a special licence.

★ ★ ★

The wedding of Hedley and Jenny was a small affair performed by Hedley's father, who had somehow persuaded his wife to attend, although Elaine made it abundantly clear that she disapproved of the match. Kate was happy for Jenny, who made a beautiful bride, although Kate knew she would miss her more as a friend than a servant. The wedding breakfast was a subdued affair in the vicarage dining room, with only Lady Lyndon, Arabella, Kate and Annie as guests. It was obvious that Elaine did not want her friends from the various committees involved, and Kate could only assume that the good ladies would look down on Jenny and feel sorry for Hedley. However, the newly-weds seemed oblivious to any undercurrents and were excited at the prospect of starting a new life together. The happy couple were due to sail on a troop ship the following day, and, after emotional goodbyes, they left to spend their wedding night in a coaching inn on the road to the East India docks.

Kate was happy to see her mother in a buoyant mood. Arabella's relationship with Giles PomeroySmith was progressing rapidly, although Kate knew that her mother was very conscious of the fact that she was still officially in mourning. However, Arabella had allowed herself to abandon the stark black widow's weeds for a gown of pale grey tussore, and Kate had persuaded her to have a dinner dress made in mauve silk. Arabella had argued at first, but when Giles continued to press his suit she had agreed to break with tradition.

Kate's liking for Giles deepened as the weeks turned into months and spring was in the air. Catkins shivered and danced on the hazel twigs and there were buds on the blackthorn bushes. The mists that had shrouded the marshes over the darkest days of winter were less frequent, and a faint haze of green on the trees that surrounded Warren House was enough to lift Kate's spirits.

She had not heard from Harry since he left Walthamstow, and she was beginning to wonder if he intended to return home, or if he had decided to keep away until Monks was finally caught. When she asked Perry about the case he had little to say except that Monks was proving a much more slippery character than the police had anticipated, and he was lying low south of the river. Despite Monks' apparent withdrawal from the criminal world, Perry thought that it was still too dangerous for Lady Lyndon, Kate and anyone who had connections to

Harry to return to London. Perry's advice was for them all to remain where they were and Kate was happy to comply with this.

There was always plenty to do, although she missed Jenny more than she had thought possible. Kate hoped that Jenny's marriage to Hedley was proving a happy one, but they were now far away and Hedley would be reunited with his fellow officers. Kate knew from experience that the tightknit military communities could make life difficult for anyone who came from a different background, and she couldn't help worrying about Jenny. In the face of such snobbishness Jenny would have to prove herself a resilient and resourceful soldier's wife, although Kate did not doubt her friend's ability to make a life for herself and Hedley, even in the furthest outpost of the Empire.

Despite all her underlying worries, one of Kate's greatest pleasures was the garden. She planned the planting of the herbaceous borders with Morrison's help, relying on his years of expertise and knowledge of plants. Ted did most of the labouring, and he seemed to thrive on working outdoors, although he was careful to defer to Morrison in all things. Ted's main interest lay in the walled kitchen garden, where he was quick to learn when to plant the vegetables and how to tend them. The greenhouse was cleaned, the broken panes mended and trays of tiny seedlings filled the racks that Ted had repaired with a hitherto hidden talent for carpentry.

Arabella liked to wander about the grounds with a sunshade and straw bonnet to protect her porcelain complexion, especially when Giles paid a visit, which was at least every other day. Kate was waiting for them to announce their engagement, but her mother was coy whenever she tried to quiz her on her relationship with the handsome landowner.

They were in the garden taking the air after a hefty April shower when Kate heard the rumble of carriage wheels and the sound of horses' hoofs on the gravelled drive.

'I think your beau has arrived, Mama,' Kate said, smiling.

'Giles is not my beau. We are just good friends.'

'I doubt if he sees it that way, Mama. He's here so often he might as well move in.'

'Don't be vulgar, Kate.' Arabella frowned, but her eyes were sparkling and there was a delicate flush on her normally pale cheeks.

'Every time he visits I expect to hear that he's proposed.'

'Even if I were to consider marrying Giles,' Arabella said sharply, 'I would have to wait at least

311

another year before we announced our engagement. I am still in mourning for you dear papa.'

'But you do intend to accept when he does propose?'

'I'm past the first flush of youth, my dear,' Arabella said, sighing. 'I don't expect every gentleman I meet to fall in love with me.'

'Oh, Mama!' Kate said, chuckling. 'You know very well that Giles is clearly smitten by you. It's quite obvious to everyone.'

'Stop it, Kate. You're putting me in a state. I won't be able to look him in the eye if you continue to tease me.'

'I'm sorry,' Kate said, laughing. 'I promise I won't say anything to make you uncomfortable. In fact, I'll go inside and see if I can find Annie. You can have Giles all to yourself.' Kate did not wait for her mother to respond. She headed for the double doors that led into the small sitting room where she knew Annie often sat in the afternoon, basking in the sun like a contented kitten.

'Kate, is that you?' Annie was suddenly alert as Kate stepped into the room.

'How did you know it was me?'

'I can tell by your footsteps. You have a certain way of walking, quite different from that of your mother or Aunt Margaret. Besides which, I heard the carriage arrive and I imagine that Lady Martin will be outside in the garden, waiting for her beau. I can tell the difference between a barouche and a tilbury.'

Kate laughed. 'I wish I had your ability to see things in my mind's eye. How clever you are, Annie.'

312

'I have to use my ears. It's amazing how much you can tell just by listening.' Annie sat back in her chair. 'For instance, I know how much you miss Harry. I miss him, too.'

'Yes, you're right. I wish I knew that he had arrived safely in Bombay.'

'You never told me why he had decided to go so far. I know all about Monks, of course, but why did Harry set sail for India.'

'You would have to ask him that yourself,' Kate said evasively.

'Well, the answer might be in this letter.' Annie held up a folded letter, sealed with red wax. 'Will you read it to me, please? I was hoping you would be the first person to come into the room. It might be from Joe.'

Kate took it from her. 'Of course.' She broke the seal carefully and unfolded the letter. For a moment she was speechless. It was from Joseph Blythe, but written by a nurse at the military hospital in Bombay. Kate read it twice before she could find the courage to speak.

'What does it say?' Annie demanded. 'I know it must be something bad or you would read it out loud.'

'It's from a nurse in the military hospital in Bombay, Annie. Your brother was badly wounded, which was why Harry set off for India. He was going to bring him home, but now Harry is very sick in hospital. The letter doesn't go into details but it must have been serious, and they're both in the same ward. It was Joe who asked the nurse to write this letter and that doesn't bode well. Harry would never have asked for help had he been in

313

command of his senses.'

'You knew that Joe was wounded and you didn't tell me.' Annie's voice rose to a cry of anguish.

'We hoped that Harry could bring your brother home as quickly as possible and we didn't want to worry you. Now it seems that they are both in trouble.' Kate folded the letter and tucked it into her skirt pocket. 'I'm going to India. I won't leave them both to die in a military hospital. I'll bring them home.'

'If you go, I'm coming with you. I won't be a hindrance, Kate. I'll do everything I can to help.'

Kate thought quickly. 'All right, we'll both go. It would be difficult for me to travel on my own, but the two of us together will be fine. I'm going to the village shop to get Mr Ruggles to send a telegram to Perry. We need two tickets to Bombay on the first ship available.'

Kate had wanted to leave immediately, but it was almost a week before she and Annie were able to obtain tickets for the ship that would take them to India. Annie had never been on a vessel of any kind, and she confessed to being nervous but excited. Perry had been reluctant to let her go, but Lady Lyndon had applauded Annie's courage, and she thanked Kate wholeheartedly for undertaking the journey to bring Harry and Joseph home. Arabella had been against the voyage, but Giles had been encouraging, and that had calmed the situation. Kate could have kissed him, but she managed to control herself. If Giles Pomeroy-Smith was to be her stepfather she was more than happy. He had brought the smiles back to her mother's face and she was like a different person. The old, sharptongued Arabella was gone, leaving someone much more amenable and kind, which made life more pleasant for everyone.

★ ★ ★

The East Indiaman was a three-masted Blackwall frigate and the passengers were mostly soldiers returning to duty, although none of them seemed to know if they would still be employed by the East India Company, or whether they had been transferred to a regiment of the British Army. The uprising had caused great confusion as well as tragedy, but the officers who shared the saloon with the small number of civilian passengers seemed optimistic. The other travellers included a missionary and his wife; a doctor, who drank too much at dinner each evening, and two spinster school teachers who were returning to Bombay after completing their home leave. The officers kept mainly to themselves, although they were affable and courteous in company, but the sound of their revelry late at night after the civilian passengers had retired to bed could be heard above the sound of the wind in the sails and the beating of the waves against the hull.

In contrast, the spinster ladies spent most of their time reading or sewing, speaking only when spoken to and they retired to their cabin every evening after dinner. The doctor's wife suffered badly from seasickness and was confined to her bunk for the first couple of weeks, and after that she either sat on deck wrapped in a couple of blankets or huddled in the corner of the saloon, leafing

315

through old copies of Household Words magazine. The doctor himself was kept busy attending minor injuries to the crew and dispensing doses of seltzer to the soldiers. He started drinking soon after breakfast, for purely medicinal purposes, he said, and continued to imbibe throughout the day. At dinner he regaled the party with accounts of his medical experiences both in India and Africa, which invariably left the two school teachers pale and unable to face the rest of their food. It was no surprise to Kate that the good doctor's wife took refuge in illness when faced with such a selfish, egotistical husband.

Kate was very glad that she had Annie as a companion, and they amused themselves by making up background stories for their fellow passengers. Annie might not have the power of sight, but her hearing was acute and she noticed things about people that Kate often missed.

Whiling away the long hours, Annie always began the game. According to her, Miss Nancy had suffered a broken heart when she was jilted by her former fiancé. Her sister, Miss Euphemia, had fallen in love with a married man and had fled to India rather than give way to the temptation of becoming his mistress. This last observation had made Kate curl up with laughter as she sat cross-legged on her bunk. The two ladies in question were so prim and proper that it was almost impossible to imagine them succumbing to any deep emotion, let alone the temptation to enter into illicit love affairs.

When it came to Dr Arbuthnot, Annie's imagination ran riot. The doctor's drink problem had been caused, so Annie said, by his wife's flirtatious behaviour. Pale, sickly and devoid of any sense of humour, Amaryllis Arbuthnot had been a dancer at the Grecian Theatre with a string of stage-door admirers. One night, during a performance, she fell off the stage, dead drunk, according to Annie, at the feet of the good doctor, who was seated in the front row. He fell hopelessly in love with her and they were married even before her broken leg had healed, but Amaryllis was not prepared to give up her many lovers and the doctor took to drink. Their passage to India was supposed to be a second honeymoon, and an escape from a titled admirer. Annie could not go on. The ridiculousness of the story had them both crying with laughter.

It was Kate's turn to improvise when it came to Mr and Mrs Skidmore, the missionary couple. Herbert Skidmore, she decided, was a reformed bank robber dragged back to the path of righteousness by Barbara, his domineering wife. It was Barbara Skidmore's voice that dominated talk at the dinner table. Well-educated, cut-crystal enunciation and the ability to make herself heard above the wildest storm made it impossible to ignore the lady, who constantly referred to her own upbringing in a vicarage and her sainted father, the late Reverend Lucius Skidmore. This always brought the conversation to a halt, and Barbara was quick to stress that her husband had chosen to take his wife's surname. She had a habit of glaring at the puzzled faces of her audience, as if daring them to question the decision.

'Of course,' Kate said, managing to keep a

317

straight face. 'Barbara Skidmore's father was really a ringmaster in a circus and when he was unable to perform his daughter took his place. I can just imagine Barbara with a top hat and a whip. I expect that's how she makes people sit down and listen to her boring husband's sermons.'

Annie clamped her hand over her mouth to stifle a burst of laughter. 'You are dreadful, Kate. I think you're worse than me.'

'It's getting late.' Kate stretched and yawned. 'But we have yet to mention our heroic captain.'

'I think he's quite young,' Annie said thoughtfully. 'I imagine that he's quite good looking.'

'Oh, yes.' Kate curled up on her bunk and allowed her imagination to take over ...

Captain Francis Langhorne, a handsome man in his thirties, was hiding a deep secret: one of his legs had been shot off by a cannonball and he cleverly concealed a peg leg beneath his uniform. The rest of his infirmities were kept hidden from the world, and his deep secrets were revealed by Kate and exaggerated by Annie until they were helpless with laughter and quite exhausted.

Sometimes, during dinner or even when walking on deck, Kate would have to control the urge to chuckle when she came face to face with one of their victims, but the silly stories helped to pass the dull evening hours and were not to be taken seriously. However, Captain Langhorne did walk with a slight limp and Miss Euphemia did have the haunted look of a star-crossed lover. The rest of the journey was quite dull by comparison, and mostly there was nothing to see but miles of ocean. The ship called in at various ports in order to take on fresh water and supplies, but the passengers were not encouraged to disembark, and Kate had no particular wish to prolong their journey. Despite the growing understanding and friendship she shared with Annie, Kate could not help worrying about Harry. At least Joseph's condition had been reported as stable, but if Harry was suffering from a bout of malaria or the dreaded cholera or typhoid, they might arrive too late. The thought of losing him now was something she pushed to the back of her mind. He had survived gang warfare, imprisonment and the hazardous sea voyage only to be struck down by some dire misfortune that had left him helpless.

The last couple of weeks of their journey seemed endless, but eventually they entered the harbour at Bombay and Kate stood on deck, breathing in the familiar scents and smells of India.

Kate's first thought was to take a tonga to the home of her late uncle's lawyer, who had helped her family when they fled from Delhi during the uprising. A group of porters offered their services and, having tipped one handsomely, Kate and Annie waited outside the dock gates for the horse-drawn carriage to take them to Audley House in an exclusive residential district. Sir Robert Audley was not at home, but his housekeeper was too well trained to show her surprise, and she welcomed the travellers as if they were honoured guests.

'Of course I remember you, Miss Martin,' Mrs Ogilvy said calmly. 'It was a terrible time but things are slowly getting back to normal.'

Kate eyed her curiously. 'You were brave to stay on, considering the circumstances, Mrs Ogilvy.

Weren't you tempted to go home?'

Mrs Ogilvy smiled. 'This is my home, Miss Martin. I was born in Poona and I met and married my husband there.'

'I'm sorry. I didn't know that.'

'Won't you come into the parlour. I'll send a servant with lemonade and perhaps you'd like something to eat?'

'A cool drink would be lovely,' Kate said with feeling.

Her stays were digging into her flesh and she could feel perspiration trickling down her back in the most inelegant manner. However, Mrs Ogilvy, in her tight-waisted grey poplin gown, looked as cool as the proverbial cucumber.

'When will Sir Robert be back, Mrs Ogilvy? I need to ask him a favour.'

'Not until this evening.' Mrs Ogilvy met Kate's anxious look with a serene smile. 'You will be staying with us, of course? I'm sure Sir Robert will be delighted to have your company.'

'That's very kind. I'm here on a mission and I might need his help.'

'He was a close friend of your late uncle, Miss Martin. I know he will welcome you with open arms. I'll have two rooms made ready for you.'

Annie laid her hand on Kate's arm. 'I need to sit down. Could you guide me to a chair?'

'I'm so sorry, Annie. I'm neglecting you.' Kate led her to a sofa. 'Are you all right?'

'It's the heat,' Mrs Ogilvy said briskly. 'I'll send for the punkah wallah, and I'll bring your drinks.' She left the room, closing the door gently.

'Are you sure you're all right, Annie?' Kate

320

asked urgently. 'Would you like to lie down?'

'No, really, I'm feeling better already. It was so hot and everything smells so strange.'

'Of course it does. This is India and I love it here. The three years we spent in Delhi were the happiest I've ever known.'

Annie laid her hand on Kate's arm. 'Do you think you will see Ashok again?'

'I didn't come here with that in mind. He might not have survived the uprising, and even if he did, I expect he will have forgotten me.'

'But you still remember him.'

'He was my first love, but it was never likely to come to anything. I realise that now. We came from different worlds.'

'I'm sorry, Kate.'

Kate patted Annie's hand. 'Thank you, but at the moment you are more important. Are you sure you feel all right? You haven't got a fever or anything?'

Annie smiled. 'I don't think I'm coming down with a dreadful tropical disease. I was just a little overwhelmed.'

A slight movement above them made Kate look up to see a large fan swaying rhythmically to and fro, creating a gentle waft of air. 'Do you feel that, Annie? The punkah is a large fan and there'll be a boy sitting on the floor outside, pulling the cord.'

'Poor boy,' Annie said with feeling. 'Is that what he does all day?'

'I suppose so. I took it all for granted when I lived in Delhi. I doubt if I gave another thought to the servants, or even the poverty that existed outside the doors of the residence. All I thought about was enjoying myself and what I would wear to the next grand occasion. I've changed so many of my ideas since I returned to London and started the soup kitchen.'

The door opened before Annie had time to answer and Mrs Ogilvy entered carrying a tray laden with a cut-glass jug of lemonade and two glasses, as well as a plate of dainty cakes, which she set down upon a brass-topped table.

'Your rooms will be ready in about half an hour, Miss Martin. Luncheon will be served in the dining room at midday.'

'You're very kind, Mrs Ogilvy,' Kate said earnestly. 'But please don't go to any extra trouble on our account.'

'It's a pleasure. We hardly entertain these days. The uprising might be over but there are deep scars that will take a long time to heal, and nothing will ever be quite the same again.'

Mrs Ogilvy left the room with a swish of taffeta petticoats, leaving a trail of a fragrant lavender cologne in her wake.

Kate filled the glasses with lemonade and handed one to Annie. 'Drink it slowly,' she said gently. 'You'll find you need to take in much more fluid in this hot climate. I used to envy the Indian ladies in their saris, but we have to keep up appearances in our tight-fitting garments.'

'It is extremely hot,' Annie said with a sigh. 'I suppose one must get used to it eventually.'

'Most of the ladies I knew spent the afternoons lying down in a darkened room. It's best to keep out of the sun in the middle of the day, but it does get a little cooler in the evening.'

Annie sipped her drink. 'I'm glad to hear it. I

don't think I'd survive long if I had to live in this climate.'

'I would have been happy to spend the rest of my days here until I lived in Warren House. Now I find myself longing for those musty wainscoted walls and the cool greenery of the gardens. Life is strange, isn't it, Annie?'

* * *

After luncheon Mrs Ogilvy showed Kate and Annie to their rooms. Kate was delighted to find that she had the same room that she had occupied while they waited for a passage to England. Having settled Annie comfortably in the adjacent room, Kate knew that she would not rest until she had seen Harry. She returned to the parlour and rang the bell to summon a servant.

Mrs Ogilvy entered the room, her brow creased into a worried frown. 'Is everything all right, Miss Martin? I thought you would enjoy a rest.'

'I need to go to the military hospital,' Kate said urgently. 'The reason we're here is because Annie's brother was badly wounded in the uprising, and a good friend travelled to India to bring Joseph home.' Kate took the letter from her reticule and handed it to Mrs Ogilvy. 'This explains everything.'

Mrs Ogilvy produced a pince-nez from her pinafore pocket and scanned the neatly written lines. She looked up, handing the paper back to Kate with a sympathetic smile. 'I'll send for the carriage.'

The journey to the military hospital on the outskirts of the city took much longer than it might have done had the roads not been so congested. Kate sat back in the landau, shaded by a large parasol, and her anxiety was calmed a little by her pleasure at being back in the country she had grown to love. The heat was intense and red dust swirled around the carriage as it disturbed the road surface, weaving in and out between donkeys struggling with overfilled panniers, lumbering elephants, carts laden with farm produce and a jostling crowd of people going about their daily business. The scent of spices mingled with the odour of dung from the skinny cows that were free to wander at will. Beautiful barefoot children ran after the carriage, holding out their hands and smiling up at Kate, who was tempted to throw them a few coins, but she knew from experience that it was unwise. Such an action would only cause a crowd to gather and the children might be in danger of being trampled in the rush to snatch the money from the dust.

It was quieter on the outskirts of the city and it was relief when the coachman drew the carriage to a halt outside the main entrance to the hospital. A young boy ran forward to open the carriage door and Kate alighted, feeling suddenly nervous of what she might discover. She tipped the boy and made her way into the building. The cloying smell of carbolic assailed her nostrils as she approached the reception desk where a turbaned gentleman listened politely to her questions.

'A moment, memsahib.' He leafed through the

pages of a leather-bound book, running a gnarled finger down the entries. 'Private Blythe is on Ward Ten, but Sahib Lyndon was discharged some time ago.'

Kate stared at him in dismay. 'Do you know where Sahib Lyndon went?'

'Not my business, memsahib. I'm very sorry, I can't help you.'

20

Kate stood in the doorway of Ward Ten, glazing down the regimented rows of iron beds. A nurse came hurrying towards her. 'It isn't visiting time yet, miss.'

'I've come all the way from England to see Private Blythe,' Kate said with a catch in her voice. 'I only arrived in Bombay this morning after many weeks at sea. Please can I just have a moment with him?'

The young woman glanced over her shoulder. 'Sister is at tiffin but she'll be back soon. You may have five minutes but please don't disturb the other patients.' She led the way to the far end of the ward where a young man lay in his neatly made bed.

'Private Blythe, you have a visitor.' The nurse backed away to answer a faint call for help at the other end of the ward.

'Joseph, you don't know me, but I'm a friend of Annie's.'

He gazed up at her with a blank expression on his pale features. 'I don't understand. Annie is in London.'

Kate could feel the eyes of the man in the next bed were on her and she felt a surge of pity for the patients who were so far from home. She moved a little close to Joseph, lowering her voice. 'Annie is here in Bombay. We've come to take you home.'

'Home?'

'To England, Joseph. We only disembarked this morning and I left Annie at the house where we're staying because she was exhausted. She's been so worried about you.'

'But I can't leave,' Joseph said dazedly. 'I'm still under orders, even though I am a helpless cripple. I had to have my leg amputated when gangrene set in.'

'I'm so sorry to hear that.' Kate laid her hand on his as it rested on the starched white coverlet. She could feel the bones through his parchment-thin skin, and was reminded of a baby bird she had once tried to rescue after it had fallen from its nest. 'I'm sure we can go through the proper channels and get you repatriated. We're staying with a lawyer and I know he'll help us.'

Joseph nodded dully. 'If you say so, miss. I don't even know your name.'

'I'm sorry, I should have introduced myself — I'm Kate Martin. I came because of your letter and I wanted to see Harry Lyndon, but I'm told he's been discharged.'

'Harry was shot and badly wounded. The uprising might be over but there are still pockets of resistance, so I'm told. Harry nearly died but he's tough and he survived the operation and the bout of malaria he suffered.'

Kate breathed a sigh of relief, dashing tears from her eyes. She was shocked by her own response to the news. 'He must have been well enough to leave the hospital. Do you know where he went?'

Joseph curled his fingers around her hand. 'He said he had some unfinished business. I don't know any more than that.'

'That's odd,' Kate said thoughtfully. 'As far as I know he'd never been to India before.'

'Look out,' Joseph muttered, releasing her hand.

Kate glanced over her shoulder. She could see the nurse advancing on them and she realised that the five minutes had flown by. 'I'm going to be thrown out, Joseph, but I'll return tomorrow with Annie. That's a promise.'

★ ★ ★

Sir Robert arrived home just in time for dinner. His surprise on being greeted by Kate and Annie was obvious, but he recovered quickly and his welcome was warm and sincere. He embraced Kate and sat down with them for a sherry before the meal. He listened patiently while Kate explained their presence in Bombay.

'Well,' he said when Kate came to the end of her narrative, 'I must say I admire you young ladies for your courage and fortitude. Your brother should be very touched and proud of you, Annie. He's a lucky fellow to have such a brave and devoted sister. As for Harry Trader, or Sir Harry Lyndon, whichever name he happens to be using, I am reserving judgement, Kate. Although it seems to me that you are quite fond of him.'

'Yes, Sir Robert, I am,' Kate said frankly. 'I was devastated when they told me at the hospital that he had left, and apparently with no forwarding address. Joseph seems to think that Harry had something important to do, but that seems odd. As far as I know, Harry had never been to India before.'

328

'I'm sorry, Kate.' Annie reached out to touch Kate's hand as they sat side by side on the sofa. 'You've done so much for me and for Joseph. I only want you to be happy.'

'Dinner is served, Sir Robert.' Mrs Ogilvy appeared in the doorway, looking approvingly from one to the other. 'I would like to say how good it is to see Miss Kate here, sir. We've been a quiet household for too long. I keep telling Sir Robert that he should entertain more.'

'Agatha takes me in hand regularly.' Sir Robert raised his glass to his housekeeper. 'But I don't know what I'd do without her.'

'Your dinner will be spoiled if you don't come now, sir,' Mrs Ogilvy said sternly. 'Sandeep announced the meal a good fifteen minutes ago. It's always left to me to make sure things run smoothly.'

Sir Robert downed the last of his drink and rose to his feet. 'I consider myself reproved, Agatha. We're coming right away.'

Kate had to hide a smile at the sight of such a prominent man being browbeaten by his house-keeper. 'I'm sorry, Mrs Ogilvy. It's my fault. I was telling Sir Robert everything that has happened to my family since we left India. I'm sure the meal will be wonderful, as always.'

Mrs Ogilvy tossed her head and marched out of the room.

'Oh dear,' Annie said anxiously. 'Have we upset her? She's been so kind.'

Sir Robert took Annie by the hand and raised her to her feet. 'She'll get over it, my dear. Agatha Ogilvy loves putting me in the wrong — it's her sole purpose in life, or so she thinks. We can talk more over dinner, and my carriage will be at your disposal tomorrow to take you to the hospital. I'll make enquiries with regard to your brother's repatriation on medical grounds.'

'I'd be so grateful if you would, Sir Robert,' Annie said eagerly. 'Surely the East India Company Army won't want to keep him on in his condition?'

'Their army has been nationalised by the British Army, so they have no say in what happens to Joseph, but we'll need to get everything done properly, and that will be my pleasure, so don't worry about a thing, Annie. Let's go to the dining room and enjoy a convivial meal. I rarely have the pleasure of the company of such lovely ladies.'

* * *

Next day they arrived at the hospital during the appointed hours, although as Kate had realised the day before, there were few enough visitors. She was aware of envious glances from the other patients as she and Annie walked to the end of the ward. Joseph was propped up on pillows and his pleasure on seeing his sister was obvious. Tears ran down his cheeks as he hugged her, and Annie sobbed unrestrainedly. Kate pulled up a chair and sat down, waiting for them to compose themselves, and eventually it was Annie who drew away first.

'You're so thin, Joe.' Annie's voice broke on a fresh sob.

'And you never have a hanky,' Joseph added, chuckling. 'Don't you dare wipe your eyes on the bed sheet or Sister Hayward will have a fit.'

This made Annie laugh and she accepted a handkerchief from Kate, who had come prepared. 'I can't believe that a brave soldier like you is afraid of a nurse.'

'Believe me, Annie, all the men in this ward are terrified of her. What Sister Hayward says goes.'

'You're looking a lot better today, Joe,' Kate said, smiling. 'Sir Robert is going to contact the military authorities about your repatriation.'

'Really?' Joe's eyes lit up and his thin cheeks creased in a wide grin. 'That would be wonderful. I can't wait to get back to London.' He grasped his sister's hand and raised it to his cheek. 'Where have you been living? I hope Aunt Margaret has been looking after you.'

Annie's lips trembled. 'I'm ashamed to say that I refused her help at the start, Joe. I suppose I was too proud to accept anything from Mama's family since they disowned her after she married Pa.'

Kate was suddenly alert. 'You never mentioned that before, Annie. I thought you had to support yourself.'

'What's this?' Joe raised himself to a sitting position. 'What were you thinking of, Annie?'

'It seems stupid now that we're all living together at Warren House,' Annie said guiltily. 'But until the trouble with Monks I had been quite happy living on my own. I had proved that I could support myself by entertaining people with my playing, and it made me feel less of a burden.'

'I'm sure you were never a burden to anyone, Annie.' Kate gazed at her in dismay. 'Why would you think that?'

'Our father was killed in a duel. He had dishonoured a gambling debt and the man he had cheated called him out. Pa was killed by a single bullet.'

'How dreadful.' Kate laid a sympathetic hand on Annie's thin shoulder. 'How old were you then?'

'I was ten and Joe was thirteen. Mama had always been delicate and she never recovered from the shock. The family disowned her and we had to live on a small allowance from a trust fund.'

'I enlisted as a drummer boy,' Joseph said, sighing. 'I only earned a little but I sent most of my wages home.'

'But why didn't Harry or his mother do something?' Kate demanded angrily. 'I thought Lady Lyndon was a kind woman.'

Annie raised her brother's hand to her cheek. 'Lady Lyndon is only related to us by marriage, Kate. Harry was away at school and then at university, so he knew nothing of our plight, and Mama would have died rather than beg the family for help.'

'It's obvious who you take after,' Joseph said with a wry smile. 'But it's true, Kate. Our mother died of a fever and I was too far away to do anything to help. Annie sent me word that she was doing well, and I had no reason to disbelieve her. But I did write to Harry and I asked him to keep an eye on my sister.'

'The rest you know,' Annie added softly. 'Harry tried to persuade me to move into the house in Finsbury Circus, but I hardly knew Lady Lyndon, and I didn't want to be the poor blind relative living on charity. It all seems rather silly now.'

'At least Harry showed some sense of responsibility and honour,' Kate said proudly. 'I need to find him, Joe. Have you any idea where he might have gone?'

Joe shook his head. 'Not really. He said he was looking for someone, but I wasn't in a fit state to press him on the subject. He promised to come back for me and I'm sure he'll keep his word.'

'I wish I knew why he had gone away like that,' Kate said slowly. 'Did he give any reason for leaving, Joe?'

'No. If I hadn't been so bound up in my own self-pity I might have shown more interest, but I can only walk a few steps with the aid of crutches. I'm a useless cripple. I'll be a burden to you Annie.'

'Don't say that, Joe.' Annie's eyes filled with tears. 'You're still my Joe, the brother I love. We'll manage on our own if needs be.'

'It won't come to that,' Kate said sternly. 'You're forgetting that you have a family now, Annie, and that goes for Joe, too. We'll return to Warren House where Joe will be more than welcome. In the meantime I'm going to make some enquiries.'

Annie clutched Kate's hand. 'I'll go with you.'

Kate shook her head. 'No, you must stay here with Joe. I'll speak to Sir Robert at dinner this evening — he'll know how I should go about finding Harry. We'll be on our way back to England before you know it, and Harry will be with us.'

★ ★ ★

'You can't go gallivanting around the city on your own, Kate,' Sir Robert said that evening at dinner when Kate told him she wanted to search for Harry. 'It would be unwise in England, and virtually impossible in this country in these unsettled times.'

'But the uprising was crushed, Sir Robert.' Kate put her knife and fork neatly back on her plate, having finished the delicious goat curry that had been served. She could see that Annie was struggling with the spicy food, but that was not uppermost in her mind. All she could think about was finding Harry.

'It will take the country many years to recover, and unnecessary travel is ill-advised.'

'That's why I thought it might be possible to find out where Harry went. He would have had to hire a vehicle and horses. Maybe he needed a guide.'

Sir Robert eyed her over the rim of his wineglass. 'This young man means a great deal to you, quite obviously. But I seem to remember your father telling me about a certain Subedar-Major Patel who had taken your fancy.'

Kate felt the blood rush to her cheeks, but she met his curious gaze with a firm look. 'That seems like a very long time ago, sir. Everything has changed since then and I realise that it was not meant to be. I don't know if Ashok survived the uprising, but if he did I hope he has found happiness.'

'Well said, Kate.' Annie clapped her hands. 'I will accompany Kate, sir.'

'I thought we'd decided that you should remain

here so that you can visit Joe every day,' Kate said in a low voice.

'You decided it for me, Kate. Of course I want to be with Joe, but we will have plenty of time together when we set sail for home, and I never want to be so far away from him again. But I know you won't leave here without Harry, so I don't see that I have any choice.'

Sir Robert refilled his glass with claret. 'I see that I have two very determined young ladies at my table.'

'You have, sir,' Kate agreed, raising her full wineglass to her lips. 'I am determined to do this with or without your permission.'

'Then it seems I can do nothing to stop you. However, I have access to information that would be denied to you. Give me a day or two and I'll make enquiries. If I am unsuccessful then I will happily put my carriage at your disposal and Sandeep can accompany you, but hopefully that will not be necessary.'

Kate could see the sense in what he was saying, and although she agreed with this in principle, she found it almost impossible to comply with his wishes. For the next three days she arose from her comfortable bed each morning wondering what the day would bring. Apart from accompanying Annie to the hospital there was very little she could do. Sir Robert left soon after breakfast and was driven to his office in the city, where he spent all day, returning in time for dinner each evening. He had nothing to report until on the fourth day, when Kate was growing more and more restive, he announced that he had spoken to an army official

335

who confirmed that Sir Harry Lyndon had been making certain enquiries, about which he was not authorised to comment. However, the official had hinted that a trip on the relatively new railway to Thana might hold the answer to their questions.

Kate was mystified by this. It was Harry's first visit to India, so why would he want to travel to Thana? She could hardly believe that this piece of information might lead to Harry, but she was determined to follow up the suggestion, even though Sir Robert said it would be a wild-goose chase.

Next morning, without telling anyone where she was going, Kate hailed a tonga and told the tonga wallah to take her to the railway station. She had hoped that the man in the ticket office might remember seeing someone like Harry, but the conversation became confused and there were people queuing up behind her. Eventually she was forced to make way for them and found herself pushed aside by angry travellers. Apparently the train was due in at any moment and then it would make the return trip to a Thana, some twenty-one miles away. She could not think why Harry might have wanted to go there, but she was growing desperate. Joe had been in hospital for so many months that he seemed to have lost all sense of time and urgency, and he was prepared to wait calmly for Harry's return.

Even though she had no interest in steam engines or railways, Kate could not resist the temptation to wait until the train came rumbling into the station. She had never travelled by rail and she was beginning to think it would be a fascinating experience, when there was a sudden rush for the gates and people waved their tickets at the guard as they hurried onto the platform. The train pulled in with a loud whistle and a gust of steam enveloped everything in its wake. Kate was about to leave, but she hesitated, hoping that by some miracle Harry would emerge from the damp cloud. But he was not amongst the passengers who pushed and jostled at the barrier where they had to hand in their tickets, and Kate struggled with a feeling of disappointment. She knew that it had been a vain hope, but she dragged her feet as she made her way out onto the dusty street, almost tripping over a small child who was clutching at her skirts and holding out his grimy hand. Kate opened her reticule and was immediately surrounded by a crowd of painfully thin urchins, begging for money.

'No,' Kate said, shaking her head. 'Go away. I haven't enough for all of you.' She attempted to escape, but she was surrounded, the clamour grew louder and the small hands grabbed at her arms and tore her skirts.

'Get away, all of you.' A man's voice thundered above the noise from the steam engine preparing to leave on its return journey, and the ugly shouts of the hungry children. 'Jaldi!' he added angrily when they refused to move. He raised his swagger stick and the children cowered and backed away.

Kate was trembling but she held her head high. 'Thank you, sir.'

The army officer smiled and proffered his arm. 'I take it that you are newly arrived in India.'

'Why would you say that?'

'Because you would not be here on your own,

337

and you would not have given alms to beggars.'

'I lived in Delhi for several years,' Kate said defensively. 'It just so happens that I am looking for someone, or I would not have come to the station alone.' She met his amused gaze with a frown. 'Thank you, sir. But I'll hail a tonga and be on my way.'

'Where are you staying, Miss — er — I'm sorry we haven't been formally introduced. My name is Francis Lambert.'

'Kate Martin.' Kate hoped he could not see that she was still trembling, although she forced herself to speak calmly. 'I see by your uniform that you are Colonel Lambert.'

'That's correct, but might I ask why you are here on your own? If you're familiar with India you must know that it's inadvisable, especially now.'

'You're right, of course,' Kate said coldly. 'Thank you for stepping in, but I'd better return to Audley House before I'm missed.'

'I have a carriage waiting. It would be my pleasure to see you safely home.'

'I'm staying with Sir Robert Audley.'

'I know him well.' Colonel Lambert proffered his arm.

Kate had little alternative but to take him up on his offer. Glancing over her shoulder, she could see some of the older boys lurking behind an iron pillar, and she knew it was not safe to remain here on her own.

'Thank you. I won't make the same mistake again,' she said as he handed her into his carriage.

'Audley House. Drive on,' Colonel Lambert

said as he climbed in beside Kate. 'Now, perhaps you'd like to tell me for whom you risked all? He must be someone special.'

Kate shot him a sideways glance. 'It's a long story, Colonel.'

'I'm sure it will make the drive back to Audley House very interesting, but I don't wish to pry.'

'Are you married, Colonel?'

'I am, as it happens,' he said with a wry smile. 'Does that have any bearing on what you might tell me?'

'Not really, but if you have a wife and family you might understand why it's important for me to find my friend. I sailed from London several months ago, accompanied by my friend Annie. Her brother was a soldier in the East India Company Bombay Army and we received a letter saying that he had been badly wounded and was in hospital.'

'That must have been very upsetting.'

'It was, sir. Annie is blind, although she is a very independent person, and she adores her brother. Her cousin, Harry, travelled to Bombay intending to bring Joe home, but apparently he was injured in a skirmish and was also suffering from malaria. He ended up in hospital with Joe and there seemed to be no answer other than for Annie and me to come to Bombay and bring them both home.'

'Are they still in hospital?'

'Joe is in the military hospital, but Harry was discharged some weeks ago and no one knows where he is now. He told Joe he had business to attend to, and Sir Robert has been making enquiries. We think that Harry might have travelled to Thana.'

339

'So it was Harry you hoped might be at the station?'

'It was a foolish idea, Colonel. I had no reason to believe that he was on that train, and no proof that he ever travelled on that line.'

'How disappointed you must feel.'

She eyed him warily, wondering if he was laughing at her, but his expression was sympathetic. 'Yes, I am. Although it was a vain hope.'

'This man means a great deal to you?'

'Yes, he does.' Kate smiled, shaking her head. 'I didn't realise how much until I found that he'd disappeared.'

'Have you any idea where he might have gone?'

'I've been racking my brains, but I can only think that he might be trying to find someone I was very fond of when I lived in Delhi with my parents.'

'That person must have been very important to you, too.'

'Yes, at the time he was. I fancied myself in love with a very handsome subedar-major, but I realise now that it was just an infatuation. However, I would like to know that he survived the conflict. He was someone very special.'

'Might I know his name? Perhaps I can help find him through army records. At the moment we are in a state of flux since the nationalisation of the East India Company Army, of which I was a part, but now we are the Indian Army, I'm proud to say.'

'He's called Subedar-Major Ashok Patel.'

'Leave it with me, Miss Martin. I'll go through

what records we have here. I can't promise anything, but I might be able to trace him for you. In the meantime I'm sure your friend Harry . . . what's his surname?'

'He is Sir Harry Lyndon, although he sometimes uses the alias Harry Trader.'

'I'm sure he will turn up when he's ready, but I will also make enquiries. Maybe I can help you to find both of them.'

That evening, sitting in the jasmine-scented courtyard of Audley House, listening to the tinkling of the water in the fountain, and the song of the cicadas, which was almost drowned out by the chatter of monkeys as they settled down for the night in the tall trees nearby, Kate felt very much at home. Annie had retired to bed early, and Sir Robert was in his study, going over a set of documents. He had apologised for leaving Kate on her own, but he had an important court case next morning, and he needed to go through his notes thoroughly before he slept.

The warm night wrapped itself around her and the skies above her were pin-pricked with millions of stars; she was on her own, but she did not feel lonely. If she could reach out beyond the stone walls she felt that the answer to everything was within her grasp. Kate sipped the last of her rapidly cooling coffee, smiling at her own folly. If she remained here in Audley House she might succumb to the idle lifestyle of so many of the ex-patriots who had chosen to spend their lives in this fascinating but dangerous country. But that was not for her: tomorrow she must face reality. Her talk with Colonel Lambert had made

341

her think hard as to Harry's motives for leaving Joe in hospital, and she could only imagine that he might have gone in search of Ashok. He knew how much she had cared for her handsome Indian soldier, and perhaps he thought by bringing her news of Ash he might lay a ghost from her past. He must have had good reason for his trip to Thana, and whatever had led him there it was likely that he would return by the same route. If it would serve any useful purpose she was quite prepared to meet every train that arrived at Bori Bunder station, but if Harry returned to Bombay he would almost certainly go straight to Joe in the hospital. She would have to curb her impatience and wait a little longer. Kate rose to her feet and made her way across the paved yard to the house. She would sleep on it and hope that in the morning a clever plan might have formed in her brain.

★ ★ ★

Next morning at breakfast Kate confided in Annie, who listened patiently.

'I agree that you can't camp on the station platform, Kate,' Annie said gently. 'If Harry has gone to Thana he might return on horseback or in a carriage, and you would have wasted your time. That's if he actually went there in the first place.'

'I know. It's all a matter of supposition, but surely Harry wouldn't simply abandon Joe in hospital. He came all this way specifically to take care of Joe and to bring him home. I can't believe that he would simply walk away.'

Annie smiled as she buttered a slice of toast.

342

'You really do love him, don't you?'

'I never said I did.'

'You didn't have to, dear. You've been fretting for him ever since we arrived at the hospital and discovered that he wasn't there.'

'Yes, well, that's true, but anything could have happened to him, and I hate mysteries. I want to know why he went and where he is now.'

A gentle tap on the door preceded Mrs Ogilvy's dramatic entrance. 'Miss Kate, there's a gentleman to see you.' She pursed her lips and folded her arms across her generous bosom, disapproval written all over her face.

'Who is it, Mrs Ogilvy?' Kate was suddenly breathless.

'Colonel Lambert, miss. He's the person who brought you home yesterday afternoon. Shall I tell him that you are otherwise engaged?'

Kate jumped to her feet, sending her starched white napkin falling to the floor. 'No, I'll see him now. Where is he?'

'I put him in the front parlour, miss.'

'Thank you, Mrs Ogilvy. I'll go and see him right away.'

'Your breakfast will get cold, miss.'

'It doesn't matter — I'll have it when I've found out what the colonel has to say. It might be important.' Kate hurried from the room and ran down the wide corridor to the spacious parlour overlooking the neat-kept front garden.

'Colonel Lambert, how good of you to come so early in the morning.'

He rose to his feet, smiling. 'Good morning, Miss Martin.'

343

'Have you news of Harry's whereabouts?'

'Yes and no. I'm sorry I can't be more specific, but my aide went through the records and found that your friend Subedar-Major Patel was born in Thana and he lived there until he joined the East India Company Army. I imagine that is what your friend Lyndon discovered.'

'So you think that's where Harry might have gone?'

'It seems likely. I couldn't find any record of the subedar-major having been wounded in battle and he was not amongst the lists of the deceased.'

Kate sank down on the sofa. 'Thank goodness. But Thana is only some twenty miles or so distant, so if Harry did go there, why hasn't he returned? Do you think something awful might have happened to him?'

'That is what we need to find out. I have sent word to the ticket office in Thana and they will telegraph my adjutant if Harry Lyndon purchases a ticket for Bori Bunder station.'

'But I could travel to Thana,' Kate said eagerly. 'If you have Ashok's home address I could visit his family and find out if Harry had been there?'

Colonel Lambert shook his head. 'That would be most unseemly and it would embarrass his people as well as the subedar-major. You ought to know that.'

'Yes, I suppose so. I wasn't thinking. Our cultures are so different.'

'Which is probably why you came up against such opposition from your parents. In time I believe things will change, but that is for the future. I can only suggest that you sit back and wait.'

'You're right, Colonel Lambert. I was never very patient, but I take your point.' Kate rose to her feet, holding out her hand. 'Thank you so much for taking the trouble to help me.'

He handed her a slip of paper. 'This is Ashok Patel's last known address in Thana, just in case you wish to contact him at any time. My wife is an Indian lady. We've been happily married for fifteen years, but we had to overcome the prejudices of both families. However, I wouldn't change a thing. I count myself a very fortunate man to have married such a wonderful woman, and I hope you find what you're seeking, Miss Martin. You're a plucky young lady and if Lyndon is fortunate enough to win your good opinion he will be a very lucky man.' He bowed out of the room, leaving Kate staring after him.

She made her way back to the dining room. 'Annie, are you ready to go to the hospital? I think we need to speak to Joe's doctor.'

Annie's eyes widened in alarm. 'Why? What did the colonel say?'

'Nothing about Joe, but what he's discovered does explain why Harry might have gone to Thana. I'm sure he'll return very soon and we need to find out if the doctors think that Joe is strong enough to undertake the voyage home.'

'Of course. I hadn't thought of that,' Annie said slowly. 'I just imagined we would arrive here and everything would be straightforward. But we have to wait for Harry, surely?'

'If we don't hear from him in the next couple of days I will go to Thana. I speak a little Hindi, so I'm not afraid to travel there alone, no matter what anyone says.'

'You mustn't even think about it,' Annie said vehemently. 'Harry would never forgive me if I allowed you to do something so rash.'

'Harry isn't here, which is the reason I'm even considering such a move. Colonel Lambert has had his adjutant go through the records and he discovered that Ash was born in Thana and lived there before he joined the army.'

'I thought you'd put him out of your mind. It's Harry you care about now.'

'Yes, you're right, and whatever Harry thinks about myself and Ashok is wrong, and that's what I want to tell him. Also I don't want Ashok to think that I sent Harry to find him. Had he wanted to, Ash could have followed me to London, or at least written to me.'

Annie did not look convinced. 'Best wait for Harry to return. At least we know where he is and why he left Joe in hospital.'

Kate sat down at the table, but the buttered eggs were cold and the toast also. She pushed her plate away. 'At the risk of offending Mrs Ogilvy I'm afraid I can't eat anything. Last night I made up my mind that I had to be patient and wait for Harry to return, but I've changed my mind.' Kate rang the bell. 'I'll apologise. She's gone out of her way to make us feel welcome.'

'You won't do anything rash, will you, Kate?' Annie said urgently. 'Please reconsider.'

Kate smiled. 'Don't worry about me, Annie. I know what I must do.' She looked up as the door opened and her hand flew to cover her lips. She jumped to her feet. 'Mira!'

346

The maid put her hands together and bowed her head. 'Namaskar, Memsahib Kate.'

Kate responded in kind before wrapping her arms around the maid in hug. 'I'm so pleased to see you, Mira. I didn't know you were still here.'

Mira smiled through her tears. 'Sahib Audley employed me. I was visiting my family when you arrived. I only returned this morning, and I found you were here. It's a miracle.'

'You know each other?' Annie asked in a dazed voice.

'Mira was my maid in Delhi. We escaped together and came here. Mira, this lady is my good friend Memsahib Annie Blythe. We've come to Bombay to see her brother, who is in hospital and, if the doctors allow it, we'll take him home to England.'

Annie smiled and nodded, but Mira was studying Kate's face with an anxious expression.

'You're not staying, memsahib?'

'Not for much longer, but I'm so happy to see you again, Mira.'

Mira backed away. 'You rang for a servant, memsahib?'

'You are my friend, Mira,' Kate said hastily. 'But you may apologise to Mrs Ogilvy for me. I couldn't finish my food, but it was delicious. We have to go to the hospital now, but you will be here when we return, won't you?'

'I will, memsahib.'

'Then we will speak again. You must tell me everything that has happened to you since I left for England.'

'I will, but I must not anger Mrs Ogilvy. I have

347

work to do.'

'Of course. I understand.' Kate reached out to tap Annie gently on the shoulder. 'We'd better go now or we might not be in time to speak to Joe's doctor.'

★ ★ ★

'The good news, Joe,' Kate said cheerfully, 'is that the doctors say that you are well enough to be discharged and you might benefit from the sea voyage home.'

Joe's expression brightened. 'Really? You can't imagine how tired I am of lying in this bed. I know they get me up and make me walk around the hospital, but I long for some fresh air and good food.'

Annie grasped his hand. 'You'll get all that when we arrive home, Joe. You'll love Warren House. It's warm and comfortable and the gardens are lovely. The scent of the roses in summer is quite wonderful.'

'But what about Harry?' Joe asked anxiously. 'I don't understand why he went off like that or why he hasn't returned. Do you think he's met with an accident?'

A cold hand of fear clutched at Kate's heart. 'Don't say things like that, Joe. We think he might have gone to Thana.'

'Why would he go there?' Joe looked from one to the other. 'What is there in Thana?'

'It might have something to do with an Indian soldier I knew when I lived in Delhi with my parents,' Kate said carefully. 'I don't know why Harry would want to contact Ashok, but that is the only reason I can think of that would explain why he went to Thana.'

'He told me how he felt about you, Kate.' Joe dropped his gaze. 'I mean he told me how you two met and it was obvious that he's in love with you, but you must know that.'

'Joe, it's none of our business,' Annie said quickly. 'Don't embarrass Kate.'

'It's all right, Annie.' Kate patted Annie's hand as it rested on the starched white coverlet. 'It's true that Harry and I have grown to know each other in dire circumstances. I expect he told you about Mad Monks and everything that went on in Whitechapel.'

Joe nodded. 'Yes, it was better than going to see a play in the theatre. I hung on his every word.'

'Well, Harry knew how much you mean to Annie and I think he felt guilty for the way the family had treated you both. That's why he came to your rescue. It had nothing to do with me.'

'I don't agree,' Annie said firmly. 'It was obvious that Harry wanted desperately to earn your good opinion, Kate. I think he fell in love with you from the start. I can understand why he wants to lay the ghost of your old love before he declares himself to you.'

Kate was conscious that she was blushing and she turned her head away. 'I can't speak for Harry, but whatever I felt for Ashok died in the flames of the rebellion. I did love him, but I knew it could never be. Harry had no need to go in search of the truth — if he'd asked me I would have told him.'

'He'll be back,' Joe said eagerly. 'You can tell him then.'

Kate smiled vaguely, but she was not convinced.

It would take less than half a day for Harry to make the return journey from Thana, and the more she thought about his continued absence the more anxious she grew. She sat in silence for the rest of their visit, allowing Annie time to talk to her brother and tell him the advantages of living in Walthamstow.

By the time that Kate returned to Audley House she had made up her mind, but she was determined to keep her plan a secret from everyone except Mira. Later that evening, when she was sitting in the courtyard after dinner, Kate was enjoying the wonders of the soft and warm India night as she made plans for the next day, and those included Mira, whom she knew she could trust implicitly.

* * *

'You must keep the dupatta over your head and cover as much of your face as possible,' Mira said anxiously as they were about to leave the house. 'Your fair hair and blue eyes will mark you out immediately.'

'Yes, I realise that.' Kate pulled the silk scarf down further, bending her head so that her face was in deep shadow. 'Remember, Mira, I am your servant, so I will walk behind you and I'll keep quiet.'

'Yes, memsahib.'

Kate giggled. 'Not memsahib. My name is Leela.' 'It's going to be difficult,' Mira said nervously.

'You can do it.' Kate stepped outside. 'It's only

for a few hours. We'll visit Thana and be back by nightfall or sooner. I had to tell Annie because I knew she would panic if she woke up to find me gone. She will make excuses for me and no one will even know we're missing.'

'It's fortunate that Mrs Ogilvy visits her friend on the other side of town today,' Mira said, glancing up and down the street. 'There's no one about who might recognise you. We'd better hurry.'

Kate hailed a tonga and when it came to a halt she stood aside, allowing Mira to take precedence. Acting the part perfectly, Mira instructed the tonga wallah to take them to Bori Bunder station, and Kate climbed in beside her. It was early morning but already the sun beat down from an azure sky, and the heat rose mercilessly from the ground. Kate, however, was too excited and nervous to feel anything other than exhilaration tinged with a little fear. They might be going on a wild-goose chase, but at least she would know for certain if this was the same path that Harry had taken three weeks previously. They alighted at the railway station and Mira purchased their tickets for Thana. Kate stood back, head bowed, clutching the dupatta tightly around her head and neck, and to her relief their fellow travellers pushed past, ignoring her as if she had suddenly become invisible.

The train was packed with standing room only, and Kate suspected that some of the passengers had climbed up onto the roof, but she huddled in a corner with Mira and neither of them spoke until they reached their destination. They were swept along by the crowd, who had leaped from the carriages, and Kate found herself standing beside Mira on the dusty road outside the station. Kate had Ashok's address tucked into the neck of the blouse she wore beneath the sari that Mira had fashioned for her. She took the slip of paper out and handed it to Mira.

'This is where we have to go. Perhaps you could ask someone for directions?'

Mira glanced at it and smiled. 'I know this street. My grandmother lives not far from there. I used to visit her often when I was a child.'

'Is it far to walk?'

'No, it's quite near. We don't need to hire a tonga. Perhaps I could visit my grandmother while you call upon your friends?'

'I need you to do the talking for me, Mira. I doubt if Ashok will be there — he's a soldier and is probably away on duty. I'm looking for Harry Lyndon, or maybe he is using the name Harry Trader. He is the one I want to find.' Kate walked on with Mira falling into step at her side.

'But I thought it was the subedar-major you loved, memsahib.'

'That was a long time ago and so much has changed since then, Mira. I will always have a place in my heart for Ashok, but I'm afraid it wasn't meant to be.'

'I am sorry.' Mira flashed her a sideways glance. 'But if you see him again it might bring back all those tender feelings.'

'That is something I will have to risk.' Kate quickened her step. 'How far now?'

'Nearly there.' Mira pointed to a small white house surrounded by peepal trees, but even as they prepared the cross the street, people dressed in their finest clothes appeared from the rear of the building.

'It's a wedding procession,' Mira said, grabbing Kate by the arm and pulling her into the shade of a coralwood tree.

Kate had seen many such processions when she had lived in Delhi and they never failed to impress her. The glorious colours of the costumes and the variety of printed cottons, silks and chiffons trimmed with gold braid, sequins and glass beads were something wonderful to see. The men were as magnificent as the women, but it was the bridegroom, riding a splendid white horse, who caught Kate's attention. She bit her lip to prevent herself from calling his name, and she leaned against the trunk of the tree, clenching her fists until the pain of her nails digging into her flesh was almost too much to bear.

'Ashok!' she murmured on a deep sigh.

'It is the one you used to see in secret when we were in Delhi,' Mira said in a whisper.

Kate nodded, unable to speak in case she choked on a sob. She had, of course, known in her heart that their love was doomed from the beginning, but she thought she had conquered the feelings she had for Ashok. However, seeing him looking so handsome and magnificent in his wedding finery brought back memories both sweet and agonising. Somehow she felt betrayed, even though the small voice of reason in her head told her that such a feeling was irrational. If she called his name he might turn to look at her and she would know in an instant if he still had feelings for her — but somehow she managed to curb the impulse. Ash had made a new life for himself, as had she. There was no going back.

'Memsahib, are you all right?'

Mira's voice penetrated the fog in Kate's brain and she dragged herself back to the present. 'Yes. I just wasn't expecting to see this.'

'Perhaps we should leave?' Mira said urgently as a small crowd of well-wishers appeared from seemingly nowhere.

'I mustn't forget why we came here today.' Kate dashed tears from her cheeks with a flick of her fingers. 'I still need to speak to someone in the wedding party. I'm sure that Harry must have been here, and I need to find out when that was. He's been missing for over three weeks, Mira. Anything could have happened to him.'

'Perhaps we should keep our distance.'

'Yes, that's what we must do.' Kate took a deep breath. The shock of seeing Ash again was overcome by a sudden urge to see the woman who had captured his heart. 'Come on, Mira. We'll follow the wedding party.'

'Is that wise, memsahib?' Mira asked anxiously. 'Some things are best forgotten.'

'You mean well, Mira, but I know what I'm doing.' Kate pulled the dupatta down over her forehead and stepped out onto the road, following the joyous procession at a safe distance.

As she had expected, the bridegroom's procession moved on until they came to the bride's home, which seemed to be the finest house in the neighbourhood. It looked as though Ash was marrying money, and somehow that hurt more than the fact that he had another woman in his life. Kate could only hope that he had fallen in love with the beautiful rich girl who waited for him patiently beneath a flower-bedecked canopy, and when the bride looked up and saw her future husband there was no mistaking the adoration on her face. Kate realised at that moment she had lost Ashok for ever.

Kate and Mira stood at the edge of the gathering. Ashok dismounted, handing the reins to a younger man, whom Kate decided must be one of Ash's brothers, they were so alike. Kate could see Ash only in profile, but it was enough to convince her that this was not an arranged match. Her heart ached and yet she was happy for him. Subedar-Major Ashok Patel was a fine man and he deserved a loving wife. Kate could see the bride's expression more clearly now, and it mirrored her own feelings during that blissful time in Delhi when she had first fallen in love. Kate turned to leave but found her way barred by a tall, bearded man.

'Who are you?' he demanded in a low voice.

'This is a private celebration and you are not one of us.'

'I-I'm sorry,' Kate murmured, uncomfortably aware that heads were turning and people were staring at her. 'I'll go now.'

The man drew her aside. 'Who are you?'

Mira stepped in between them. 'Let her go at once. Memsahib Martin is a guest of Sir Robert Audley.

Even in this small town you must have heard of him.'

'You are impertinent, girl. Know your place.'

'Mira has just told you my name,' Kate said angrily. 'We will be on our way.'

He closed his large hand around her slender arm. 'Come with me.'

Despite the fact that they were in the middle of a happy occasion, Kate felt a sudden chill. 'Not until you tell me where we're going. Who are you, anyway?'

'My name is not important. Don't make a fuss.' He glared at Mira. 'You must come, too.'

'I think I know you, Bikram Patel.' Mira shook off his restraining hand. 'You're Ashok's brother. We used to play together when I stayed with my grandmother.'

'That was a long time ago,' Bikram said with a hint of a smile. 'But you must both come with me now. People are looking at us. Do you want to ruin my brother's wedding?'

22

'No, of course not,' Kate said hurriedly. She allowed Bikram to lead her away from the wedding party and out into the street. The heat was oppressive and she swayed on her feet as a feeling of faintness overcame her. Seconds later she felt herself lifted in a pair of strong arms, and she closed her eyes in an attempt to stop the world from spinning around her.

When she opened them again she was seated on an old and saggy armchair in an unfamiliar room. A strong scent of sandalwood and crushed rose petals was secondary to the fumes from the oil lamp placed on a brass table at the side of her seat. The blinds were lowered to keep out the heat, but despite this, it was stiflingly hot. Mira was fanning Kate energetically but it did little to cool the air.

'Where am I?' Kate murmured anxiously. 'Where is Bikram?'

'I don't know, memsahib. He brought us here and he said you were to wait.'

Kate struggled to her feet, but the feeling of dizzi-ness and nausea made her sink back onto the uncomfortable seat. 'He might intend to keep us here until after the wedding ceremony, but I'm not here to make trouble for Ashok.'

Mira increased her efforts with the palm leaf fan. 'Don't upset yourself, memsahib. I know Bikram.

He's not a bad man. He won't harm us.'

'I'm not afraid of him, I just want to find Harry.'

'Then you have come to the right place, mem-sahib.' Bikram beckoned them from the doorway. 'Harry will see you now, but I should warn you that he has been suffering from a severe bout of malaria, which overcame him soon after he arrived in Thana.'

'Harry is here?' Kate rose unsteadily to her feet. 'Let me see him.'

Bikram led the way to a back room, which was also in semi-darkness. He moved a smoking oil lamp a little nearer to the charpoy where Harry was propped up on coloured cushions, their brightness at odds with his sallow skin and sunken cheeks. Kate kneeled at his bedside.

'Harry.' She reached out to brush a stray lock of hair back from his damp forehead. 'Why didn't you return to the hospital when you were taken ill? They would have taken care of you.'

'I thought you were safe at home.' He clutched her hand. 'What are you doing here, Kate? Are you real, or has the fever returned?'

'She is real, sahib,' Bikram said, smiling.

'I received a letter from Joseph, written by one of your nurses. It said that you were both very ill, so I decided to come to India and bring you home.'

'You travelled across the globe on your own?'

'No, Harry. Annie is with me. We're staying with Papa's old friend Sir Robert Audley.'

'Joe was doing so well. I was going to book our voyage home when I went down with the first bout of malaria. Then Joe developed gangrene and had to have an amputation.'

'I know, Harry,' Kate said gently. 'He told us about it. You've both had a terrible time.'

'I was perfectly well until I arrived in Thana, and then I became ill again.'

'You are much recovered from when you first went down with the fever,' Bikram said firmly. 'It is thanks to my mother's medicines that you are still alive.'

'I am most grateful to you and your family, Bikram.' Kate rose to her feet. 'When will Harry be well enough for me to take him home?'

'I can speak for myself,' Harry said irritably. 'The fever has gone, although to be honest, it's left me so weak that I can hardly stand.'

'I'm not surprised.' Kate pulled up a stool and sat down again. She was still shaky, and seeing Harry in such a weakened state had shocked her to the core. 'We must get you back to Audley House, Harry.'

'How is Joe? I didn't mean to leave him for such a long time.'

'He's doing surprisingly well, although he's desperate to leave the hospital. I'd have come here sooner, but no one knew where you were, even Joseph. It was only when we discovered that Ashok was born in Thana that we wondered if you'd come here to find him, but I don't understand why you would do such a thing.'

'I knew I had to lay the ghost of your first love, Kate. What chance had I got if you still harboured feelings for the fellow? I needed to meet him and see what I was up against.'

'Instead of which you arrived on our doorstep

359

and passed out,' Bikram said with a wry smile. 'My brother still doesn't know why you came to us, Harry.'

'I'm sorry I gave you so much trouble, Bikram. I think I would have died had it not been for your mother's expert knowledge of herbs and medicines. But if I was off my head with fever, how did you find out who I was?'

'I sat with you during your ravings, sahib. I pieced the story together, but I kept it to myself. My family had a wedding to plan.'

'Is it today?' Harry asked dazedly. 'Do you know about this, Kate?'

'I arrived here in time to see the wedding party setting off. I admit it was a shock, but then I realised how much things have changed — how much I have changed. It simply was not to be, Harry.'

He reached out to take her hand in his and squeezed her fingers. 'That's all I wanted to know.'

'Joe will be so relieved to learn that you're safe. Which reminds me,' Kate said, turning to Bikram, 'you ought to be with your family. Your brother's wedding is too important for you to be spending it here with us.'

'It was necessary to bring you to Harry,' Bikram said with a wry smile. 'Now you know how you really feel and you can live your life in peace. My brother will be happy enough with his chosen bride, but I must ask you to leave here before the others return. Only I know about you and Ashok. It is better that way.'

'I understand.' Kate raised Harry's thin hand to her lips. 'Can you find some sort of transport to take us to the railway station? We'll catch the next train for Bori Bunder.'

'Of course.' Bikram moved to the doorway where Mira had been standing quietly. 'Will you pack the few things that Harry brought with him, Mira? I'll show you where they are.'

'You always did like to tell me what to do,' Mira said with a pert smile. 'It's like old times, Bikram.' She followed him from the room.

Kate could hear them chatting amicably until their voices faded into the distance. 'I think Mira has rekindled an old friendship. I'd like to think she had someone to look after her.'

Harry smiled weakly. 'You were always a little matchmaker, Kate.'

'Me?' She stared at him in astonishment. 'Name one match I've made.'

'Annie and Peregrine Harte.'

'I had nothing to do with that. They fell in love all by themselves.'

'With no encouragement from you?'

'Not really. Perry is a good man and Annie is a sweet girl. They were meant for each other.'

'What about your maid, Jenny, and Hedley Courtney?'

'How do you know about these things, Harry? You were away when Jenny and Hedley were married.'

'Annie wrote to Joe, or rather she dictated the letters to my mother, who was pleased to pass on the gossip, often adding little extras herself. Joe let me read them.'

'You can't lay all of it at my door,' Kate said, laughing. 'I can see you're back to your old self, and here was I, feeling sorry for you. I think you're a bit of a fraud.'

'I've made you smile, Kate. That's what I've been missing all these months. Now I'm happy.'

She leaned over and dropped a kiss on his forehead. 'Don't exert yourself. Save your strength for the journey back to Bombay. I think I should take you straight to the hospital.'

'No, please. I will go there tomorrow or the next day, but I need to sleep in a soft bed, and I want to make sure that you are really here and not one of my fevered dreams.'

'I am here, I assure you of that. I'm going nowhere without you, Harry.'

She turned her head to give Bikram a grateful smile as he walked into the room. 'I can't thank you and your family enough for taking care of Harry. But what will you tell Ashok? He will know that Harry couldn't have made the journey back to the hospital on his own.'

'I will tell my family that Sir Robert sent his servant to fetch Harry. They won't think to question me — why should they?' Bikram's stern features creased in a wide grin. 'And it gives me an excuse to visit Mira. I will, of course, have to thank her properly for relieving us of our sick guest.'

'You and Mira?' Kate shot a sideways glance at Harry, trying not to giggle. 'She's obviously very fond of you and your family, Bikram. And her grandmother lives quite near here, so Mira might visit her more often.'

'Kate,' Harry said firmly, 'I think it's time we left.' He struggled to a sitting position. 'Bikram, old chap. Will you help me up?'

It was not an easy journey, but Harry had lost a great deal of weight and with Mira's help Kate managed to get him settled in a corner seat on the train. When they reached Bori Bunder station Mira went out to hail a tonga, and the tonga wallah half-carried Harry to the vehicle and hoisted him into the carriage. Sandeep rushed out to assist them when they arrived at Audley House and then Mrs Ogilvy took over, seemingly delighted to have someone too weak to argue with her. She put Harry to bed in one of the guest rooms and issued orders to the cook that light nourishing meals must be created for the invalid. Harry put up with this on the first night, but after breakfast in bed next morning he insisted on sending for Sandeep to help him get washed and dressed.

'I'm being treated like a baby,' Harry said with a heavy sigh when Kate found him in the front parlour, seated in a cane chair with a blanket wrapped around his knees. 'I feel like an elderly invalid.'

Kate chuckled. 'You can't be a baby and an old gentleman. Make up your mind, Harry.'

'You know very well what I mean. I need to exercise and get my muscles working again. I can hardly walk two steps without someone holding me up.'

'You must be patient, Harry. You've been very ill. Anyway, the doctor is coming this morning. Sir Robert insisted on sending for him to make sure that you have everything you need to get you fit again.'

'At this rate I might well have to run away,' Harry said, sighing. 'Although I doubt if I could run anywhere at the moment, even if the house was on fire.'

'Stop grumbling and be thankful that you're alive and on the mend.' Kate was about to leave the room when Harry called her back.

'Where are you going? You can't leave me here on my own.'

'I'm going to the hospital to see Joe and tell him that you're here. Annie is just finishing her breakfast and she's going to sit with you until the doctor comes. You are to do what you're told, Harry Trader, or Harry Lyndon, whichever you choose to be today.'

'Petticoat government,' Harry said, pulling a face. 'Hurry back, Kate.'

★ ★ ★

The doctor visited Harry later that morning and was pleased with his progress, so Annie told Kate when she returned from the hospital. Another week or two of rest and good food and Harry would be able to undertake the voyage home to England.

'That's wonderful,' Kate said, taking off her straw bonnet and flinging it onto the bed in her room. 'Thank you for sitting with him, Annie. I know you'd rather be at the hospital with Joe, but there's good news there, too. I saw the doctor who's been treating your brother and she said that Joe is strong enough to leave hospital. He'll always have to walk with crutches, but you knew that anyway.'

'Yes, of course, and Sir Robert came to see me earlier with Joe's discharge papers. We can all travel home together.'

Kate sat down on the window seat overlooking the courtyard. 'It's been lovely staying here, but we mustn't impose on Sir Robert any longer than necessary. I'll ask Sandeep to drive me to the shipping office this afternoon to purchase our return tickets. That will give us something to plan for.'

'It must have been so hard for you seeing Ashok in his wedding finery. Do you regret not speaking to him?'

Kate shook her head. 'No. It wouldn't have been right. He's making a life for himself and I've no right to upset him or his bride. I've said goodbye to him in my heart, and as far as I'm concerned it's over.'

'Mira seems quite taken with Bikram,' Annie said, chuckling. 'I think there might be a budding romance between them.'

'Harry said I was a matchmaker; now you're doing it.'

'I think we all want to see people happy,' Annie said dreamily. 'I really miss Perry, and I hope he misses me.'

'I'm sure he does, and in four months or so you'll be able to tell him how you feel.'

'Yes, I will. I just hope you're not making a mistake by leaving India without talking to Ashok.'

'What good would that do now, Annie? He's a married man and I love Harry. There, I've said it, and I think Harry loves me. The past is over and done with.' Kate stood up and went to the dressing table to tidy her hair. 'I'm going to give Harry

365

the good news that we'll be leaving very soon. We should be home in time for Christmas.'

★ ★ ★

Two days later Kate alighted from the tonga outside Audley House. She left Mira to pay the tonga wallah, and was about to walk up the path to the front door when she heard someone call her name. She froze on the spot, turning her head slowly at the sound of the familiar and once-loved voice. Ashok was standing on the pavement with Bikram at his side.

'Go inside, memsahib. I will deal with this,' Mira said urgently.

Kate laid her hand on Mira's arm. 'No, it's all right. You can spend a little time with Bikram. I will speak to Ash.'

Reluctantly, Mira walked towards the servants' entrance accompanied by Bikram, leaving Kate and Ashok facing each other on the steaming pavement. At that moment the monsoon rain began to pour from a leaden sky.

'Come with me, Ash.' Kate hurried up the path and stepped into the shelter of the portico.

'I had to see you, Kate.'

She tugged at his sleeve. 'You're soaked to the skin, Ash. I can't ask you into the house but you must take shelter.'

'Why didn't you make yourself known to me when you were in Thana?' Ash demanded angrily. 'I thought we meant something to each other.'

Kate was suddenly breathless. She had imagined coming face to face with Ashok so many times in the past, but the reality was different and she was suddenly tongue-tied. 'How could I spoil your special day?'

'You can't say that. You have no idea how I might feel about you now. We swore to love each other for ever.'

'I remember that,' Kate said mistily. 'But it's different now.'

'I haven't changed. I still love you, Kate.'

'You're a married man. You have to forget me, Ash.'

'As you have forgotten me,' he said bitterly. 'Your words meant nothing.'

'That isn't fair,' Kate protested. 'I didn't know if you were alive or dead. I had no alternative but to return to my own country and make a life for myself, but that doesn't mean that I forgot you.'

He bowed his head. 'That man who stayed with my family while he was sick — is he your lover?'

'This is ridiculous, Ash. I'm glad that you survived the fighting, but why did you come here today?'

'I had to see you. I wanted to know if there was anything still between us.'

'Your brother should not have told you about me.'

'I knew there was something he was keeping from me. I dragged it out of him. Perhaps I sensed that you had been there that day. My marriage was arranged by her parents and mine.'

'Then I hope you will be happy, Ash. I really mean that.'

'You came all the way to Bombay to find that man? You didn't think to come looking for me?'

'Ash, this is getting us nowhere. You are a married man and I am spoken for. At least I think I am.'

'You are not certain? You wish to marry that sick man?'

'Ash, I loved you very much, but it was a long time ago now — it was another life. We are not the same people we were then.'

'I still love you, Kate.'

Kate hesitated, gazing into his tragic, dark eyes. 'The girl I was then still has a place in her heart for you, but the rebellion changed our lives for ever.'

He dashed the rain from his eyes. 'In my heart I am still the same.'

'I'm returning to London, Ashok. We didn't have a chance to say goodbye before, but I'm saying it now. You have a beautiful wife and I hope you have a happy marriage. I'll never forget you, and I'll always be grateful to your family for taking care of Harry.'

He backed out into the teeming rain. 'I will always love you, Kate. But you are right: I have my path in life and you have yours.' He walked away, shoulders hunched, his clothes sodden.

Kate brushed the raindrops from her cheeks, or perhaps they were tears — she did not know which — but she had made her choice. Her future was not in India, much as she loved the country and its people. She clutched her reticule with both hands. It contained the tickets that would take them home. In four months or maybe a little less, depending on the strength of the trade winds, they would arrive in London.

Kate's last mission was to visit the graveyard where her beloved uncle's ashes had been interred. It had taken her some time to pluck up the courage to say farewell to the man who had made her a very rich woman, but having seen the quiet surroundings, she knew that he was at peace. She draped a garland of marigolds over the stone that marked his place, and whispered a final goodbye before leaving. Harry was waiting for her in the carriage and Sandeep drove them back to Audley House.

Harry raised her hand to his lips. 'Your uncle would be proud of you, Kate.'

'I don't know why you say that. I've done little enough with the money he left me.'

'Nonsense. You'd already started the soup kitchen and it was only circumstances that forced you to give it up. From what I saw of Warren House you've spent your money well, even though it doesn't belong to you. If that's not altruistic, I don't know what is.'

She leaned against his broad shoulder. 'I want to do more, Harry. When we return to London I want to do more for the poor and needy. I'd like to think that Uncle Edgar would be proud of me.'

'I don't think there's any doubt of that, Kate. My mission will be to put Monks behind bars for the rest of his miserable life.'

Kate laid her hand on his. 'But first you must get completely better. I hope the long sea voyage will be good for you and for Joe.'

★ ★ ★

Despite the cramped conditions on a sailing ship, built mainly to carry cargo but fitted out to take a few passengers, Kate was happy in the small world she inhabited with those closest to her. She had always been fond of Annie, and as she grew to know Joe better Kate realised that he was very much like his sister. Her relationship with Harry deepened with every passing day. What she had felt for Ashok seemed like a youthful dalliance when compared to the feelings she had for Harry. But although they had grown so close that they seemed to think alike, there was a hint of reserve in Harry's manner that baffled her.

On their final night at sea, in the cold waters of the Thames Estuary, Kate had seen Annie tucked up safely in her bunk, and she had returned to the small saloon where they ate their meals and spent much of their spare time. The other passengers had retired to bed, wanting an early night before disembarking at the East India Docks next morning, and Harry was there on his own.

'I thought you'd turned in, Kate,' he said, smiling.

'I'm so excited that I doubt if I'll sleep a wink. I can't believe that we'll be home in time for Christmas.'

Kate sat down at the table where they had eaten their supper. 'It will feel strange to be back on land after so many months at sea. I know we had brief trips ashore when we took on fresh supplies, but that hardly counts.'

Harry cleared his throat, eyeing her warily. 'I won't be coming to Walthamstow with you tomorrow, Kate.'

She stared at him in astonishment. 'You're staying in London? Why?'

'I have some business to attend to, but I will be with you on Christmas Day.'

'But surely you could leave whatever it is until after Christmas? Everyone will be so looking forward to our return. You did send a telegram from our last port of call, didn't you?'

'Of course I did. Don't upset yourself, my love. I need to find out what's been happening with Monks — you know that as well as anyone — but I promise I'll come to Warren House on Christmas Day.'

'But that's the day after tomorrow, Harry. Can't you come with us and leave Monks until later?'

Harry reached across the table to grasp her hand. 'If word gets round that I've come home and Monks hears of it, I'll be a marked man, and so will all of the people I love. The whole reason for my mother, you and the others hiding away in Walthamstow is because of Mad Monks. That man is a vicious criminal and he knows that I was working with the police to bring him in.'

Kate withdrew her hand, fixing Harry with a stony stare. 'Is that the only reason? Or have we grown too close during the last four months at sea? Are you afraid to come home with me, Harry? I won't hold you to any of the wonderful things you've said to me during our time together. I realise that being confined for so long in each other's company can make people say things they don't mean.'

'I meant every word I've ever said to you, Kate. I love you with all my heart, but our relationship has to end here, at least until I know that Monks is safely out of the way. If we announce our engagement it would mean that you are even more of a target for Monks and his men. It would be like signing your death warrant. You do understand that, don't you?'

23

Kate had hardly slept that night, but in the morning she was able to say goodbye to Harry with a brave smile, even though she knew he might be heading into danger. The last four months had been a respite from the real world, but now she knew there were hard truths to face. Warren House had been a perfect hideaway, not too far from London, but not close enough to come under the scrutiny of Monks or any of his remaining gang. As she sat in the hackney carriage with Annie and Joe, Kate was reminded of the last time she had returned from India, and had faced the reality of the East End streets, the poverty, the filth and the industry that polluted the very air she breathed. The world seemed to have lost all its colour in the black and grey of an English winter, compared to the blaze of sun and brilliance of Bombay.

'Kate, I asked you a question.' Annie's voice broke into Kate's reverie.

'I'm sorry. What did you say?'

'I wanted to know if you thought that Perry would come to Warren House for Christmas.'

'I can't say. I mean I asked Harry to send him a telegram when we called in at Southampton, but I didn't think to check.'

'Oh, well, if Harry said he'd do it I'm sure he wouldn't let you down. Why isn't he with us, Kate? I was shocked when he said goodbye at the docks.'

'He has things to do that don't concern us,

'Annie.' Joseph leaned back in the corner of the cab. 'How far is it to Warren House? My bones ache already in this damp atmosphere. I'd almost forgotten what an English winter was like.'

'I suppose it will take an hour or so. The cabby wasn't too pleased to be taken so far out of town, but I offered him double the fare and that persuaded him.'

'I can't wait to be with Aunt Margaret and the children,' Annie said, smiling. 'I've missed them all.'

'We'll have to move on sooner or later. We can't stay at Warren House for ever, Annie.' Joseph stared gloomily out of the rain and mud-spattered window. 'Harry said it wasn't safe for Aunt Margaret to return to Finsbury Circus, but you and I will have to rent rooms somewhere else.'

'Aunt Margaret made it very clear that she wanted us to live with her,' Annie protested. 'She's getting on in years, Joe. We can't abandon her. Besides which, we haven't any money now that you've left the army, and I can't earn enough to keep us both.'

Kate threw up her hands. 'What a miserable party we are, to be sure. There's no question of either of you having to leave Warren House. Heaven knows, it's big enough for all of us, and Lady Lyndon is the most hospitable person I know.'

'Harry won't throw us out,' Annie insisted, pouting. 'You will have to grow stronger, Joe. The country air will do you good.'

'We might as well face facts, Annie,' Joe said with a heavy sigh. 'I'm a cripple and no use to anyone. I've no profession and the best I could hope for is a poorly paid clerk's position in the city.'

'Joe, it's nearly Christmas.' Kate reached across Annie to pat Joe on the hand. 'Do please cheer up. I'm sure you'll find something better than that. Maybe Perry can help.'

'I don't want to be beholden to him. He wouldn't want to be saddled with a crippled brother-in-law, as well as a blind wife.'

Kate slapped his hand. 'That's uncalled for, Joe. And it's unkind.'

'How can you say things like that, Joe?' Annie said tearfully. 'Perry hasn't asked me to marry him. We've been away for months and he might have changed his mind or met someone else. And I'm not a burden.'

Joe wrapped his arms around his sister. 'I'm sorry,

Annie. I don't know what made me say that. I didn't mean it. Any man would be lucky to have you for a wife.'

'Let's change the subject,' Kate said firmly. 'Remember the season, Joe. We've bought presents for everyone and they'll be longing to hear about our time in Bombay and our voyage home. You'll be all right, I won't let you and Annie starve.' She faced him with a meaningful frown. 'And don't say that you won't accept charity. I'll help you because I love you both, and Annie is the nearest thing I have to a sister, so that makes you my brother, and family look after each other.' She sat back in her seat, silently daring him to argue, but Joe was obviously chastened by their words, and he kept his thoughts to himself for the rest of the cab ride.

When they reached the road that crossed the marshes the rain turned to sleet and then to snow, and by the time they reached Warren House large wintry flakes were settling on the ground. Kate gave the cabby a large tip and he grunted a response, refusing her offer of a hot drink before he undertook the journey back to London. He drove off, sending flurries of snow from the horse's hoofs and the carriage wheels.

It was Tilly who opened the door and she forgot herself enough to give Kate a hug. 'Oh, miss. It's so good to see you. We was hoping you'd make it, even though the snow started falling over an hour ago. Let me take your cape and bonnet, and Miss Annie's, too.'

'Where are my mother and Lady Lyndon?' Kate asked, smiling.

The weather might be awful but Tilly's welcome was genuine and her enthusiastic greeting brought a smile to Joe's lips.

'In the drawing room, miss. The nippers are in the kitchen having their supper with Ivy and Mrs Boggis.'

'When they've finished their meal we'd like a tray of tea in the drawing room, please, Tilly.' Kate turned to Joe. 'Would you like something stronger? Something to keep out the cold.'

He handed his greatcoat, hat and gloves to Tilly. 'Tea will be very welcome. I don't suppose there are any muffins or crumpets in the kitchen, are there, young lady? I've been dreaming of hot buttered muffins all the time I was in hospital.'

376

Tilly blushed to the roots of her mousy brown hair. 'I'll ask Mrs Boggis, sir. If there are I'll bring you some with lots of butter.'

'Good girl,' Joe said with a disarming smile. 'I love it here already.'

'Behave yourself, Joe.' Annie gave him a gentle push in the direction of the drawing room. 'Mind your manners in front of Aunt Margaret and Lady Martin, and don't go on about your injuries; they don't want to know.'

'Stop nagging me, woman,' Joe said, chuckling. 'I've had my moan. I'll make an effort to be cheerful now.'

A log fire blazed in the grate, sending out the familiar fragrance of burning apple wood, and in the corner of the room a decorated Christmas tree was surrounded with presents. The children had obviously been busy making colourful paper-chains, which they had draped over the portraits of sternlooking dignitaries who must once have held prominent positions, but were now simply part of the festive décor. Lady Lyndon remained seated in an armchair by the fire, but Arabella rose to her feet with a welcoming smile.

'Kate, my dear. We were beginning to think that the weather had held you up.'

Kate dutifully hugged her mother. 'We were determined to get home for Christmas, Mama.' She smiled down at Lady Lyndon. 'I've brought someone to see you, ma'am.'

Lady Lyndon glanced past Kate and her face lit up when she saw Annie with Joe lingering in the doorway. 'Annie, my dear. I'm so glad to see you safe and sound, and is that Joe loitering behind you? Come forward, Joe. Let me look at you.'

Joe limped into the room, leaning heavily on his crutches. 'I'd kiss your hand, Aunt, but I'm hampered by these dreadful wooden things.'

'Don't be silly, Joe,' Lady Lyndon said sharply. 'I don't expect you to kowtow to me, but you were always a rebel, just like your father.'

'I'm a soldier, Aunt. Or I was . . .'

Kate sent him a warning look. 'Take a seat near the fire, Joe. You look perished. It's quite difficult to get used to an English winter after the heat of India. I should know.'

'Yes,' Annie added hastily. 'But you'll soon get acclimatised, and you'll love it here, Joe.'

Lady Lyndon glanced over Kate's shoulder. 'Where is Harry?'

'He's following later,' Kate said, improvising wildly. 'He had a few things to settle in London before he came home.'

'I do hope he isn't going to start up that gaming club business again.' Lady Lyndon sighed, shaking her head. 'And I hope the police have caught that dreadful creature who forced us out of our homes. Perry visits occasionally, but he never tells me anything.'

'I'm sure they have everything under control.' Kate pulled up a chair and sat next to her mother. 'How have you been, Mama? I quite thought I might come home to find that you and Mr Pomeroy-Smith had eloped to Gretna Green.'.

'Don't say such things, Kate. Not even in jest.' Arabella raised her left hand to her cheek, exhibiting an expensive-looking diamond ring. 'We are officially affianced, but will wait until your papa has been gone for two years before we get married. It's only proper.'

Kate leaned over to give her mother a hug. 'I'm so glad, Mama. You deserve to be happy and Giles is a good man.'

'And very wealthy,' Lady Lyndon added, chuckling. 'Not, of course, that it had anything to do with your decision, Arabella. Giles is a very presentable man, and quite charming. If I were a few years younger I might have been a serious rival.'

Arabella opened her mouth to comment but a knock on the door and a rattle of teacups announced Tilly's arrival with a laden tray. Kate jumped to her feet to help her.

'I'm longing to see the children, Tilly,' Annie said wistfully. 'Are they all well? They must have grown a lot since we went away.'

'They're shooting up, miss.' Tilly smiled proudly. 'Shall I send them to you when they've finished their meal?'

Annie bit her lip. 'Do you mind, Aunt Margaret? I can always go to the kitchen if you'd rather they didn't come to the drawing room.'

'Nonsense,' Lady Lyndon said cheerfully. 'They're always welcome, aren't they, Arabella?'

Kate shot a sideways glance at her mother, knowing very well her dislike of children in general, but Arabella was smiling, even if it was a little forced.

'Of course they are. Anyway, I have to go to my room to change for dinner. We're expecting Perry to come down from London, providing the roads are still passable, and Giles is coming, too. Tilly, I'll need your help since I allowed Mrs Goodfellow to spend the evening with her husband.'

'Mrs Goodfellow is your maid, Mama?' Kate stared at her mother in surprise. Bold, brassy and not afraid to speak her mind, Marie Goodfellow was hardly the sort of person her mother would have chosen in the old days.

'Needs must, Kate. Needs must.' Arabella rose to her feet and whisked Tilly out of the room before she had a chance to speak.

Lady Lyndon smiled benignly. 'It's so good to have you all home safe and sound, but I won't rest until Harry returns. I have a feeling there's something you are not telling me, Kate.'

'Harry will explain everything when he joins us,' Kate said diplomatically. She turned her attention to the tea tray. 'Look, Joe. Hot buttered muffins, just what you wanted.'

'If you can't explain Harry's absence, you can at least tell me about your experiences on the journey.' Lady Lyndon shook her head when Kate offered her a cup of tea. 'No, thank you, my dear. I'll wait and have a glass of sherry wine when Perry arrives. He's always so amusing and he's missed you very much, Annie.'

Annie almost choked on her tea. 'Did he say so, Aunt?'

'Not in so many words, but he was always asking if I'd received word from you or Kate. You could do a lot worse, my dear. He's not a rich man but he has a steady income, and it's obvious that he's devoted to you.'

Kate could see that Annie was embarrassed.

'Perhaps it would be better if you told us what's been happening here in our absence, Lady Lyndon. We've been looking forward to coming home ever since we left Bombay.'

'Yes, indeed,' Annie added hastily. 'I've been telling Joe all about Warren House and the lovely times we've had here.'

Joe took a bite of buttered muffin, closing his eyes and smiling with obvious enjoyment. 'Mm, that was so good. You have an excellent cook, Aunt Margaret. No wonder you are happy to live in the country.'

'I can't wait to return to London, as it happens, Joe.' Lady Lyndon shot him a sideways glance. 'I'm not a countrywoman, although I have to admit it's been quite pleasant living here. However, I want to return to my house in Finsbury Circus, though you and Annie may live here as long as you wish.'

Joe hesitated with the other half of the muffin poised ready to take a bite. 'But I can't live here for ever, Aunt. How would I earn my living?'

'That's something you will have to decide for yourself, my boy.' Lady Lyndon rose somewhat creakily to her feet. 'I must go and change for dinner. You three had better do the same when you've finished your tea, although you will have to unpack your things yourselves. Since Jenny left it has been impossible to find anyone with her skills. Marie Goodfellow does her best, but she has fingers like sausages when it comes to doing one's hair or fastening tiny buttons.'

Kate stifled a giggle as Lady Lyndon swept out of the drawing room. 'Oh dear, I can see that this household needs a small adjustment, Annie. Maybe we ought to send for Mrs Hattersley, since your aunt is obviously desperate for a proper lady's maid.'

Annie nodded. 'As it happens I know that she went to stay with her sister in Epping. It's not too far from here. Maybe Goodfellow could take the carriage and fetch her, when the snow clears, of course.'

'Maybe I could train as a lady's maid,' Joe said gloomily.

'That would be very funny.' Annie put her head on one side. 'I think I can hear a carriage approaching. Maybe it's Perry.'

Kate stood up and crossed the floor to pull back the curtains. 'I don't know if it's Perry or Mr Pomeroy-Smith. Stay here, Annie, and if it's Perry I'll send him to you.' She hurried from the room before Annie could protest, and Joe was fully occupied, munching his way through the plate of muffins.

Kate arrived at the front entrance just as Tilly opened the door. Perry handed the reins to Bob, who was in his shirtsleeves, despite the bitter weather. 'Take good care of Tarquin and there's half a crown in it when I leave.' Perry took the steps two at a time, bringing a flurry of snow with him as he stepped into the hall. 'I thought I wasn't going to make it for a while. There was quite a blizzard as I crossed the marshes.' He shrugged off his great-coat and handed it to Tilly, together with his hat and gloves. 'Kate, this is wonderful. I wasn't sure if you'd be here.' He grasped her hand and held it tightly. 'You're back safe and sound.'

'And Annie is waiting for you in the drawing room.' Kate nodded to Tilly, who was eyeing them both expectantly. 'That will be all, for now, Tilly.'

Kate tucked her hand in the crook of Perry's arm.

'I want a word with you before we join them, Perry.' He gave her a quizzical smile. 'That sounds ominous.'

'No, it's just a matter of common sense and decency, if it comes to that.'

'Are you asking me if my intentions towards Annie are honourable?'

'Yes, I suppose I am. I'm very fond of her and she has no one to stand up for her, unless you count Joe, but he's so wrapped up in his own affairs that he's unlikely to even think of challenging you.'

'A challenge?' Perry's hazel eyes twinkled with amusement. 'Come, Kate. You know me better than most people. I was honest about my feelings for Annie from the start, or are you telling me that she has had a change of heart?'

'No, not at all. She adores you, Perry, and she's a thoroughly decent person. Don't break her heart.'

'I've no intention of doing anything of the sort. I love her, Kate. My feelings for her have deepened during our time apart and I intend to marry her, if she'll have me.'

Kate reached up to kiss him on the cheek. 'That's wonderful, but now you can tell me what I want to know.'

He met her gaze with a candid look. 'If it's Monks you're asking about, I'm afraid the answer is that he's still a problem. As you probably remember, he went into hiding south of the river and he's managed to evade captivity even now.'

'That's what worries me. Harry insisted that he had business in town, and I know exactly what that would be. He'll have gone after Monks on his own and I fear for his safety.'

'I was hoping he wouldn't do that. If he went straight to the police they will have told him to leave Monks to them.'

But if he went in search of Monks on his own — what then?'

Perry laid his hand on her arm. 'If that's so I'm afraid there's nothing that you or I can do about it, especially now. It's Christmas Eve and soon the roads will be all but impassable. I'm afraid we're likely to be stuck here for a while.'

'There's one other thing, Perry,' Kate said as they walked slowly towards the drawing room. 'Joe is quite badly crippled. He'll never be fully fit again, but he needs to find some sort of employment, and he knows nothing apart from soldiering. Can you help him without making him feel that he's being treated like a charity?'

'I'll have a chat with him. I'll do whatever I can for Annie's brother, and that's a promise.'

'I knew I could rely on you. And if you hear anything concerning Monks, please tell me. I'm very worried for Harry's safety.'

'When I return to London I'll speak to one of my contacts in the police force, and if Harry should get in touch with me I'll let you know.'

'Thank you, Perry.' Kate squeezed his arm as they came to a halt outside the drawing room. 'I'm going upstairs to change for dinner. I'll leave the rest to you.'

Kate walked away, but before going to her room she made her way to the kitchen where the children were just finishing their evening meal. They left the table, despite instructions from their mother to remain seated, and they danced around Kate, demanding to know if she had brought them anything from India.

Four-year-old Emma was convinced that Kate had packed an elephant in her cabin trunk, much to the amusement of Frankie and May. Six-year-old Nellie asked shyly if Kate had brought them a monkey for them to play with, and was obviously disappointed by the answer she received. However, with the promise of telling them stories of her travels when they were in bed, and reminding them that next day was Christmas Day, Kate eventually managed to escape from their demands and she went straight to her room.

For a while she sat in the dressing room, amongst Harry's belongings, watching the snowflakes fluttering against the cold glass windowpanes. She wondered where he was at this particular moment and she could only hope that he was safe and warm. She had become used to seeing him every day during their voyage home and it would be a strange Christmas without him.

Eventually, hearing the soft chimes from the clock in her room, alerting her to the fact that it was seven o'clock, she rose to her feet and went to start unpacking. When she had sorted out the clothes that needed to go to the laundry room, she changed out of her travelling garments and took a velvet evening dress from the clothes press. There had been no call for such finery during her time on board ship or in Bombay, and the last time she had worn it was for Jenny's wedding. The silk velvet was soft to her skin as she slipped it over her head, and it absorbed the heat from her body. She wished that Harry was there to see her dressed in such finery. In a pensive mood, she went to sit on the dressing table stool, gazing into the mirror with a silver-backed hairbrush clutched in her hand. She thought of Jenny and wondered how she was adjusting to married life. Jenny and Hedley must have reached their posting by now and it would be a huge change from rural Walthamstow or the bustle and comparative sophistication of Finsbury Square. Kate brushed her hair and knotted it carefully at the back of her neck. It was, after all, a family meal and there was no need for an elaborate coiffure.

She was about to return to the drawing room for a sherry before dinner, when she remembered her promise to tell the children a bedtime story. Not wanting to disappoint them, she climbed the stairs to the floor where the old nursery suite was situated, but when she opened the door she was enveloped in a cloud of feathers from a burst pillowcase. The children stopped bouncing on their beds and froze, gazing at her with guilt written all over their faces.

'It was Frankie who started it,' May said urgently.

'We're going to get into ever such a lot of trouble.'

'I think you're right.' Kate tried hard to keep a straight face. 'It looks as if the snowstorm has come inside.'

'Are you going to tell Ma?' Frankie asked sheepishly. 'We won't get our presents if you do.'

Kate put her head on one side, looking from one to the other. 'Well now, that wouldn't do,

386

would it? I tell you what. If you clear up this mess right now we'll say no more about it.' She perched on the edge of Charlie's bed and lifted him onto her lap. 'Perhaps it would help if I told you a story while you're stuffing all those feathers back in the pillowcases.'

'Yes, please.' Nellie bent down, scooping armfuls of feathers back into the cotton ticking. 'Come on, Frankie. You started it, so you can do most of the hard work.'

Grumbling beneath his breath, Frankie went to help her, with May and Jimmy doing their best to assist them. Kate made up a story about an Indian elephant who saved the Maharajah from being eaten by a tiger. It was all make-believe, but she described the colourful costumes of the villagers and the intense heat with such feeling that Nellie began to fan herself, complaining that she was hot. With perfect timing, the story ended as the last few feathers were packed away.

Kate placed a sleepy Charlie in his bed and rose to her feet. 'I'll sew up the seams in the morning and no one will know any different. Now I want all of you to get into bed and go to sleep, and that includes you, Frankie.'

He opened his mouth as if to protest, but seemed to think better of it and reluctantly climbed into the bed he shared with Jimmy.

Kate drew back the curtains so that moonlight flooded the room. Outside the world was white and sparkling. She picked up the candlestick she had brought with her. 'Good night, children. It's good to be back home with you.' She left the room, closing the door softly behind her.

★ ★ ★

Downstairs the family had assembled in the formal dining room by the time Kate joined them. She was pleased to see that Giles Pomeroy-Smith had made it through the snow and he was seated next to her mother at one end of the table, with Joe and Annie on either side of Lady Lyndon. Perry held out a chair for Kate before resuming his seat next to Annie.

Ivy, assisted by Tilly, served the food and it was a pleasant meal, although as far as Kate was concerned it would have been more enjoyable had Harry been present. Conversation flowed and there was plenty to talk about after their absence for the best part of a year. Joe was the only one at the table with little to say, and Kate felt for him, but there was nothing she could add to the conversation that would bring him out of his torpor.

When they retired to the drawing room for coffee, the gentlemen having decided to forgo their brandy and cigars, Giles took Joe aside. Kate could not hear what they were saying but Giles had an easy way with him and Joe began to look more relaxed.

'What did he say to you, Joe?' Kate asked when Giles returned to the sofa to sit beside Arabella.

'He offered me work,' Joe said, grinning. 'He's bought more land and he needs an agent to go round collecting rent and sorting out problems. He said that as I'm a military man I'm just the sort of person he's looking for. He needs someone disciplined and above all, honest. I wouldn't cheat anyone, least of all the man who was paying my wages.'

'That's wonderful, Joe. I'm so pleased for you.'

He nodded. 'And there's a cottage to go with the job. I'll have a home of my own, and for Annie, if she chooses to live with me.'

'Then you'd better discuss it with her, Joe.' Kate smiled as she watched him cross the room to sit by his sister. She was happy for them both, and it would be a good Christmas, but for the fact that there was someone very important to her, who was missing.

24

Christmas was over, but it had ended with the announcement from Giles and Arabella that they planned to get married at Easter. Kate was delighted for her mother, and Lady Lyndon was full of plans for the wedding to be held in the village church with the reception at Warren House. Giles agreed that St Mary's would suit both him and his fiancée, but he insisted that Pomeroy Park would be a much more suitable venue for the wedding breakfast than Warren House. The guest list seemed to grow by the minute as he included all the notable families in the area and beyond. The whole village would be welcome and he planned to have entertainment that would astound and delight everyone. Kate was not so sure about that, but her mother was so excited by the whole idea that Kate did not like to cast doubts on the practicality of her future stepfather's plans.

They had to wait for the thaw, which took place at the end of January, and then Arabella insisted on returning to Finsbury Square so that she could order her wedding gown from one of the top modistes in London. Kate was worried about her mother's safety if she returned to their town house, but Arabella was determined to make her mark as the bride of Giles Pomeroy-Smith.

'What is the point of marrying the wealthiest man in the county if I dress like a country bumpkin, Kate?'

There was nothing that Kate could say that would persuade her mother to remain at Warren House until the wedding, and Lady Lyndon did not make matters easier.

'If dear Arabella thinks it's safe to return to London, then there's nothing to stop me from moving back to Finsbury Circus. I think you worry unnecessarily, Kate. I'll get Hattersley to pack my things. We're going home.'

It was an unstoppable tide and there was nothing that Kate could do or say that would prevent either her mother or Lady Lyndon from returning to their former residences. The only person who listened to Kate was Annie, who was persuaded by Joe to remain at Warren House. He had started working for Giles, and was learning the job of a land agent. The cottage he had been allocated needed some renovations, and Ted had set about mending the roof, while Ivy, with the help of two village women, cleaned the place from top to bottom. Joe moved in on his own, but Ivy promised to help out if needed, and a girl from the village went in daily to cook and clean.

Ivy and Ted were happily settled in their cottage in the grounds of Warren House and neither of them wanted to return to the city. The children thrived and were doing well at school, and Martha was delighted to have her kitchen to herself once more. Kate did her best to persuade her mother to remain at Warren House, but in the end she knew she had lost the battle and in some ways it suited her to return to London, too. Harry was somewhere in the city and she was determined to find him, no matter how dangerous it might prove.

* * *

The move back to London went smoothly enough, Kate having sent a telegram to Mrs Marsh, giving her warning so that the house could be made ready, and it was. Everything was sparkling as if cleaners had been working night and day to ensure that Lady Martin was not disappointed.

Mrs Marsh was obviously delighted to have the house reopened, but her main concern was for Jenny, and at the first opportunity she bombarded Kate with questions about India. Kate was careful to stress the beauty of the country, and the fact that peace had been restored, and though she knew very little about life in the military she assured Mrs Marsh that Hedley was a good man and Jenny was a resourceful woman. They would do well together, of that Kate was certain, and Mrs Marsh seemed happy with that. She went about her work humming a cheerful tune, and Kate could only hope that Jenny was finding life as an army wife lived up to her expectations. Two days later both Kate and Mrs Marsh received letters from Jenny, and it seemed that all their fears had been groundless. Jenny had settled happily into married life and Hedley had received a promotion. They were expecting their first child in late spring, and Jenny could not be more content. Kate remembered Harry's words when he had accused her of matchmaking, and if that were true it seemed she had done her job well. Now all that remained was for her to find Harry.

In the days that followed Kate felt bound to accompany her mother to various fashion houses and modistes where the wedding dress and trousseau were discussed at length. She herself was expected to act as maid of honour, and that entailed poring over fashion plates with her mother. They had decided that although traditionally still in mourning, they would choose fabrics in neutral colours so that they did not cause offence to anyone. Kate was growing bored with the whole process, and despite a visit to Perry's chambers in Lincoln's Inn, she was no nearer to finding out what had happened to Harry. The police were saying nothing about the case, and Kate was becoming increasingly frustrated. In the end she made up her mind to go to look for him on her own.

On the fifth day since their return to Finsbury Square Kate was up early. She dressed in some of Jenny's old clothes that had been set aside for charity, and she wrapped an old cloak around her head and shoulders before venturing out on a cold, wet February morning. She was always conscious of the threat posed by the Monks gang, and keeping in character as a poor woman, she walked to Cable Street where she had opened the soup kitchen. The fire damage appeared to be minimal, but the windows were filthy and boarded up in places where they had been broken, and the front door looked as though someone had attempted to kick it to pieces. She knocked in the vague hope that Spears might still be living above the shop, but there was no response. She backed away, standing on the kerb, looking up at the grimy windows of the meeting room and she caught a fleeting glance of a familiar face. She went to hammer on the door with her fist.

'Spears, I know you're in there. Let me in. It's Miss Martin.'

She was vaguely aware of curious looks from passers-by but she was determined to speak to Spears. If anyone knew where she might find Harry it would be Augustus. She knocked repeatedly until she saw a shadow on the other side of the glass and heard the sound of bolts being drawn back. The handle turned and the door opened just a crack.

'Are you alone, miss?'

'Yes, Spears, and I'm perished. Let me in.'

Augustus opened the door just wide enough to allow her to slip inside. 'What d'you want? Haven't you had enough trouble here?'

'Where is Harry?' Kate faced him with a determined lift of her chin. 'I'm not leaving until you tell me everything you know.'

Spears backed away. 'I don't know nothing, miss.'

'And I don't believe you. If anyone can help me to find Harry it's you.'

'I'm flattered, but I tell you I don't know where he is at this moment in time.'

'But you've seen him recently? I always know when you're lying, Spears.'

'I've had enough problems trying to live here without getting meself killed by one of Monks' men. I don't want you bringing more trouble to me door.' Kate paced the floor in an attempt to get warm. An icy draught blew in from the old kitchen and the smell of charred wood and smoke hung in the air like a pall. 'I don't suppose you've got the range going, by any chance. I could do with a cup of tea.'

'Tea? I ain't had a hot drink for months. I got no coal and I was about to starve to death when Harry turned up just before Christmas. Not that I had what you might call a Christmas. I probably wouldn't be here if he hadn't bought me some food and drink.'

Kate smiled in spite of the fact her face was stiff with cold. 'That sounds like Harry. But where is he now? Where is Monks? I want to find Harry before he does something he'll regret.'

'You left it a bit late for that, miss. He's been back here for nigh on two months, where've you been all this time?'

'You're right. I should have come looking for him sooner, but I'm here now and I need to speak to him. Is he upstairs?'

Spears shook his head. 'No one in their right mind would stay here. As for me, I got nowhere else to go.'

'Are you expecting him to call on you again? You must know something, Spears.'

He leaned closer and she recoiled at the smell of his unwashed body. His straggly hair was lank and greasy and he had grown a beard. 'What's it worth?'

'I'm not stupid enough to carry a lot of money on me in this neighbourhood.'

'But you got some, I know that.' Spears cast his eyes over the reticule she clutched in her hand. 'I'm starving, miss. Get me a pie and a jug of ale and I'll tell you everything I know.'

Kate eyed him warily. She had no way of knowing whether he was simply using her or if he actually had some information as to Harry's whereabouts.' She sighed, shaking her head. 'If you're having me on, Spears, I won't forgive you.'

'I won't be here to repent if I don't get some vittles inside me soon.' Spears raised a skeletal hand to his forehead. 'I'm faint from lack of nourishment.'

'All right. I'll go to the pie shop and the jug and bottle, but you'd better give me some news when I get back or I'll go straight to the police station in Leman Street and report you for being here illegally. I assume the property still belongs to Harry.'

'I ain't lying,' Spears said feebly. 'Two pies would be better than one, miss. I got to keep body and soul together.'

Kate walked past him and went into the kitchen, where she and Ivy used to make the vast batches of soup for the needy. It was, as she expected, filthy and there were rodent droppings everywhere, although what they found to eat was a mystery. She plucked a chipped china jug from one of the shelves and hurried back into the shop where Spears had slumped down on the only chair in the room.

'I'm going, Spears, but I'll be back as quickly as I can. Let me out, please.'

He stumbled to his feet and staggered to the door, leaving her in no doubt as to his weakened state. Kate knew the area quite well and she walked to the Brown Bear pub where she had the jug filled with ale. She went on to a nearby pie shop where she purchased three pies — two for

Spears and one for herself. She had not bothered to have breakfast before she left home that morning, and the cold weather, together with the long walk, had given her an appetite.

She returned to the shop and Spears let her in. He grabbed one of the pies and returned to his chair, stuffing the food in his mouth as if he had not eaten for days.

'Give us the ale,' he said through a mouthful of pie. 'This tastes so good. You can't imagine what it's like to starve, miss.'

Kate passed him the jug and he drank from it, gulping down the ale and belching loudly. Kate nibbled her pie, but she was no longer hungry and she gave it to Spears, who downed it in seconds.

'I'll save the other one for me supper,' he said, grinning and exposing a row of blackened and broken teeth. 'That went down well, and the ale. Thank you, miss.'

Kate moved closer. 'I've done my part, now tell me what you know. Where can I find Harry?'

'He's lying low, miss.'

'Yes, I understand that, but where will I find him?'

'He moves around so that Monks never knows where he'll be next, but the last I heard he was lodging at the Town of Ramsgate pub, next to Wapping Old Stairs. But it ain't the sort of place you should go to, miss.'

'I want to find Harry. I need to know what's happening and why he hasn't returned home. If it was up to me I'd have left Monks to the police.'

'If you say so, miss.' Spears lifted the jug to his lips and drank deeply once more.

397

Kate took a sixpenny bit from her reticule and placed it on the table next to Spears. 'That should feed you for a day or so, and I'll speak to Harry about finding you somewhere safer to stay. That's if I find him.'

'Good luck, miss.' Spears gave her a tipsy grin, waving to her as she let herself out of the shop.

Kate headed towards the river. She knew Nightingale Lane, of course, which was where she had first met Ivy and the children, and it was easy enough to find the pub that Spears had mentioned. However, she was not prepared for the hostile reception she received from the men, mostly dockers and seamen, who crowded round the bar. She pulled her cloak more tightly around her and pushed her way through to speak to the barman.

'This ain't the sort of place for you, miss.' A burly man with shaggy red hair and tattoos on his forearms and neck, leaned towards her. 'Unless you're touting for business, of course.' He roared with laughter, as did the men around him.

'I'll give you a penny for it, love.' A younger man wearing workmen's overalls and a woollen hat over his forehead, laid his hand on her shoulder.

Kate pulled away, glowering at him. 'Go away and bother someone else.'

'Ho, we've got a lady in our midst.' The tattooed man raised his glass to her. 'How much d'you charge, your ladyship. I ain't never had a lady.'

'And you won't now,' Kate said, edging away towards a young serving girl, who was collecting glasses.

'I'm looking for a friend,' Kate said in a low voice. She took a silver shilling from her reticule under the cover of her cloak. It would be fatal to let the present company see that she had money on her person.

The girl eyed her fearfully. 'I don't know your friend.'

'His name is Harry and I was told that he's lodging here.' Kate pressed the coin into the girl's hand. 'Can you help me?'

'I dunno.'

'But you do know Harry?'

'Maybe.' The girl glanced fearfully at the barman, but he was busy serving ale, and her gaze flicked back to Kate. 'Who's asking?'

'Is he here now? If he is, tell him it's Kate.'

'I can't promise nothing, but you'd best get out of here. If they lay hands on you I don't fancy your chances.' The girl jerked her head in the direction of a group of rough-looking labourers, who were obviously the worse for drink. 'It's low tide, wait at the foot of the old stairs.' The girl picked up her tray and headed for the back of the bar, leaving Kate with little alternative but to make a hasty retreat.

The watermen's stairs the girl had mentioned were at the side of the building down a narrow alley that led to the river. Kate glanced up at the pub windows as she made her way carefully down the worn stone steps. The aroma of tea from a nearby warehouse mingled with the various smells of tobacco, roasting coffee beans and the odour from the detritus washed up on the foreshore and sewage that floated downriver. A bitter east wind ruffled the surface of the water and tugged mercilessly at Kate's cloak as she waited, hoping that the serving maid would have given Harry the message.

She stood there for what seemed like an eternity, and the tide had turned causing the water to rise rapidly. Kate was about to climb the steps to the High Street when she looked up and saw Harry. He was dressed as a seaman in a pea jacket, with a cap pulled down over his brow, but she would have known him anywhere and she started up the slippery, well-worn steps. They met halfway and he enveloped her in a hug and a kiss that took her breath away, making it almost impossible to think. She laid her hands on his chest and pushed him away.

'Someone might see us, Harry,' she said, glancing nervously up at the side windows of the pub.

'What the hell are you doing here, Kate? Why did you leave Warren House?'

'Can we go somewhere safer?' Kate said breathlessly. 'One false step and we'll end up in the mud and the tide has turned.'

He put his arm around her waist guiding her up the steps in silence. When they reached the street he led her to St John's church where they found a secluded spot in the churchyard. He leaned against the wall.

'Now tell me why you came looking for me, Kate. You knew what I was about when we parted on the docks.'

'That was nearly two months ago, Harry. I didn't know if you were alive or dead, and Perry wouldn't tell me anything. What was I supposed to do?'

A wry smile curved his lips. 'A sensible woman would have remained at Warren House where she was safe, but I should have known you wouldn't abide by the rules. How did you find me?'

'I went to my old soup kitchen. Where else would I go? I bribed Spears with a jug of ale and a couple of meat pies. He's in a bad way, Harry.'

'Spears is not my problem. He chose to stay on and he knows the score. Don't waste your pity on him.'

'But he was starving and filthy, as well as being chilled to the bone. You can't leave him like that. He used to work for you.'

Harry acknowledged this with a nod. 'You're right, of course. I should have done something for Spears, but I've put everything into catching Monks. The trap is set now, which is why you must return home immediately.'

'What do you mean? How are you going to catch him?'

'You're shivering.' Harry slipped his arm around her shoulders. 'Have you come all the way from Walthamstow today?'

'No, my mother insisted on opening up the house in Finsbury Square because she wanted to get her outfit for her Easter wedding. Your mother has returned to Finsbury Circus. I tried but I couldn't dissuade either of them.'

'It's still not safe. If my plan fails Monks will be even more dangerous.'

'But the police should be handling this, Harry. Come home. Come to Warren House and leave all this behind.'

He touched her cheek with the tip of his fore-finger. 'You called Warren House "home". Is that how you see it?'

'Yes, I mean, no. Don't put words in my mouth, Harry. And you've changed the subject very cleverly.

I asked you what your plans were regarding Monks.' 'I couldn't tell you even if I wanted to, my love. I'm working with the Metropolitan Police and they want to bring Monks in with as much evidence as they can gather. They need the case for the prosecution to be watertight.'

'And Perry knows all about this, I suppose?'

'He does.'

'Well, he wouldn't tell me anything. He's allowed me to suffer since Christmas. I didn't know if you were alive or dead.'

He drew her to him and kissed her until her senses were reeling. He released her gently, brushing a stray lock of hair from her forehead with the tip of his finger. 'I'm sorry, my darling girl. But it wasn't safe for you to know the details and it still isn't. I'm begging you to return to Finsbury Square, and if you can't persuade your mother to return to Warren House, at least you must be aware of the danger you're in.'

The touch of his lips on hers had left her dizzy with desire for more, but his words sent cold shivers down her spine. 'Why is that man so important to the police? He can't be an ordinary gangster. There must be more to it than that.'

'Monks is the head of an international gang who have stolen works of art and jewels worth thousands of pounds. His London thuggery was simply a cover to divert the police in this country into thinking just what you've called him: a local villain who might get away with a short prison sentence. Monks' gang are ruthless killers and they'll stop at nothing to keep themselves free from arrest.'

'But why have you put yourself in danger, Harry? Haven't you done enough? Can't you leave it to others and come home to lead a normal life?'

'I will, but only when this is finished. I have a personal score to settle with Monks. He shot and killed Annie's father and her mother died of a broken heart.'

'I was told it was a duel, fought over a gambling debt.'

'George Blythe was my uncle and he was good to me when I was a boy, but he had a weakness for gambling and he became involved with Monks. He lost heavily and when Monks put pressure on him to pay back his debt of honour, it ended in a duel. Monks supplied the pistols and I've always suspected that the one George used had been tampered with, but it was a long time ago and impossible to prove.'

'Are you certain? I mean it could have been that Monks was a better shot.'

'Never. George was an army officer, trained in the use of firearms. One of the reasons why I started up the gaming clubs, apart from the obvious need to make money, was to keep Monks within my sights. If I couldn't catch him any other way I had to make him think that I was a criminal, too.'

'And the police knew about this?'

'Not at first. I had to be very careful with my cover, but eventually I had to tell them what I was doing or face arrest. When I was sent to prison it was all arranged, as you know. Monks is no fool and he was getting suspicious.'

'What are you going to do now? What is this trap you're talking about?'

He shook his head. 'I can't tell you, Kate. I want you to return to Finsbury Square and stay there until I tell you it's safe to leave.'

'But we'll be prisoners in our own home.'

'If you can't persuade your mother to be careful then you should take her back to Warren House.'

'For how long, Harry? This could go on for ever.'

'No. I told you, Kate. I am working to bring a case against Monks that is watertight.'

'You say he's a jewel thief and he steals works of art.'

'Yes, what of it?'

'Well, the simplest way I can think of is to put temptation in his way that he simply can't resist. If I wanted to trap a jewel thief I would bait a trap with a priceless item of jewellery or an art collection and wait. Sooner or later he would be bound to take the bait.'

'There's only one flaw in that theory, Kate. Precious jewels are hard to come by, as are great works of art. Monks isn't a fool. He'd see through something like that in an instant.'

Kate eyed him thoughtfully. 'Not necessarily. We don't need to possess the articles, Monks simply has to believe they are there for the taking. Where do you think he gets his information from?'

'I've never thought about it like that.'

'It must be someone who is quite high up in society. Perhaps that person travels abroad quite often and that would account for Monks knowing when and where to strike.'

'It would take time to follow up that idea, Kate. It's a good one, but I've managed to infiltrate the gang and I'm hoping to get the details of their plans very soon. I know how these people work and I don't want you to get involved.'

Kate could see that arguing was pointless. When it came to protecting those closest to him she knew that Harry would not be swayed. 'I understand, but I'd better start walking back to Finsbury Square. It looks like rain and it might even snow.'

He wrapped his arms around her and held her close. 'Don't do anything foolish, Kate. I'll sort this out very soon now and we'll be together again.'

She allowed herself a few moments of respite, leaning against him and breathing in the scent of him, which was achingly sweet and so familiar. The months they had spent on board ship had been precious and she was not going to let their closeness slip away, but if Harry had a stubborn streak then she had one to match. She drew away reluctantly.

'I must go now, Harry.'

He grasped her by the hand. 'I'm sending you home in a cab.'

'I'm supposed to be incognito, Harry. Servant girls walk everywhere or take a bus.'

'My future wife is not going to walk from Wapping to Finsbury Square, Kate Martin.'

'Your wife? When did you propose to me? I think I might remember something like that.'

'I thought we had an understanding, my love.'

'All the more reason to get this done quickly, Harry. I think you're placing yourself in great danger. I'm sure there is an easier way.'

He proffered his arm. 'Let's get you home. The weather is taking a turn for the worst.'

'You can avoid the truth as often as you like, but I think you need my help, Harry, and I'm not giving up.'

He kissed her briefly on the lips. 'That's why I love you, but I won't allow you to put yourself in danger. Leave it to me, Kate. It will be over soon and then we can get on with the rest of our lives, but please, if you love me at all, persuade your mother to return to Warren House. I'll pay a call on my mother and see if I can make her see sense.'

25

Mrs Marsh answered Kate's knock on the door in Finsbury Square. She stood aside to allow Kate to enter, but her gaze was fixed on the garments that Kate had chosen to wear.

'If I might be so bold, Miss Kate, why are you wearing my daughter's old clothes?'

Kate slipped off her rain-soaked cloak and handed it to her. 'I had a private mission to undertake, Mrs Marsh. I didn't want to be recognised.'

'Something is still amiss. I know it's not my place to question my betters, but closing the house and running off to Walthamstow was just the start. I've known you since you were a child, and you can't pull the wool over my eyes. Something bad has happened or is going to happen. I'm glad my Jenny isn't here.'

Kate laid her hand on Mrs Marsh's arm. 'You are part of the family, Mrs Marsh. You've always been there to take care of me when my parents were too busy. I owe you an explanation, but it will have to wait until later.' Kate paused, sniffing the air. 'Can I smell cigar smoke?'

'Mr Pomeroy-Smith arrived a couple of hours ago. He's in the morning parlour with your mother.'

Kate nodded. 'I'd better change out of these damp clothes and then I'll let Mama know that I'm home.'

'If you leave Jenny's things out I'll see that

they're laundered and put back in the bag for the missionaries. Unless, of course, you might need them again.'

'I don't think so, thank you.' Kate headed for the staircase. She had no intention of risking such an expedition again. This was the time to take matters into her own hands and Giles's arrival in Finsbury Square seemed like the answer to the questions that had been buzzing around in her brain since she parted from Harry in Wapping.

★ ★ ★

Giles rose to his feet when Kate walked into the room.

'Kate, your mama has been telling me that everything is in hand for our wedding.'

'Yes, indeed.' Kate acknowledged her mother with a nod and a smile. 'I'm sorry I wasn't here when you arrived, Giles.'

'Where were you, Kate?' Arabella demanded crossly. 'You shouldn't go off like that without a word to me.'

'I'm sorry, Mama, but I had something very important to undertake.'

Giles went to stand with his back to the fire. 'Is there anything wrong, Kate?'

The arrival of the new parlourmaid put a stop to conversation while she set the tea tray on a table by the window.

'You may leave it, thank you, Lizzie.' Kate went over to the table and poured the tea. 'Would you like a cup, Mama?'

'No, thank you. We had coffee after luncheon,

which you missed. What have you been up to now? I hope it has nothing to do with that man Monks.'

Kate waited until Lizzie had left the room. 'He was the reason why we had to leave our home, Mama.'

'I'm fully aware of that, Kate. It all happened because Harry Lyndon was involved with some gangsters, and we were supposed to be in danger. Margaret Lyndon believed it, but I always thought it was a ridiculous story.'

Giles went to sit beside Arabella, taking her hand in his. 'Kate told me all about it, my dear. I believe that there was, and probably still is, very real danger. I've heard about Monks and his disreputable gang. They are not the sort of people to trifle with.'

'Don't tell me that you're mixing with these people again, Kate,' Arabella said, sighing.

'Not exactly, Mama. Anyway, I think I have a way to end this whole business to everyone's satisfaction.' Kate moved to a chair by the fire, taking her tea with her. 'Giles, I need your help.'

'Of course, Kate. I'll do anything to make you and your mother safe. How I can be of assistance?'

'You know many wealthy people, don't you? I mean, you have connections with the rich and famous.'

He smiled modestly. 'I suppose so. I've never really thought about it in that light.'

'Well, I was thinking of giving a grand ball. Only this house isn't really large enough for what I had in mind, and it would be very costly.'

'I don't understand. What are you planning, Kate?' Arabella clutched Giles's hand. 'Why would

409

we want to hold a ball?'

'To celebrate your engagement and to announce your forthcoming marriage,' Kate said glibly. 'It would be a way for Giles to introduce you to society. After all, I believe you wish to return to London to live, Mama. I've heard that you own a large town house, Giles.'

He chuckled. 'Is this your way of suggesting that I throw the ball at my property in Berkeley Square, Kate? I'm staying there for a couple of days, but it is usually closed until the start of the London season. It's a tradition started many years ago.'

'But I'm sure you have kept staff on there, and I imagine you have a collection of valuables and fine paintings.'

'I have a few. What's this all about, Kate?'

'I'll be honest with you both. The police, together with Harry Lyndon, have been trying to catch Monks and his gang for a long time. They are ruthless jewel thieves and they also steal works of art. I want to set a trap for them by announcing a grand ball to be held in your mansion in Berkeley Square. I think the temptation would be too much for Monks. After all, he and his gang have been lying low for months, and they must be getting a bit short of money by now. What do you say?'

'I'd have to consider it carefully,' Giles said slowly. 'It's true that I have many wealthy friends and acquaintances, but I would be deliberately putting them in harm's way. That simply isn't on.'

'In the usual way of things I'd have to agree with you,' Kate said earnestly. 'But Monks has to have a good reason to risk stealing jewels and works of art. He's clever and he's managed to evade the police for far too long. None of us is safe until he's behind bars.'

Arabella paled alarmingly. 'Oh, Giles. Say yes. We can warn your friends —'

'No!' Kate said firmly. 'No one must know. Harry will inform the police and they will lie in wait for the gang. Your engagement ball will be the talk of the town for years to come.'

'It's a risk.' Giles patted Arabella on the hand. 'But I think Kate is right. If this is the only way to catch a villain like Monks, so be it.'

'Then you agree?' Kate could hardly contain her excitement.

'In principle, I do, but I'll have to give it a lot more thought. I don't want to endanger anyone.'

'I agree,' Kate said fervently. 'I suggest we ask Perry's opinion. He's been liaising between Harry and the police. They've been working hard to catch Monks and this seems too good an opportunity to miss.'

Giles nodded. 'I'm returning to Berkeley Square after dinner. I suggest that you and I pay Perry a visit at his chambers tomorrow morning.'

'What about me?' Arabella demanded. 'Am I to be left out of this?'

'No, my love, of course not.' Giles resumed his seat at her side. 'I suggest that you make a list of all the rich and influential people you know, and even those you've never met. We'll work out who to invite from that, and if Perry thinks it's a sound idea I'll have invitations printed. I imagine we need to work quickly from what you've said,

Kate?'

'Yes, the sooner we get this done the better.'

But we will still go ahead with arrangements for our wedding at Easter?' Arabella said anxiously.

'Of course, my dear. That's another good reason for getting Monks and his men caught, tried and convicted as soon as possible. I don't want anything to spoil our special day.'

Arabella smiled happily. 'I'll need a new ball gown, Kate. If the celebration is in my honour I need to be the best dressed woman present.'

'Of course, Mama. You will eclipse them all.'

'And you must have a new gown, too,' Arabella said, warming to the theme. 'You might meet a wealthy gentleman with good connections. I'm afraid your romances have proved quite disastrous in the past, if you count that Indian soldier and then a man who's been in prison. Much as I like Margaret Lyndon, I don't think her son is a suitable husband for you.'

Kate exchanged meaningful glances with Giles. 'I don't think you need to worry about me, Mama. I know what I'm doing.'

'I should hope so. You're twenty-three, Kate. Soon you'll be on the shelf — just think of the disgrace. Anyway, I suggest that we visit the modiste in Bond

Street tomorrow or the day after.' 'Yes, Mama,' Kate replied automatically.

* * *

After a few moments of quiet reflection Perry agreed that the suggestion had its merits. He wrote

412

a message for his clerk to take to the chief inspector at Scotland Yard. It was then that Kate realised how much importance the police put on rounding up Monks and his gang. They waited an hour for a reply and were about to leave when the chief inspector himself arrived at Perry's chambers. Kate sat quietly during the discussion, leaving Perry and Giles to do the talking. She had been schooled by her father to speak when spoken to on matters of such importance, although she was ready to step in and say her piece should the conversation not go her way. However, after half an hour it was decided that her plan might work and it would have the full backing of the Metropolitan Police. The date was set in agreement with Giles and it was left to Kate to persuade her mother that there would be time to make the necessary arrangements.

That afternoon Kate had little choice other than to accompany her mother to Madame Jolyot's salon in Bond Street, where the need for a ball gown designed, fitted and delivered in three weeks was discussed at length. Arabella refused to ask the price of such speedy service, but Kate knew it would not be cheap. However, if it made her mother happy and if the ball attracted the attention of Monks, she considered that whatever it cost was a price worth paying. A more modest gown was ordered for herself, and when they left the salon Kate hailed a cab and they went for a celebratory tea at Gunter's in Berkeley Square. Arabella could hardly contain herself when they alighted.

'Look, Kate. Over there — that mansion

belongs to Giles. I'll be able to entertain royally when we're married. This is just the beginning of the sort of life I could never have imagined when I was married to your dear papa.'

'Yes, Mama. Shall we go into the tea shop? All the talking today has left my throat dry as dust.'

'Don't be vulgar, Kate. In high society we don't mention bodily functions. It's simply not done.' Arabella marched into the tea shop. 'Those cream cakes look so delicious. I might put in an order for several dozen for supper at the ball.'

'Yes, Mama,' Kate said dutifully as they were shown to a table, but her thoughts were elsewhere. Perry had promised to contact Harry, and although she was longing to see him again and to give him the news in person, she knew it would be a mistake to return to the pub in Wapping. No doubt Monks had spies everywhere. Kate ordered an ice cream and cakes for her mother, but all the while she was thinking of her next step.

★ ★ ★

Kate had not planned to visit Whitechapel again, but if anyone could get a message to Harry it would be Spears. He would be able to call in at the Town of Ramsgate pub and not draw attention to himself, and so she set off next morning for Cable Street, but this time she took a cab.

Spears peered at her from an upstairs window. Moments later he opened the door and dragged her unceremoniously over the threshold.

'Why have you come here again, miss? You know it ain't safe. Monks is back in town. Maybe

414

it got too hot for him south of the river.' Spears slammed the door and bolted it.

'Have you seen Harry recently?' Kate asked anxiously. 'I really need to speak to him.'

'I ain't seen him for days. I dunno what's going on and that's the truth.' Spears put his head on one side, eyeing her expectantly. 'I don't suppose you brought me any vittles, did you, miss?'

Kate had come prepared and she placed a wicker basket on the table. Spears snatched a pie wrapped in a piece of butter muslin, barely unwrapping it before he took a huge bite.

'This is good,' he said, spitting crumbs of pastry onto the floor. 'I dunno how I'm going to keep going. Monks has got his men watching every move I make. They think Harry will come here and if he does they'll get him. Word got round that he's working with the coppers. Monks won't stand for that.'

'Last time I was here I took your advice and went to the pub in Wapping. I spoke to him and he said that it wouldn't be long before Monks was caught, but I have a better plan.'

Spears munched the pie, barely paying attention to what Kate was saying. He nodded, smiling blissfully.

'Are you listening to me, Spears?'

He swallowed convulsively. 'Yes, miss. This is the best pie I ever tasted.'

'I'm sure Mrs Pugh will be delighted to hear that,' Kate said drily. 'But I need your help, Spears. I want you to find Harry and tell him that I need to speak to him urgently.'

'If I go out they'll get me for sure.'

Kate could not argue with that, but an idea came

to her and she smiled. 'I want you to come back to Finsbury Square with me. A bath and a shave, clean clothes and a haircut will work wonders. Then I'll send you to Wapping in a cab. Monks' men won't recognise you.'

Spears almost choked on a mouthful of pastry. 'You want me to dress up like a toff?'

'Something like that, but we must get word to Harry and I can't think of any other way.'

'This ain't a ruse to get me arrested, is it? I done some things that the law don't approve of in the past.'

'The police aren't interested in you, Spears — I have it from the highest authority — and if you do this and help to bring Monks and his gang to justice you'll be free to live your life as you choose.'

'That ain't saying much, miss. I've been living like a hermit in this place. I don't care if I never see Whitechapel again in me whole life.'

'Perhaps there's another way. Leave it to me, but will you do this? It's very important.'

Spears puffed out his chest. 'I never been that before.' He reached for a slab of cake and took a massive bite. 'I'd like to marry your cook. D'you think she'd have me?'

'Not while you look and smell as you do at the moment. Do you agree to help us?'

Spears nodded. 'If there's more of this cake I'll do almost anything.'

'That's good. I'll go out and hail a cab. Wait in the doorway. The sooner we get away from here, the better.'

★ ★ ★

Lizzie almost fainted when she set eyes on Spears and Mrs Marsh stood arms akimbo in the entrance hall, glaring at him suspiciously.

'Why have you brought this vagabond into the house, Miss Kate? Your mama won't be too pleased.'

Kate drew her aside. 'This is police business, Mrs Marsh. This man is a valuable witness in a case that is so important the chief inspector is handling it. I want a bath filled with hot water, with clean towels and soap ready. Are there any of my papa's old clothes that have not been given to charity?'

'There is a trunk filled with them in one of the attics, miss.' Mrs Marsh pursed her lips, folding her arms across her chest. 'But if you don't mind me saying so, is it right to give them to someone like him? I'm sure there are more worthy people.'

'Not in this case, Mrs Marsh. I'll take Mr Spears to my father's dressing room where he can wait while Lizzie fills the bathtub. I'll go to the attic myself and search for the appropriate garments.'

'If you say so, miss. But I don't think Lady Martin will approve.'

'My mother has gone for a drive with Mr Pomeroy-Smith. By the time she returns I'll have Mr Spears looking and smelling like a gentleman.'

'Better tell him to keep his mouth shut, then,' Mrs Marsh said, tossing her head. 'I'll see to it, miss. But if your mama creates a fuss, I won't take the blame.'

'Don't worry. It's my responsibility.' Kate moved

417

away to where Spears was standing awkwardly at the foot of the staircase. 'Come with me. I'll take you where it's quiet and you can have a bath in peace, while I look for some suitable clothes for you to wear. You're about the same size as my late father.'

Spears rolled his eyes. 'I dunno about wearing a dead man's clothes.'

'He's hardly likely to complain, is he?' Kate gave him a gentle shove towards the bottom step. 'Think of a life free from Monks and then you'll see the benefit of what you're about to do.'

Spears was still protesting when she settled him in her father's old dressing room where Lizzie had already begun to fill a tin bathtub with hot water. She scurried from the room, taking the two large ewers with her.

'I want you to sit there, Spears.' Kate pointed to a nearby chair. 'It will take a while to fill the bath. Our old footman has just been reinstated and he'll give you a hand to wash and shave.' 'I ain't a baby,' Spears protested.

'No, of course not, but you will need someone to shave off that awful beard, and Henry will trim your hair. We'll have you looking like a gentleman before you know it.'

'I don't want that young girl ogling me in the tub.'

'I'm sure that's the last thing Lizzie wants. She won't be there to watch you, and neither will I. Just remember that this is all about finding Harry and bringing him here without Monks' men recognising you. Your life might depend upon this, Spears.'

'It's all right for you to try to change me life for me, miss.' Spears eyed her suspiciously. 'But what happens when I've done me bit and I'm no use to you or Harry?'

Kate moved to stand in the doorway. 'Maybe you'd enjoy living in the country, Augustus. I might even have a person in mind who is in need of an old soldier. That is how you started out in life, isn't it?'

'Who told you that?'

'You did, Augustus. The first time we met you told me you'd been a soldier in Her Majesty's army. I'll see you when you're finished here.' Kate left the room before Spears had a chance to argue.

★ ★ ★

The person who entered the morning parlour an hour and a half later was nothing like the shabby scarecrow Kate last saw. Spears was dressed smartly in her late father's clothes and now he was cleanshaven. His hair had been washed and brushed and she could see that he might once have been a goodlooking man.

'I feel like a fool, dressed up in these duds, miss.'

'Augustus Spears, you look like a proper gentleman. No one in Cable Street will recognise you. In fact I think you'll take Harry by surprise.'

'I've come this far. What d'you want me to do?'

'Find Harry and bring him here after dark.'

'What then? I can't go back to Cable Street looking like this, and I got no money.'

'You can sleep here tonight. I'll ask Mrs Marsh to have a room made up for you and tomorrow

I'm planning to visit Warren House in Waltham-stow. I was thinking of taking you with me.'

'You said you might have a job for me? I need to know, miss. I'm a marked man as far as Monks is concerned.'

'Annie's brother is a soldier, or rather he was until he was badly injured. I thought you two might get on well together and he needs someone to do things that present a problem to him.'

'Sounds all right, I suppose.'

'You don't have to make up your mind now. Just find Harry and bring him here. That's all I ask.'

'Yes, miss.' Spears was about to leave the room when Perry breezed in, almost knocking him over.

'I beg your pardon, sir,' Perry said hastily. 'I was in such a hurry that I didn't see you.' He paused, staring at Spears. 'Is that really you, Spears?'

Kate clapped her hands. 'That's excellent. You passed the test, Augustus. You can be assured that no one will recognise you.'

Spears jumped to attention and saluted. 'Yes, miss.' He marched out of the room leaving Perry staring after him.

'I wouldn't have believed the transformation. I've only met Spears once or twice, but had I seen him in passing I would not have recognised him. What are you up to, Kate?'

'Sit down, Perry. I'm glad you're here. I've sent for Harry, but I don't want Monks to get wind of our plans. If Harry can spread the word that there'll be rich pickings at the ball, I want Monks to think it's too good a chance to miss.'

'Can you give me a copy of the guest list? The police will need to know who will be in attendance.'

Kate moved to her mother's escritoire in the corner of the room and lifted the lid. 'I have one here. I made a fair copy because I knew you would need one.'

Perry took it from her, smiling. 'You think of everything, Kate.'

'I do hope so,' she said fervently. 'It feels as if this will be our last chance to live a normal life again.'

'I plan to propose to Annie when this is all over.' Perry glanced at her nervously, as if expecting her disapproval.

Kate flung her arms around him. 'About time, too. It was obvious from the start that you two were a wonderful match.'

'You don't feel put out? I mean I know I led you to think that . . . '

'Perry, it doesn't matter. That is all in the past. You met and fell in love with Annie and that's all that matters. I might have felt a little piqued at the start, but now I see it is the best thing that could have happened. You and I were not meant to be together.'

He raised her hand to his lips. 'You are a very special person, Kate. Harry Lyndon will be a very lucky man if you decide to take him as your husband.'

Before Kate had a chance to respond the door opened and her mother walked into the room, coming to a sudden halt when she saw them. She threw up her hands. 'Oh, how wonderful.

Have you two come to your senses at last? Kate, I couldn't be more pleased. Now we'll have another announcement to celebrate at the ball.'

26

It took Kate and Perry some time to persuade Arabella that they were not romantically involved, and even then Kate doubted if her mother was entirely convinced. However, the subject of the ball was closer to Arabella's heart and she was quite open about her wish to become a leader of fashion. Kate made an effort to sound encouraging, but entering society was the last thing on her mind.

After a brief meeting with Harry that evening, Kate was even more determined to see an end to the activities of Monks and his gang. Harry agreed that the ball was an excellent idea, but he insisted on returning to Wapping that night.

'If I don't go back to my room at the pub they will get the wrong idea. Some of Monks' men are suspicious because I was released from prison so early. I've worked hard to get their trust, but it's like walking a tightrope — one slip and it's all over. If I return there now I can continue to spread the word about the valuables that will be there for the picking at the ball.'

'Yes, Harry,' Kate said. 'But I think you've done enough. I'm planning to go to Warren House in the morning. Why don't you stay here tonight and travel with me tomorrow? The people in Wapping won't know where you are.'

'No, my love, they won't, but if I don't return word is sure to get back to Monks and he'll be on the alert. He's not stupid, Kate. I don't want to leave you, but I must. For now, anyway.'

She nodded. 'All right. I understand what you're saying, but I don't like it, Harry. As you said, one slip and they won't have any mercy. Spears has told me something of the way they treat people who cross them. It's not pretty.'

Harry took her in his arms and kissed her. 'Don't worry about me, my darling. I can take care of myself. I just want you to be safe.' He left through the servants' entrance and Kate made her way slowly to her room. As she undressed and slipped her nightgown over her head her whole body ached for more of his caresses. The touch of his lips on hers still very real, and she realised how much she missed the intimacy they had shared on board ship. The ball was only a week away and yet it felt like an eternity of waiting and worrying. It would be a relief to leave London and spend a day or two in Warren House, but at the back of her mind was the nagging fear that if Monks had any suspicion that he was being led into a trap it would be the worse for Harry. She climbed into her cold bed, and lay shivering as the dark night wrapped itself around her. Eventually she fell into a fitful sleep.

★ ★ ★

Spears was not the most cheerful travelling companion. He grumbled all the way to Warren House and Kate could not wait to alight from the carriage. They were greeted by Frankie, May and Nellie, who appeared as if from nowhere.

424

'Mr Spears,' Frankie said, grinning, 'you look like a proper toff. What are you doing here?'

'Have you come to stay?' Nellie asked shyly.

'Not if you youngsters persist in asking questions. Ain't you supposed to be in school?'

Frankie grinned cheekily. 'We come to the big house every morning. Tilly gives us cake, but don't tell Ma.' He winked and raced off towards the road, with May and Nellie chasing after him.

Spears followed Kate into the house. 'You don't want me to look after them nippers, do you? If that's the case I'll be on me way back to London. I prefer Monks' men to them kids.'

Kate laughed and patted him on the shoulder. 'No, they live with their mother and father in a cottage on the estate. If you see Ivy don't tell her you saw them or they'll be in trouble and so will Tilly. But that's by the bye . . . I'll take you to the kitchen and introduce you to Martha and her husband. She is a wonderful cook, so you'd better be nice to her if you want some tasty treats, and Arthur looks after the property. He may seem stern, but he's a very nice person when you get to know him.'

'So I'll be working for Annie's brother. Is that right, miss?'

'We'll have breakfast and then I'll take you to the cottage where he lives. You're both old soldiers, so I'm sure you'll get along splendidly.'

'I ain't said I'm staying yet,' Spears said gloomily. 'I'm town born and bred. I don't like the countryside.'

'Everything looks better on a full stomach.' Kate led the way to the kitchen where they were welcomed by the aroma of baking bread and sizzling bacon.

Spears sniffed appreciatively. 'I ain't smelled anything like that since me ma died twenty years ago.'

Martha looked up as they entered the room. 'Miss Kate, it's good to see you back, but who's this?' 'Martha, I want you to meet Augustus Spears. He's going to work for Joe, or at least that's the plan. I'll have to see if Joe agrees.'

Martha looked him up and down. 'I suppose you'll be wanting to be fed then, Augustus. Or do I call you Gus?'

'You calls me Mr Spears until we get to know each other better, Mrs, er . . . I didn't catch your surname.'

'It's Boggis.' Martha unhooked a side of bacon from the inglenook where it had been smoking gently for some months. She brandished a vicious-looking knife and sliced the bacon with a meaningful down stroke. 'Don't get cheeky with me, Gus. I'm the head of the kitchen, so unless you want the burned leftovers or things I don't deem fit for the pigswill, you'd better show some respect.'

Kate tried not to laugh. The look on Spears' face was so comical, and she could hear Tilly giggling in the scullery. 'I'll leave you two to get acquainted, but I'd appreciate some breakfast when it's ready, Martha. We were up very early, and I want to introduce Augustus to Joe before he goes out on his rounds.'

Half an hour later Kate and Spears were on their way to Joe's cottage.

'I dunno what exactly I can do for him,' Spears

426

said warily. 'I mean, it sounded like a good idea yesterday, but the more I think about it the less likely it seems that he'll want to have me hanging around.'

'You don't know him, Augustus. He's very proud and he doesn't like to ask for help, but he's limited physically and even tacking up his horse must prove quite difficult.'

As if to prove her point a large black horse came cantering towards them, with its saddle coming adrift. In the distance Kate could see Joe standing in the middle of the path, leaning heavily on one crutch.

'Whoa there.' Spears held out his arms and the horse came to a halt, snorting and pawing the ground. 'Steady there, old fellow.' Speaking gently in a tone that Kate had never heard him use, Augustus soothed the agitated animal.

'I couldn't fasten the girth properly and he bolted,' Joe said apologetically. 'I don't know if I'm fit for this job, Kate. I think Mr Pomeroy-Smith will have to find someone better suited.'

'I don't think that will be necessary. I may have the answer for you.' Kate waited until Spears was within earshot. 'Joe, this is Augustus Spears. He's a military man like yourself and he's looking for work. You need someone to assist you and I thought you might be able to help each other.'

Spears came to a halt, clicked his heels together and saluted in a dramatic way that seemed to impress Joe. 'Good morning, Captain.'

Joe grinned. 'No need for formalities, Spears. I was only a private.' He held out his hand. 'Joe Blythe.'

'I know your sister, sir. Me and Annie are old friends.' Spears shook hands and the horse nodded as if in approval.

'As you can see, I do need some help if I'm to continue working for Mr Pomeroy-Smith, but I can't afford to pay you, Augustus. It wouldn't be fair to keep you from getting a better position.'

'Money doesn't come into it,' Kate said hastily. 'There's a grant available for ex-soldiers. I know someone who applied for it and is now in full employment, all expenses paid for by a grateful government.' It was, of course, pure fabrication, but Kate could see that they believed her. She would fund Spears' wages herself, but there was no need for anyone to find out, and she would be putting her uncle's legacy to good use. It was a well-intentioned lie and surely she could be forgiven for that. She looked from one to the other. 'Well? Are you willing to give it a try?'

'I am, most certainly,' Joe said with feeling. 'What about you, Spears?'

'I'm very willing, sir.'

'Wonderful.' Kate patted Spears on the back. 'Now both of you can do something for me and for Harry. I want you to attend the ball in Berkeley Square, which is being given to celebrate my mother's engagement to Mr Pomeroy-Smith.'

Joe stared at her, shaking his head. 'Why would I attend a ball, Kate? I can hardly walk, let alone dance.'

'It's going to be a trap to catch Monks and his gang and put them in prison where they belong. We think, or rather we hope, that the lure of expensive jewels and priceless artworks will be enough to tempt Monks out of hiding. I think Harry and the police will need all the help they can get.'

'Look at me, Kate.' Joe lifted one of his crutches. 'I'm not much use with these things.'

'I dunno, mate,' Spears said, chuckling. 'A hefty swipe with one of those would do the trick. You look as though you know how to handle yourself in a set-to.'

'I haven't any suitable clothes,' Joe said stubbornly. 'Unless you want me to wear my uniform.'

'Me neither,' Spears added. 'I only got these duds because you gave them to me, miss.'

'There's a shop in Covent Garden where Mr Moss sells very good second-hand garments,' Kate said firmly. 'I want you both to come to London as soon as possible and we'll get you kitted out.'

'If you put it like that I suppose I can't refuse,' Joe said, grinning.

Kate smiled. 'That's settled then. Hopefully you won't have to do anything but stand by, looking impressive.'

'I want to see Monks get his comeuppance,' Spears said grimly. 'Nothing would please me more.'

'I'll leave you two to get acquainted, and in the meantime I'm going to see Ivy. She wasn't at the big house so I expect I'll find her at home. I think Ted would be a handy man to back you two soldiers up.'

'Ted's a good chap,' Joe said earnestly. 'We'll be there, Kate. After everything you've done for Annie and me, I owe you my life.'

'Nonsense,' Kate said briskly. 'We're as good as family, and that means we stick together.' She was about to walk away but she hesitated. 'You'll need a horse, Augustus. I'll tell Goodfellow to find you a suitable mount.' She did not wait for an answer and she set off again, this time heading for Ivy and Ted's cottage at the edge of the spinney.

Ivy was in the garden hanging the washing on a clothes line, her breath curling round her head in the cold air. Kate called her name and Ivy took a peg from her mouth to answer with a cry of delight.

'Kate! I didn't expect to see you today. What a lovely surprise.' She picked up the empty willow basket. 'Come inside where it's warm.' She entered the cottage, leaving the basket and bag of wooden pegs in the porch. 'I'll make a pot of tea as it's you. I have to be careful with money now that we're supporting ourselves, but I'm not complaining. We're doing very nicely, thanks to you.'

'I'm glad.' Kate pulled up a chair and sat down at the table. 'You seem to be very comfortable here, Ivy.'

'It's wonderful being a family again, and living here there's no temptation for Ted to get in with the wrong people.' Ivy busied herself making a pot of tea. 'But what's happening in London? Why have you come back so soon?'

'That's partly why I've come to see you.' Kate accepted a cup of tea with a nod and a smile. 'Harry and Perry have been working with the police and they have a plan to catch Monks and his men. I've explained it all to Joe and he's willing to be a part of it. Do you think Ted will help?'

Ivy took a seat opposite Kate. 'I dunno. You'd better tell me exactly what this plan is and whether it would put my Ted in danger of being on the wrong side of the law.'

'It won't do that, I promise.' Kate leaned her elbows on the table, fixing Ivy with a serious gaze. 'I'm going to tell you everything, but it mustn't go any further.'

You know you can trust me. What can my Ted do for you?' Ivy listened in silence while Kate outlined the plan.

'So, you see, Ivy,' Kate concluded. 'We will all be able to live a normal life when Monks is locked up. Harry will get a full pardon and Lady Lyndon will be able to return to her home in Finsbury Circus. My mama and Giles will be married at Easter and we can breathe easily again.'

'And what about you?' Ivy said earnestly. 'Will you marry Harry?'

Kate felt herself blushing and she looked away. 'That depends.'

'On what?' Ivy asked, chuckling. 'Come on, Kate. You can tell me.'

'Life has been so uncertain and I've hardly seen Harry since we returned from India. Ask me again after the ball, and I might be able to give you an answer.'

'Are you going to the ball, Kate?'

'Yes, of course, I am. I wouldn't miss it for the world.'

'Then you'll need a lady's maid in attendance. Preferably one who can keep calm in a fight, and I've seen enough of those when we lived in Wapping. Them villains won't get close to you while I'm around. I can use me fists if I have to.'

'Of course I'd like you to come, but who would

431

look after the children?'

'Tilly is a good girl. She can stay here overnight. The nippers love her and Tilly loves them. I could do with a bit of excitement. You can count me in.'

★ ★ ★

Kate left Ivy's cottage filled with plans for the upcoming event. She went straight to the stables to see Goodfellow, and she gave him permission to purchase a more suitable mount for Spears at the next horse sale. According to Goodfellow, there was an ageing horse that would do very well for Spears until he was a more proficient rider, and Kate left him, satisfied that it was a job well done. Joe had the help he needed and Spears had found employment and a more healthy way of life. Out of politeness, Kate called briefly on Marie Goodfellow, who was as loud and cheerful as ever, although she did complain about the size of their cottage and the smell from the stables. Kate nodded politely and when Marie stopped to draw breath Kate took the opportunity to wish her well and backed away. She returned to the house where she found Martha looking ill at ease.

'Will you be coming back to Warren House soon, Miss Kate?' Martha eyed her curiously. 'I mean it's not my place to ask questions, but Lady Lyndon didn't give me any instructions when she left. It was all a bit sudden.'

'Yes, I know it was, but you mustn't worry, Martha.'

'I'm sorry, miss. But of course I'm concerned. I've served Lady Lyndon and the family all my life. If she isn't coming back ever, will they sell the property? It does happen, you know. My friend Elsie Brown used to work at Chestnut Grove and the owners fell upon hard times. The property was sold, and with no family of her own, poor Elsie ended up in the workhouse.'

'That won't happen to Warren House, I can promise you that, and should Lady Lyndon decide to sell, which she won't, I would buy it myself. I love this place and the village. I'd be more than happy to make my home here.'

Martha breathed a sigh and smiled with tears in her eyes. 'Thank you, Miss Kate. That's put my mind at rest. Arthur and I are too old to start afresh with a new family. It would be my pleasure to serve you and Sir Harry if you . . . ' Martha covered her mouth with her hand. 'I'm sorry, I didn't mean to presume.'

Kate laughed. 'You're the second person today who has suggested that Harry and I might make a match. Don't worry, Martha. If we do decide to marry, you will be among the first to know.'

'I have known him since he was born, miss. I couldn't want for a better outcome.' Martha blew her nose loudly on a hanky she took from her pocket. 'Will you be staying for the night? I'll have your room made ready if you are.'

'I think my business here is done. I'll get Goodfellow to drive me back to London as soon as I've had a bowl of the delicious-smelling stew you have bubbling away on the hob. I've missed your cooking, Martha.'

'Of course, miss. I'll send Tilly to light a fire in the dining room.'

'Don't trouble her. I'm quite happy to sit here at the kitchen table. Tilly can take a message to the stables so that Goodfellow is ready when I want to leave.'

★ ★ ★

Kate was so busy that she did not have time to worry about the success or failure of their plans for the capture of Monks. To her its success was a foregone conclusion and the first thing she did when she returned to Finsbury Square was to order invitations to be printed as a matter of urgency. Giles saw to it that the event was mentioned on the front page of The Times, leaving nothing to chance. It might not be an obvious choice of reading matter for someone like Monks, but as Giles explained, it was where society functions were announced. Monks would follow the money, it was as simple as that.

Ted, Joe and Augustus rode up to London and Perry accompanied them to Moses Moss's shop in

Covent Garden where he purchased suitable outfits for them, at Kate's expense, although Perry had been instructed not to tell them who was paying. Kate knew it would hurt their male pride to be beholden to a woman, and Perry reported back to her that all three had been quite happy to believe that Giles had footed the bill. Kate herself took Ivy to Peter Robinson's store in Oxford Street, where she was also fitted for a new gown.

Caterers were booked, and at Arabella's request a special order was given to Gunter's for their delicious fancies and ice cream to be served in the supper room. Harry kept away from Finsbury Square and Kate had to be content in knowing that soon all these cat-and-mouse games would be over. Her dearest wish was to lead an ordinary life without fear of being abducted or even murdered by Monks.

Arabella seemed to have forgotten the main reason for the ball and had convinced herself that it was a genuine introduction to the society that she longed to embrace. Lady Lyndon had been let into the secret and she was eager to get the whole thing over and done with, while Annie was quietly supportive. Kate worked hard to make sure that everything went to plan, leaving Perry to liaise with the police. There was nothing more she could do now but hope that Monks would be unable to resist the temptation of easy pickings.

27

Everything was ready. Kate was dressed in a ball gown of ivory satin over a wide crinoline. The low-cut décolletage was framed by a waterfall of Honiton lace and the sleeves were trimmed with glistening glass bugle beads that caught the light every time she moved. Ivy had put Kate's hair up in a coronet of curls interspersed with loops of pearls, but despite the grandeur of her gown, Kate's mind was not on her own appearance. Her one thought was for the ball to be a success in bringing about the capture and arrest of Monks and his gang. She had only met him twice, but she knew she would recognise him the moment she set eyes on him. She was excited but she was also apprehensive. So many things could go wrong, but at least the house in Berkeley Square was a wonderful setting for such an occasion. She had been there since early morning, supervising everything down to the smallest detail in order that her mother could enjoy being hostess without the worry it entailed. The drama that was to unfold would make Arabella's debut in society memorable, even if for the wrong reasons.

Kate walked the length of the ballroom with its highly polished wooden floor surrounded by tables set with pristine white damask cloths, gleaming silverware and cut-crystal glasses that winked and shone in the light from sparkling chandeliers. Everything was perfect, from the exquisite floral arrangements that filled the air with their exotic perfume to the musicians from the newly arrived orchestra, who were just tuning their instruments. Kate made her way to the supper room and was dazzled by the array of delicious dishes set out on long tables. The aroma was so tempting that at any other time it would have made her mouth water, but tonight she had no appetite. It felt as if her whole life was dangling on a thread as fine as the silk from a spider's web. She turned with a start at the sound of a familiar voice calling her name.

'Kate.'

'Harry! What are you doing?' Kate glanced round to see if any of the servants were looking, but fortunately they were being harried by Giles's butler as they added the final touches to the banquet. 'You mustn't be seen.'

He was at her side in two steps and he held her at arm's length. 'You are so beautiful, Kate. You always look lovely to me, even when you're dressed as a poor serving maid, but tonight you are truly breath-taking.'

'Thank you, but please keep out of sight. The guests will start arriving at any moment.'

'I've been waiting for the opportunity to get Monks for a long time. We're ready for him.'

'Someone's coming, Harry. You have to leave now.' He leaned over and kissed her briefly on the lips. 'I'm going, but you have Ted, Joe and Spears on hand to keep you safe. We don't know when Monks will put in an appearance, but it's my guess that he'll wait until the guests have drunk too much champagne to be aware of what is happening. Don't take any risks.'

'That goes for you, too. Now please, leave me to handle this my way. Go.' His comic expression made her laugh, but she pushed him away and turned her back on him. She could hear her mother and Giles in the ballroom and she went to join them.

Even though she had seen her mother's gown during the fitting sessions, this was the first time Kate had seen her mother wearing the exquisite creation in magenta silk trimmed with black lace. A necklace of rubies and diamonds shone like fire around Arabella's slender neck, with matching earrings and flower-like diamond pins in her fair hair.

'Mama, you look amazing,' Kate said earnestly. 'But I don't recognise your jewels.'

Giles slipped his arm around Arabella's waist. 'A wedding present from me, Kate.'

'But you're not . . .' Kate looked from one to the other and realised that they were smiling blissfully. 'You're married already. When? How? I don't understand.'

Arabella broke away from her new husband and slipped her arm around Kate's shoulders in an unusual gesture of motherly affection. 'My dear, neither of us have to ask anyone's permission, but I am still supposed to be in mourning, so we thought it best to get a special licence and marry quietly.'

'I don't know what to say, but I suppose congratulations are in order,' Kate said dazedly. 'But this ball was supposed to celebrate your engagement. What will you tell your guests?'

Arabella moved to Giles's side and tucked her

438

hand in the crook of his arm. 'I realise that it's rather unusual, but as long as everyone enjoys themselves I don't think it matters. I just hope that things don't get out of hand.'

'That won't happen, Arabella,' Giles said firmly. 'The police are here now, as is the chief inspector, who is an old friend. Everything is in place and all we have to do is to welcome our guests as they arrive, but Kate, if things get too hectic I want you to promise me you'll see your mama to safety before anything else.'

'Of course I will.' Kate turned towards the stairs where Giles's butler cleared his throat loudly before announcing the first arrivals.

Kate stood in line with her mother and her new stepfather to receive the guests, most of whom were unfamiliar to her, but she managed to smile and nod as if she did this every day of her life. Her hand was aching and her face felt as though it was set in a rictus grin when the last couple had been warmly welcomed, and she could only admire her mother for acting as though she were accustomed to entertaining on a grand scale. Even so, and although she had sent out the invitations herself, Kate was amazed to see so many people, and so much obvious wealth. If Monks missed this chance he would be either stupid or extremely clever. Kate tried to enjoy the evening but all the time she was waiting for something dire to happen.

Ivy was stationed in the small parlour adjoining the ballroom where the ladies' capes and wraps were laid out, and Joe was in the next room attending to the gentlemen's coats, hats and gloves. Ted and Augustus, looking very smart in their evening dress, stood to attention on either side of the door, apparently to prevent gate crashers, but Kate could tell by their rigid stance that they were prepared for trouble.

The orchestra struck up a grand march and couples paraded solemnly round the floor, the women's jewels gleaming in the candlelight. The air was heavy with expensive perfume and pomade, and a hint of Havana cigar smoke wafted in from the terrace. Couples whirled around to the strain of waltzes and the more formal cotillion and quadrille. Kate was claimed by several good-looking, well-bred gentle man, whose names she had already forgotten. She danced and responded half-heartedly to their attempts at conversation but she was on edge all the time, waiting for something to happen. Champagne was flowing and as the evening progressed the guests wandered into the supper room to sample the sumptuous banquet spread out before them.

Kate had worried at the start that Monks would appear too early and ruin everything, but now when it was getting late, she was beginning to fear that he might not turn up at all. When one of the gentlemen, with whom she had danced twice, asked her to accompany him to the supper room, Kate could hardly refuse without looking petulant, but nerves were causing her stomach to churn uncomfortably. She allowed him to pile delicacies onto her plate, even though she knew she would not be able to eat a morsel, but when he led her to a small table at the side of the room she accepted his offer to fetch her a glass of champagne.

She sat down, gazing despondently at the food, which at one time she would have eaten and thoroughly enjoyed, when suddenly she was aware of someone standing very close to her. She looked up, thinking it was her dance partner, when her heart gave an uncomfortable leap in her chest. The welldressed gentleman who was looking down at her sported an ugly scar on his right cheek, which even the neat beard, moustache and sideboards could not quite disguise.

'Don't make a sound, Miss Martin,' Monks said with a wolfish grin. 'You'll do as I say or it will be the worse for your dearest mama. Look how happy she is.' He jerked his head in the direction of Arabella, who was chatting to a woman whose diamonds flashed and winked in the candlelight. 'One wrong word from you and your mama goes to heaven, or the other place.' He shot a sideways glance at a man standing close to Arabella. 'He's one of my men. We're all here and we are armed in case you're thinking of summoning help.'

'What do you want?' Kate demanded in a low voice.

'Come with me. Act normally as if you and I were about to join in the country dance.'

'What if I say no?'

'Then I signal to my men and they will shoot the first person who challenges them.'

Kate rose to her feet. She could see her dance partner approaching with a glass of champagne in each hand, but she walked straight past him with Monks so close behind her that she could feel his breath hot against her neck.

'Miss Martin, I . . . ' The young man took one

441

look at Monks and stepped aside.

Kate stared straight ahead. She could see her mother and Giles on the dance floor and she managed to catch Perry's eye, but she did not dare to call out. Then suddenly, without warning, Monks drew her into the midst of the dancers and he pulled a pistol from beneath his frock coat, brandishing it in the air and barking an order for everyone to stop where they were.

Kate tried to break away from him but his grasp on her tightened painfully. 'Stand very still,' he said in a loud, clear voice. 'No one will get hurt if you do exactly as I say.'

A cry of fear rippled around the room and some of the gentlemen made as if to rush at Monks, but his men emerged from the crowd, forcing them back.

'As you see,' Monks continued calmly, 'we are armed and not afraid to use our weapons. I want all the ladies to stand in the middle of the room — gentlemen move away.'

There were muttered protests but Monks' men formed an armed circle around the centre of the dance floor, and the women huddled together, some of them sobbing while others faced their aggressors with silent fury.

'Ladies, take off your jewels and drop them in my colleague's hat. I want everything so don't try to conceal your valuables or we might be forced to search you.'

One of Monks' men walked round slowly, holding out a top hat into which the terrified women dropped their priceless pieces of jewellery.

'And the gentlemen, take off your stick pins and

442

gold pocket watches, but make one sudden move and you will face the consequences.'

Kate caught sight of Harry at the far end of the ballroom and she could see Ted and Augustus standing either side of the main doors with Joe close by.

'I can see you, Harry Trader,' Monks said in a loud voice. 'Don't imagine I haven't planned for all contingencies, but I have the trump card.' He tightened his grip on Kate, clenching his arm under her chin, so that it was almost impossible for her to breathe, let alone to call out. 'Miss Martin will be the first person to suffer if you make a move.'

Kate found herself pressed to Monks' body but she managed to draw her right foot back far enough to deal him a sharp kick on the shin, and at the same moment she sunk her teeth into his wrist. He released her with a yelp of pain and she collapsed onto the floor. The women around them screamed and in their panic they moved as one body, pushing through the ring of Monks' men in an attempt to reach safety. At the same moment the police rushed through the double doors and a scuffle broke out. Kate dragged herself to her feet and managed to reach Annie, who was crouched in a corner, obviously terrified.

Kate put her arms around the frightened girl.

'You're safe now, Annie. The police are here.'

'What's happening? Where's Perry?' Annie whispered through chattering teeth.

'I'm sure he's all right, and the police are gaining control.' Kate looked up to see Ivy coming towards them. 'Ivy, will you look after Annie? I

443

want to find my mother and Lady Lyndon. I can't see them anywhere.'

'Your ma is safe,' Ivy said in a low voice. 'I think Lady Lyndon is with her, but I never saw such a to-do in all me born days. My Ted got one of Monks' men. He knocked him down with one swipe to the jaw.'

'Stay here and don't move,' Kate said urgently. She had seen Monks edging towards the only way of escape and no one else seemed to have noticed. After everything he had put them through she was not going to allow him to get away and, regardless of her own safety, she managed to dodge flailing arms as she tried to reach Joe, who was standing guard by the double doors.

'Look out, Joe,' she cried in desperation. 'Stop Monks — he's trying to get away.'

Despite the uproar in the ballroom, Joe heard her warning cry. Wielding one of his crutches like a battle axe, he caught Monks a blow to the head that sent him crashing to the floor. With a victorious shout, Joe launched himself on top of the fallen man, pinning him to the ground until a burly police sergeant came to his aid. The sergeant helped Joe to his feet while a constable tied Monks' wrists behind his back. Kate found herself caught up in the tumult once again, and it was almost impossible to distinguish between the men who had come to rob them and the gentlemen who were guests. The screams of women echoed off the high ceiling together with the muted sobbing of those who had managed to scramble to safety.

The musicians had stopped playing at the first

sign of trouble and they snatched up their precious instruments, keeping them out of danger. Kate managed to get to the edge of the fray by following the cellist, who carried his instrument on his back like some bizarre tortoise. She stumbled over an insensate body and would have fallen, but was caught in a pair of strong arms.

'Kate, are you all right?'

Harry's voice was like music to her ears and she breathed a sigh of relief. 'They've got Monks, Harry. It's over.'

'Thanks you to, my darling. Monks won't be going anywhere except the police cells.'

Kate moved aside as a woman dived down to rescue her pearl necklace. She waved it in Kate's face.

'This is a precious family heirloom. We were invited to a grand ball, but we were robbed at gun point.'

Kate had no idea who this woman was, but she felt obliged to apologise. 'I am so sorry, ma'am.'

'Don't apologise, my dear. I've never had such an exciting evening in my life. I hope there is plenty more champagne. Fasten my necklace for me. The evening isn't over yet.'

Kate fastened the triple strands of pearls around the woman's neck.

'Thank you, my dear. I'll have so much to tell my friends.' The woman beckoned to a gentleman, who appeared to be her husband. 'Champagne, Frederick. I need several glasses to get over the shock. Tell those idiotic musicians to play something lively. Where's Giles? He needs to take charge.'

Kate turned to Harry, shaking her head. 'I don't

445

think anyone who attended tonight will forget this party.'

He smiled and brushed her cheek with a swift kiss. 'I want to make sure that Monks is safely locked up in the Black Maria before I do anything else. But I claim the last waltz with you, my darling.'

Kate took her cue from the woman with the pearl necklace and she signalled to the conductor, who dutifully led the musicians back to their places. Acknowledging him with a nod and a smile, Kate beckoned to a waiter.

'Please serve the members of the orchestra with drinks. I think they've earned them.' She glanced round the ballroom to see some ladies being led away by their husbands while others had resumed their seats and were sipping champagne as if nothing untoward had occurred. A police constable was trying to convince one of the titled ladies that her jewels were evidence and police property until after the trial, but Kate could see that he was losing the argument. She was hardly surprised when the imposing dowager wrested the diamond tiara from him together with a sapphire and diamond choker, which she clasped to her large bosom.

'Take them, if you dare, but the Duke will hear of this and you will lose your job, my good man.'

The constable looked to his superior, who shrugged and rolled his eyes. 'Don't worry, Perkins. We've plenty of evidence to go on. Allow the lady to keep her jewels.'

'I should think so, too.' The dowager turned her back on them, addressing herself to a pale young man who had accompanied her to the ball. 'Eustace, fetch me a brandy and something to eat.

I'm not leaving until I've had supper, and despite everything, the food looks delicious.'

Kate went in search of her mother, half expecting to find her prostrate with shock, but Arabella and Giles were seated at a table in the supper room, toasting each other in champagne.

'Are you all right, Mama?' Kate asked anxiously.

'Oh, yes, Kate. It was frightening at first, but Giles had warned me what to expect.'

'You did understand that this was an elaborate trap to catch Monks?'

'Of course I did, Kate. Don't forget I met that dreadful creature when he broke into our house, and I endured months and months in the country because of him. I even had to put up with Ivy's brood of children, but that's all in the past now. Giles and I plan to live part of the time in Pomeroy Park and we'll spend the season here, in Berkeley Square.'

'But first we're going to have a honeymoon in Italy,' Giles added, patting Arabella's hand.

'Although we'll be home in time for your wedding at Easter,' Arabella said happily.

'My wedding?' Kate turned to Harry, who had just joined them. 'Do you know anything about this?'

'I haven't had a chance to propose yet,' Harry said mildly.

'But you will, of course.' Arabella smiled benignly. 'At one time I would have said that you could do better, Kate, but now I have to admit that Harry Lyndon might make a good husband, and as Giles and I are already wed, I suggest you take our place at St Mary's for an Easter wedding.

We've decided that you may use Pomeroy Park for the wedding breakfast.'

Kate held up her hand. 'Mama, I'm very happy for you and Giles, but please will you allow me to run my own life? After tonight all I want to do is to go home to Warren House and enjoy a good night's sleep.'

'You still call Warren House home?' Harry said softly.

'I meant Finsbury Square, of course. I'm exhausted after all this excitement.'

'The house in Finsbury Square belongs to you, Kate,' Arabella said firmly. 'After all, you inherited it from your uncle and I no longer need to live there. You are a woman of means, and won't have any reason to return to Walthamstow.'

Kate was about to answer when Lady Lyndon bore down on them, holding Annie by the hand. 'Harry, there you are. I want you to take us home. After all the excitement poor Annie is exhausted, and I don't know where Perry has gone.'

Harry hesitated. 'I should take Kate home first, Mama. Perry is probably dealing with the police but he'll see you and Annie safely back to Finsbury Circus when he's ready.'

'I hope that young man isn't simply amusing himself with you, Annie,' Lady Lyndon said wearily. 'The youth of today seem to think they can do what they please, and never mind the consequences.'

'Aunt Margaret! How can you say such things about Perry?' Annie's cheeks reddened and her eyes flashed. 'Perry has already proposed to me, but I said he must ask your permission first. He

448

would have done so this evening if it hadn't been for all the excitement.'

'Oh, well, that's different.' Lady Lyndon beamed, patting Annie's hand. 'Of course I want to see you happy, my dear. We'll talk about it in the morning.'

'You could stay here for the night, my dear.' Arabella turned to Kate, smiling. 'The rooms have been made ready and you don't want to return to an empty house, do you, Kate? I know we've had our differences in the past, but we can start afresh.'

'Of course we can, Mama. But you needn't worry about my safety. There are plenty of servants to look after me in Finsbury Square. Ivy, Ted and Augustus will be staying, too. We can all fit into the barouche and Goodfellow will drive us.'

'You can't travel in the same carriage as your servants, Kate.' Arabella's eyes widened in horror.

'They are my friends, Mama. Anyway, I'm too tired to argue.' Kate turned to Harry. 'Look after your mother, I'll be perfectly fine.' She reached up to kiss his cheek. 'I'll see you tomorrow.'

He nodded. 'All right, if that's what you want. We have a lot to talk about.'

* * *

Despite the fact that she was exhausted, Kate could not sleep. The house in Finsbury Square seemed even larger than ever, and haunted with echoes from the past. The memories it held were not particularly happy ones: living with a domineering father and a mother who had shown little

449

interest in Kate as a child had not made for a warm and comfortable home. What she had found in Warren House was priceless, and that was where her true destiny lay. She fell asleep eventually but awakened early and she knew exactly what she must do. Harry would understand.

She dressed quickly and sent a startled kitchen maid to the mews to rouse Goodfellow and tell him to be ready to leave for Walthamstow in half an hour. Kate made her way to the morning parlour where her mother's workbox had been left open, and an abandoned piece of embroidery was still stretched on its hoop. She smiled to herself — Mama was too busy with her new life to bother with such trivialities now. It was a good thing, but without her mother's presence the room was cheerless and oddly impersonal, like a stage set or an arrangement of expensive furniture in a shop window. Kate closed the door and went to wait for Goodfellow in the entrance hall. There was nothing to keep her here now that her mother and Giles were married and had their own home, but one day she would find a good use for the house in Finsbury Square. Perhaps it would be a shelter for widows and their children, or a home for women who had fallen upon hard times. To make use of her uncle's legacy for charitable purposes would be a fitting tribute to a good man, but for now she would leave everything in the capable hands of Mrs Marsh and the remaining servants. No one would suffer from her sudden decision to leave London.

Kate went to her mother's escritoire and sat down to pen a quick note to Harry, explaining that she had left for Warren House. She rang the bell for Agnes, but it was the young housemaid who appeared at the door, her face and apron smudged with soot from cleaning out the grates. Kate gave her the note and asked her to make sure that she gave it to Sir Harry Lyndon, but she did not have time to go through her instructions again as the girl scuttled off in the direction of the servants' staircase. Then, through a side window Kate saw the carriage come to a halt outside and she picked up her reticule. Taking one last look around the grand entrance hall she let herself out of the house, and closed the door firmly behind her.

Goodfellow climbed down from the box and assisted her into the carriage. 'You're up bright and early, Miss Kate.'

'Take me home, please, Goodfellow.'

'Of course, miss.' He glanced over his shoulder. 'Are we to wait for the others?'

'No. Let them sleep. You can come back for them later.' Kate settled herself in the corner and as the carriage set in motion she turned her head to catch the last glimpse of the old house. This was goodbye to the past. Her new life beckoned.

★ ★ ★

When Kate entered Warren House later that morning she felt the warmth of home wrap itself around her. Martha fussed over her, insisting that she must have something to eat, while Arthur saw to her luggage. Tilly regaled her with stories about the children's antics during their parents' stay in London, while Kate sipped a cup of tea in the kitchen and toyed with a slice of bread and butter. It was Martha who came to Kate's rescue by sending Tilly off to make the drawing room ready, and then Marie Goodfellow burst into the kitchen, beaming with pleasure.

'Seth told me you'd come home, miss. He had a bite of food and now he's gone off to London to fetch Ivy and Ted. Shall I take some hot water to your room? I expect you'd like to wash the dust of the road off and change out of your travelling clothes.' She bustled into the scullery before Kate had a chance to respond.

'She wants to be a lady's maid,' Martha said in a stage whisper. 'You could do worse, miss.'

Kate smiled. 'It's good to be home, Martha. I've really missed your cooking.'

'Get on with you, miss.' Martha's plump cheeks reddened. 'We was all afraid you'd stay in London.'

'No, never! This is where I belong.' Kate rose from the table and made her way to her room, where Marie pounced on her. With boundless energy and good humour Marie helped her to wash and change out of her travel-stained gown.

'Martha suggests that you might like to have me as your maid, Miss Kate,' Marie said hopefully. 'I done well when I looked after her ladyship. You won't have no cause to complain.' She took a deep blue merino gown from the clothes press. 'You look a treat in this colour, miss. It matches your eyes.'

Kate smiled at Marie's eagerness to please. 'I dare say you and I will do very well together.'

'I promise you won't regret it, miss.' Marie stood back to admire her handiwork. 'No doubt you'll have a gentleman caller before the day is out.' She tapped the side of her nose. 'I have the gift of second sight. My grandmother was a gypsy.'

'Then you know more than I do,' Kate said tiredly. The excitement and pressure of the past few days was suddenly overwhelming. Harry had promised to come for her, and she could only hope that the young maidservant had given him the note. Perhaps she should have waited for him in London, but the desire to come home had been overwhelming.

Marie took a woollen shawl from the press and wrapped it around Kate's shoulders. 'Some fresh air is what you need now, miss, if I may be so bold. It will put the colour back in your cheeks. My grandmother always swore that good country air was the best medicine.'

'I'm sure she was right.' Kate had a sudden desire to see the gardens that she had helped to rescue from the wilderness.

★ ★ ★

The view from the terrace was breath-taking now that Ted had pruned back the overgrown shrubs and bushes, and the sun was shining. The air was redolent with the scent of spring flowers and damp earth. A cool breeze ruffled Kate's hair, but her mother was not there to tell her she must wear her bonnet in order to protect her complexion against the sun and she felt a wonderful sense of freedom. She came across Morrison outside the walled garden and received such a warm greeting that she felt like hugging the old man, but she did not want to embarrass him. She smiled and listened attentively to his ideas for planting new rose bushes, standards and climbers. He beamed with delight when she told him to order what he thought they needed, with no thought to the cost. She adored roses and could not think of a better way to spend her money. She wandered on, admiring the cultivated beds with plants ready to burst into flower, and she ventured into the spinney at the bottom of the garden. It was carpeted with daffodils, and she could not resist picking a large bunch, even though they would last just a few days indoors. Their glorious scent made her feel drunk with delight as she made her way back to the terrace, where she came to a sudden halt at the sound of horse's hoofs on the gravelled carriage sweep. Her heartbeat quickened and she stood very still. It seemed as though she had spent her whole life waiting for this moment.

Seconds later Harry rushed onto the terrace. He paused, gazing at her as if seeing her for the first time. Kate took a step towards him, and as she opened her arms a shower of daffodils cascaded onto the paving stones.

Harry crossed the terrace in long strides, taking her hands in his. 'The sight of you in that blue dress, surrounded by a sea of golden daffodils will stay with me for as long as I live, Kate my darling. I want an artist to paint your portrait just as you are now.'

Her eyes filled with tears, but they were tears of sheer happiness. 'I didn't know you were such a romantic, Harry.'

'There's a lot we don't know about each other, but it will be wonderful finding out.' He took her in his arms. 'I was worried about you staying in London on your own last night, but when I called this morning Mrs Marsh told me that you had sent for Goodfellow and had left without telling her where you were going. Why did you run away?'

'I didn't run away, Harry. I left a note.'

'I didn't get it.'

'I'm sorry, Harry. I just wanted to come home.'

'You must have known that I would come for you.'

'I had to get away. I couldn't bear to stay in London a moment longer.'

He answered her with a kiss that said more than words. 'We should be together,' he said softly. 'I need you with me now and always, my darling.'

She leaned against him with a contented sigh. 'I know. I feel that way, too.'

'Then marry me, Kate. We'll live here, at Warren House, if that makes you happy.'

'Won't you get bored with country living?' Kate smiled, raising her hand to trace the outline of his firm jaw. 'You led such a different existence in London. How will you fill your days?'

'I'll do what I was always meant to do, and I'll run the estate. I might even buy more land and take up farming. I've sold my clubs in London and money will never be a problem from now on. Besides which,' he added, chuckling, 'I hope to marry an heiress.'

'I never wanted to inherit my uncle's money, but I'll try to do some good with it.' Kate gazed up at him, frowning. 'I know you said you'll be happy living here, but are you sure you won't find it dull after a while?'

'Life with you will never be dull, my darling. I don't imagine you will sit by the fire with your embroidery. You are a born reformer, Kate, now you have the means to make a difference in the world.'

'And you don't mind?'

'I'd be very surprised if you haven't thought of a project to help those who are not as fortunate as we are.'

Kate wound her arms around his neck. 'You know me so well, Harry. I saw what a struggle Ivy had when Ted was sent to prison, and there must be many more women like her who have young families to raise on their own. The house in Finsbury Square would make a wonderful home for dispossessed and desperate women. My mother can make it one of her charities, and all those wealthy ladies who attended the ball last evening will be able to salve their consciences by contributing to such a good cause.'

'You've thought it all through, haven't you?'

'It took me a long time to go to sleep last night, but all I wanted was to be with you and live here for ever, Harry. The first time I saw Warren House I knew that I'd come home.'

'Is that an answer to my question, Kate? I love you with all my heart. Will you marry me?'

She smiled up at him. 'I love you, too, Harry. Of course I'll marry you.'

We do hope that you have enjoyed reading this large print book.

Did you know that all of our titles are available for purchase?

We publish a wide range of high quality large print books including:
Romances, Mysteries, Classics
General Fiction
Non Fiction and Westerns

Special interest titles available in large print are:
The Little Oxford Dictionary
Music Book, Song Book
Hymn Book, Service Book

Also available from us courtesy of Oxford University Press:
Young Readers' Dictionary
(large print edition)
Young Readers' Thesaurus
(large print edition)

For further information or a free brochure, please contact us at:
Ulverscroft Large Print Books Ltd.,
The Green, Bradgate Road, Anstey,
Leicester, LE7 7FU, England.
Tel: (00 44) 0116 236 4325
Fax: (00 44) 0116 234 0205

Other titles published by Ulverscroft:

THE COUNTRY BRIDE

Dilly Court

Little Creek, 1879. For most of her life Judy Begg has been a loyal servant at Creek Manor, and to Jack Fox, its future lord. But just as their childhood friendship blossoms into a secret engagement, he abandons her. And with Creek Manor up for sale, Judy and her family lose everything. Devastated, Judy is nonetheless determined to make the best of her life. Resolving to forget about Jack, she battles to keep her family from poverty's door and her mother from the hands of her violent husband. Rob Dorning, the new owner of the manor, seems to be the answer to all of Little Creek's problems, but Judy isn't convinced. And when the ghosts of her past resurface, Judy will need to find more courage than ever before . . .

NETTIE'S SECRET

Dilly Court

London, 1875. Thanks to her hapless father, Nettie Carroll has had to grow up quickly. While Nettie is sewing night and day to keep food on the table, her gullible father has trusted the wrong man again. Left with virtually nothing but the clothes they stand up in, he's convinced that their only hope lies across the English Channel in France. Nettie has little but her dreams left to lose. Even far from home trouble follows them, with their enemies quietly drawing closer. But Nettie has a secret, and it's one with the power to save them. Does she have the courage to pave the way for a brighter future?

THE CHRISTMAS ROSE

Dilly Court

Standing on London's Royal Victoria Dock with the wind biting through her shawl, Rose Munday realises she's been abandoned by her sweetheart. She had risked everything to get to London but, stumbling through the pea soup fog, she has nowhere to go, and no one to turn to.

Scared and alone, Rose steps straight into danger, only to be rescued by a woman of the night and her young sidekick, Sparrow. With all hope of her sweetheart's return fading, Rose finds herself forging a new life with her unlikely companions. But a dangerous enemy threatens to ruin them all . . .